THE WAY of the SWORD-WORLDS

John F. Carr
& Mike Robertson

Pequod Press

THE WAY OF THE SWORD-WORLDS
A Pequod Press Adventure Novel

Printed in the United States of America

First Printing, 2021
V 10 9 8 7 6 5 4 3 2 1

ISBN: 978-0-937912-79-9

Cover at by James Wu
Layout by Delaney-Designs

Pequod Press
P.O. Box 80
Boalsburg, PA 16827

Available from Pequod Press:

Paratime

Time Crime
Paratime Trouble
The Paratime Police Chronicles, Vol. I
The Paratime Police Chronicles, Vol. II
Great King's War
Kalvan Kingmaker
Siege of Tarr-Hostigos
The Fireseed Wars
Gunpowder God
Down Styphon!

TERRO-HUMAN FUTURE HISTORY

The Merlin Binary
Fuzzy Ergo Sum
Caveat Fuzzy
Fuzzy Conundrum
Fuzzy Logic
The Way of the Sword-Worlds
Space Viking
The Last Space Viking
Space Viking's Throne

SPACE VIKING Era Chronology

The Atomic Era is reckoned as beginning on the 2nd December 1942, Christian Era, with the first self-sustaining nuclear reactor, put into operation by Enrico Fermi at the University of Chicago. Unlike earlier dating-systems, it begins with a Year Zero, 12/2/'42 to 12/1/'43 CE. With allowances for December overlaps, 1943 CE is thus equal to Year Zero AE, and 1944 CE to 1 AE, and each century accordingly begins with the "double-zero" year, and ends with the ninety-nine year—H. Beam Piper.

782	Foxx Travis born.
839	System States Alliance secedes from the Terran Federation.
842 - 854	System States War.
855	Ten thousand refugees from Abigor flee the Terran Federation. They end up in a star cluster several thousand light-years from the Federation and settle an earth-like world, Excalibur.
895	Sword-Worlds Joyeuse, Durendal and Flamberge colonized from Excalibur.
915	Sword-World Haulteclere colonized from Joyeuse.
935	Sword-World Gram colonized from Haulteclere.
950	Aditya abandoned by the Federation, as it pulls back from the frontiers.
1000	The Interstellar Wars begin, a series of wars and uprisings which lead to the break-up of the Terran Federation.
1100	The final dissolution of the Terran Federation as war breaks out on Terra and the Sol System. The colony worlds turn on the mother world.
1200	The Interstellar Wars come to an end, more through exhaustion than desire. Only a dozen or so worlds still have the capability for interstellar flight.

SPACE VIKING Era Chronology continued

1359 First Sword-World ship returns from the Old Federation. Aditya occupied by Morglay.

1450 First Sword-World raid of the Old Federation.

1533 Wulf Hellmut raids Baldur and a dozen planets in the *World Smasher* and brings home over a billion and a half stellars of plunder back to theSword-Worlds.

1572 Captain Erlic Sanchez, the Planet-Buster's, raid on Isis is one of the richest Space Viking raids ever made in the Old Federation.

1595 Prince Havilgar of Haulteclere takes six ships against Aton. Two ships got back, but his didn't.

1602 Aditya is abandoned during a dynastic war on Morglay.

1615 Skathi, a Space Viking world, is abandoned.

1643 Xochitl is the first true base world. It's created by the Liebig Royal Family of Haulteclere. It becomes the template for future Space Viking base worlds.

1650 Marduk-Odin "fake war." Both navies make a lot of fireworks, then each side goes home and claims victory.

1665 Planetary Nationalist Party takes control of Aton during the crisis after the war with Baldur.

1677 Otto Harkaman is born on Colada.

1680 Lucas Trask is born on Gram.

1695 Otto Harkaman joins the independent Space Viking ship, *Devil's Mace*, as an ordinary ground trooper.

1702 The Oskarsan-Elmersan dynastic war begins on Durendal, when Frydrych Elmersan is assassinated.

1707 Angus becomes Duke of Wardshaven.

table of contents

PART ONE

TROOPER

MIMIR

I

1696 A.E.

Otto Harkaman pushed his helmet visor back and grimaced, looking at the men in his two troop sections. There were only a few of his fellow ground fighters he trusted. A few more that were inexperienced but one day might be worthy of trust; the rest were nearly worthless. This was his second raid as a Space Viking troop section leader since his promotion from ordinary trooper. During the previous assault on Volund, the locals had hardly fought at all before they turned tail and ran, so that one had been easy. However, it turned out the locals had nothing worth fighting for since they had found zilch worth stealing. Space Vikings referred to those kinds of raids as chicken-stealing because there was so little profit to them.

The city in front of them was surrounded by a stone curtain wall some twenty feet in height with drum towers set approximately every hundred feet. It looked as if its inhabitants were made of sterner stuff than the troops on Volund even though the military technology level was lower. From what he'd seen, he would place it at the pre-gunpowder stage.

He gestured to Ranjit Chaudhry, one the few men he trusted, to peer around the wall his men were crouched behind. He took a quick look and quickly pulled his head back. Two arrows whizzed by half a second later.

"Spearmen on the wall and at the gate," Ranjit noted, "with archers every ten feet or so along the parapets."

Harkaman grimaced again. He had been the one who had suggested raiding Mimir to the Captain. The world wasn't on any of their usual charts. He had found out about it during the previous raid on the nearby world of Volund. While the other crewmen had been celebrating the end of the raid, he had been poking through an old library. Studying history was his hobby and he was always searching for new material; a lot of it was useful in his new career and he enjoyed learning about the past. He'd found an atlas describing a number of nearby worlds. Most of them were known but Mimir was not. There was a notation about Mimir's trade in gems, such as rubies and diamonds during the Federation Era, which caused him to bring it to the attention of the Captain. Because it was Harkaman's suggestion, he had let him lead the raid.

Nial Burrick, Captain of the *Fortuna,* had been a successful raider in the past but was going through a streak of bad luck with too many unprofitable raids. Consequently the investor/owners of the *Fortuna* had pushed him to go farther into the Old Federation seeking more lucrative worlds. Having served on several voyages with Burrick, Harkaman knew that the Captain was a large part of the problem. He was a cunning man, but he was getting sloppy and his crew was following right behind.

A lot of the men serving under him hadn't received enough training. Too many were more interested in getting drunk and finding women, than fighting for loot. Few of them had what it took to be successful Space

Vikings, but he did and he planned to go far. He didn't know how far, but he was not satisfied with just being a troop section leader any more than Otto had been as a junior machinist back on Colada.

They were all Space Vikings, inhabitants of the Sword-Worlds, located over two thousand light-years away from the nearest world in the Old Federation. Their ancestors had fled the Federation, after being on the losing side in a civil war, traveling far enough away that no one would follow them. When their descendants had returned to the Old Federation five hundred years later, they found the vast majority of worlds had collapsed into anarchy and barbarism. They had started raiding those worlds for plunder and for some, a new home.

"All right listen up men," Harkaman said. "We've blown the gates open but these natives are sheltered behind stone walls."

The cities and towns on this world are peculiarly designed, he thought. The curtain walls that protected the city had sharpened stakes that pointed downward. All the cities and towns they had observed on Mimir had been built since the collapse of the Old Federation. The few Federation era cities on this planet had been nuked long ago, and now were nothing but ruins and slag piles.

"Carlos," he said to one of the men. "I want you to contact the ship and tell them to send down an air-cavalry mount." The *Fortuna* was hanging a few miles over them but there were several pinnaces, two hundred foot spherical auxiliary vessels, a few hundred yards away waiting to be loaded with whatever plunder they found inside the city. One of the pinnaces had fired the missile which blew open the gate. No other heavy weapons would be used because they would bury valuable goods under the ensuing rubble.

Harkaman wasn't worried about protecting the local population since Captain Burrick wasn't a slave trader—one of the few things he admired about the man. No civilized world wanted to purchase slaves; only barbarian worlds, with little to offer, would buy them. Now they were going to have to take the city the old-fashioned way, street by street and building by building.

"Once you're onboard, I want you to stay at a hundred feet," he continued. "As soon as you're overhead, cut loose and take out the bowmen. The moment you start shooting, we'll charge and take out the remaining spearmen."

Carlos got up and ran, twisting and turning every few feet. There was only one arrow fired and it missed him by several feet.

One of the other men swore. "They're just Neobarbs; let's get 'em." With that he leapt to his feet and charged around the wall, which was about fifty feet outside the city walls. Another man followed him before Harkaman could shout out halt.

Within seconds the first man came staggering back into sight, gasping with an arrow through his throat. He fell to his knees, his body convulsing, stretching out a hand in a mute appeal for help. One of the men ran to help, then fell backwards with two arrows in his chest armor. He twitched a few times and lay still.

"I told you to maintain your positions!" he yelled.

The indigenes were using bodkin arrows, not hunting arrows. *They're a well-disciplined lot*, he thought. *More in control than my own men, I'll have to do something about that.*

Only a few of the archers had fired, so they hadn't wasted many arrows. Their compound bows were powerful enough to penetrate the light battle armor most of the men wore. Armor was a matter of personal preference and what each man could afford. Some opted to not wear any at all; they claimed it made them faster, but he wondered if they just didn't like the extra weight. After his first raid, he had purchased the best personal armor he could afford.

If I were captain, I'd pay for decent combat armor or even bulletproofs for all my troops.

"Anyone else want to charge the gate without cover?" he asked, scornfully. "These walls were obviously placed to provide range markers for the bowmen."

That still puzzled him. He could understand range markers, but why five-foot high walls that could shelter an enemy? Unless for some reason their enemies weren't the kind to hide behind walls: however, he couldn't think of any human attacker who wouldn't use them as cover during their approach to the city.

Initially, the Captain had refused to let them use the one-man air-cavalry mounts because he didn't think there would be any real opposition once the gate was blown open. He was also a cheapskate and didn't want them to use any more ammunition than absolutely necessary. Harkaman disagreed, but hadn't wasted his breath saying anything; he and the Captain were already at loggerheads on other issues. In his mind, men's lives always trumped weapon and ammunition costs. However, Captain Burrick knew that he could always get replacement fighters at the next Viking base world, so he wasn't worried about their longevity and spent their lives freely.

A few minutes later, Carlos flew back on one of the egg-shaped air-cavalry flyers, soaring a hundred feet above the walls on its contragravity lifters, his hands on the controls of the machine guns mounted in front.

As soon as Carlos opened fire, Harkaman bellowed "Charge!" and rose to his feet.

With the bowmen either shot or diving to the walkway floors behind the parapets, they concentrated their fire on the spearmen. He felt his pistol buck in his hand as he shot a man, wearing a high-combed morion helmet, who appeared to be an officer.

In a few moments, they were at the rubble-filled gate and entering the city. The few spearmen behind the wall who tried to engage them were quickly cut down. Most threw aside their spears and ran away. Harkaman kept a wary eye out for bowmen, as he divided his squad, sending them down the three streets that radiated from the entrance.

Carlos stayed overhead on the air-cavalry flyer, firing occasional bursts from his machine guns or auto-cannon when he saw any movement on the upper stories. In less than an hour they were in control of the city.

II

"Not bad, Otto," Ranjit said, showing him a metal box full of diamonds, rubies, gold rings and necklaces. "We've got five more just like this one."

Harkaman grinned, while mentally calculating what they could be sold for. There was nothing like a bank in this city but they'd been going through the larger homes searching for jewelry and other valuables. They'd only knocked down a few men who objected to giving up their rings or having necklaces and other jewelry taken from their wives.

"How are the others doing," he asked.

Ranjit frowned. "Some of the men found a bar and have started their drinking."

Nifflheim, he thought. He considered going to the bar and trying to get them to focus on looting first, but they were just as likely to take a shot at him as follow his orders. Since Captain Burrick never objected to such behavior, discipline was poor on raid aftermaths. Not for the first time, he thought it was time for him to find another ship.

"At least no one's started any fires," Ranjit noted, looking around at all the wooden structures. "This whole city could easily burn down to the ground."

"Right," he replied. "Some firebug will get started shortly. Spread the word that if I catch anyone setting a fire, I'll shoot them where they stand."

Ranjit grinned. "Will do, Otto." He repeated Harkaman's orders into his helmet comm. When he was finished, he said, "I'll take a walk thought the city and make sure they received and understood your orders."

He nodded, thinking, *it might even help.*

"Add that to the rest of the pile," he told the man behind him, as he handed off the box of jewels he'd gotten from Ranjit. There was a small mountain of plunder building just outside the walls where the front gate had been located. Even now crew members were loading some of it aboard the contragravity lifters to haul it to the waiting pinnaces. There were the usual odds and ends of a successful raid; consumer goods looted from stores, paintings and statues from museums and wealthy homes, metals, fancy-looking furniture or clothing and anything else anyone thought might be worth something. No doubt the *Fortuna's* assayist would probably throw a quarter of it out as not worth transporting. However, the gems had lived up to the world's reputation.

It was the morning after their raid. Harkaman had just finished breakfast, when he picked up a distant vibration. He stepped out of the former temple that they were using as a temporary dining hall when heard one of the locals shouting.

"*Panya*!" a local woman cried out.

He approached her in an attempt to find out what the problem was.

"*Panya, Panya*," she continued, as she looked at him. She pointed outward beyond the city walls, her face terror stricken.

He tried to ask her what a *Panya* was, but was unable to make any sense out of her words. The locals still spoke Lingua Terra, but with a thick accent. The woman shook her head in exasperation and took off running.

It was a pleasant day and warm enough that he was happy to sit in the shade of the wall. After a few minutes, he noticed the vibration was growing louder. He rose to his feet, looking around for the source. Suddenly another woman burst out of a nearby hut and ran frantically toward him.

"*Panya, Panya!*" she screamed as she reached him, grabbing at his armorall vest, pointing toward the horizon. He thought at first she was pointing at trees but the spot seemed to grow as he watched.

"Guards, Guards!" he bellowed. There were six men just inside the gate who got to their feet, some of them obviously aroused from sleep. He thrust the woman aside while she ran into the streets, continuing to shriek "*Panya*" at the top of her lungs.

"What is it?" one of them grumbled.

He pointed. In seconds the dark spot had grown in size but he still couldn't see what it was, it was too hazy and indistinct.

"Get your guns out, damn you!" he demanded as they just stared, blinking as they woke up. He pulled his gun out if its holster, then slid a clip into it as an example. The others hastily brought their guns to bear. He looked again, gaping for a second as the dark cloud resolved itself into its individual components. It was a horde of black, hairy animals. They looked like four-foot long rats.

"I don't have any more clips," one of the men cried.

Harkaman grabbed him and pushed him through the gate. "Get to the nearest pinnace and call the ship," he ordered. "Tell them we need help."

"Form a line," he ordered the other five. When the creatures were about a hundred and fifty feet away he cried, "Fire!"

Some of the animals staggered but only a few went down. As their firing continued more of them began to drop. That didn't slow the charge as most of the creatures behind them simply leaped over the dead bodies. Without thinking he slipped another clip into his pistol and when the beasts less than fifty feet away, he began to pick off individual targets.

Two men ran up with sonic stunners and fired at full power. They took down hundreds of the approaching animals until they ran out of power. One of the other guards cursed as he ran out of ammo. Another tossed him one of his clips.

Harkaman had just reloaded when the first creature reached him and leapt at his throat. His shot blew half the beasts' head off, but another one was following right behind causing Harkaman to jump out of the way.

The creatures had pushed them back inside the city, and he watched in horror as they ran into buildings and huts, attacking anyone inside. There was nothing he could do to help the screaming city dwellers.

He fired rapidly, clearing the creatures in front of him. He was peripherally aware of one of his men going down shrieking under several of the beasts, when his pistol clicked on empty. He reached quickly into his pocket for another clip, when he saw one the animals leaping straight for him, its sharp fangs glistening in the sun. He could smell its rotten breath as he tried to slap the clip into his pistol, knowing it was going to be too late.

Suddenly a spear point thrust into the beast's neck, knocking it to one side and causing blood to splash all over him. He staggered back, using his left sleeve at wipe his eyes. A few dozen native spearmen had joined them and the beasts' charge ground to a halt on their spear heads. He looked down and saw that the crewman at his feet was just stunned. He pulled him to his feet, firing at any nearby animals as he did so. One of the most frightening things about these creatures was they didn't growl or howl; they only made a barely audible hiss.

He ordered his men to move behind the spearmen, who had obviously been through these attacks before. A few more ground fighters arrived and they started firing volleys into the attacking horde, while the spearmen thrust their weapons, pushing them back. The increasing growing pile of dead creatures in front of them slowed the attack for a few minutes until the beasts started to circle around, trying to encircle them.

Then one of the air-cavalry mounts arrived and fired its machine guns into the attacking horde, throwing bodies and bloody parts into the air. Both the spearmen and the beasts were startled, and spearmen wavered, backing up.

"Keep your places!" he shouted, pushing them forward while continuing to fire. "They won't hit us." He hoped he was right. If the spearmen ran away now, there were more than enough creatures left to tear them all apart.

All at once the surviving beasts turned and fled, trying to escape the firing guns that come out of sky. The air-cavalry flyer fired a few more rounds at them and then stopped, letting hundreds escape.

Probably under orders to save ammunition, he thought wearily as he watched the big rat-looking creatures scamper away. If they'd been allowed one air-cavalry mount at the gate to begin with they probably wouldn't have had any problem. He turned and looked at the nearby huts and swore. They were all overturned, human bodies mixed almost indiscriminately with dead creatures. He looked behind him and swore again: all of his books had been trampled and torn up during the battle.

He turned to the spearmen who were busy binding wounds on two of their number. "Thank you," he said, wondering how his thanks would be received. He wasn't long in finding out.

"If those *Panya* had breached the walls," said one man in an unfriendly tone, "they could have done irreparable damage. More than you did, Starman," he finished.

Harkaman nodded wearily in assent. He noticed that some of the natives were dragging the carcasses of the beasts into the city. He pointed at them, his eyebrows raised quizzically.

"Good eating," said one of the men. "Especially, when barbequed."

He snorted and began to walk away. He heard one of the natives say to another, "They nearly killed all of the slinkers. It's almost worth everything we lost."

III

Harkaman hoped he was right; he'd used up a lot of his capital with the Captain when he told him his plan. Now he was approaching the largest city on Mimir in an open aircar, ten feet off the ground on its contragravity, while waving a white flag. Ranjit Chaudry sat next to him driving the vehicle. A pinnace was grounded fifty yards behind him; the *Fortuna* hung about a thousand feet above, its shadow blanketing the city. When the aircar reached about five hundred feet from the city gate, he got out and walked slowly toward the gate, a white flag held prominently in his hand.

Thinking further about the chance remark he'd overheard in the aftermath of the *Panya* attack, he had approached the Captain after the raid and suggested that they offer to destroy the *Panya* lairs near the bigger cities in trade for their gems.

Captain Burrick was dubious at first: "Why should we do the Neobarbs any favors. We're Space Vikings, not Gilgameshers," referring to the itinerant traders of the galaxy, who were not regarded fondly by Space Vikings.

After he noted that they would be spending less lives and ammunition by trading, the Captain scratched his unshaven chin and looked up at him. "All right, Harkaman, if you're so damn smart," he declared, "you try it."

It's clear the Captain thinks I'm committing suicide, he thought, as he got out of the aircar and walked toward the city gate. And he might be right, as he noticed the cold. It appeared to be winter on this continent and while only a slight breeze was blowing his coverall wasn't that warm. There was a large sign on the gate which spelled Brunner, which must be the name of the city. It was encircled with a curtain wall as was the previous city. Unlike the other city this one was big enough to have half a dozen gates but the one he was approaching looked like the main entrance. When he was about fifty yards away one of the men on the wall, obviously an officer, with a tall plumed helmet yelled, "That's far enough, Starman. What do you want?"

They used the same term for him as the previous city, he thought. They couldn't possibly have heard of their earlier raid as this planet didn't have either telegraphs or radios, and they were on a different continent than the first city the *Fortuna* had looted. *Starman must be their term for off-worlders*, he decided, although as far as he knew they had never been raided by Space Vikings. Of course, Space Vikings weren't the only raiders or traders, for that matter, in the Old Federation. The planet did show evidence of having been nuked in the past but that was limited to old Federation cities and probably dated from the Interstellar Wars eight or nine hundred years ago when the Federation collapsed.

Keeping both hands in the air with the white flag clutched in one, Harkaman replied. "I want your gems."

The man on the wall, wearing the plumed helmet, laughed sardonically. "Try and take them, Starman!" he yelled, then started to turn away.

"I'm willing to trade," he said.

The noble stopped, showing a look of confusion, which was echoed by the other men around him on the wall. "What do you have to offer?" he asked.

With the lessening of hostility, Harkaman lowered his hands and dropped the white flag, moving slowly toward the gate. He was careful not to make any sudden moves that might cause alarm. "I'm offering to destroy the nearest nest of Panya," he replied.

"Panya?" said the man quizzically. One of the other men on the wall spoke up, "The black slinkers, sir."

That's right, he thought; he'd also heard one of the previous city's soldiers call them slinkers. "Yes the black slinkers," he said. He turned, pointing up at the *Fortuna*, "We have mighty weapons that can do this."

The officer looked up at the *Fortuna*, which was hovering a half mile or so overhead, but she still dominated the daylight sky. The officer shrugged, and said, "Wait here." It appeared he had decided to kick any decision upstairs.

He stood patiently. After a short wait, the man returned and opened the single door that was part of the larger gate and motioned for him to enter the city.

He followed the officer down board-covered streets to the palace where he was taken past the guards to a large chamber. It was a richly appointed throne room. There were large fires set in fireplaces along the wall; it still felt cold to him, but not as bad as it was outside. He knew these stone mausoleums were a bitch to keep warm.

There were scores of locals, including the young man, sitting on a raised dais at the end. Several appeared as if they had hastily dressed, and were still adjusting their clothes. If this was supposed to be their best dress, he wasn't impressed. Most were wearing furs and clothing of homespun cloth. A few men wore trousers, but most of the inhabitants wore long robes that came down to their ankles. He could see plenty of bejeweled rings on the men and necklaces on the women. There was very little gold visible, but what was in evidence was prominently displayed. That confirmed his reading that there wasn't much gold on the planet. Other than a half a dozen guards with halberds in front of the dais, he did not see any weapons beyond what appeared to be dress daggers in the men's belts.

A herald announced the presence of King Jasper the VI of Brunner. Harkaman decided that was most likely the young man, seated on a throne on the upper dais. He appeared to be in his late teens, although appearances were often deceiving on Neobarbarian worlds. There were five older men standing on the dais just below the king and their appearance and dress screamed senior advisor. He walked slowly toward them, noticing that each of the columns holding up the roof were intricately carved thick wooden posts. Some were recognizable as people or animals while others were abstract, with complex designs meaningful only to the inhabitants.

There were murmurs running through the richly dressed crowd as he advanced. Whether because of his height or his utilitarian green spaceman's battle dress coverall, he didn't know. He'd left his combat helmet behind but he was towing a metal box on a contragravity lifter. The lifter might be what was drawing their attention.

As he reached within ten yards of the dais, he stopped as he saw the guards rise up on their toes. The herald pounded his staff into the floor.

"Who is this who approaches us?" the young man asked. His voice was high and he was trying to act as if he were not scared, but failing miserably. His furs were more opulent than the other men. He wore gems on every finger including his thumbs, an ornate necklace and a thin gold torc around his neck. He gave his name and said he was from the starship *Fortuna*.

"The sky monster!" someone whispered.

"I am here to trade," he announced, loud enough so everyone could hear him. "I will destroy the nearest black slinker nest in return for gems and gold."

That set the crowd off. One of the men on the lower dais stepped forward and spoke. He noticed the annoyed look on the King's face. Apparently this man wasn't following protocol. "How many gems?" the man asked.

Harkaman turned and took the metal box off the contragravity lifter, opening it while turning so that many in the crowd, as well as those on the dais, could see its size. "Enough gems and gold to fill this box," he said.

That brought forth an explosion of noise. Several of the men on the dais cried out and made angry gestures at him. Some in the crowd yelled "No" and other words he couldn't make out but whose meaning was quite clear. He stood still and said nothing.

The middle man on the dais stepped forward and waved his hand. From the rich robes he wore and the gold lining, he was an important figure. The crowd quieted down almost immediately. The man was middle-aged, broad shouldered and stocky with a pot belly. His beard was thick and grey, but his hair was still dark brown. He had an intelligent and self-possessed look about him. He turned and bowed slightly to the king. "Sire, if I may?"

With a look of relief the king made a motion to him to continue. "Please, speak, Chamberlain."

"You ask for all of our wealth," the Chamberlain said.

He kept a straight face, but he doubted that was true. This city held at least fifty thousand inhabitants, ten times what the previous city had held. If the amount of gems they had were similar they could probably fill two of the strong boxes he had brought with him without a problem.

"What I offer is more than worth a single box of gems," he replied. "The scourge of the slinkers will be removed from your lives. You can plant crops outside your walls, expand your city, do whatever you wish without fear of attack. Trading with other cities will become easier as well."

There were more murmurs from the crowd at this statement. He assumed they had some way of trading with other communities as he doubted that the variety of gems they displayed could come from just this area. The man's expression was thoughtful. "How do we know you can do what you say?"

Harkaman had been expecting this question. He drew his pistol out of his holster, turned and fired at the wood pillar that was carved into a representation of a giant slinker. It only took a few bullets for the face to dissolve into splinters before he re-holstered his weapon.

This caused more than a few screams from the crowd and a lot of excited yelling. Many people drew back while others turned and ran out of the room. The halberdiers in front of him raised their halberds at the same time as they backed away. The king shank back on his throne, while the minister who had spoken stood still, trying his best to look unimpressed but not succeeding.

Once the noise died down, Harkaman continued. "We have even greater weapons that can destroy the slinkers' nest. Are you interested?"

The older man turned around and faced the King. Their conversation took no more than a minute.

"How do we know you will do what you say," he asked.

He had also been waiting for this question. "You may designate two men to travel with me in the vehicle I arrived in. We will fly above the slinkers' nest so that they can see it destroyed."

He could tell from the reactions of the people in the presence chamber that the notion of flying through the air was frightening to most of them. He continued, "You must fill this box with gems before I leave, but it will stay under guard here until I return once the nests are destroyed." He planned to leave a guard of his own so that even if they tried to renege on the deal, the *Fortuna's* crew could take the gems.

The older man did not even bother to turn to the king before he spoke. "Your terms are agreeable to us but we have one other condition."

After that pronouncement, the Chamberlain walked down from the dais and removed four of his rings, depositing them in the strong box. He gestured to the crowd to do the same. Only a few followed his direction, until the King stood up and removed half a dozen rings and his necklace as well and added them to the box, although he stayed out of Harkaman's range and quickly returned to his throne. After that, most of those in the chamber hastened forward to add their jewelry as well, eager to be seen cooperating with the King.

He noticed that the king and his senior advisor were carefully watching who did and did not contribute. He suspected that those who didn't donate were going to receive an armed visit from the King's Guard.

He motioned for the senior advisor to approach him and said, "Let us talk about your additional condition."

The additional condition that the senior advisor, who turned out to be an uncle of the king, asked for was easily granted. Harkaman had been afraid he would ask for his gun or some other weapons, but all he wanted was a second Slinker nest destroyed.

IV

As he walked out of the Brunner city gates, he received numerous friendly comments from the people he passed to which he responded with a wave. He suspected the commoners didn't have anything worth contributing and so were pleased, for once, to see the nobility having to give up some of their wealth. The commoners were going to benefit, at least initially, by not having to fight against the slinkers. Although, in the end he was certain the nobility would come up with a way to tax the commoners to get their wealth back. *Not my problem*, he thought.

The nearest nest was only two miles away behind some low hills. However it was a small one. Most of the slinker attacks on the city came from a very large nest that was almost ten miles away.

It hadn't been hard to convince the Captain. While he had been in Brunner negotiating with the king and his advisors, some of the crew had been going through the weapons inventory. They had found half a dozen old-style burrowing bombs. They drove a hundred feet or so into the ground before igniting, sending out an explosive pulse that had turned both of the slinkers' nests into a pile of earth, dead slinkers and rubble.

No one knew their original purpose. The bombs predated even Captain Burricks' tenure on the *Fortuna*. There was speculation that they were in the weapons stockpile in case it became necessary to attack some buried installation, but they hadn't been used for the purpose in a long time—if ever. Others thought they were intended for mining operations. It didn't matter since they were perfect for taking out slinker nests. The

Captain said they could repeat Harkaman's visits to other cities until the bombs were used up.

The King's uncle, along with an alchemist, who passed for a scientist on this Neobarbarian world, had ridden along on the air car and been suitably impressed. They had reported excitedly to everyone within earshot when they returned to Brunner.

The strong box was delivered to Harkaman as he waited just outside the city gate. After opening the box, he dug through it to be certain that they hadn't filled the bottom with earth or otherwise added fake gems and jewelry. A few of the nobles in attendance made scandalized noises. The king's uncle silenced them with a brief comment, nodding to Harkaman as if he were impressed with his thoroughness.

As he returned to the pinnace, which would take him up to the waiting *Fortuna*, he couldn't help but think about all the ways he might use this to get ahead in the world. He'd left the Sword-Worlds because none of the paths available to him for advancement seemed as attractive as being a Space Viking. On the other hand, he didn't intend to be a troop section leader for the rest of his life.

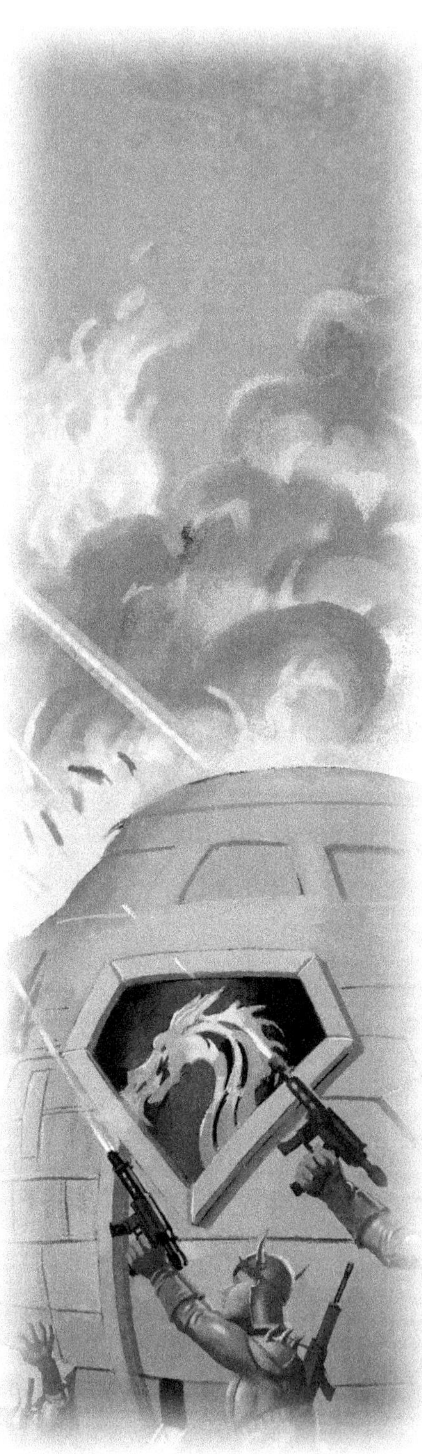

Excalibur

1699 A.E.

The Viking's Lair was crowded and loud with the sound of celebration. Located next to Camelot Spaceport on Excalibur, the Lair was the local port of call and catered to Space Vikings. When Space Viking crews had money they were prone to spend it quickly. And now, after a successful voyage, it was full of men eager to throw their money around as well as women eager to benefit from that fact. The room smelled of spilled beer, piss and vomit. Tobacco smoke hung like a cloud below the ceiling. A man at the back of the room wearing a Space Viking jacket with no ship insignia was playing strange electronic music that no one was listening to, which only added to the background noise.

In one corner however, there was a small group of men who weren't quite so boisterous. "They're saying nine hundred, maybe even a thousand stellars apiece," said one man, gulping at his drink.

"No, Carlos," another replied. "It'll be more like six hundred. Seven hundred tops. You take it easy," he continued, putting his hand on Carlos's arm as he started to raise his glass to his lips again. "No need to drink it all up before you've gotten your share in hand."

Carlos Ericsan calmed slightly. Even though Otto Harkaman was no more than a year or two older than he was, he had an authoritative manner that gave his words weight. Beyond that, he was a good five to six inches taller than anyone else, even though Space Vikings tended to be larger than the average man in Terro-human occupied space. He had a large chest and arms the size of most men's thighs; he was not a man to be trifled with.

They were all Space Vikings from the Sword-Worlds, a cluster of a dozen worlds in a stellar cluster often referred to as the Helm due to its shape. They were located more than two thousand light-years from Old Federation space. At a light-year per hour, travel to the Old Federation took at least three months. Despite the distance, like the Vikings of old Terra, they had raided those worlds that could not defend themselves, taking much of their loot back to the Sword-Worlds. Excalibur, the oldest and most populated of the Sword-Worlds, was the most popular destination for selling plunder, although, not always the most profitable port of call.

Harkaman smiled and added a little more beer from the pitcher of Durendal draft, most Space Viking's favorite swill, to Carlos's glass. "The captain or his executive officer will be back soon enough," he said. "We'll find out then just how well we did."

"By damn, this was a profitable voyage," said one of the other men at the table. "I'm glad I signed on with the *Fortuna*."

"Couldn't do much better than we did," another muttered, draining his glass for emphasis and stretching it out for a refill.

Harkaman shook his head while picking up the pitcher in one giant hand and smoothly refilling the other man's glass. With the other hand he removed the pipe from his mouth, exhaling a puff of smoke. He looked around carefully before replying, noting there wasn't anyone within hearing distance of their table.

"I believe we could have done a lot better," he said, and began giving examples of what he meant, starting with, "there's been too much partying and drinking, when the men should be focused on raiding..."

The others listened, some slack-jawed, some amused, one intently, as he analyzed the *Fortuna's* raids from beginning to end, giving examples of alternative measures which might have brought them more plunder.

"Harkaman, you're full of it!" Olaf, another ground troop section leader, shouted derisively.

"You can't maintain that kind of control over a crew," added another. "We're Space Vikings, not Space Virgins! No one joins a ship because he's an angel."

"The boys have to be able to let loose planet-side," said a third. "After all the time we spent cooped up on a ship, by Odin's Spear, we deserve to have our fun!"

Harkaman had noticed that more and more Space Vikings were using so called Viking oaths and curses from Old Terra. Some were even worshipping the Old Norse Gods. The Neo-Paganism movement had started on Morglay, and now it was sweeping its way through the other Sword-Worlds.

He grinned, waving a hand the size of a baseball glove to forestall any more objections. "I'm not objecting to anyone cutting loose. I'm just saying that if they're doing it during a raid, they aren't making us any prize money."

He emptied the last of a pitcher of Durendal draft into his glass. He turned around, trying to attract the attention of a barmaid for a refill. Typically, in the Sword-Worlds, most bartenders were robots; but here at the Viking's Lair, the owners realized that men, after a long voyage, were more eager to spend their money if attractive women served their drinks—the less-clad, the better.

Failing to get the barmaid's attention, Harkaman started to stand up to go to the bar.

"I'll do it," Alvyn Karffard volunteered, taking the pitcher from Harkaman's hand. Karffard was six feet tall, a half-foot shorter than

Harkaman. He was slender and muscular. Unlike Harkaman's reddish-brown hair and clean-shaven face, he had short black hair, olive skin and a neatly trimmed beard. He found the discussion worthwhile and didn't want Harkaman distracted by one of the barmaids. As the most junior member of the Ship's Stores department, he hadn't had much contact with Otto Harkaman, who was a ground troop section leader. Most of the others at the table occupied similar junior positions, although nearly all had several years more experience than he did.

Karffard's previous interactions with Harkaman on the *Fortuna* had been during the long trip from the Sword-Worlds into the Old Federation for the current raid. He had found out that Harkaman was from Colada, one of the poorer Sword-Worlds, and the son of a machinist with only a secondary education. However, he had discovered that Otto was very well-read, particularly in history. In fact Harkaman had given him a couple of books on ship operations that had filled in a few gaps in Karffard's knowledge. Their discussions of those books and other topics had developed a lasting respect for each other's intellect and their desire to improve themselves.

"Chasing the local girls, drinking booze to get drunk and seeing how fast you can burn a building down is fine," Harkaman continued. "But not until the raid is over and done with."

"Maybe you should share your great suggestions with the Captain," Olaf said sarcastically. "I'm sure he'd appreciate them."

A shadow crossed Harkaman's face. A barmaid arrived at that moment with a new pitcher of beer and he didn't say anything. Instead, he took the pitcher and began refilling everyone's glass.

"Well," interjected another man, the only one present with braided-shoulder length hair, identifying him as a member of the old Sikh faith. "Are you going to talk with the Captain, Otto?"

"I already did, Ranjit," Harkaman replied, grimacing. "He told me what I could do with my recommendations."

Several of the men laughed and Olaf stood up. "That shows you exactly what they're worth." Throwing a few coins on the table for the beer, he picked his glass up and headed for the main crowd at the bar. One by one the other people at the table looked at one another and followed his example. Finally there were only three men at the table.

"Go ahead, Carlos," Harkaman said kindly to the young man fidgeting nervously next to him. "I don't mind."

"Sure…sorry, Otto." Carlos rose and left.

He turned to Alvyn Karffard. "No need to hang around a man who's obviously howling up the wrong tree."

Karffard reached into his pocket and pulled out a package of cigarettes, tapping one out and lighting it. He didn't offer one to Harkaman, who'd already made it clear he preferred his pipe.

"I don't think you're wrong," he said. "All of those ideas were good, and none of them were based on the benefit of hindsight. Ever since I became a Space Viking, I've wondered about some of the crazy stories I've heard, about what happened during ground raids."

Karffard had always been shipboard during the *Fortuna's* raids, since he was part of the ship's crew of three hundred odd men; not one of the five hundred ground troops that went planetside for raids.

"It always seemed to me, Otto," he continued, "that too many of the troops were focused on having a good time instead of finding the best loot. If we did it your way, the men could still have fun later—and maybe we'd make a few stellars more."

Harkaman grinned, raised his glass and drained half of it. "Thanks," he said.

Karffard took a deep breath, then plunged in further. "Have you ever thought about holding a command position?" he asked. "I've served with plenty of officers who don't have half your abilities."

Harkaman started to speak, then paused and reached into his jacket pocket, pulling out a pouch of tobacco. He methodically repacked his pipe and lit it before he responded. He'd always liked Karffard but they'd never had this kind of conversation before and he wondered where it was headed; he decided to respond honestly.

"I've given a lot of thought about commanding my own ship,"

Harkaman said seriously. "I've seen the same things you have on the ships I've been on. But everyone I've ever talked to about it has laughed at me, telling me I don't know what I'm doing, or I don't have the background, education or connections." He smiled a little, "You're the first one who hasn't."

Karffard inhaled deeply, while nodding his head. He'd been around a lot of senior officers in his few years of Space Viking life, and not many of them had impressed him with their knowledge, intellect or drive. In fact, most of the captains he'd served under were less impressive than Otto Harkaman and he told him that.

"Thanks, again," Harkaman replied, a little embarrassed. He'd never found Karffard to be a brown-noser and knew his words were sincere. "But what about you and command?" he continued. "I've noticed, even though you're the bottom man in Ship's Stores, it's running a lot better on this voyage than it ever has."

Now it was Karffard's turn to appreciate a compliment. He decided it was time to lay his cards on the table. "I don't know how I'd do in a command position," he said. "But I know I can organize things. I've done it all my life." He thought of his well-meaning but hapless parents and how he helped them while growing up on Haulteclere. He gave Harkaman a few examples. "Any good captain needs a good exec," he finished, watching Harkaman closely to see how he reacted. He wanted this conversation to be more than just typical bar banter.

"I agree," Harkaman said. He was silent for a few moments. He liked Karffard but he had never thought about working with him as part of a team until this moment. "But we've got a lot to do before that can happen. You've got to get some experience outside of Ship's Stores to be certain your skills translate. And I've got to move into a more senior command position before anyone would consider me as a captain." He wondered how Karffard would react to that statement.

"That won't happen aboard the *Fortuna*," Karffard said, putting the rest of his cards on the table.

Harkaman agreed again. In that moment he decided that Alvyn

Karffard was the kind of man he wanted by his side. He began suggesting possible ships they might consider transferring to. Karffard nodded, making some suggestions of his own. Since there were almost two hundred Space Viking ships currently operating in the Old Federation and more than a dozen currently at the spaceport here on Excalibur with lots of turnover, so there were a number of choices. They considered the possibilities until both their glasses and the pitcher was empty. Still feeling thirsty, Harkaman waved over the barmaid.

"This calls for something more than beer," he said, ordering two shots of Red Whiskey, Excalibur's best.

They stood, swaying slightly as they got up after a long time sitting. The bar was much quieter, the crowd having thinned out during their talk.

"To a future captain!" Karffard toasted.

"And his top exec!" Harkaman cried out.

They tossed back the whiskey and bumped fists, Karffard grimacing as Harkaman's giant hand crashed into his. Ignoring his look of pain, he clapped him heartily on his back.

"Now I need to make use of the head," he said, looking around for the proper door.

Karffard pointed to the opposite corner. "You go ahead. I want to find out what this music is we've been listening to," he said, pointing toward the man in the back of the room who had continued to play, even as the room cleared out. The man was of average height but his long, thick curly hair, broad shoulders and barrel chest made him seem larger.

They both listened for a few moments.

"I'm not sure I'd even call that music," Harkaman said dismissively, as he turned and headed resolutely toward the opposite corner.

Karffard strode over to the musician. He was always curious and one never knew what you might learn.

Rimmon

I

1702 A.E.

The first floor room was large and ornate-looking. Even on a barbarian world, which Rimmon certainly was, it looked like a high-class bank, or, at least a bank that wanted you to think it was high class. The ground troop section leader saw him and came over to report. The look on his face told him the report wasn't going to be very good.

"There's some gold and silver here, Otto, but not much," he said, indicating the two contragravity lifters that men were towing out.

Otto Harkaman, raid commander on the *Manticore*, looked around, trying to hide his disappointment. They had come to Rimmon, the third world of a G5 star, looking for heaven-tea, which was in big demand back on the Sword-Worlds due to its taste and healing properties. He remembered when his older sister had been very ill, his father had spent most of his money for a week's worth of heaven-tea which had cured her.

Unfortunately it turned out they had arrived on Rimmon several months before the harvest and the warehouses in Tucuman, the largest city, held very little tea. He had been among the crew members who had tried to talk the captain out of raiding here for just that reason. The only time to successfully raid Rimmon was right after the heaven-tea harvest. If you were too late, the harvest was already dispersed throughout the world; it was impractical to rob every little city and town on the planet.

Rimmon was an uncivilized world; its development level was at the equivalent of the Industrial Revolution, Third Century Pre-Atomic Era back on Terra. The locals had rifles and small cannon and were just starting to develop steam engines. The only land transportation was by horse-drawn carts, so the major cities were located on rivers or coastal ports for water transport. It was not a rich world.

However, Captain Kowalski had a friend who claimed that he could calculate exactly when the harvest would occur and that they could fill the ship with heaven-tea. Harkaman hadn't seen the Captain's friend for the last two days. He suspected no one would see him until the *Manticore* was safely back in the Sword-Worlds star cluster, where he could slip off the ship undetected.

They'd hit another city before Tucuman without any better luck. From what he'd heard the crews looting this city's warehouses weren't finding anything more worthwhile than what was at this bank.

He looked around curiously. His men had pushed all the customers and bank employees into a corner at gunpoint.

"What's in all those vaults?" he asked, pointing to several that lined the wall behind the counters and tellers' workstations.

"I'll show you," the section leader said, gesturing for him to follow. "Nothing but a bunch of worthless paper," he said, pointing to a pile of bank notes neatly stacked in an open vault. "The others are much the same."

"Too bad," Harkaman said disappointedly, turning to leave. It had been an unprofitable voyage so far and this world, their fourth stop on the trip, didn't look like it would change the stench of failure that saturated the ship. There were already grumbles of discontent from the crew, according to Alvyn Karffard, who had found a junior position on the engineering staff when they had signed on with the *Manticore* at Excalibur.

"Well, wrap everything up here and head back to the ship. No one's found anything better anywhere else in this city."

The section leader nodded and repeated the order to his men. As raid commander, Otto Harkaman had retrained all the ground fighters of the *Manticore* until he was satisfied with them. There were a few that he didn't think were suited to being Space Vikings but at least now they carried out his orders promptly.

As he turned to leave, he noticed a large attractive sculpture that took up part of one wall of the city's biggest bank. Maybe this would be worth something he thought, moving closer to examine it further. Most Space Vikings considered only gold, silver, jewels, metals and consumer goods worth stealing. He knew that sometimes you could get lucky with barbarian art works, depending on the quality of their craftsmanship and the rarity of their materials.

Upon closer look, he realized it was a map of the continent which he remembered seeing from orbit. A prominent bronze star, probably representing the location of the bank, was located in the northern part of the continent. There were other, less prominent stars on the sculpture, probably representing other cities or branches of the bank. Although an example of fine workmanship, he doubted that it would have much value on the Sword-Worlds, since no one would recognize the subject matter.

Then it hit him. He turned around and saw the bank employees, who had been herded into one corner, standing there frightened out of their wits. He gestured to one of his men, who was helping to guard the employees.

"Bring me fancy-pants," Harkaman ordered, pointing to a man wearing an elaborate coat and suit with hair teased up in an elaborate swirl. He assumed from his appearance that he was in charge of the bank. One of the crewman seized the man by the arm and dragged him over to Harkaman without much concern for the man or his fancy coat.

The man looked up at him fearfully; his greater size had the man thoroughly intimidated.

He asked if those stars on the sculpture referred to other cities. The man replied that they did. In response to further questioning, he confirmed that the stars represented cities where the bank had branches. The larger stars denoted most prosperous branches.

Harkaman pointed to a large star on the southeast coast of the continent which appeared isolated from the other cities. "Is that city very prosperous?" he asked.

"New Cottesloe? Yes sir," the man said quickly, though he pronounced sir more like "sire." "But," he continued, trying to be helpful. "Even that far south the heaven-tea harvest will not happen for at least two months."

He grimaced. Apparently, the locals had been asked enough questions about the heaven-tea harvest to know that that was what the Space Vikings wanted. After a few more questions he motioned fancy-pants back to the corner where the other employees remained huddled together. Grateful nothing had happened to him, the man moved quickly back to where he'd been standing before.

Harkaman took another look back at the bank vaults filled with worthless paper. An idea was stirring around in his mind and he stood there for a few moments more as it became fully formed. Making his decision, he called the section leader over and gave him an order.

The section leader looked at him uncomprehendingly for a moment. "You want: what? All that useless paper!"

He quickly explained what he had in mind. He was aware he was about to try something totally outside of anything he'd ever heard of. The section leader finally nodded as if he understood why he wanted him to collect the currency.

While the men looted the vaults, Harkaman walked out of the bank toward the waiting troop transports. He pulled his pipe from his pocket, recharged it and lit up. Inhaling deeply, he wondered if the Captain would approve of what he'd done, or if he had just shoot his young career in the foot.

II

In fact his career hadn't been shot in the foot; at the moment, it was thriving to his immense relief.

"This is really something," Otto Harkaman said. "Thanks, Lauren," he added, raising his glass toward her, finishing his drink.

They had left Tucuman City and it was now their seventh day in New Cottesloe. After spending a few days roistering among the bars at the water's edge of this port city, he and Alvyn Karffard had gotten bored and started exploring. In a combination library, art gallery and coffee house, he had met Lauren. Besides being a red-haired beauty with striking green eyes, a rare combination on the Sword-Worlds, she was also the daughter of a prosperous local manufacturer. Lauren also had a larcenous streak. She not only knew all the richest people in town, but where they kept many of their valuables, as well as how they might be persuaded to part with them.

Their attraction was mutual, and he suspected that she made a habit of dating "dangerous men," because of her knowledge regarding the New Cottesloe underworld. Their lovemaking was hot and heavy. Lauren understood that since he was a visitor, there was no possibility of commitment, which added to the excitement.

He was still a little surprised when Captain Kowalski readily accepted his suggestion that the crew take some of the bank notes they'd stolen from the bank in Tucuman and take a couple of days of shore leave. "It'll be easier to pay the locals with worthless paper, than trying to take it from them," he'd told him. "Besides, it'll keep them friendly."

The Captain agreed, probably because he'd heard about all the grumbling from the lower decks. Other than money, drink and easy women were the fastest way to calm a restive crew down.

Originally, he had thought they would only stay at New Cottesloe for three to four days, but the Captain had found a curly-haired beauty he was utterly enamored with and he showed no sign of leaving. The Executive Officer, tired of drinking and wenching, had left three days ago with a couple pinnaces of men to raid some of the more distant cities on Rimmon. The locals believed the *Manticore* was a merchant ship and it would be a while before this isolated port town would hear anything that would change their minds, since they hadn't yet rediscovered radio. By the time they heard about the robberies, they'd be long gone....

Lauren had shown him one of the nicer restaurants, hidden away in a more residential part of town, and he'd expressed his appreciation for its excellent food and good service. Besides his stories of exotic worlds she would never see, she told him she appreciated his height. Though half a foot shorter than he stood, Lauren was taller than most of the native men and was pleased to find a man who made her actually feel dainty.

She had also informed him about several stashes of heaven-tea owned by individuals or businesses. He had used the Tucuman bank notes to add another few hundred pounds to the small amount of heaven-tea in the *Manticore's* hold, even if in one case he had to convince a reluctant owner to sell by adding a few more local notes and, at the same time, letting his coat fall open to display his pistol. The man had hastily completed the transaction.

Several other crew members had been just as enterprising. Alvyn Karffard had obtained a few kegs of heaven-tea by trading some advanced metallurgy techniques to a local blacksmith, a man they would have never suspected of having a cache of tea in a typical raid. Others had shown the locals some advanced medical or construction knowledge and been rewarded in turn.

"I know a place that has some great art," Lauren said, continuing the conversation while he waved for a refill. "Different stuff," she continued. "Not the usual trash," she added, as she considered herself quite the connoisseur.

Harkaman knew that Lauren had worked in an art gallery and had a degree in art history. Still, she might be an expert judge of art produced on Rimmon, but he'd seen great art on a dozen worlds. He evidenced only mild interest until she mentioned that some of sculptures were made of gold. Hastily draining his glass, he rose from his seat, throwing a few of the banknotes on the table.

"Let's go see this art gallery of yours," he told her.

Lauren hadn't been kidding, either about the gold or the quality of the art. Most of the people in the warehouse at the edge of the commercial area were young and had the dress and air of well-to-do people determined not to be respectable. Respectable or not, they were happy to take his paper banknotes. On several occasions, it was all they could do not to let on that they thought they were taking advantage of him. He kept a stone-faced demeanor throughout. He wasn't going to let them know that their paper money was worthless to him, whether the number on it was ten or ten thousand.

Harkaman called Alvyn Karffard on his handheld to bring a lifter, as he had accumulated a lot more valuables than one man could carry. The natives stared at him while he talked. *Radios probably seem like magic to them*, he thought. Even Lauren, who had grown blasé about some of the advanced technology Space Vikings used after five days at his side and in his bed, was watching closely. She had told him that she never got tired of watching him talk into a small box and hearing another voice reply. At least she'd become comfortable enough in its presence not to jump in fright, as most of the other locals did, whenever his handheld beeped.

Karffard arrived a quarter-hour later with a couple of crewmen and a few lifters. "Nice haul," he commented with a smile, as they loaded the various pieces onto the lifters.

After he had directed the crewmen where to stow it on the ship, he turned to Lauren: "Any more like that around here?" he asked.

Lauren started to speak and then stopped, looking at the people crowding around them. “Let’s go for a walk,” she said with a serious expression, taking them each by arm. Going outside, she turned toward a section of the port that neither of them had been in yet, shaking her head when they started to speak. After a few blocks she turned away from the water onto a residential street.

“What’s wrong, Lauren?” he asked.

“I didn’t realize you were so interested in gold and silver,” she said, looking upset. “I thought all you wanted was heaven-tea. If I’d known I would have brought you here much sooner.”

“Yes, we’re very interested in gold and silver,” Harkaman said, hastily adding that it was his fault for not mentioning it.

Mollified, her face relaxed. She smiled and increased her pace.

“Where are we going?” Karffard asked. They’d left the port area and now were walking uphill, where the homes kept getting larger, many surrounded by high fences.

“We’re going to the Majolas,” she replied. “That family is the primary dealer in gold and silver in New Cottesloe.” Her faced turned grim. “They are the most powerful members in the *Nauntana*,” she used a local word that they couldn’t pronounce, even though they’d heard it a few times before.

Lauren explained that New Cottesloe was run by an oligarchy of wealthy residents, called the *Nauntana*, comprised only of merchant traders and ship owners. Even though Lauren’s father was as rich as any of them, the members of the *Nauntana* looked down on him because he was a manufacturer rather than a trader. All her life, Lauren had been made to feel like a second-class citizen. And now she had an opportunity with her new Space Viking friends to knock them down a notch or two.

“Here we are,” she said, coming to a stop before the largest house they had run across in New Cottesloe. The house was made of stone and several stories high and covered roughly half a block; the fence surrounding it was well above even Harkaman’s height. She reached into a nook in the wall and removed a bell, which she rang five times.

“How many people live here?” Karffard asked, swinging around to eye the imposing building.

“Most of the structure is a warehouse,” said Lauren dismissively. “The family lives in the front. The back of it doesn’t look as impressive,” she noted, referring to the part of the house hidden by another fence.

After a few minutes, a well-dressed man came out of the front door and strolled slowly down the walk to the front gate. He stopped when he saw Lauren and her friends.

“What do you want?” he asked haughtily.

Her face colored but her tone remained even as she replied. “Hello, Arico. My friends are visitors from the space vessel,” which was how all the locals referred to the *Manticore*. “They wish to trade for gold and silver,” she finished.

The man managed to look even more dismissive. “With what?” he asked.

He opened his pouch to show a wad of bills. It was arranged so that the larger bills were on the outside.

The man shook his head. “Not interested,” he said, turning to leave.

“Why not?” he asked, genuine surprise in his voice. Every New Cottesloe native he’d met had been thrilled the moment they saw the large wads of bank notes the Space Vikings were willing to throw around. They hadn’t had a problem with anyone accepting them before.

“We don’t sell our work for paper money,” the man said, disdain in his voice. He turned again to leave. “Try some of the other merchants,” his tone showing that he was clearly talking about a lower class of people. “Or maybe some manufacturer has something to sell you,” he finished contemptuously.

Lauren made a rude noise. The man didn’t stop walking, but made a gesture with his finger that seemed to be universal on all the worlds Harkaman had visited.

He took Lauren by the arm, and said, “Don’t make a fuss.”

“I don’t take that kind of crap from anyone!” she cried.

He just laughed. “Remember, turnabout is fair play.”

“Oh…” Lauren said, as the penny dropped and she stopped

struggling.

Karffard chuckled as he walked alongside them. "Well, she has a Sword-Worlder's attitude, that's for sure."

Sword-Worlders were disdainful of paper money. The only currency that had retained its value over the centuries were Excalibur stellars, which were redeemable in gold—one Excalibur Stellar being worth an ounce of gold. Every other Sword-World currency was debased—either from too many bouts of inflationary excess or too much currency manipulation—usually by rulers trying to enrich themselves or shore up their flagging reigns. This was why there was such a strong demand for monetary metals and jewels throughout the Helm. Most people considered tangible assets a more reliable and trustworthy source of wealth than paper currency or bank notes.

"Let's come back tomorrow," Harkaman mused. "We might get lucky and someone else might answer the door that would be more reasonable."

Karffard looked uncomfortable. "I'm sorry to bring this up now," he said. "But the Captain issued orders that we're going to space out just after breakfast."

Lauren turned red. "And when were you going to share this news with us!"

Karffard's cheeks colored but he didn't back down. "I thought it would be better if I told Otto, then let him tell you himself."

"He's right, darling," he said to her. "Give us a moment, will you?"

He promptly pulled Karffard away, leaving a baffled-looking woman staring angrily after him. "This means we have to hit that place tonight," he said urgently.

Karffard's mouth gaped. "Are you crazy!" he exploded.

"When someone says something you don't understand, ask him what he means," he replied, annoyed. "Don't call him crazy."

"Well…then, what do you mean, Otto?" Karffard wasn't intimidated in the least by his manner. "The raiding crews are off with the Second. Or they're having one last drunk, a final tryst like the Captain, or both."

"I know, that's why you're going to put a raiding party together," he replied, turning to look at an impatiently waiting Lauren. "Like the Captain, I want one last fling."

"Me!" exclaimed Karffard, a worried look creasing his face. "What do I know about raiding? I've always been crew, not a ground fighter."

"Well then it's time to start," he said heartily, clapping him on the back while Karffard looked anxiously at him. "Listen, here's what I want you to do."

Harkaman gave him a detailed list of everything he wanted, then sent him off before turning back to Lauren. With anyone else he would have had to write everything down, but Alvyn's memory was near photographic. He'd get everything organized, while he enjoyed his last night on Rimmon.

III

Alvyn Karffard had returned to the ship and brought all of the equipment and most of the men Harkaman had requested. He was already dressed and ready when Alvyn knocked discreetly at the back door of Lauren's home. She wasn't there with him, saying it would be too hard to watch him leave after she'd already said goodbye. As he came out the door, Harkaman looked around the back alley and nodded to Alvyn with approval. It was about an hour or so before dawn.

"Do you think there's a chance Lauren might call ahead and let them know we're coming?" Alvyn asked.

"Not a chance in hell. She hates the Majolas. They act like they're better than anyone else in town."

Alvyn had brought some two dozen men with him; some of them like Ranjit and Carlos were members of what they already considered their crew. Others were the ones Harkaman had put on his list; they were the men Harkaman had led as raid commander and whom he'd learned could be trusted do their jobs. Since he couldn't find all the men Harkaman had requested, Alvyn had brought a handful that he had found either at the *Manticore* or on his way back into town. One or two had looked a little unsteady on their feet when he found them, but the walk to Lauren's home and then up to the Majolas' mansion had helped sober them up.

One of the men was Guatt Kirbey, who looked even more worried than Karffard did. Alvyn had met Kirbey at the Viking's Lair on Excalibur when he'd asked him about the strange music he was playing. Kirbey was an apprentice astrogator and a superb mathematician, two traits that went well together. As a hobby he wrote music which was based on his mathematical knowledge, which was why it sounded so different. He had struck both Karffard and Harkaman as both knowledgeable and solid.

Kirbey had also been unemployed, his last berth having ended when the ship failed to produce enough profit on last raids and was seized by its investors. They had recruited him to join the *Manticore* and he had become a member of their personal group. Like Alvyn, he had always been a crew member and never taken part in a raid. But Kirbey was a trained small vehicle operator so Alvyn had put him behind the controls of the landing-craft. The landing-craft was designed so that it could open on all sides for quick loading and unloading. It also carried a variety of contragravity powered lifters and three egg-shaped one-man air cavalry mounts with machine guns.

All the rest of the men carried personal weapons or machine guns.

Alvyn gripped his pistol a little tighter, trying not to show how anxious he felt. He was standing right where Harkaman had told him to, behind his broad back. He was suddenly very happy his friend was such a big man. Harkaman turned to him with a serious expression.

"What's your number one job?" he asked him again.

"Not to shoot you in the back," Alvyn replied.

"Good," he grinned. "Try and relax."

They were standing before a doorway in the back alley behind the Majolas' property, where Lauren had said the warehouse was located. Alvyn moved back when he realized that the man ahead of them had just finished pressing a small amount of plastic explosive into the door lock. He turned and nodded in readiness.

"All right boys," Harkaman said with a smile. "These people have been good hosts to us so let's try not to burn the town down."

That got a good laugh.

Harkaman motioned everyone back. Alvyn hastily joined the other men in pressing himself against the warehouse wall, trying to keep his breathing down. Though it was a cool morning he was sweating profusely. He looked around and was surprised to note that most of the men, even the experienced ones like Ranjit, seemed equal parts worried and excited.

Suddenly an explosion went off and he felt a rush of burning hot air singe his face. *If this is a "quiet explosive,"* he thought, *I wonder what the Cataclysmite sounds like!*

As soon as the debris settled, Carlos and another crewman quickly rushed through the smoke-filled doorway with their guns drawn. Two other men with portable lights quickly followed. After long seconds, he heard Carlos' shout: "There's no one in here!"

Harkaman waved the air-cavalry mounts ahead and followed behind, with Alvyn in his wake. Along with Kirbey, five men remained alongside the landing-craft, with guns drawn.

The room was only about sixty feet deep but contained a variety of merchandise stacked along the walls. Harkaman waved their explosives expert forward to a large metal door that took up much of the eastern wall. The others continued opening and searching the boxes and kegs along the side walls.

As soon as the explosives' man at the door indicated he was ready, one of the other men spoke up: "By Satan, this whole wall appears to be filled with heaven-tea." There was elation in his voice.

Alvyn saw grins breakout on everybody's faces. Here in one spot was ten times more heaven-tea than they had previously collected during the last few hundred hours.

Then, they heard voices on the other side of the wall.

"Let's give them a wake-up call," Harkaman laughed, holding up the detonator.

Everyone hastily dived on the floor or pressed up against the wall. The explosion that followed was even louder than the previous one in the confined space. Smoke and debris filled the room.

Alvyn rose up from where he'd crouched against the stone wall, a little disoriented and coughing. After waiting a minute or two for the smoke to disperse, several Space Vikings charged through the blasted out doorframe with guns in their hands, while one of the air-cavalry mounts followed overhead. He heard a few shots followed by hammering of a machine gun, then a call for lights. The men carrying the portable lights hastily moved through the door, followed by another air-cavalry mount.

Harkaman stopped the third air-cavalry mount as it began to follow. "Stand guard outside," he ordered. Then turning to the rest of his crew, he said, "Grab the lifters and start loading the heaven-tea."

As they jumped to obey, Harkaman motioned for Alvyn to follow. They advanced down a short corridor about ten feet wide which opened into another large room. Alvyn saw two dead bodies lying near the doorway and catching a whiff of blood, he hastily averted his eyes. He'd never seen a corpse blown apart by explosives and didn't want to see one now. There was a third body about a dozen feet inside the door.

This room was much larger than the outer room. It appeared to be a good hundred and twenty-feet deep. The walls were stacked with a mixture of boxes and crates. Carlos went over and began to open one of the boxes.

"They're not the right size for heaven-tea," one of the men said; disappointment in his voice.

Carlos was having a difficult time trying to open the box. "It's heavy," he said, finally throwing it on the floor in frustration. The box burst open and a dozen ingots, reflecting golden light spilled out.

"By the gods!" Ranjit exclaimed. "That's a box of gold ingots."

Harkaman turned and grinned at him. He had instructed Alvyn not to mention gold or silver when he brought the men. He hadn't wanted to disappoint them if Lauren had turned out to be wrong.

Everyone gaped at the gold, and then several men started moving toward the stack of boxes. A second later they were hastily trying to dig themselves into the floor as a shot rang out from behind the inner door. Karffard heard a variety of guns go off, the yammering of the machine guns of the air cavalry mount drowning them all out. Then Harkaman was yelling for everyone to cease firing. "Anyone hurt?"

In the silence that followed, they heard the air cavalry-man's voice: "Just one. I got him, sir."

One of their men was on the ground groaning and holding his leg. Alvyn started toward him but Harkaman grabbed him and pushed him toward the outer door.

"Call the ship," he ordered. "Tell them that we're going to need a medic, more landing-craft and lifters."

Harkaman ordered the two air-cavalry mounts to cover the inner door. Karffard went out to the landing-craft and made the call. He had just finished arguing with a somewhat incredulous junior officer, when the injured man, his leg bent at an unnatural angle, was carried out, swathed in bandages leaking blood.

Alvyn looked at the crewman, his stomach heaving with the effort of not losing his dinner. Guatt Kirbey looked like he was having an equally difficult time keeping his last meal down. Despite this Karffard assisted in lifting the man into the vehicle. He turned and told Kirbey to take him back to the ship.

"No," Ranjit Chaudry interrupted; he had just come out with another lifter full of gold. "Wait until the landing-craft is full."

Alvyn was astonished that no one objected to this statement. He started to complain, and then realized he was forgetting one of Harkaman's prime tenets: Everything is secondary to getting the loot on the ship as fast as possible. They didn't know whether the Majolas had more men in the house that might attack them, or whether the neighbors or someone else would show up in force to investigate all the noise.

Everyone continued to haul out boxes of gold and kegs of heaven-tea, loading them onto the landing-craft as fast as they could. Two more landing-craft arrived before the first one was full. He hopped off and waved to Kirbey as he lifted off. Then he turned and went into the house to help bring out the remaining valuables inside the mansion.

No one came out of any of the nearby houses to challenge them; apparently, they had learned their lesson after the first exchange of gunfire.

It sure felt longer, he thought wearily, looking up at the sun. The sun was almost directly overhead when they left the building and boarded the last landing-craft.

"So this was a raid," Alvyn said.

"And, not a bad one," Harkaman replied, stretching his long legs out around some kegs of heaven-tea. "Only one casualty. I'm sure he'll be fine once they set the broken bones in his leg. I'd bet we got over a million stellars worth of loot out of this house alone."

Yes, Alvyn thought, *not a bad raid at all.*

PART TWO

OFFICER

Junrojin

1704 A.E.

The *Hungry Dragon* emerged from hyperspace about five light-minutes from Harley's star. Two microjumps put them ten thousand miles from Junrojin's only moon. They'd hid behind the moon until nightfall when they descended toward the middle of a vast ocean. They came out of the darkness, swooping down on the port of New Otago just as dawn arrived.

Captain Raynard Dampier sent the pinnaces out, with orders to hit the major banks, jewelry stores and department stores. There was only scattered resistance from the local police force, which they quickly silenced, by bombing their headquarters. Their air-cavalry mounts shot up any police vehicles traveling along the streets. Although, Junrojin did not have radar, it did have radio. So they worked quickly to loot the banks and stores before the local military had time to respond.

Harkaman led one of the parties tasked with robbing jewelry stores. There were five major stores in the downtown area and they hit them hard. First, they blew out the windows, then forced their way inside with guns blazing. They left the employees alone unless they tried to resist, usually one or two killings silenced the rest. Then they herded the survivors into the stockroom where they were tied-up and made to lie on the floor until they left.

If there was a safe, one of their trained safebreakers would go to work while the rest of the team removed rings, necklaces, pendants and bracelets from the display counters. They worked quickly and efficiently and were done with the last store well before it was time for the recall buzzer to go off.

They went back aboard the pinnace and flew it directly to the city center, which held city hall, the library and the local museum. Harkaman ordered men to loot the museum, while he went into the nearby library. The library was deserted; their gunfire had emptied it out. He started his search by going to the reference desk and looking for the local atlases. Once he had a good atlas, he began to search for books referencing nearby worlds, as well as any older history volumes, especially those pertaining to the Terran Federation. He had almost an uninterrupted half hour, before the recall buzzer on his handheld went off.

Back aboard the bridge of the *Hungry Dragon*, Alvyn Karffard turned and said loudly, "Hey, turn that down!" However his grin belied the tone of his voice.

The junior astrogator, Sharll Renner, complied with a grin of his own. Renner was a short man with black hair and pockmarked brown skin that he tried to hide with a sparse beard. Karffard, a junior officer in the Damage Control department, and Renner, the assistant normal-space astrogator, were stuck on duty on the bridge with some of the other junior officers. The rest of the crew was celebrating in the ship's large mess hall. Renner had just tuned the bridge radio into the dining room to see what they were missing, resulting in Alvyn's mock complaint.

All of them were feeling pretty good, even if they weren't celebrating with the rest of the crew. Junrojin was a world with plenty of chemical weapons, artillery and rockets, so a lot of Space Vikings avoided raiding it. Captain Raynard Dampier was not one of them.

They had made a big haul looting New Otago, while his friend Otto Harkaman had done his usual investigation of the city's library once the raid was over. Harkaman was always looking for new material. He had found an atlas of the world and had determined that the wealthiest city, Lucindale, was located on another continent. Since it had been over thirty years since the last time Junrojin had been raided by Space Vikings, it was not surprising that their local knowledge was out of date. Captain Dampier had accepted Harkaman's information and as soon as the looting of New Otago had finished they had set off for Lucindale.

By the time they arrived, Lucindale was aware that Space Vikings were on the planet and their military forces were on alert. Coming down on the city the *Hungry Dragon* had been subjected to a relentless barrage of rockets and cannon fire and had the scars to prove it. Even with their overwhelming firepower, it had been a hard-fought battle to subdue the city—entire city blocks had been bombed into rubble.

Once the fighting had died down, Harkaman had led a force of air combat cars and landing craft to the sites he had identified. One was at a large bank and the other vaults underneath the government palace. They had spent a day and half unloading gold, jewels and other valuables. Meanwhile, the rest of the ground troops were looting stores and warehouses of jewels, furniture, machinery, metals, furs and anything else that held possible value.

"What do you think, Otto, three hundred million stellars?" Vann Larch asked, the junior guns and missiles officer, taking a break from discussing some of the art they he had removed from the Lucindale museums and art galleries. Most Space Vikings had hobbies to pass the time during long periods they spent in hyperspace. Larch was a painter and a good one, which was an odd contrast to his tall, thick-bearded, blond frame. Harkaman had once said he looked like a classic Viking from the Dark Ages on Old Terra. The Captain was happy to follow Larch's recommendations on taking any art he thought might be worth selling back in the Sword-Worlds.

"We might do that well, Vann," Harkaman said with a grin. As the highest ranking junior officer he was in command of the bridge at the moment. He turned back to some of the other crew and finished his story of how they had come to join the *Hungry Dragon*.

Harkaman had impressed the Captain on his previous ship the *Manticore*. Not having any open positions for promotion on his ship, the Captain had recommended him to several other captains while selling loot and relaxing on the Space Viking base world of Hoth. Captain Dampier had interviewed him and hired him. Harkaman had also convinced him to hire Karffard and Guatt Kirby, currently sitting in the assistant astrogator's chair. As the most senior of the junior officers, he was also put in charge of filling the other openings on the crew. He had taken this opportunity to hire some of those troopers he had been impressed with on other Space Viking ships.

Three hundred million stellars, Alvyn thought. That would make his share a little under two million depending on ship expenses, because the *Hungry Dragon* had so few crew rated as junior officers. The most lucrative raid they had ever participated in would help them on their way to their goal of saving up enough money to eventually get their own ship.

He was distracted by a look of concern on the signals and detection officers' face as he turned away to look at his board. "What is it, Paul?"

Paul Koreff shook his head. He was short, with black hair, brown skin and a black pencil mustache. "There was a beep as if something had been detected off-planet," he said. "But I don't see anything. If it was a ship, she would have had to have come out of hyperspace and almost immediately drop into the shadow of one of the moons."

He laughed. "Well if it's a Space Viking ship, they're welcome to some of the cities we didn't raid. But, I think they'll discover that everyone is on their guard."

Alvyn relaxed and put his feet up on his console, lighting a cigarette.

They were currently sitting on an uninhabited island in the middle of Junrojin's largest ocean. The island wasn't much more than a beach and enough flat area to land a ship but it was nice to breathe real air and look at a sky. The Captain liked to stretch his legs outside after a long voyage so he always stayed on the planet for a few days after a raid was over if he could do so without any more fighting.

"Looks like just a false alarm," Koreff said, pushing various buttons and not finding any satisfactory results. "I'll give the equipment a thorough checkup once we're in hyperspace."

Koreff is probably right, Harkaman thought. It would be an incredible coincidence if two Space Viking ships raided a planet independently at the same time. While there were some two hundred independent Space Viking ships, there were several thousand planets in the former Federation, spread out over more than ten thousand light-years; enough so, that it wasn't unusual to hear of some new planet being discovered that no one had ever heard of. The distances that Space Vikings had to travel from the Sword-Worlds just to reach the Old Federation made it even more unlikely two ships would show up at the same place. He smiled and listened to the tales that the bridge crew was sharing of past voyages. It was about seven hours until the end of their shift, then they could look forward to joining the party.

Otto Harkaman grinned as he noticed everyone casting more glances at the bridge clock. "Relax, everybody," he said. "It's a little less than an hour before we're relieved and can join the celebration."

Someone said that they hoped there'd still be some booze left and everyone had a laugh at that. Koreff suddenly turned to his instrument board with a surprised look on his face. Before he could ask him what it was, he had turned back to face him.

"Unknown ship detected, Otto," he stated. "She's just coming over the horizon line. Half an hour away at current speed."

"Send her the standard Sword-World impulse code and our screen combination," Harkaman ordered.

After a few seconds Koreff, turned back to him. "No response."

Well, that's curious, Harkaman thought. Even ships that weren't from the Sword-Worlds knew the code. Then he began to get concerned.

"Check the long range telescope," he ordered. "What do you see, Paul?"

"She's a fifteen-hundred footer," Koreff said, after a few moments. "Nothing else is visible."

"Keep looking." Harkaman turned to the junior comm officer: "Contact the Weapons Control rooms and see who's awake."

"Could this be what you detected a few hours ago?" Karffard asked Koreff.

"Maybe," he replied. "But why would they approach this way unless they were trying to conceal themselves."

"Why indeed," Harkaman mused out loud. One of the crewmen reported that only two of the eight Weapons Control rooms had responded.

"Try again," he ordered.

Harkaman was debating whether he should note in the ship's log that some of the crew had left their stations, undoubtedly to join the celebration, when someone else spoke up.

"Ship's insignia visible," someone announced. "I'm transferring it to the main screen."

The main screen wavered a moment until the picture steadied. The ship had a skull and crossbones imposed over a planet. He heard Karffard swear as he hit the ship wide announcement button.

"Battle Stations, Battle Stations!" he announced. "This is not a drill. Captain to the bridge, all missile crews to the Weapons Control rooms. Repeat, Captain to the bridge, all missile crews to Weapons Control. This is not a drill."

"Take us up as fast as possible," he told Sharll Renner, who quickly started pushing buttons.

"Wait a moment," one of the crew members cried. "The Captain said we were to stay on the ground."

"We're sitting ducks on the ground," Harkaman replied. "That's where they were hoping to catch us."

In less than a minute the *Hungry Dragon* was rising up into the atmosphere.

"What's going on?" Kirbey asked, alarmed. "Do you know that ship?"

Seeing Harkaman was too busy to reply, Karffard spoke up: "That's the *Jolly Roger*." When he saw the blank look on Kirbey's face, he continued. "We heard about her on Hoth. She's known to have forced two Space Viking ships to give up their loot by doing what she just tried to do to us; catching us on the ground by surprise where a lot of our weapons would be useless and we'd have to surrender."

Going over the weaponry reports, Harkaman discovered that two of the empty Weapons Control stations had missile tubes fully loaded as did the two that were manned. The others were empty. They could load the missiles from the bridge but that would mean taking someone away from other important duties.

"*Jolly Roger* is accelerating," Koreff announced. "She'll be here in less than two minutes."

"Alvyn, start loading the empty missile tubes." That would take Karffard away from monitoring the incoming ship but it couldn't be helped.

"Harkaman!" the junior comm officer cried out. "The Captain is demanding to know what's going on; he says to put the ship back on the ground."

Harkaman swore. "Tell him to get up here to the bridge as fast as possible!"

He hoped that the Captain was sober. He'd been very impressed with Captain Dampier so far. His crew was well trained and disciplined, and he'd found him very willing to share his knowledge and experience on the trip from Hoth to Junrojin. And the Captain hadn't objected to his recommendation to raid Lucindale, even though he was aware that the locals would be prepared for their attack. However, he'd also heard that the Captain and his officers could be serious drinkers when it was time to celebrate.

"Incoming message," Koreff announced. "But they're not sending any video."

That's not surprising, he thought. Space Vikings who preyed on their own kind wouldn't want to identify themselves. He wondered who the crew of the *Jolly Roger* might be and where they could sell their loot. *Could there be a Space Viking base planet we don't know about*, he wondered.

"*Hungry Dragon*," the voice came over the radio. "You are outgunned. All we want is your loot. Land and let us transfer your cargo to our ship and we'll let you live. Otherwise we'll destroy your ship. This is your only warning."

Harkaman snorted. "Are we within range?"

"Coming up now," Larch replied.

"Fire an offensive spread," he replied. "Sharll," he turned to the normal-space astrogator, "begin evasive maneuvers."

There was a slight lurch as the ship shifted course. "Missiles incoming," Koreff yelled.

Harkaman watched as the *Jolly Roger's* missiles closed in on the *Hungry Dragon*. Some of them missed due to Renner's maneuvering. The majority of the rest were intercepted by defensive missiles but two of them got through. He felt slight jolts as the ship took the hits.

"Gaining altitude," Renner announced. The *Jolly Roger* had tried to pin them against the ground but failed due to Renner's quick action. Now she was going too fast to turn with the *Hungry Dragon*.

"See if you can get above them, Sharll," he said. "Let's see if we can turn the tables on them."

Suddenly the bridge door opened and the Captain bustled in with the Second and Third officers following him.

"What in the hell's going on?" the Captain yelled. "I told you to keep the ship on the ground, Harkaman."

Renner chose that moment to make another maneuver. Though the Captain only swayed, the Second officer actually fell to the deck and the Third officer looked as if he were going to throw up.

"We're under attack by the *Jolly Roger*, Captain," Harkaman replied.

"I took the ship up to prevent them from catching us on the ground."

He started to get out of the command chair when Koreff yelled "Incoming!"

"Give them another spread," he ordered, while the Captain just stood there with a bewildered look on his face.

Larch began pressing buttons on his board. The ship shook again as a few more missiles struck it.

"What the Nifflheim!" sputtered the Captain. Before he could say anything else, the Third officer, who normally handled guns-and-missiles, yelled "Belay that order, Larch!"

Larch ignored him and continued to press buttons. Harkaman reached out and grabbed the Captain's arm and tried to guide him into the command chair. This proved impossible when the Captain jerked away from him, trying to help the Second to his feet. The Third officer pawed at Larch, who ignored him. There were a few more jolts as more of the *Jolly Roger's* missiles struck them.

"Damage report," Harkaman ordered. He could see a few lights blinking red on the main board but nothing appeared to be too serious. Without the collapsium plating on the hull, the nuclear-tipped missiles would have vaporized them. Ordinary Sword-World nuclear missiles could typically penetrate about five to seven decks into a collapsium plated ship, which was why nothing vital was stored in those areas. After a hit, the decks were automatically sealed off and the Damage Control Department crew and robots would be working to seal those openings. At least he hoped the crew would be working and not recovering from overindulging like the Captain and senior officers.

The biggest concern was if the *Jolly Roger* could target a missile into one of the areas damaged by the Junrojin natives' cannon fire. With the outer hull already broken open, a penetrating missile could go deep into the ship and could do serious damage.

"We're good, Captain," Karffard reported. He didn't know if Alvyn was speaking to him or to Dampier, who was at this moment trying to help the Second to his feet. "The *Jolly Roger's* taken more damage than we have."

"She's hair-pinned on us," Koreff swore.

"Turn the ship, Sharll," he started but Renner was already doing so. They had to keep the side of the ship with the most damaged areas away from the *Jolly Roger's* short-range guns. Then the two ships passed with a few miles of each other, while missiles exploded between them and their short-range guns hammered at each other.

"Ray, we've got to surrender," the Second said looking up at the Captain, his face frightened. The Captain swayed again, looking uncertain and indecisive. Harkaman looked at the main board again, seeing a lot of blinking red lights showing missile strikes but nothing showing dangerous damage.

"I'll fix that!" Larch yelled, pressing a variety of buttons. Half a minute later the *Hungry Dragon* shook violently.

That didn't feel like a missile hit, Harkaman thought. "What happened?"

"I just sent him our Hellburner," Larch replied. "They detonated it just before it hit their ship."

Of course, he thought. They were still in the atmosphere and the explosion's shock waves would have been transmitted to them. *If it hit us that bad I wonder what it did to the* Jolly Roger. He was just about to ask when Karffard yelled triumphantly.

"She's fleeing!"

The bridge erupted in cheers. Harkaman sighed with relief and grabbed the Captain's arm again; this time he was able to maneuver him into the command chair.

"Do you want us to pursue?" he asked the Captain.

The Captain blinked uncertainly for a few moments. "Uh, no," he finally said.

Harkaman stepped over to the drunken Second Officer and helped him to his feet. "Command crew resuming stations," he announced to the bridge." He guided the Executive Officer over to the seat Karffard had just vacated. Larch stood up, but before he could move away the Third Officer shoved him to one side and sat down.

Harkaman stood there waiting for the Captain to regain his composure. His eyes were red and he looked as if he still didn't quite know what was going on. He started to report but the Third Officer interrupted him.

"What the hell do you think you were doing, Harkaman?" he shouted. "Why didn't you call us earlier? The Captain gave explicit orders to stay on the ground. And you," he said, turning to Larch. "I told you not to fire those missiles. Look at all the damage to this ship!" He acted as if Larch had personally blown holes in the ship.

"Sir," Harkaman said, looking straight at the Captain, "if the *Jolly Roger* had caught us on the ground, they would have had us. We would have been outgunned and had to give up our loot the same as the *Mandrake* and *Tiger's Claw* did."

The Third Officer continued to complain about him and the other bridge officers. Harkaman looked at him and replied. "Sir, everything anyone on the bridge did was under my command. I take full responsibility. However, if we hadn't taken action, we'd be surrendering to the *Jolly Roger* right now. Mr. Larch and Mr. Renner performed superbly, and I commend their actions."

He turned and looked at Captain Dampier. The Captain blinked at him owlishly for a few seconds.

Wow, he's really smashed, he thought.

Finally the Captain spoke. "Get the hell off my bridge, Harkaman!"

Shocked, his mouth dropped open. He'd just saved the man's ship and he expected to be congratulated for it. Not condemned. His face turned red and he bit off an angry reply before he got himself into *real* trouble.

The Captain gestured to the other junior officers on the bridge. "The rest of you, as well. Get off my bridge and stay off."

As he walked over to the bridge entrance, he looked at Alvyn. He had a look on his face that he was sure was mirrored on his own. Apparently they weren't going to have a long tenure on the *Hungry Dragon.*

Jagannath

I

1704 A. E.

"Thanks, Gareth, I appreciate this," Otto Harkaman said during a brief break between visitors. They were at the mercantile center adjacent to Odisha spaceport on Jagannath. Around them were displays of the loot they had accumulated on their recent voyage. Various merchants and independent traders had been coming by and examining the samples. Some had made offers for a number of the items. So far they had rejected most of the offers as too low.

"It's the least that we owe you, Otto," said Gareth Lozalic, Executive Officer of the *Hungry Dragon*. "You saved our butts on Junrojin, even if the Captain won't admit it."

Lozalic had been celebrating so hard he'd been passed out during the battle with the *Jolly Roger* on Junrojin. When he recovered and reviewed the tapes of the battle, he had tried to talk Captain Dampier into changing his mind. But the Captain refused: he wanted Harkaman and the junior officers who'd followed his orders off his ship. At least Dampier had not put any negative ratings on their ship's papers, which most captains wanted to examine before hiring anyone. Lozalic had also written letters of recommendation for all of the dismissed officers and had vouched for them verbally as well.

They had been on Jagannath for the past five days. At his request Lozalic had allowed him to sit in on the efforts to sell the booty they had gathered. There was an art to getting the most value for loot and Harkaman wanted to learn all he could of it. Being fired for defending the *Hungry Dragon* had only fueled his desire to be a captain and have his own ship one day. Knowing how to value and sell loot was an important part of being successful. With them was Ship's Services Officer, Adrian Madligoza, who besides assisting with selling the ship's loot was also in charge of restocking supplies for the next voyage. There were three other Space Viking ships currently on Jagannath along with four merchant ships, so there were a lot of items for sale with plenty of wheeling and dealing going on.

Just then, another man came up to them to see what they had to sell. "Gaurav Harrier, independent trader *Bucephalus*," he introduced himself to Lozalic, who introduced them in turn.

"I like these gems," he said, before launching into a series of questions about how many they had and whether they matched the quality of those displayed. He also had an interest in some of the machinery and furniture they had picked up. He indicated that he traded on a wide variety of worlds and was certain he could find buyers for the machinery, which would be very advanced for many worlds in the Old Federation.

He offered platinum and Excalibur stellars in trade and bargained more realistically than anyone they had encountered that day. Excalibur stellars were accepted almost everywhere, issued and backed in gold by the Trans-World Bank of Excalibur, the only bank that Sword-Worlders truly trusted. Because of this they were very receptive and managed to conclude a deal, contingent upon final examination of all merchandise.

As the hour grew late and there didn't seem to be anyone left in the center they hadn't already spoken with, they began locking everything up making plans to return the next day. They had rented the space for a week because they wanted to get the best prices they could for their cargo. Madligoza said that he was going to see about purchasing some supplies for the *Hungry Dragon* and left. Harkaman was planning to meet his friends for dinner. Several of them had been talking to the crews of other Space Viking ships on Jagannath and he wanted to see what they'd found out. Lozalic stopped him as he was leaving.

"I've heard the *Black Hawk* and *Star-Breaker* came into orbit a couple hours ago," he said.

That was news to Harkaman and he said so. He had never met anyone from either ship. He didn't know anything about the *Star-Breaker* but he'd heard that the *Black Hawk* was a good ship with a history of successful raids.

"I know the Captain of the *Black Hawk*," Gareth Lozalic said. "I don't know if he's hiring, but I'll put in a good word for you when I see him."

He thanked him and said he'd see him the next morning. He'd already talked to the captains of two of the Space Viking ships that were hiring but had quickly determined that neither was a good fit. His share of the loot from the Junrojin raid was going to be the highest payout he'd ever received. He was determined to spend months on Jagannath, if necessary, to find the right fit for his next berth.

II

Alvyn Karffard waved as he saw Harkaman enter the restaurant. After several days of hanging out in the bars next to the spaceport of Odisha, they'd decided they wanted better cuisine and this place came highly recommended by a lot of Space Vikings.

He expected all of what they now thought of as their group to join them eventually. Sharll Renner was there already. He clearly had something he wanted to talk about but said he wanted to wait for Harkaman. He joined them and filled them in on his experiences selling the *Hungry Dragon's* loot while he reviewed the menu. They decided to wait for the others before ordering food and just ordered their drinks.

"So Lozalic has lived up to his promises," Renner said. "Well, at least one of the officers has been decent."

While all the men who'd been fired from the *Hungry Dragon* by Captain Dampier were unhappy about it, Karffard thought Renner had the hardest time of any of them letting it go. Even the normally sour Guatt Kirbey hadn't taken it as hard as Renner. He'd confided to Karffard that it was the first time in his life he had been fired from anything. The same drive that had made him such a good pilot threatened to undo him as he was spending too much time brooding about what had happened. Karffard and Harkaman, by contrast, had been just as upset but had been able to let it go after a while, preferring to focus on what they could control. Then Renner brought up what he'd been thinking about.

"I've been asked to interview for the assistant pilot position on the *Starhopper*," he said without any preliminaries. "They said the position would rate at the junior officer level."

That made it more attractive as it would be compensated at a higher level than a regular crewmember. Harkaman kept his face passive, but Alvyn could tell he wasn't happy. They had all discussed trying to stay together no matter how long it took to find new berths.

Alvyn had wondered how long such an agreement would last but he certainly thought it would take longer than five days for that pledge to fray. Their discussion was interrupted for a moment as the bar tending robot served drinks.

"What do you think, Otto?" Renner asked. Harkaman sipped his drink thoughtfully, giving an appreciative smile. "I think there's a couple of questions you should ask Sharll," he said. "There some stories I have heard that make me wonder if you would like it there."

"Why?" asked Renner. "Isn't Teodor Vaghn a good captain?"

"He's known as a successful captain," Harkaman replied. "But he's also known to be atrocity prone."

Harkaman described what was known about the *Starhopper* along with Vaghn's penchant for using locals for target practice: "I heard he once gathered up a few hundred or so young men after one of his raids, and had them run one at time across a field. He let his ground troops practice their shooting by using them as moving targets. If the any of them made it across the field, they could live. Not many did," he added grimly, while taking another sip of his drink.

Karffard had heard the same story from a *Starhopper* crewman who seemed to think it was a helluva good time. He could tell Renner didn't care for the practice. What Harkaman said next nearly caused him to drop his drink.

"I still think you should go through with the interview, Sharll," he added. "It doesn't hurt to gain that kind of experience."

"Thanks Otto," Renner said appreciatively, looking embarrassed. "I feel bad for even thinking about it after what we've talked about. At least, now I know what to ask."

"If we're going to be partners, it has to be voluntary," said Harkaman seriously. "Otherwise, it's not going to work." He could tell Harkaman was talking to him as much as he was to Renner. "Our partnership will only work if we all believe it is in all our best interest."

They were saved from any further discussion of the topic by the arrival of Vann Larch, Guatt Kirbey and Paul Koreff. If anyone was going to interview for a position on a ship without the rest of the group, Karffard thought it would have been Koreff. Renner and Vann Larch had enthusiastically pledged themselves to the idea of working together with the thought that they one day would serve under Harkaman as captain, while Guatt Kirbey had already made that pledge a few years before. Koreff had been a little more reserved in his acceptance. Though, as he got to know him, he realized that could just be his personality. Other than the battle with the *Jolly Roger* on Junrojin, he had been very low-key about everything else that happened. He'd also been the one who had the easiest time getting over being fired from the *Hungry Dragon*.

"We have some news," Vann Larch announced before even ordering drinks or looking at the menu. "We're not the only ones that had an encounter with the *Jolly Roger*. They succeeded in catching the *World-Eater* off guard about five months ago and hijacked their entire cargo.

That would have been just before the time we were previously on Hoth, Karffard realized. *That's why we haven't heard of it until now*. Then he wondered: *How had the* Jolly Roger *known where we were headed?* When he shared that thought with the others, it was clear Harkaman had been thinking along the same lines.

"Everyone's going to have to be more careful about discussing where they are going to raid in the future," Harkaman offered.

"I noticed that they've attacked only raiding vessels and not any traders," said Kirbey as he punched in his drink order. "I wonder why that is?"

That set off another round of speculation, which continued while everyone ordered dinner from the table robot. Though Space Vikings thought of themselves as raiders, many of them traded just as much or more as they raided. Some worlds were too decentralized to raid; it was easier to trade with them. And civilized worlds were nearly impossible to raid but would allow trading under certain circumstances.

"Do you think it would be worthwhile to serve on a ship that mainly traded?" Renner asked during a lull in the conversation. "Could such a ship be successful?"

"I wouldn't knock trading under the right situation and especially the right captain," Harkaman opined. "Wulf Hellmut and the *World-Smasher* did well a few centuries ago on Ithavoll. Shortly after the Vollers declared independence from Marduk, he showed up with a ship full of gold that they paid through the nose for. They wanted backing for the currency they were establishing."

They'd all had heard that story. That might be why Ithavoll was one of the few civilized worlds happy to trade with Space Viking ships, Karffard decided. Though given their high landing fees one only went there if they had a very valuable cargo to sell.

"Speaking of successful Space Viking traders," Koreff said with a laugh. "I understand we missed seeing the *Honest Horris* by just a few days."

That brought a belly laugh from everyone. The *Honest Horris* was regarded as one of the most decrepit ships in space. Her captain was from the Sword-Worlds and styled himself a Space Viking, but no one had ever heard of them raiding any planet with anything worth stealing. They traded only and not too profitably, hence the run-down ship.

"What about hiring your ship out to some of these planetary kings or rebel groups?" said Renner, exhaling a small cloud of cigarette smoke. "There always seems be some faction or another looking to hire a ship at any Sword-World or base planet I've been at. I've always wondered if it's worthwhile."

Yes, and they don't pay worth squat, Karffard thought, then said so, adding "And they're always trying to get you to take the job on spec."

"Probably hoping you'll get blown to Em-See-Square in the process so they don't have to pay you," said the pessimistic Kirbey to a general laugh.

By common consent everyone took a break to order another round of drinks when the bartender robot came by.

"I would consider that under certain circumstances," Harkaman said. "The *Curse of Cagn* did real well on the Morglay civil war thirteen years ago. They got paid twenty million stellars of gold and silver and then they were allowed to loot the losing side for all the contragravity machinery and consumer goods they could load on to their ship. I heard they came away with a hundred and seventy million stellars all told."

"And they didn't have to pay off any ground fighters," Larch added. "So they had fewer people to split the money with."

"I don't think it's worth getting involved in any of these Sword-World rebellions," stated Karffard. "It's like trying to raid a civilized world. There are too many things that can go wrong."

The last Space Viking raid of a civilized world had occurred over a century ago. Six ships from Haulteclere raided Aton. Only two returned—without any loot. No one had tried since. Competing opinions on these topics were thrown around throughout dinner. A successful Space Viking, they concluded, was one who seized every good opportunity to make a profit, no matter where it came from.

III

They avoided the people clustered around the bartending robot as they made their way to a table in the corner. They were back at the restaurant they had eaten at three days ago since they hadn't really liked the any of the other places they'd tried. Given that it was a weekend night and the place was popular with locals, Harkaman and Kirbey had come early to get a large enough table. Soon after they were able to order a pitcher of Durendal draft beer, Karffard and Ranjit Chaudry joined them. Ranjit had served with him on the *Fortuna* as well as the *Happy Dragon*. He had decided to join their group.

"Where's Carlos?" Harkaman asked.

Chaudry lowered his eyes. "He decided to take a berth on the *Star-Breaker*," he said apologetically. "They offered him a troop section command."

He was sorry to see Carlos Ericsan go and said so. He had always liked the pleasant natured man. He did think that being a troop section leader was probably about the top level of his skills but he deserved a chance to prove himself.

"To Carlos," he said raising his glass. The other three joined him in the toast.

At this point, Carlos departure appeared to be the only loss in their group. Karffard had told him earlier this afternoon that Renner's interview with the *Starhopper* had not gone well. Apparently Captain Teodor Vaghn did not like to be questioned about his crew's behavior and had terminated the interview early. He was looking forward to hearing about it directly from Renner. He didn't have to wait long as Renner, Larch and Koreff walked in the door. Karffard ordered another pitcher of Durendal as they were making their way to the table.

Renner gulped half his beer before giving them a description of the afternoon's interview. He concluded it with the statement that "Vaghn was pissed as hell that I had even dared to ask about his crew and their behavior. When I tried to ask a second question, he called me a Neobarb lover and told me to get the hell off his ship. I was glad to leave," he concluded, draining the rest of his glass for emphasis.

Everyone laughed at that, telling him he'd made the right choice.

"How things are things going at the mercantile center?"

"They've finished selling all the loot from Junrojin," Harkaman said. "The take after expenses was a little over three hundred million stellars."

They all made appreciative noises. That was the most lucrative raid any of them had been on. In fact, Harkaman had made enough money that he finally decided to establish a bank account and when he brought it up, they all agreed to do likewise. Before this, he'd just carried his money with him on each ship like a lot of Space Vikings did. The only bank a Sword-Worlder would trust was the Trans-World Bank of Excalibur. They had branches on every Sword-World and base planet; in fact, you weren't a true base planet until they established a branch.

After dinner they went to the local branch and set up their savings accounts. Trans-World issued them a credit chit based on their deposits that was redeemable on any Sword-World or Space Viking base planet.

Having a bank account also allowed him to send some money to Marta back home on Colada. Since his parent's deaths, his sister was his only remaining relative. And if he died or disappeared for a period of five years, his funds would automatically be transferred to her as his beneficiary. A good arrangement since few Space Vikings lived to a ripe old age.

As they were walking back to the hotel, Alvyn Karffard said, "We'll receive more than enough interest income from our accounts so we'll be able to wait and pick the right berths from now on. I think that should put everybody at ease."

Both Harkaman and Karffard thought that even with plenty of money in the bank, they'd have to keep an eye on Renner and support him if he got any more depressed about being unemployed. Then everyone got back to discussing the news and gossip they'd heard that day as they made the rounds of bars and talked to some of the thousands of Space Vikings and traders that were currently hanging out on Jagannath.

"Everyone's up in arms about the *Jolly Roger*," Harkaman said. "That's four ships she's hit now. They're all wondering where she's from and where she sells her loot. I think from now on everyone's going to wait until they're off-world before they start celebrating."

"There was talk that the *Starhopper* was looking for someone to team up with," Kirbey said. "They said Vaghn has a tough target in mind that will need at least two ships. Naturally no one's saying where it is."

"Vaghn shouldn't have any trouble finding a partner. The Everrards got greedy and raised Hoth's landing fees," Harkaman noted. "That's why there are so many ships at Jagannath now."

"People are wondering if anyone else is ever going to establish another base planet," Kirbey added, "since Barragon is struggling at Dagon and the Everrards aren't making enough money on Hoth."

Back at the hotel, they all gathered at the bar where Harkaman ordered a round of drinks and continued their discussion. "I think Sword-World base planets are the wave of the future and there should be more of them. Why should our ships continue to make the six-month journey to and from the Sword-Worlds when they can get everything they want here in Old Federation territory?"

"What do you mean, Otto?" Karffard asked, taking the pitcher and refilling his glass along with Harkaman's. He thought he was crazy but had learned saying that just made Harkaman mad. "Two of the five base planets are struggling and having trouble drumming up business. Why would any more be needed?"

"I think they're struggling for three reasons; bad management, for one. The Everrards raising landing fees was stupid. Everyone else is charging the same fee. Why would you think you could get away with charging more?"

"Plus, they need more money because they're spending so much on building their palace," said Larch.

"That's the second reason," Harkaman agreed.

"It's already nicer than the Royal Palace on Excalibur," Renner said, who was from there and had seen it on tours. Since Excalibur had been occupied over eight hundred years and Hoth less than fifty that was worth noting.

"And Barragon's a cut-rate chiseler," Harkaman noted, referring to the man who ran the Dagon base world. "He's always cutting corners and trying to get an edge on you rather than dealing with people fairly. The only ones that deal with him for repairs these days are the chicken thieves who can't afford to deal with anyone else."

"Yeah," Karffard offered. "He offers desperate captains in need of repairs credit; then tries to confiscate their ship if they can't pay their liens off."

"What's the third reason, Otto?" Chaudry asked, extending his glass for a refill.

"The base worlds are too close together, and, with the exception of Dagon, located too close to the edge of the Old Federation nearest the Sword-Worlds. To be successful, a new base world has to be deeper into the Old Federation."

"I agree," Karffard said. "And not just another two or three hundred light-years or so."

"No," exclaimed Harkaman. "Five hundred or a thousand would be better. A lot of that area is somewhat unknown and there are good worlds to raid."

They digested that while their robot tender approached with two more pitchers of beer.

"Otto, what do you think a base world needs to be successful besides good management and location?" Karffard asked. As Harkaman swallowed his drink, Larch spoke up.

"A decent spaceport that can be fixed up and refurbished pretty easily."

"Reliable sources of fissionables," added Kirbey.

"Plenty of metals, gold, iron ore, aluminum, etcetera," Chaudry said.

"Plenty of nearby good worlds to raid," Renner added.

"Those are all good points, but I think some sort of support is the most important," said Harkaman, when he finally had a chance answer to the question. "A good base world needs support or investment from a more prosperous world that can supply it with the items one might need quickly."

Seeing questioning looks, he continued. "Look at Xochitl, for example. They've had a connection with Haulteclere from the beginning. They could get what they needed: machinery, personnel, weapons, ammunition and credit because of that. Prince Thom is considered a Haulteclere noble by King Konrad so they're an extension of the realm in the Liebig family's minds."

"That's true, said Karffard. "But they had an advantage, being the first base world established over a hundred years ago. No other base world is as old or developed as Xochitl is."

"What about Skathi?" Larch asked, with a chuckle.

They all had a good laugh about that. Some Space Vikings claimed that Skathi was the first base world. It was actually a chicken-stealing world where several Space Vikings maintained informal homes due to its primary attributes; it manufactured several potent brews and its women were considered more attractive than the average world. It had no real spaceport or repair facilities.

"When you look at the big picture," Koreff said, thoughtfully, "even though they have a lot less population than Haulteclere, Xochitl is really more prosperous."

While they were digesting that statement a man approached their table. He looked around fifty years old and even though he was dressed as a civilian, he had that indefinable air of command. He was about six feet in height, a little stocky, with short black curly hair that was just starting to go grey. His skin was even darker than Kirbey's.

"Are you Otto Harkaman?" he asked.

Otto replied affirmatively.

"Trevor Mavuso, Captain of the *Black Hawk*. May I join you?"

They hastily agreed, Koreff pulling out the vacant chair for him. *Maybe it's a good thing Carlos didn't show*, he thought.

"Durendal draft?" Karffard offered, picking up the pitcher, while Vann Larch extended an empty glass.

"Please," Mavuso replied. He waited until his glass was full and took an appreciative sip. "Ahhh," he said with a grin. "Always hits the spot." Then his face became serious. "I spoke with Lozy about you Mr. Harkaman," he said.

They all smiled at that. Although they had heard Gareth Lozalic called Lozy by Captain Dampier on the *Hungry Dragon*, none of them had felt comfortable enough with him to call him by his nickname.

"We served together over thirty years ago on the *Sword of Doom*," he said by way of explanation. "I heard about your battle with the *Jolly Roger*," he continued. "I'd like to hear your side of the story."

They all turned to look at Harkaman. He took a deep breath and began telling how it happened. While recounting the ship-to-ship battle, he called on each of the men at the table at the appropriate time to share their versions of what they had done and seen. "And that's what happened, sir," he finished.

Mavuso looked at each of the others, who nodded in turn. "Well," he said, "that matches up with what Lozy told me and what I heard some of the crew spreading around town. I have to say that I agree with Lozy: you guys got a raw deal."

As Captain Mavuso took a sip of his beer, Renner took advantage of the pause to lean forward. "Excuse me, Captain, but maybe you have some insight as to why that happened. Otto, and everyone else here, they saved the ship. Why was Captain Dampier so mad?"

Mavuso laughed heartily. "Because he doesn't own his ship," he replied. Seeing their blank looks, he continued. "I know you think ships' investors are just faceless people who take twenty percent of the loot but in some cases they're more than that. Often they have a strong say in who runs the ship. I think Reynard Dampier was afraid that if the word got out that he had a junior officer,"—he paused to toast Harkaman with his glass—"who had fought a battle, defeated an attacker and saved his ship as well as anyone could"—again he nodded in Harkaman's direction, who blushed at the praise—"all while his captain was off drunk, I seriously believe that some of the investors might start to think Captain Dampier needed replacing. Especially those investors who thought they could get a new captain and officers at a cheaper price than the old ones."

They looked blankly at one another until Karffard spoke up. "Cheaper, captain? But, shares are the same on every ship."

Standard shares on a Space Viking ship for any raid were twenty percent to the owner/investor(s); ten percent to the captain; twenty percent to the other officers (with the senior officers receiving a double-share); and fifty percent to the crew (again with crew chiefs and troop leaders receiving a slightly higher share). Shares had been that way on every ship they had served on.

Mavuso laughed heartily. "I can see that none of you have ever negotiated bonuses."

They all shook their heads. Harkaman had heard talk of bonuses but whenever he had asked about them, the people he asked had said it was just chatter; he hadn't pushed it for fear of upsetting the proverbial apple cart. It was clear the others hadn't heard anything.

"Well, I'm not surprised," Mavuso said. "A lot of captains and owners keep that information close to the vest. You'll find I'm not one of them."

Hearing that, they all looked around at each other, some surprised, some expectant.

"I need to hire some new officers on my ship," he said authoritatively. "Everything I'd heard has told me you could be the kind of men I'm looking for, and this discussion has confirmed it." He drained his glass and looked at them expectantly. Karffard grabbed the pitcher and refilled it.

"Well, thank you for the compliments, Captain," Harkaman said. "Could you be more specific as to what you are looking for?"

Captain Mavuso indicated that his second and fourth officers had just announced their retirement. The fourth officer was staying on Jagannath while the second would book passage on the next ship for his home world of Morglay. Several of his junior officers were leaving the ship, too, he noted. "I'm promoting one of my junior officers to second officer. He's been an officer for a decade and has been waiting patiently for a deserved promotion."

He must have a pretty good relationship with the man he promoted, Harkaman thought. Most qualified people wouldn't wait that long without changing to another ship. That was another point in his favor.

It wasn't unusual for personnel changes to occur whenever a ship stopped at a Space Viking base world or arrived at the Sword-Worlds. A surprising number of men got tired of the robberies and violence which was a big part of a Space Viking's life and wanted out. Some just got tired of spending most of their lives cooped up on a ship, making long boring voyages between worlds. Others had a specific financial goal and once they reached it, they were ready to do something else. He'd known crewmates, who once they achieved a little financial success, wanted to return home to buy a business, a farm or a minor peerage and settle down in one spot.

"And what about your third officer?" Harkaman asked, wondering why he hadn't been promoted.

Mavuso sighed. "I've told the third officer his services will no longer be needed."

There was a moment of silence until Karffard asked why.

"He's been with me five years, over two as third officer. He wants to be liked by everyone, especially by the people underneath him. We've had several conversations about that but he still hasn't changed. I should have removed him sooner but," he sighed again. "You always think you can teach people how to improve."

They all nodded, especially Harkaman. Many decisions had to be made on a ship and some of them, especially on a raid, were life and death. It was much better to have the men under you respect you and jump to obey than it was to have them like you—especially if your attempts to get them to like you cost their respect.

"So, Mr. Harkaman, I'd like to offer you the position of third officer," Mavuso said.

"Thank you, Captain," Harkaman said with a smile, trying to not show how excited he was. Being a senior officer put him that much closer to becoming a captain one day. Everything he'd heard from Captain Mavuso during this discussion indicated that he was a good man to work for. He was especially impressed that he had talked to them informally rather than requiring a formal interview. "I'll accept that provisionally while I hear what you'll offer these men."

"Good. I'm aware based on my discussions with Lozy that you all come together as a package deal. I think you should all tour the ship and meet my other officers before you make a final decision."

He turned to Vann Larch. "My guns-and-missiles officer has left and I would like to offer you the position."

Larch told him his answer was the same as Harkaman's. He offered the rest of the men the same or similar positions to what they had held on the *Hungry Dragon* with the exception of Karffard.

"Mr. Karffard, I also understand from Lozy that when Harkaman becomes a captain you intend to be his exec. I can offer you the opportunity to work directly with my Executive Officer, Hamid Jorgensans, so you can learn from him. He's been with me for almost twenty years."

"Thank you, Captain," Karffard replied. "I appreciate that offer. However, I'm wondering, in light of our recent experience, why you're so willing to hire people who might want to leave one day for their own ship."

Captain Mavuso chuckled. "I've found it's better to have smart people around me than people who just do what I say, without bothering to think or ask questions. And I own my ship, so I don't have to worry about investors. Besides, I didn't start out as a captain, though I was lucky enough to have the right connections to begin as an officer. I did sufficiently well to convince investors to back me as captain on a ship, and then I was successful enough at raiding to pay off all those investors and purchase my ship outright. I'm impressed with people who want to do the same."

He rose to his feet and raised his glass. "Men, I've kept you up late enough. Let me see you on the ship tomorrow at local noon time. And let me say, provisionally, welcome to the *Black Hawk!*"

They all rose and drained their glasses with him. He bumped fists with each of them in turn and said good night.

Ereshkigal

I

1706 A.E.

They stood in a group waiting, some patiently, others impatiently. Harkaman wished he'd remembered his pipe so that he could at least smoke. Although, now that he thought of it; the air here was so thin there might not be enough oxygen in the air to keep his pipe lit. He'd thought they'd be on the planet less than an hour but their stay had already stretched into its third hour.

While raiding the nearby world of Jutrovit, he had made his usual library visit and in an old captain's log he'd read about two nearby worlds that were not in the *Astrogator's Guide to the Worlds of the Federation* or any Space Viking log he'd run across. The first world, Koresh, had been settled late in the waning years of the Federation by a religious sect and named after their founder. Like all habitable worlds located around a red dwarf sun, it was close enough to the sun that it was tidally locked, with one side perpetually turned to the sun and the other side in permanent darkness. Unlike some similar worlds, Koresh didn't seem to have much to recommend it, which was probably why it had slipped under the radar of other Space Vikings searching for planets to raid.

Signals and detection had confirmed there were no more than a few hundred thousand people on Koresh, and those were living barely above a Stone Age level of existence. The majority of the population was located in the twilight area where the normal rotational wobble of the planet provided a short day and night cycle.

The second world, Ereshkigal, a moon orbiting the fifth planet of an A7 star, appeared more promising. There was another nearby yellow sun, but it was too far away to impact the planet or its moon. Ereshkigal had been a source of gadolinium during the Federation era. Gadolinium was a rare earth metal and about fifty pounds of it were needed in every hypership engine. It was many times more valuable than gold. They had sent a pinnace down to check the industrial site where it was produced. A brief review of the rest of the world put it at a low level of development so it didn't seem to offer much in the way of raid-worthy targets.

Once they had determined that there was no finished gadolinium on site, they took down several industrial engineers from the Engineer Department so they could examine the facility to see if it could easily be put back into production. The *Black Hawk* was unusual as very few Space Viking ships included industrial engineers. Harkaman was impressed; Captain Mavuso was a leader who was prepared for almost any eventuality that might arise while raiding the Old Federation.

He had been wandering through the buildings with them until the senior engineer had said pleasantly but firmly. "Our review will go a lot faster, sir, if you don't interrupt us with questions every few minutes."

He had acquiesced, acknowledging that engineering was not among his skills and left them to their examination. Stafan Mavuso had already come to the same conclusion and was waiting outside. Stafan was the second officer on the *Black Hawk* and the Captain's son. He had started as a cabin boy on the ship over twenty years ago. Harkaman had figured out that was why the captain had wanted them to meet all his officers before making a decision on whether or not to join the crew.

Normally Harkaman would have been concerned about joining a ship where the captain's son was one of the officers. Meeting Stafan had assuaged those concerns. He found him to be a serious and knowledgeable officer. He had an encyclopedic knowledge of the *Black Hawk*, since he had served in every department and practically every position from Engineering to Hydroponics to Weapons Control to Ship's Services to Damage Control to Med Tech as part of his training over the last two decades.

Stafan in turn had been very impressed with Harkaman's raiding experience as his father had not allowed him to take part in ground actions. They'd many productive discussions about the best way to run a ship and raid planets during the two years they served together.

"Here they come, Otto," Stafan said, noticing that the engineers had left the building. The rest of the crew started to gather around. None of them had wandered very far away from the facility during the wait. The nearest local village was about a half mile away up a hill and so far had not reacted to their presence; however, the elevation was over nine thousand feet so no one had the energy to walk that far. The rocky area around them was spotted with patches of grass, but he could see terraced gardens just below the nearby village.

"Gentlemen, this facility could be made to function with a little bit of work," the senior engineer told them. "There's already a pile of material in the factory that has been separated out into cerite and other metals. That just needs to go through the final processor to be concentrated into worthwhile metal. And there's another chamber full of material that can go through the separation process when the first chamber is processed into gadolinium."

"And there's another pile of earth," he turned and pointed to a large mound of material, "that could be processed when the first two chambers are emptied."

"Do you mean the facility just needs to be turned on?" Harkaman asked.

"No sir," the engineer explained patiently. "The power plant is fine, but we'll need to bring some plutonium down to power up everything. We've found that most of the power cartridges were removed as well. And we didn't examine all the robots. We won't know how much work we'll need to do with the robots until we examine each and every one of them."

"How long will this take?" Stafan asked.

"Once we've got the power plant going, we should be able to get the robots up and running in two to four days, depending on what condition they're in. We've got enough plutonium, power cartridges and robotic equipment on the ship to get everything ready to start production."

"And once it's running?" Harkaman asked, wondering how long they'd have to stay there.

"To process the existing material will take at least a month. I've never worked at one of these types of factories before, but based on what I've read there should be at least half a ton of finished gadolinium when we're done."

Half a ton would be enough for twenty hypership engines. *That was certainly worth a month of their time*, Harkaman thought.

Stefan ordered the engineer to make a list of everything he needed and told him he would talk to the Captain.

II

Otto heard loud voices from downstairs. Mom and Dad are fighting again, *he told himself. They had been arguing constantly since his father had lost his previous job. Now, his they were both worried about his new job at the machine shop. He got out of bed, quietly opened his bedroom door, then tiptoed to the staircase and leaned over to listen at the furnace vent.*

"You've gotta stop spending so much, damn it!" yelled his father.

"The kids need new clothes. What am I supposed to do, let them go out looking like beggars?"

"Begging! That may be next; my job is on the line—again. I lost my last job at Colada Metal Stamping when they replaced everyone with those damn robots."

"You're a machinist and tool and die maker; you used to claim there'd always be a need for them."

"That was before the new fabrication computers came out last year. They've already replaced all the punch-press operators at Allied Metals with robots, now we're next."

"You should have joined up with your Uncle Mort. He's been after you for years to work on his ship."

"I'm not going to ship out as a Space Viking, Alana. You and I both know they're not spacemen, but robbers and murderers. I have my self-respect."

"I know you're a hard worker, but your self-respect isn't going to put food on the table! The Old Federation is full of petty tyrants and corrupt dictators. The Space Vikings are only doing the same things the Neobarbarians are doing—and making good money while they do it."

"I'll find another job, somewhere, somehow...."

Otto felt a hand on his shoulder, and just about jumped out of his skin.

"It's just me," whispered his sister, Marta. "Don't be scared."

"Mom and Dad are fighting again," he said, his voice trembling. "When Rolf's parents did that, they divorced. Now, he lives with his mother and his daddy's gone."

"Our parents aren't going to get a divorce. Dad will figure out something. Or Uncle Mort will find him something to do. He owns businesses all over town."

"If you space out with Mort," his mother said, "you wouldn't be one of the ground fighters. You'd be part of the crew. What's wrong with that? It's not like you'd be getting your hands dirty."

"I refuse to support murder and robbery on any level. It's just wrong!"

"Why doesn't dad wanna be a Space Viking?" Otto asked his sister.

"Mom says it's because he's squeamish."

"What's 'squeamish' mean, Marta?"

She put her arms around her little brother. "It means he doesn't like to see blood."

"Oh. Like when Bobby got drove over by a ground car. There was blood all over. It made me feel sick in my stomach."

"Yes, that's it."

"I still wanna be a Space Viking. So I can go to different worlds and fight and find gold and treasures, like on my favorite show, Raiders of the Old Federation. *Uncle Mort is always telling me stories—"*

"That's why Mom and Dad stopped going over to his house. Dad says Uncle Mort's a 'bad influence.' If you want to be a Space Viking, don't talk about it so much. It only makes Dad angry. Keep it to yourself, Otto."

"Okay. And, don't worry; I'll take care of you, too, Marta."

His sister gave him a big hug.

Harkaman woke up and for a moment wondered where he was. Then he saw the rocks that made up three walls of the house he was sleeping in and remembered that he was in the small village of Padul. He got up from the pallet he had shared the night before and went to the rock shelf where a basin of hammered iron held water. He drank some and splashed some in his face to wake up. He looked around for a towel; not finding one he picked his shirt up from where it had ended up on the floor the night before and wiped his face. As he finished his morning toilet, a pretty woman, with black hair the color of a raven's wing, entered the room.

"Good morning Sky Lord, Otto," she said with smile. Her pronunciation made his name sound more like Ah-tow.

"Just Otto," he replied.

"Good morning, Just Ah-tow ," she said. He was about to correct her again when he saw she was grinning and he laughed in return.

The *Black Hawk* had left four days ago. Captain Mavuso hadn't wanted to wait around for the ore to be processed so he had left to raid several nearby worlds. Harkaman was left in command of the engineers and a dozen crewmembers who were working to get the gadolinium facility back into production. After a few days of eating carniculture meat and stale fruits and vegetables, they had killed one of the sheep grazing nearby. The meat was tough and unappetizing.

Some of the crew had wanted to raid the nearby village for food. Both because they wanted some variety but also because they weren't used to being on a world where they weren't stealing something. Harkaman had told them there was no reason to loot such a poor little village. He left to see if he could work out some way to trade with them for their some of their food. His past dealings with locals on many worlds had made him more comfortable than most Space Vikings when interacting with local populations.

He had not gotten far on his walk to the village when he started regretting not taking the aircar. *Even at this elevation, I shouldn't be this winded,* he thought. *I've got to keep in better shape; I'm not yet thirty, I shouldn't have this much trouble.*

Then he'd seen a woman walking down the mountain path to meet him. He slowed down, breathing heavily, until they met. "Greetings, Sky Lord," she intoned, bowing slightly.

That was how he had met Kristel. She had been very willing to trade food, stating that the village had more than it could use. When they reached the village, with many pauses so he could catch his breath—which she found highly amusing—he began to see why. Although there were forty to fifty homes dug into the soft rock of the cliffs, there weren't very many people about.

Kristel said that most of the adult men had been taken away a few years ago by the Empire to work in the mines. He perked up when he found out the mines were silver mines. He asked how far away these mines were and what was done with the silver.

"About four day walk," she replied. Then she added, "Though for you it might be six or seven days"—she put her hands over her mouth to smother her laughter—"then they carry the silver to the Swazi Empire, which is another twelve day walk."

He interrupted her, before she was about to add with a smile how much longer the walk would be for him, by asking her more questions about the Swazi Empire.

Kristel told him that most of the silver went to Swazi City, which apparently was the name of the Empire's capital city. It was located in a broad river valley several weeks walk away. He didn't recall any such city during their initial reconnaissance of the local area.

Kristel went on to explain that like the village, Swazi City was dug into the rocks of the river valley and very little habitation was outside. He asked why.

"To survive when a Hot Time comes," she explained. Questioning her further didn't yield many details. Apparently the land would periodically get so hot that nothing could survive outside; wooden structures would burn and even stone structures wouldn't protect the inhabitants. He wondered if she meant this occurred during their summer. However she said the Hot Times came infrequently and would only last for a few days.

"The last one was when my mother was but a girl," she said, "The Learned Ones in Swazi have said that the next one will come when I am an old woman, may I live that long."

As she prepared food for their breakfast, he called the crew. Most of them were staying aboard the pinnace that the *Black Hawk* had left behind; Harkaman had insisted on having a pinnace left in case something went wrong during the *Black Hawk's* raid. Captain Mavuso had acquiesced and they had agreed that if the *Black Hawk* had not returned in three months' time, they should return to the nearest base word.

"Is there anyone groundside who works in astrogation?" he asked Guatt Kirbey, who he'd left in command in his absence.

"Yes, Anvil Straller, he's an apprentice."

"Put him on."

There was a squawk from the receiver, then a high-pitched voice replied, "Straller, here."

"I've learned something interesting about this world. From what the locals say, there's a major climate event every eighty or so years. They call it the 'Hot Time.' My suspicion is that that nearby yellow star has an oblong orbit that brings it in close to Ereshkigal's orbital path; at least close enough to affect the temperature. Can you check that out?"

Straller hemmed and hawed about not having the *Black Hawk's* computer available, but finally admitted he could do the same calculations on the pinnace's smaller machine—it would just take a whole lot longer.

"Then get cracking!" Harkaman ordered. "It may prove to be helpful. Now, put me through to Pablo."

"I'm here, boss," Pablo replied. "What do you need?"

"Bring a lifter with a large pot of carniculture," he ordered. "I'll tell you why when you get here." Carniculture steak would be unique and tasty enough that it should feel like a fair trade to the villagers.

When he got back inside the hut, Kristel was putting food on the small wooden table. "Now you will see what properly prepared mutton tastes like," she said, as she set a bowl before him. It looked like a stew of meat and vegetables. Gingerly he tasted it, then made sounds of appreciation.

"It is said whenever the Sky Lords come to see the old mine they will kill one of the great rams," she said, smiling at him. "By this, we have learned that while the Sky Lords are mighty, they are not all-knowing—for the smallest child knows that old rams are not fit for eating."

He almost choked on his mouthful of food. "Sky Lords have come here before?" he asked, surprised. "When were they here last?"

"It is said the Sky Lords come once every generation," she intoned. *This sounds like a story told around the campfire*, he thought. As she continued, he wondered just how Sky Lord Ah-tow would be added to any future tale. "They stay but for a few hours, kill a great ram and then leave. Usually they do not visit the village but sometimes they do. Some of them are regular-looking people and some are very pale such as you."

The villagers all had very dark skin. He didn't know whether that was because the original colonists were dark-skinned or because they had adapted over time to the harsh A7 sun. Maybe both. The crew had quickly learned to stay out of direct sunlight during their short visit. Fortunately, it had been cloudy during most of their time on-planet. Kristel said it was because it was winter, but they were very close to the equator so they had found the weather pleasant.

"Did the Sky Lords steal anything?" he asked. When she looked at him blankly he continued, "Either from the villagers or from the Swazi?"

"No, why do you ask?"

"Some of the worlds we visit have been visited by Dark Sky Lords," he said. "Not like those of us who come in peace."

This gave him much to think about. Apparently spacemen had occasionally stumbled on the fact there was a gadolinium mine here. But they must not have been Space Vikings, just regular traders looking to see if any processed gadolinium had been left behind.

"A city of silver," Guatt Kirbey remarked, after Harkaman finished telling everyone what he had learned. "I wonder why we didn't see it."

"According to Kristel, cities here are dug into the cliffs to avoid the Hot Time, whatever that is," he replied. "And it's not summer," he added before anyone could ask. "She said the last Hot Time came when her mother was a little girl."

"Their year wouldn't be anywhere near our Galactic Standard year anyway so it wouldn't help to know how long ago it was," someone said.

"I've got that wise-ass kid Straller looking into it."

"Why does this matter, Otto?" Kirbey asked. "There are only a dozen of us and most are crew not ground troops, so we don't have enough men to raid the city." Seeing the look on Harkaman's face he became apprehensive. "Uh-oh, what are you planning?"

Harkaman leaned forward, certain he had their undivided attention. "Here's what we're going to do," he began.

III

Their pinnace landed in one of the fields less than a quarter mile from the entrance to Swazi City. *I bet we just crushed somebody's potato crop*, Harkaman thought. It took roughly fifteen minutes before anyone left the city to see what was going on. The party that came out seemed to be a combination of what passed for an army along with some colorfully dressed men he guessed were nobles. The city had multiple levels of dwellings carved into the cliffs based on the windows and porches he could see. The height of the rows of windows seemed to vary a bit across. He wondered if it was because the softness of the rock was not consistent, or it was a sign of status.

Once the army was finished assembling, he left the pinnace and walked slowly toward the city; not due to lack of oxygen since the air at this lower elevation felt oxygen rich after a week at the mine, but because he didn't want to frighten the inhabitants into any premature action.

The soldiers carried spears and swords. Their armor appeared to be made thick leather, but their helmets were made of felt. A handful of what he assumed to be officers wore metal helmets. The lone combat car left the pinnace at the same time he did. It remained about fifty feet in the air and to his right. The soldiers and nobles seemed to have trouble deciding whether to look at him, the slowly moving combat car or the pinnace.

When he reached some fifty feet away, he stopped. By that time he'd seen that the spears were roughly twelve feet in length. No one was going to be throwing one of them at him. In fact, he saw no missile weapons anywhere.

"I am one of the Sky Lords!" he announced in a loud voice. He waited for their murmuring and questioning glances at each other to subside before he continued.

"You will bring to me all of your silver and gold!" he continued. "If you do not do this, I shall destroy you and your city. Your women and children shall be slaves and I will have your silver and gold anyway!"

"You mean you're going to try and bluff them?" Kirbey had exclaimed when he explained his plan to the crew. "You know at times, I've wondered, Otto, if you're crazy but this, this is—" He was at a loss for words.

"Yes, that's exactly right," he said.

"Well, Otto, what are you going to do if they call your bluff?"

"Shoot a missile at whoever greets us to show we mean business and leave. When the *Black Hawk*, comes back we'll pay them another visit. One way or another we'll get what we want."

After some talk between the military officers and the colorfully dressed men, one of the nobles stepped forward. *Good they want to talk*, he thought. *If they wanted to fight, the nobles would have retreated into the city*.

"How do we know you're a Sky Lord?" the man asked. His manner was respectful but questioning.

Harkaman raised his hand and made a prearranged signal to the combat car. There was one area of the city that due to a lack of windows did not appear to consist of multiple levels of dwellings. A missile from the combat car slammed into that section.

The crowd screamed as rocks showered them and part of the cliff face slid down. Some of the soldiers turned and ran into the main entrance followed by most of the colorfully dressed nobles. It took a few minutes for the officers to get the remaining soldiers under control. The man who had spoken to him remained, shaking so much he could barely stand up. He hurriedly consulted with the few remaining nobles and one of the officers.

The noble walked slowly towards him, then dropped down to one knee and bowed. "Sky Lord, we shall do as you ask."

"Make sure you bring all of your silver and gold," he announced. "Do not try and cheat us or you shall suffer."

One of the other colorfully dressed men walked slowly toward him, stopping a pace or so behind the other man before he went to his knee and extended his arms.

"Sky Lord, we have little gold." He paused for a moment then continued. "If you wanted gold, you should have gone to Kaura. They have much gold. All of our gold comes from there."

"Where is Kaura and how may I find it," he asked.

The man stood and pointed vaguely to the northeast. "It lies across the ocean. There is a great river that drains that land. Kaura City lies over eighty miles up the river. The gold mines are two hundred miles north of the city."

He felt in his pocket for the small coins he always carried. Taking them out, he selected a small gold one and tossed it to the man.

"Thank you for your information. Now bring all of your silver and gold to me."

"Yes, Sky Lord," said the man with a smile, turning away to shout orders to the soldiers. The other nobleman stared angrily after him.

For the rest of the afternoon men carried silver bars, coins, sculptures, rings and necklaces out to them. There wasn't much gold, only some gold rings and a dozen gold necklaces, but there was a lot of silver. He had all the booty taken to the lifters and then quickly transferred to the pinnace.

As the white sun was starting to set, the man who had received the gold coin came out. Once again he advanced to within ten yards, took a knee and bowed. "Sky Lord, that is all the silver and gold we have," he said.

"You were wise to comply," he said, as the last of the lifters was loaded into the pinnace. Then he turned and left.

IV

Everyone off duty was eating lunch in the pinnace when one of the crew came charging into the room. He was so excited that he was gasping for breath as he tried to talk.

"Calm down, relax," Harkaman said. He hadn't heard anything from the watch officer so he wondered what the man was so excited about. Ever since the *Jolly Roger's* attack on the *Hungry Dragon*, he made certain there was always someone on watch, even on the pinnace. If the *Jolly Roger* or some other raider did come, they probably would be disappointed. After three weeks they had processed only about two hundred pounds of finished gadolinium, though the engineer said the pace of processing should pick up now that they had worked out all of the bugs; inevitable in restarting machinery that had stood idle for nearly a thousand years. He doubted that anything made today in the Sword-Worlds would last even a century.

In comparison to today, the engineers and scientists of the Federation must have been wizards.

They did have about fifteen million stellars worth of silver they had taken from the Swazi kingdom and with astute trading he thought they might double that. He had scouted the city of Kaura and found it much larger and its military much more organized than that of Swazi. They had a stone palisade fifteen feet high in front of their city. They had spotted his aircar and their military had assembled out in front of the wall within minutes. Archers lined the top of the wall walkway. He decided that they were much better prepared than Swazi City and were unlikely to be bluffed; he determined to wait until the *Black Hawk* returned before he tried to raid it.

"There's a woman running towards the ship," the man said when he found his breath. "I think it's your woman, Otto."

Almost half of the crewmen, besides him, had taken up with some of the women of Padul village. Kristel wasn't the only one who missed having a man. And several of them, like Kristel, still wanted to have children. It was something that he and his men were happy to help with.

As he went outside, he noticed that he was adjusting to the elevation and the lack of oxygen. He no longer felt out of breath, walking to and from the village every day. However, he couldn't run for more than twenty yards or so without running out of breath so he never would equal the speed at which Kristel was approaching.

"Ah-tow, please help us," Kristel said as she came to a halt. She looked upset, which he had never seen before. She had confided to him that she didn't really miss her husband. As was typical in these primitive cultures, the men were the bosses and the women their property. He had noticed that she seemed to enjoy being the informal leader of the village, although there were still a few old men around who were nominally in charge.

"One of the shepherd boys just came in," she said. "Men from Postrel are approaching, many men. We think they are here to steal our food and more of the village's women."

He had already learned from her that men from Postrel, a village further up in the mountains, had come down from the hills last season and stolen six young women from the village along with some of their food. What she had not said, but he had learned from a crewmember who had taken up with one of the other women, was that her daughter had been among those stolen. He had learned that the only reason Kristel wasn't taken was that she was out among the flocks when the men came.

"Of course, we'll help you," Harkaman said. He'd been getting bored, as were most of the other men. Although he'd brought plenty to read, this isolated location didn't have any of the other distractions that the *Black Hawk* had. He'd even found himself joining the crewmen playing cards, which normally he avoided. He'd been thinking about taking the aircar and exploring some of the other continents to relieve his boredom. Now that he knew what to look for, he might spot some cities that were worth raiding.

He stood on a slight rise from where he could watch the group of men from Postrel advance across a large open area toward him. The combat car was behind the rise where no one could see it. Then someone spotted him and they slowed their pace from a trot to a walk. He really didn't consider the group an army. A few of the men had swords and wore padded leather vests. Most carried clubs or staffs. There were no bows and arrows or missile weapons that he could see. Nor were they weren't in any kind of formation.

As they got closer, they slowed when they noticed his height, pale skin and different clothing. They stopped about thirty feet away and he could hear them muttering among themselves. There were from fifty to sixty men between the ages of about fifteen and forty five. That would mean their village was probably three or four times the size of the one just behind him. Finally, one man—probably the village headman, advanced.

"Who are you and what are you doing here?" the headman demanded.

"I am a Sky Lord," he bellowed. "This village is under my protection. Return to your village immediately!"

That caused the headman to turn back to the group, where a furious discussion arose. Harkaman noticed that the younger men, who were on the left side of the group, seemed eager to come to grips with a legendary Sky Lord. Finally one of them made a sound of exasperation, pushed the headman out of the way and strode forward about ten yards. He appeared to be in his early twenties and was one of the men with a sword and a leather vest.

"I challenge you, Sky Lord!" he cried. He pulled his sword out, swung it back and forth, passed it from hand to hand behind his back and twirled it overhead again like a bad actor in an old historical Tri-D.

Harkaman smirked, pulled out his pistol and shot him through the head. As the rest of the men were gasping and falling back a step, he talked into his radio. "Fire a two second burst into the left side of their formation."

The combat car rose and fired. The left side of the group dissolved, as men fell and died. The rest of the warband turned and started running back the way they came. *They really have some lungs on them*, he thought since they didn't slow down after thirty to forty yards. Then he waved his hand at the combat car. As he had previously arranged, the combat car flew well ahead of the group and fired into the ground in front of them, bringing them to a halt. With the cliff wall to one side, a few of them tried to run down the opposite slope but most lost their footing and tumbled down.

That looks like it's got to hurt, Harkaman thought, striding toward them. Those who remained fell to their knees or threw themselves flat on the earth, crying out or beseeching their gods.

He waited for a short while until most of the screaming and crying ended, then and spoke: “Because you disobeyed me, I have killed many of you.”

The headman, who was down on his knees, raised his arms to him beseeching, “Please Sky Lord, forgive us!”

He waited awhile to give them time to ponder what terrible fate he had in mind for them. “You must return to your village,” he intoned. They started to rise to their feet, nodding agreement. Clearly, this was a desire they all shared.

“Once you are there you will gather up all your silver and gold and bring it back to me.”

They stared at each other in wonder at his request. They hadn’t expected it, but no one was inclined to argue.

“In addition, you will also return to me all of the women and young girls you took from this village last season,” he demanded.

This caused them to look at each other in wonder. Clearly this Sky Lord must be all-knowing if he knew they had taken women from this village. The headman quickly gave his agreement.

“And, then you will never return to Padul again except in peace. If I return and find you have failed to honor my request, I shall burn your village to the ground and kill everyone there.”

The men rose to their feet, quickly heading up the slope for home, not waiting to hear anything further demands from him. He signaled to the combat car to move out of the way. The headman assured him again that they would follow his commands. He signaled they could examine the pile of wounded and dead men the combat car had left behind. However, he ordered them to leave their armor, such as it was, and weapons behind.

Several of them gingerly walked past him, trying to stay as far away as possible, while examining their wounded neighbors.

He turned and walked back toward the village, happy that there’d been some excitement on what he thought might be a boring day. He was certain the people of Padul could use the abandoned weapons. They, along with his threats, would help protect the village from any further attacks after the Space Vikings left.

V

"Otto," one of the crewmen announced, sticking his head into the hut. "The *Black Hawk* is back."

Harkaman stretched out, putting his book down. He was pleased to learn the ship had finally returned; he was starting to worry. They'd been on Ereshkigal for almost seven weeks which was several more than he'd expected. He was looking forward to being back on the ship. He wondered how well the *Black Hawk* had done. He suspected the Captain would be pleased with how much they had accomplished on Ereshkigal.

A crewmember exploring deeply in one of the old mine tunnels had found a contragravity bulldozer someone had left behind. They had managed to get it started, after they removed a power cartridge from one of the other machines and temporarily stopped production to do so. After processing the ore that was left inside the industrial plant, they had started moving the large mound of ore outside the facility into the first chamber for processing. They had finished processing all of the ore five days ago. Between the additional ore and what had already been in the facility, they had produced one thousand, six hundred and sixty pounds of gadolinium. That was enough for thirty-three ships. They would have to stop at several worlds to sell that much.

Plus, there was more than gadolinium to report. Besides the silver taken from Swazi and the tiny amount contributed by the village of Postrel, Harkaman, now that he knew what to look for, had found three other cities worth looting. On each of them, he had run the Sky Lord bluff again. Two of the cities surrendered their silver and gold after one missile demonstration. The third one had required several missiles before they surrendered. And there was still the city of Kaura which he would need the ground fighters and the fire power of the *Black Hawk* to subdue. Between the gadolinium, silver, gold and what they could get from Kaura, he figured that Ereshkigal would end up yielding seventy to ninety million stellars worth of loot.

"Do you want to say goodbye to your gal, Otto?" Guatt Kirbey said as he came into the room. Kirbey had suffered less than anyone from boredom on this world. He was close to finishing his magnum opus, as he called his latest painting, and wanted to spend every spare hour working on it. Harkaman had insisted that Kirbey come on daily walks with him to get some exercise as he tended to put on weight if he wasn't active.

"No," he said with a shake of his head. "I don't think that's necessary."

Kristel had been very grateful that he had protected her village from their neighbors. She was even happier when her daughter arrived in the village five days later when the stolen women were returned. Her daughter was six Galactic Standard months pregnant. So her first grandchild would be born four months before her next child. She had informed him two weeks ago that she was pregnant. Though she was still happy to have him visit, it was clear to him that there was nothing more she wanted from him; Sky Lord Ah-tow had performed all the duties she needed.

That was fine with him. He'd learned long ago that extended relationships weren't for him. He had only one long-term relationship with a girl and that was back on Colada as a teenager before he left to become a Space Viking. If he'd stayed with Delia, or any other woman on his homeworld, he either would have remained on the lowest rung of society or forced to do things he didn't care to do to improve his status.

Nor did he have a home base where he could keep a woman or wife. It was unusual to find women aboard Space Viking ships, other than the occasional captain's wife—and even that could be problematic. With the long hyperspace trips between worlds, there were too many opportunities for trouble and ships that allowed women onboard didn't last long.

Not everyone felt the way he did including some of the crewmen who'd remained with him on Ereshkigal. The women here were far more attractive than the usual slatterns they encountered on the base worlds;

and six members of the crew who were tired of fighting or the boredom of hyperspace travel had decided to stay.

He wasn't surprised when Anvil Straller approached him with a sheepish grin. "Otto, I've decided to stay at Padul. Here I can teach the locals things and be of real value. It'll be years before I become an officer on the *Black Hawk*."

Given that he was lazy and unmotivated, it would take longer than that, Harkaman thought, but he didn't say anything. Instead he laughed, "Yes, and you'll have the lovely Sinja as your wife."

Straller turned beet red. "What about you, Otto? Sinja says that Kristel is pregnant. Aren't you going to stay and take care of her?"

He shrugged. "She was doing a pretty good job of protecting herself and the village before I came along. Besides, I'm not husband material, and Kristel knows it. I'm a born wanderer and it'll take more than a good woman to tie me down. Furthermore, I've got my own star to follow."

Straller shrugged as if he didn't get it. "How do you think the Captain will react?"

Harkaman sighed. "We're a bit crew heavy as it is. I don't think he'll mind unless one of the officers decides to jump ship."

"You're the only ranker that stayed behind when the ship left so I don't know why any of the others who haven't been here would stay." Straller then began to hem and haw.

He was running out of patience, so he asked, "What else is on your mind?"

"Well, the Captain's not going to pay us if we leave before he pays out shares, right?"

"You're right, Straller. Captain Mavuso goes strictly by the book."

"Well, I was talking with the other guys who've decided to stay and we agreed that we'd sign over our shares to any of the crew members who will trade us gold and silver jewelry. We could also use some weapons...."

Harkaman knew a number of crewmen who'd be more than willing to trade their personal jewelry and weapons for shares on what appeared to be a very profitable series of raids. However, the pistols would only be good for as long as their ammunition lasted.

He nodded. "Fine, I'll talk to the crew first chance I get and see what I can work out. In fact, I'll give you three of my own rings and two of my pistols for a share."

Along with the nice deal with Straller, he had learned a valuable lesson on Ereshkigal as well; previously, he had believed that barely civilized worlds were worthless to raid. Now he knew that if you looked hard and deep enough you might find wealth where you least expected it. Such worlds would never be the centerpiece of any of his future voyages, but he resolved that he would always check them out thoroughly to see if there was anything worthwhile to steal.

nergal

1708 A. E.

Alvyn Karffard laughed as he shut off the communication screen. "Good news everyone," he announced to the bridge crew. "We've finally sold the last of the silver." That drew shouts of derision from most of those present. It had only taken several years.

After the successful raid at Kaura City, they had left Ereshkigal. It had been Alvyn's suggestion that they head to Imhotep to trade. Imhotep was currently undergoing extensive glaciation. Because it was winter for three quarters of their year, there were numerous pelted animals, whose furs were considered among the finest available. There was only one small city of about fifteen thousand or so and the rest of the population was so dispersed it was not worth raiding. The city would spread the word via radio of a ship arriving and everyone would come in on contragravity to trade. For some reason they considered silver more valuable than any other metal so it was a logical place to trade their silver.

Unfortunately, the *Black Hawk* was the victim of bad timing. Just a few months before they arrived at Imhotep, the Space Viking ships, *Starhopper* and *Star Breaker*, had landed with large cargos of silver they had obtained raiding Agni. They had bought up almost every available hide. The only furs left were to be found in isolated settlements that had been too far from the city to come in and do business. They had sent their pinnaces down to those settlements to trade, but didn't dispose of much silver that way. The bad timing continued when they went on to Jagannath. Recent traders and Space Vikings had sold enough silver that there wasn't much demand and consequently they were offered a very low price. Captain Mavuso decided they'd just hang on to it for a better deal. Happily the gadolinium, gold and other merchandise turned out to be very profitable.

That was the story for their next few voyages. At Xochitl, and later Hoth, there was a similar lack of demand. Some of the crew had joked about the silver being cursed. At least their other loot continued to sell and their other raids were profitable. The amount of funds accumulated by their band of adventurers continued to grow. So did Harkaman's reputation, as Captain Mavuso was more than willing to give him credit for his profitable recommendations and ideas. The guys believed they were over a third of the way to having enough funds to purchase or construct a ship of their own.

The *Black Hawk's* luck finally changed on Nergal due to a big demand for monetary metals. An independent trader was the primary source of the demand. Though closed mouthed about why he need the specie, rumor had it that he was looking for monetary metals for an industrial baron in the Sword-Worlds who wanted to finance a rebellion against his king, which left just about every Sword-World—other than Excalibur—as a prime candidate. The trader was selling a lot of industrial machinery, power units and other finished manufactured products and was happy to trade them for the *Black Hawk's* silver.

The Captain, Harkaman and the other senior officers met at the Nergal branch of the Trans-World Bank of Excalibur. With the cargo from Ereshkigal finally sold, there were a variety of financial transactions to complete. The standard payout of death benefits for crewmembers, who had died on a voyage, was made whenever the ship stopped at a base world. In addition while some crew members who left the *Black Hawk* after the raid on Ereshkigal had accepted a financial settlement for the unsold loot, others had been willing to wait for it to be sold in hopes of a better payout. Those that waited had made the right choice and the funds were being dispersed to their bank accounts for future pickup.

While this was going on, Alvyn had been putting together a summary of all the information and gossip the crew had heard during their stops at the various watering holes and other sources of amusement they had visited on Nergal. There was only one Space Viking ship currently on-world but there were four traders, two independents and one each from Morglay and Xochitl, so there was a lot of information to be had. However, there was no mention of the *Jolly Roger*. She seemed to have dropped out of sight, perhaps due to the damage they had inflicted to her on Junrojin. Although the officers had probably heard same talk, they would only review it when they got back before they decided which targets to raid next.

What started as a gossip session of all officers, junior and senior, had morphed into a strategy session and then morphed again into cocktail hour. They had gone over all of the information they had gathered on Nergal and a discussion of which worlds to raid was next. By common consent they were staying on the *Black Hawk* for drinks and dinner so that there would be no possible leakage. Harkaman had an idea but he had waited to let everyone else make their suggestions.

"Would we want to partner with some other Space Vikings to hit a tough target like Beowulf?" Vann Larch asked, after several other possible targets had been thoroughly discussed.

Captain Mavuso shook his head. "The only other Space Viking in port is the *Doombringer* and I wouldn't want to work with them." He paused to sip his drink.

"Would it be worth seeing if Tobbin would want to commit a ship on a raid?" Stafan Mavuso suggested. Tobbins ran the Nergal base world, which his father had founded over thirty-five years ago. They always had a ship or two orbiting their world plus a couple of missile launching stations on Nergal's three moons to discourage anyone from thinking about raiding them.

"There are only a few captains I'd think of partnering with," Captain Mavuso said. "And they aren't one of them. Furthermore I'm not interested in raiding Beowulf. It's far too much like a civilized world for my taste."

He wondered how the healthy the Captain was feeling. His hair had gone completely grey in the last two years and he seemed tired more often. He'd told him that he'd been checked out by the medical facilities on Xochitl, and now Nergal, and they'd found nothing wrong with him.

"Just old age creeping up on me, I guess," he'd said early that day. Mavuso was much older than Harkaman had thought when they first met. Chronologically, he was in his mid-nineties. However, since much of Mavuso's time had been in hyperspace, where time was more relative, determining his actual age was difficult. Most Space Vikings and merchants who traveled in hyperspace stayed with their ships until death, or some injury or infirmity sidelined them.

Once everyone had exhausted their ideas, he spoke up: "What about Susano?"

Susano was a world with a technological level similar to Terra about the time it developed nuclear energy. It was also a world Trevor Mavuso had raided when he was on the *Sword of Doom* almost thirty five years ago. It was a raid the Captain talked about with fondness: the success of that raid had led to him having the reputation and funds to buy the *Black Hawk*.

"That's a great idea, Otto!" Stafan turned to the Captain, "We'd be going back to your roots, Father."

It was a symbol of how excited Stafan Mavuso was about the idea that he referred to the Captain as father, something he rarely did in front of the crew. Harkaman could tell the Captain liked the idea. He also was trying to see if there was anything wrong with the idea for that reason; one of the many things he liked about Trevor Mavuso was he did his best not to let his emotions lead him into making hasty decisions.

"Didn't I hear about someone raiding them recently and doing poorly?" the Captain asked.

"Yes," Harkaman replied. "It was the *Fortuna* about a dozen years before I joined your crew. When I reviewed the raid with some of the crew who'd taken part, it was clear that the captain was too cautious. They hit one of the smaller cities without much to offer in loot. Once some of the major powers showed up and started peppering them with missiles and bombs, they fled. That's why it hasn't been raided since; the *Fortuna* gave it a bad rep by getting so little plunder while taking some serious damage."

The Captain laughed heartily. "Let's do it, then." Everyone grinned at that. Some people started to get up to leave, thinking that the meeting was over and they could get dinner. Harkaman stopped them.

"We have another suggestion that we think would work well," he said. "Alvyn came up with this so I'll let him tell you himself."

"I was at the Golden Nugget," Karffard said, "when I ran into the captain of a merchant ship who had just stopped by on a whim to see if they had anything worth trading on Epona."

Epona had been a major world that had been heavily damaged in the Interstellar Wars that had occurred after the fall of the Terran Federation. The last Space Viking to hit Epona raided it almost two centuries ago, and had found so little wealth that it was considered a chicken-stealing world.

"He said they had operating atomic power plants," Karffard reported. "When Epona was first settled during the late Federation era, they found the planet was chock full of fissionables. The locals must have technologically advanced enough in the last two centuries to recover those skills. The trader sold them machinery and received plutonium and diamonds in return."

He reached in his pocket and took out a document. "Otto and I were able to find a map of the world in the library on Nergal. The city he traded with was located here on one of their southern continents," he said, pointing to the spot. "So we know where to go," he finished. "And," he added, "It's right on the way to Susano."

Everyone congratulated Alvyn on his research. Then all eyes turned to the Captain.

"We've got a plan," he said with a grin. "So what are we waiting for!"

Epona

1708 A.E.

Epona was almost too easy. It was the second planet of an orange K2 sun. They were detected a few hours after their last microjump as they were just beginning their descent from orbit. The city of Oriente, which was the city that the trader had described to Alvyn Karffard, welcomed them with open arms. They told the Eponans they were a merchant ship and eager to trade with them.

While they were descending, the cities of Latrobe and Matlosana also contacted them, offering to trade as well. Captain Mavuso spoke to each of them, asking what they had to trade in turn. When each offered plutonium, he asked if they had gold, jewels or silver. Another city, Arica, contacted them during this discussion. They were eager to describe their nearby gold mine and the amount of gold they had to trade. Everyone wanted machinery. The Captain slowed their descent to allow the cities to keep bidding against one another. This also allowed them to tour the world so they could get an idea of the size of the cities contacting them.

Some of the original Federation cities were still hotspots of radiation easily detected from low orbit. Oriente was the largest city at an estimated three million in population so they decided to target it first.

As they descended over the city they were directed to the airfield where the previous ship had landed. The person they spoke with also responded to their queries by directing them to the sites where they could trade for plutonium. When they were just a mile over the city the *Black Hawk* launched pinnaces, combat cars, one-man air cavalry mounts and landing craft full of heavy duty lifters and manipulators. One third of these were directed to the two plutonium sites and the other two thirds attacked the area of the city where the stores and banks were located.

The locals were caught totally by surprise and there was little resistance. They seemed completely flabbergasted by being robbed by people whom they believed to be friendly traders. Of course, no Space Viking cared what a Neobarb thought. Whatever political entity they belonged to didn't seem to have any military forces nearby. The local police were soon killed or cowed into submission.

The two plutonium sites took hours to strip, primarily because the plutonium needed to be carefully loaded into the collapsium-plated containers they had brought. This was a precise operation requiring a lot of remote robot work to avoid any radiation leakage. Once this was completed and the plutonium loaded on to the *Black Hawk*, the pinnace joined the rest of the ground troops looting the warehouses, stores and banks of the city. This went on throughout the day and into the next morning before they were finished. Ranjit Chaudry, as raid commander, coordinated everything. They lost only two men; one of whom was killed when he fell down some stairs trying to carry too much booty.

Harkaman, accompanied by enough troops to keep him from being bothered, did his usual tour of the local libraries, leaving them dozens of books and journals poorer. Vann Larch toured the various museums to take any paintings and sculptures he thought would be salable. Once they were done the *Black Hawk* rose into the air. Any local watching the ship depart and seeing the blazon of a black hawk descending on a planet with a sword in its beak and talons outstretched would have a better idea of just what that emblem meant; that is if they could see it through the smoke of the many fires lit while the city was sacked.

As they rose up from Oriente, the Captain noticed Paul Koreff, the signals-and-detection officer, looked worried. "Paul, what have you uncovered?"

"All of the big cities on the planet are frantic, Captain," Koreff said. "They are calling out their military forces and asking help from other cities." He pointed to one of the screens showing a dozen or more jets heading their way.

"Vann, give those aircraft a good spanking," the Captain ordered.

A flight of ship to ship missiles went out and suddenly most of the red lights disappeared from the screen. Two more missiles ended the threat, although the fighters got off a few missiles of their own. The *Black Hawk* didn't even notice their impact, since they were chemical rather than nuclear warheads.

"Which cities are the best protected?" Harkaman asked.

"Matlosana," Koreff replied. "Then Latrobe. Both have called out their armed forces and have lots of tanks, artillery and planes ready. Other cities are requesting their help, but from what I'm hearing, they're going to get it."

"What about the city with the gold?" Stafan Mavuso asked. "What was its name?"

"Arica," Alvyn Karffard said.

Koreff grinned. "They don't seem to have much in the way of military forces. They are frantically asking for help from Matlosana and one or two other cities on the same continent."

Harkaman turned to the Captain. "I suggest we alter course for Matlosana as a ruse. They'll think we're going to attack their city and won't let any of their military depart to help anyone else. We can change course at the last moment and hit Arica."

The Captain agreed and directed Sharll Renner accordingly. "It will take several hours Captain," Renner said, after he reviewed their course. "But the sun will just be rising when we get there, so we should have plenty of light."

"Good," the Captain replied. "Tell the ground troops to relax for a while." He turned to Harkaman and his son. "You two supervise the resupply of all the ground vehicles so they're ready to go when we reach the city."

Before he could give any more orders his Exec, Hamid Jorgensans interrupted. "Trevor, you've been up for over twenty hours. Why don't you get some rest? I'll have Koreff call you when we reach Arica."

"That sounds like a good idea, Ham," he said, rising from the command chair, suddenly looking very tired. "The rest of you carry on and get some sleep if you can."

As he left the bridge, the Exec directed all of the bridge crew, except Renner and Koreff, to take a breather as well, then called in their backups to take their places.

Arica was just as easy as Oriente and even more lucrative. What few troops they had were scattered after a few chemical missile strikes. They had apparently received the news about what happened in Oriente. There was plenty of gold in the warehouses adjacent to the mine. Apparently, it was stored there for shipping. There was even more in the banks located in the commercial area of town. Since the city only had two hundred thousand or so inhabitants, there was only a small commercial area but it was a very wealthy community. They spent the rest of the day looting all the banks, stores and high-end shops.

Harkaman and Larch visited the libraries and museums. While Harkaman didn't find much material of interest, Larch had better luck. There was a large sculpture exhibit in one of the museums and many of the figures were made of gold. The museum would have a lot of room for new exhibits in the future after they emptied out most of the floor space. Due to the lack of resistance, there were few fires obscuring the *Black*

Hawk blazonry as it rose into the sky.

“Do we want to hit another city, Captain?” Karffard asked.

The Captain shook his head. “We’ve made a huge haul so far. The remaining cities are ready and lying in wait. We could loot them but we’d take a lot of casualties doing it. I say, quit while we’re ahead.” He rose to his feet, grinned and extended his hand. “Congratulations Alvyn! You’re due an extra half share for this.”

“Thank you, Captain,” Karffard said, shaking hands with a big smile.

The Captain turned to the rest of bridge.

“Congratulations men, this was a great way to start a raiding trip.”

SUSANO

I

1708 A.E.

Ranjit's face appeared in the combat car's communication screen. "Otto, Karma is really a bitch!" The rest of his statement went unheard due to the bass-drum boom of explosive shells detonating against the vehicle.

"Any damage?" Harkaman asked the pilot.

"Just dents so far, sir," he replied. "No penetrations. That's not counting my ears, though!" He turned the combat car suddenly to avoid an incoming rocket, throwing Harkaman against the straps of his seatbelt.

The *Black Hawk* had approached Susano slowly; Guatt Kirbey had brought the ship out of their last microjump masked from the planet by the larger of its two moons. Susano had radar so once they moved out of the moon's shadow they were detected. They had gathered in the mess to discuss their strategy.

"Thirty-five years ago, we sacked their largest city, Kaipara," Trevor Mavuso said. "Then about a dozen years after us the *Curse of Cagn* looted it again. I don't know whether it's still a worthwhile target."

Harkaman had reviewed all the information he had found in various libraries about the planet, noting that the information was centuries out of date. Others talked about what they had heard from other Space Viking ships. The planet was thought to have a unified government which meant no matter where they attacked they'd likely get an armed response.

"They have chemical-powered aircraft, missiles and plenty of artillery," Captain Mavuso noted. "And they're very fierce fighters. When you think you've beaten them, don't let up because they'll regroup and come right back at you."

Ranjit Chaudry would lead again as the raid commander in one of the pinnaces. But the Captain wanted Harkaman out there, as well.

"Otto, you take another combat car," Mavuso ordered. "Years ago we found that there was so much going on that we needed several people to coordinate our response."

So Harkaman now found himself several hundred yards above the city of Sergipe, where they had decided to begin the raid. The *Black Hawk* had made one quick circle around the planet as they descended. The city of Kaipara had not looked particularly prosperous viewed from orbit on their highest powered telescopes. Much of it looked as if it hadn't been rebuilt since previous raids. However Sergipe, which was located a few hundred miles north of Kaipara across an ocean, appeared to be flourishing. So they had aimed toward Kaipara, then turned toward Sergipe.

As Sergipe was a port city, he was concentrating on the warehouses lining the harbor while Ranjit was hovering just above their commercial area. None of the buildings were more than six hundred feet tall, with narrow streets between them. The warehouses were all less than half that size.

"Watch out for enemy action," Ranjit called out from the pinnace.

Ranjit's comment was ringing in his ears as the combat car turned toward what looked like troops gathering in an open, park-like area. A couple of missiles, followed by a few bursts from the port gunner's machine guns had dispersed the crowd, leaving dead bodies strewn haphazardly over the verdant grass. Ranjit had told him on the way down to the surface that he was certain they were going to have to pay for the easy time they'd had on Epona. He'd have to tell him he was right.

A missile slammed into the combat car, rocking it violently. *That is, if I make it back in one piece to tell him.*

After defeating the initial attack in the warehouse area, they had hovered above in the combat car to provide protection to the ground troops as they looted the warehouses. Half the troops were now focusing on emptying two of the warehouses below. Others were fanning out through the area to see if there were any other valuables.

"Report from Trooper Rodriguez, sir."

The pilot patched Harkaman through. Rodriguez reported that he had found a street with a number of jewelry stores, but was asking for help. "They took out our air-cavalry mount," he was saying. "There are four of us pinned down in one of the stores. Their heaviest weapons appear to be rocket-propelled grenades and bazookas. Get some more people here. This place is loaded with rubies, diamonds and emeralds."

The pilot banked and flew around the city, while he called the *Black Hawk*. A reserve ground troop section was dispatched his way. Given the fierceness of the fighting, he wondered how many reserve troopers were left.

Then the pilot called out, "There they are, sir."

He spotted the ground fighters a few blocks ahead; there were numerous people firing on them from the tops of the surrounding buildings.

"No missiles, just machine guns," he ordered. "We don't want to bury any nice jewels in the rubble."

"Yes, sir!" the starboard gunner said happily, as he let loose with a blast.

As Harkaman watched the soldiers on two of the buildings almost dissolved before his eyes. Just as he was thinking everything was going well a huge jolt rocked the combat car. The pilot swore, fiddled desperately with his controls, then activated the radio.

"Combat car Two, calling Mayday, Mayday. We have lost power and are going down!"

Otto saw the ground coming rapidly toward them on one of the screens. *This is it*, he thought. Then the pilot gave a yelp of surprise as the controls started to work again and he began punching buttons. Their descent began to level off, but they were still slewing. They struck the ground at an angle and slid along the roadway until they crashed into a building.

The world went dark for a moment.

Dazed, he sat frozen in his seat while trying to get his bearings. He undid his seat belt straps and started to get up. The combat car was tilted to the left. Then a series of shells hit the left side. He heard the port gunner scream and saw something pass in front of his eyes.

When he looked again the port gunner was lying sprawled in his chair. One of the shells must have made a direct hit on the gun. Shrapnel had come through the tiny opening and taken off part of his head. There was a jagged piece of shrapnel stuck into the wall in front of him. He didn't have any time to congratulate himself on his good luck.

The starboard gunner's machine guns were pointed uselessly up in the air. He and the pilot were out of their seats and the gunner started to reach toward the door. "Let's get out the Nifflheim out of here!" he cried, beating against the door until it opened.

"No, wait!" Otto Harkaman shouted, but the gunner already had the door open. He saw a half dozen men charging toward them, one of whom was aiming a rocket-propelled grenade.

"Get down!" he yelled, reaching out and pulling the pilot down with him. There was a huge explosion that rocked the combat car, filling it with smoke and debris and setting his ears ringing. He was tossed back against his seat, smacking his ribs with enough force to knock the breath out of him, then he was thrown against the wall as the combat car slid off whatever was tilting it to the left and came to rest tilted slightly to the right.

It seemed like an eternity before he could raise himself up. He wondered briefly how he was still alive, then looked out the open door. Three soldiers were rushing toward him from about fifteen yards away. He realized he still had his pistol in his hand; he kept firing until they were all down. There were other men behind them who suddenly took cover in a tobacco shop. He rose into a crouch, jammed in another magazine, then fired blindly out the door, hoping to keep their heads down. He quickly launched himself past the door to the starboard machine gun, tripping on the pilot who was just rousing himself.

Settling into the starboard gun pit, which he'd always found cramped for someone of his size, he quickly scanned the street. Seeing no one in the open areas, he looked up toward the roof tops. He swung the gun up when he spotted several troops looking down at him, one aiming a bazooka. He couldn't tell whether he hit anyone with the gun burst but there was no longer anybody in sight.

The pilot was staggering to his feet. He reached out and pulled him away from the door and thrust him toward the pilot's seat.

"See if the radio is working and let them know we're alive," the pilot ordered.

Harkaman took a quick look around but didn't see any movement out on the street. Then he heard the pilot retch. He turned and saw why.

The starboard gunner was splayed across the pilot's seat. Just his body. His head was lying on the floor below and one of his arms was tangled in the gun rack. The bazooka shell must have hit him as he was going out the door and blown his body to bits; that bit of cover had saved him and the pilot from a blast that would certainly have killed them. He reached out again and grabbed the pilot's shoulder.

"Pull yourself together," he said, urgently. "I need you! We've got to get a message out or we're dead!"

The pilot looked at him and gulped. With a visible effort he steadied himself. He reached out and pushed the gunner's body off the chair. After a moment's hesitation, he sat down in the pool of blood he'd left behind.

"Combat car Two reporting, we are down but alive. We're in the northeast quadrant, where the jewelry shops are. We're pinned down by local troops and need assistance."

After a moment there was a reply:

"Acknowledged, combat car Two. We're on our way."

With the message sent, he looked up at the roofs, pausing for a moment to wipe the sweat out of his eyes. He couldn't see any movement. Peering down the street, he saw a score of soldiers headed their way. He gave them a burst from the machine guns and hit several before they took cover. At the same time the surviving combatants across the street from the combat car fired. He fired a burst back at them. Then he checked the gun, noting it still had plenty of ammunition.

"Try to close the door," Harkaman ordered. The pilot moved over cautiously, grabbed the handle and gave it a yank. It closed about three quarters of the way before it jammed against the street.

"Grab one those machine guns," he said, indicating the guns stored in a rack. "Get behind that seat and fire at any movement you see through that opening."

The seat didn't provide much cover, but the pilot did as he ordered and signaled that he was ready. His fear was that someone could get close enough to toss a grenade through the opening. If that happened, they were finished. Then he got an idea.

"Bring that lifter over here, the small one," he qualified. "Lay it on its side in front of the door and turn it on."

The pilot immediately grasped what he was up to. When turned on the lifter's contragravity field would repel any thrown grenades or bullets. And not a moment too soon as bullets started pinging off the vehicle.

Suddenly, he heard voices to the left side of the combat car. He saw movement to the left of the port side gun. The pilot saw it too, moved over and fired out the small opening.

They heard a scream and saw someone fall away. He thought about warning him to be careful but decided he'd rather be hit from a ricocheting bullet from the pilot's gun, which he might survive, than by a grenade someone shoved through the portside gun opening. He heard the troops outside calling to one another.

"Get ready!" he told the pilot. "They're going to rush us."

The locals started their charge. Before he could decide who to fire at first, he heard the yammering of machine guns and saw the troops down the street start falling, shot from behind. He quickly turned his guns on the people coming at them from across the street and cut them down with several bursts. He heard swearing on the left side of the vehicle; then machine guns sounded again from down the street. More screams. Then everything was silent.

"Did the cavalry arrive?" the pilot asked, wonderingly.

"If so, I didn't hear any coming in," he replied.

"Combat car Two, this is Trooper Rodriguez," crackled the radio. "Anyone in there alive?"

Harkaman looked at the pilot and they both laughed a little hysterically—the laugh of men who'd thought they weren't ever going to have a chance to laugh again.

"Rodriguez we're, fine," the pilot replied. "What are you doing here?"

After a few seconds, Rodriguez replied. "Everyone shooting at us left. We figured they were going after you and decided to follow them."

"Hey," he added, after a moment's delay, "Are we ever going to get any help grabbing these jewels?"

Harkaman was about to reply when he heard the sound of another combat car coming down the street. He sighed and relaxed. The cavalry had finally arrived.

II

The party was starting to slow down a little towards the end of the second day. They were in hyperspace on their way back to Nergal. The Captain had decided that since they'd had good luck selling their previous loot there, he'd try it again. And they had a lot of plunder. The estimates were between six hundred and fifty and seven hundred million stellars combined from the Epona and Susano raids. They had everything from gold, silver, emeralds, diamonds and rubies to plutonium, uranium, platinum, metals, fine art and consumer goods. It was the biggest score any of them, including Trevor Mavuso, had ever been a part of.

Harkaman had missed the first day of the celebration when he decided his bruises were a little too painful and spent the time in the robomedic. Now he was feeling good and several drinks into the party. He was sitting with Alvyn and the rest of their band; they had started discussing whether they had enough funds combined to get a ship of their own. The consensus was that they did; then the discussion was over the best place to either buy or build a ship. They had settled on Xochitl. As the oldest of the base worlds it was the most developed and had the best construction facilities and financing options, outside the Sword-Worlds of course. If they couldn't find what they wanted there they could always go to one of the Sword-Worlds, but that would mean a three-month travel delay. He was just about to order another drink from the bartender robot when a crewmember came up to him.

"Sir, the Captain would like to see you in his quarters," he said.

Excusing himself he left and took the lift to the Captain's floor. He knocked on the door and was given permission to enter. Inside the Captain was sitting in a chair with Stafan Mavuso standing next to him. Stafan had an expression on his face he'd never seen before; what it meant became clear in a moment.

"Otto," said Trevor Mavuso. "I'm announcing my retirement."

His jaw dropped. Although the Captain had seemed a little more tired lately, he had never given any thought to the idea that he might one day retire. Mavuso seemed to enjoy the planning and carrying out of a successful raid too much. Their recent expedition was proof of that.

He dropped into a nearby chair in surprise.

"Otto, I'm sure you've noticed that I don't have the energy I used to," Trevor Mavuso said ruefully. "When I can't stay in the Captain's chair for the duration of a raid, no matter how long, it's time for me to give it up to someone who can. I'll be turning the ship over to Stafan when we reach Jagannath."

"I don't know what to say, Trevor. I've really enjoyed serving under you. I've learned so much from you and Stafan."

"I've talked it over with my son, and we'd love to see you and your people continue on as part of the *Black Hawk's* crew. But, I suspect the six of you, after this trip, have enough funds saved to pursue your own dreams."

Before he could say anything Stafan Mavuso spoke up and echoed his father's thoughts, ending with, "Otto, there will always be a place for you and your comrades on the *Black Hawk*."

"Thank you, both," he replied. "We just confirmed that we will be leaving the *Black Hawk* at the end of this voyage to seek our own ship."

They didn't act surprised at this. They must have been expecting it and offered their congratulations.

"We figured we would go to Xochitl and see what we can find."

They both nodded at that. It made as much sense to them as it had to him and his comrades. "Though," he added with a smile, "if we find anything to our liking on Nergal or Jagannath I won't be disappointed."

They laughed at that. "Don't feel you have to stay with us until Jagannath," Captain Mavuso said. "And I'll be happy to confirm with any investor that contacts me that you're worthy of having your own ship."

"You've earned the right to go off on your own," Stafan Mavuso added. "The bunch of you are going to be damned hard to replace."

"I'll drink to that," his father said, making a toast: "To good friends, good fortune and Lady Luck!"

They all clinked glasses.

Harkaman rose to his feet. "Thank you both, again. I can't express enough how much I've enjoyed working with you."

He extended his hand.

Trevor Mavuso rose and shook it. Space Vikings being notoriously unsentimental, at least when sober, only the extra length of time they held each other's hand conveyed the depth of their feelings. He turned to Stafan and did the same thing with him.

"Can I let the rest of the guys know, or would you prefer that I keep it quiet for a while?" he asked.

"No, go ahead," the Captain said. "I've told Stefan that we will be letting everybody else know through a general announcement."

He thanked them again and left the cabin. Clearly it was best for all parties to make this transition now. Stafan Mavuso would be the unchallenged captain of the *Black Hawk* with officers he'd hired, not inherited. And he would soon be captain of a ship whose name was not known yet. He couldn't wait.

NERGAL

1709 A. E.

It was fascinating to watch all the figures as they added up on the screen at the Nergal branch of the Trans-World Bank of Excalibur as the bank manager walked them through it. Although Harkaman had a rough idea of how much they had in their join account, it was still a shock to see it documented on the screen.

The banker, a small well-dressed man with a goatee, finished with a flourish. "There you are," he said. "Unless I missed something, I'd say that combined you men have around three quarters of the funds necessary to construct a ship. As for purchasing one, you might be able to find a used ship for the funds you've accumulated, but I'm not familiar with that market."

They looked at each other with smiles and even a little wonderment. He and Alvyn had been talking and planning for this moment for a decade. Now they were finally in sight of their goal of having their own ship.

"What do you think, Otto?" asked Alvyn Karffard, the first man who'd joined with Harkaman on this endeavor.

He chose to focus on the task in front of them, rather than what they had accomplished. "There's enough demand for Space Viking ships that I've never seen them sold at much of a discount; unless they've had a lot of damage or deferred maintenance, that is."

The banker handed each one of them their credit chits, after reviewing and verifying the funds contained in accounts with each of them. Another one of the reasons the Trans-World Bank of Excalibur was trusted was that they were meticulous in their record keeping. Their fees were substantial and upfront but they delivered.

The banker was a native of Nergal and in his mid-thirties. The natives were easy to spot. Unlike most planets which typically had a wide variety of skin, hair and eye color the Nergalers were a uniform lot. They had mahogany brown skin, coarse black hair and unique maroon eyes. Whether the eyes were a mutation caused by the F5 sun that Nergal orbited, he didn't know.

Nergal had been established as a base world by the Tobbin family over thirty-five years ago. He had seen a lot of the native people during their time groundside over the past few days, which showed that the Tobbin family had made a real effort to educate the natives so that they didn't have to import all their skilled workers from the Sword-Worlds. On most Space Viking base worlds, like Dagon and Xochitl, the local peoples were given the low-paying jobs, while the better paying ones went to immigrants from the Sword-Worlds. He'd have to remember this if and when they decided to establish a base world of their own.

The banker also offered them half a dozen names of people or firms they could contact about ship financing. They still were going to need a loan of around fifty million stellars if they were to obtain a ship. Unfortunately, he had already talked to three investors and found the discussion unsatisfactory.

A number of investors were willing to loan them the money based on Captain Mavuso's recommendation and their own considerable experience. However, the investors wanted to receive their twenty percent share of any proceeds of their raids in perpetuity. They weren't interested in any mechanism whereby they could be paid off and have to give up their part ownership. Two of them also wanted any loot they obtained sold on exclusively on Nergal and run through firms they had an interest in, which would allow them another rake-off from each sale. Harkaman had turned them all down with the other partners' approval,

"Well, do we celebrate or do we continue to talk to financing firms?" Vann Larch asked.

"I'm willing to leave the finance talk to Otto and Alvyn," Paul Koreff said. The others indicated agreement with that as well.

"We have a few days before the *Black Hawk* leaves for Jagannath," he said. "Alvyn and I will continue to meet with potential financiers. Why don't the rest of you look around and see if you can find some sort of hyperyacht for sale; it would be nice to be able to travel independent of the *Black Hawk*."

"It sounds like you don't have much hope of getting a loan," Guatt Kirbey said.

Harkaman shook his head but Alvyn spoke up before he could respond: "The terms everyone offered were so similar that I suspect there was some collusion going on between them. We'll talk to everyone, but I have a feeling we'll either be going on to Jagannath or direct to Xochitl, if we can find a hyperyacht."

Those words proved to be prophetic. There was no hyperyacht worth buying on Nergal and the terms offered by financing firms didn't change either. They rode with the *Black Hawk* to Jagannath. There were more financing firms on Jagannath but their terms weren't much better. Some were willing to see their loans paid off but the pay-off process was onerous. It would have taken ten raids as good as the one on Susano to accumulate enough money. However, they were able to find a decent hyperyacht they could purchase. Saying goodbye to all their shipmates on the *Black Hawk* and wishing Trevor Mavuso well in retirement, they left for Xochitl.

Xochitl

I

1709 A.E.

On Xochitl, they found there were dozens of banks, investment groups and financing firms competing for business; in addition, several companies that repaired and constructed ships were also willing to offer financing. There were a bewildering variety of terms offered, which they discussed thoroughly among themselves, trying to understand which one was the best deal for them. Two investor groups they were working with tried to sneak in unmarked changes to proposed contracts which would have given the investors control of any ship they purchased. They promptly ceased talks with those groups as soon as their deceit was revealed, but that had created some paranoia in their negotiations. They were reviewing various options with the Xochitl banks with the rest of their party when they were approached by a man wearing the uniform of a palace guard.

"Are you, Otto Harkaman?" he asked. Upon affirmation he added, "Crown Prince Viktor would like to see you."

He was surprised, and looking at his comrades, they were just as surprised as he was. He'd never had any dealings with Sword-World royalty. The Liebig Royal Family was not known for its duplicity, at least, in regards to fellow Sword-Worlders, so he was more intrigued than concerned as he joined the guardsman in an aircar outside.

As their rented aircar rose up above Icacan spaceport and made its way to the palace, he tried to think of everything he could recall about the family. Viktor's father, Prince Thom, was King Konrad of Haultclere cousin and they were considered part of the Liebig Royal Family. They were also considered smart businessmen, which was why Xochitl had prospered since its establishment two generations ago; although the prosperity was mainly limited to the royal family and their close local allies. It certainly hadn't spread as far as the Xochitl natives. Prince Thom was in his late-fifties, so the crown prince had to be somewhere in his twenties or early thirties.

Their aircar pulled into a landing stage near the upper part of the palace. This was an office building which had been built as part of the original spaceport over a thousand years ago. It had been converted into the royal family's living quarters and offices. He took an elevator down a few stories and he was directed into a luxuriously appointed outer office. Once there, another staffer conducted him through several rooms, each equally luxurious. The staffer knocked on a door and then held it aside while he entered.

Crown Prince Viktor was small man with fine features, like a Tri-D star. He appeared to be about five or six years younger than Harkaman. He wore his black hair down to his shoulders and had a Vandyke beard. That explained to him why he'd seen so many men with shoulder-length hair in the last few days. Apparently the Crown Prince was a fashion-setter. Or, the men who dealt with him were trying to curry favor by imitating him.

Viktor greeted him and directed him to a seat, retaking his own. He noticed that the part of the room where Viktor was seated sloped upward and that his seat was also raised. *Another small man overcompensating*, he decided, while maintaining a poker face.

In his favor, Viktor got right to the point without small talk. "I understand you're looking for financing for a ship, Captain Harkaman."

"Thank you, for the title, Your Highness; however, I'm not a captain yet."

Viktor waved his hand dismissively. "A mere formality," he stated. "I've had a thorough investigation made into your background. Captains Mavuso and Kowalski, as well as first officer Lozalic, have written laudatory statements regarding your abilities. Even men who've never served with you have heard of you and think highly of you. I think you're going to be a very successful captain and I'd like to back you."

As Harkaman thanked the Crown Prince, he realized that he was going to have to handle this request very carefully. Viktor was certainly not acting like he was giving orders, more like a businessman wooing a client. However, it was one thing to say no to a finance company or group of investors, and another thing to say no to someone who would be ruling a major Space Viking base world someday.

"Your Highness, most of the companies I've spoken with want to take twenty percent of what we make in perpetuity," he said. "Or, if they are willing to have their loan retired, the terms are so onerous that the loan would be almost impossible to pay off."

Viktor's face was impassive, so he was unable to tell if he intended to propose the same type of terms to him. *If I played high stakes cards, I wouldn't want to play against him.* "So," he concluded, "I'm looking for a loan that can be paid off one day in the future. My goal is to be the owner of a ship, not just its captain."

They discussed a variety of ways to structure a deal between the two of them. Viktor had some interesting suggestions which they discussed in detail. There was one sticking point.

"Tell me, why wouldn't you want to sell your loot exclusively on

Xochitl?" Viktor asked testily. "Our facilities are the best of any Sword-World base planet, and better than you'll find almost anywhere in the Helm. We always have a lot of Space Vikings and independent traders here, so there are always good markets for anything you might bring back to sell. Where else are you going to get such a good deal? Why would you want to travel all the way back to the Sword-Worlds, considering what I'm offering here on Xochitl?"

And you would get a percentage of every deal, he thought, but of course he wasn't going to say that. Every base world had landing fees for the use of their spaceport and also typically taxed all merchandise that was sold there. They kept these fees low, or otherwise everyone would take their business elsewhere but the fees were a major source of planetary revenue. It was smart of Viktor to want more.

"It's not always that simple, Your Highness," he said. He reviewed the problems the *Black Hawk* had selling the silver they had acquired on Ereshkigal. "As you can see," he concluded, "we were forced to travel to five different worlds before we were able to unload all the silver in our holds. So it's just not good business to restrict oneself to a single market."

Viktor looked thoughtful. "You have made some very good points, Mister Harkaman. I shall take them under consideration. You'll receive a proposal from me within the next day or two."

He stood up, indicating the meeting was over.

Harkaman stood as well, shaking the Crown Prince's extended hand. "Thank you, Your Highness. I'm staying at—"

Viktor waved his hand. "I know where you're staying. You'll hear from me."

He turned to leave, not sure at all about how he felt about that statement. He had a feeling that if he took Crown Prince Viktor up on his offer, there might be a lot of unspoken strings attached to the deal.

II

That pretty much described the view his partners had, when they went over the Crown Prince's proposal. Since it was a fine spring day, they were eating lunch at an outdoor plaza while reviewing various offers. Space Vikings spent so much time aboard ships that they enjoyed being outdoors and looking at the open sky whenever they had the chance.

"The Captain shall make all best efforts to trade on Xochitl," Sharll Renner said. "What does 'best efforts' even mean?"

"Whatever the Crown Prince wants it to mean," Vann Larch opined.

"Which would not be good news for us," Alvyn Karffard said. He turned to Guatt Kirbey. "How do those figures come out?"

Kirbey was an expert mathematician, a necessary characteristic of any good astrogator. They had him check every calculation in any proposed agreement. He had already caught firms trying to slip in requirements that they had not discussed beforehand. "All the figures are accurate," he said.

"Well, at least Prince Viktor's not trying to pull a fast one on us," Renner said, "unlike some of the people we've dealt with."

"Don't be too sure of that," the often pessimistic Guatt Kirbey replied. "I don't like this option where he gets his twenty percent before any ship expenses. If we suffered heavy damage during a raid and weren't able to pick up much loot, why, that could break us. Viktor would end up owning our ship."

"Which might be his long-range plan," Karffard replied.

"I don't like it either, and we're not going to agree to it," Harkaman said. "I do like this option of us having a partial ownership share and receiving five percent of the profits of any voyage on top of our regular shares."

"But that option removes the 'best efforts' clause and requires us to trade all our loot on Xochitl," argued Karffard. "I don't like tying our hands that way."

"Agreed. I suggest we rewrite the contract, keeping the parts we like and rejecting the rest," Harkaman said.

"Are you actually thinking of making an agreement with Viktor?" Larch asked, incredulously.

Harkaman removed his pipe and reached for his pouch to repack it. He'd picked up a large parcel of tobacco on Susano from a store adjacent to where his aircar was shot down. He'd fallen in love with it and was smoking it whenever he could. "No, I'm not," he replied, lighting his pipe. "But we can't just turn him down. We've got to make it look like we're actually negotiating. That way we won't run into troubles when we land on Xochitl in the future."

A lot of Space Vikings concentrated most of their trading and selling at one base world or on one of the Sword-Worlds, either because they had some sort of alliance with the ruling family, an agreement with one of the local trading companies or some other connection. Trevor Mavuso of the *Black Hawk* owned a home on Jagannath so he liked to get back and visit it. Some Space Vikings just became comfortable with the people they dealt with or felt they got a better deal on a particular base world and tended to return. At this point, Harkaman wanted to keep their trading options open and not be tied to any one world.

"I agree," Karffard said. "Let's accept the partial ownership option, reject Viktor's requirement to trade solely on Xochitl and suggest terms that would allow a much faster payoff of the loan. That should cause him to reject the proposal, but not come to the conclusion that we're stonewalling him."

There were nods of agreement from everyone present, even Paul Koreff and Ranjit Chaudry, who had not shown any prior interest in being involved in the loan negotiations.

"What about the other firms you've contacted, Otto?" Koreff asked. "Are they offering any better terms?"

"Slightly," Alvyn Karffard said, who only answered because Harkaman had a mouthful of sandwich. "Word's gotten around about us. The fact that we've rejected the initial offers shows people that we're not naïve or easy marks. The terms are getting better. Some firms have even come back with more realistic options after we rejected their initial offerings."

"Are we close?" Larch asked.

"Not yet," Harkaman replied, after swallowing. "But we're getting closer to a deal. We have a meeting with a new party,"—he paused to look around until he found a clock with the local time on the building wall—"in an hour. This is someone we haven't talked to yet." He looked around at the group. "Is anyone getting anxious?"

They all shook their heads. Each of them had enough money that they could live for years without working, if necessary. But if that was all they had wanted, they could have retired years ago. Kirbey agreed to redraft the proposed agreement with the changes they wanted and send it back to Viktor. Then the partners picked a place to meet that evening where they would review their next steps.

The afternoon meeting turned out to be with a representative of the Royal Bank of Excalibur, something that had not been revealed to them initially. The Manager apologized immediately: "We're one of the smaller banks on Xochitl and we're usually not interested in competing with the big banks on these kinds of loans, so we keep a low profile. However this is a special case."

The Manager was a slim man of about forty years, well dressed as every banker seemed to be. He explained that almost a decade ago, the former King of Excalibur had decided that he wanted to try to increase Excalibur's trade. He was seeing more and more Space Vikings trading on the base worlds established in the Old Federation rather than making the long voyage back to the Sword-Worlds; consequently Excalibur was losing business. The monarch had decided that financing some ships would bring increased commerce as they would be more inclined to return to Excalibur to trade their loot as well as rest and refit.

"His plan never worked the way he intended," the banker admitted. "The returns never justified the investment. When King Teodor died and Rodolf ascended to the throne, he stopped the practice and decided to concentrate on increasing trade within the Sword-Worlds cluster. I've been involved in winding down all the loans ever since."

Harkaman looked at Karffard, who gestured that he should respond. "That's an interesting history lesson, but what does that have to do with us? If you're not loaning any more funds for Space Viking ships, why did you want to meet with us?"

The banker looked a little embarrassed. He leaned forward slightly as if wanting to quietly impart a confidence. "Because we have one last loan remaining, and this one isn't performing at all."

Seeing their look of mystification, he continued. "We recently had to seize the *Corisande* for lack of payment. Its last few voyages have hardly produced any profits. In fact, the last one didn't make enough money to cover expenses."

"You want to sell us the *Corisande*?" Harkaman said, surprised. He looked at Karffard, who looked equally baffled. It was clear neither one of them knew anything about the *Corisande* being in trouble, nor had he ever heard of the ship before. She was probably one of the ships that returned to the Sword-Worlds to trade after every raid, so they had never crossed paths. This brought up a question.

Karffard asked, "How is it you're on Xochitl instead of Excalibur?"

"Captain Bartley came to Xochitl because he knew if he returned to Excalibur, we would have seized his ship. It would have worked too, except that he didn't have enough money to service the ship. He tried to get a loan to make repairs, but was turned down when the loan company found out he was behind in his payment to us. They contacted our agent here, who runs the small Xochitl branch, and we were able to get the *Corisande* impounded."

Harkaman grinned to himself. He was sure that the Xochitl Spaceyard was charging them a pretty good fee to hold the ship for them, which meant they were anxious to unload it.

As he recalled, the captain of his old ship the *Fortuna*, had faced the same issue. After several raids that brought in little to no profit, Captain Burrick knew he couldn't pay his investors. If he'd taken the ship to a base world, it would have been seized. Instead, he had spaced out to Melkarth, a Neobarbarian world that even chicken-thief raiders avoided. There he lived in some opulence, compared to the locals, with what remained of his crew. He supposed Burrick would continue to live there until his ship fell apart.

Harkaman wondered why they hadn't heard about the *Corisande*. Apparently they had been so focused trying to line up financing, they had missed out on some of the gossip. He finally understood why, when the banker said that he had been summoned from Excalibur to handle the sale of the ship. That meant the ship had been seized at least six or more months ago, which made it old news. He focused on the issue at hand. "How much do you want for the ship?"

"Two hundred million stellars, minus the cost of resupplying the ship."

Karffard shook his head. "That's the cost of a new ship. Not one that's decades old."

Harkaman was impressed that Alvyn knew that because he had no idea how old the *Corisande* was. He added his concern to Alvyn's, indicating he'd have to inspect the ship before agreeing to anything.

The banker looked like they caught him in a lie. "All right, I'll level with you," he said sheepishly. "You're attractive buyers because no one else I've spoken to has as much money for a down payment as your partnership does. We'd be willing to finance the rest of the cost on very good terms."

Now they were on familiar ground, they immediately began discussing financing terms. The banker really wanted the value of the ship established at two hundred million stellars. That must have been an order from either his boss or the King. However, the banker offered to pay the entire cost of resupplying and rearming the ship. Harkaman succeeded in adding the costs of hiring the crew and making any repairs and updates.

Alvyn hid a grin. He knew that Otto, based on their many discussions on the long trips between worlds, had some expensive ideas on how ships could be improved and refitted to increase their raiding abilities.

They quickly came to agreement on everything else but the terms of how they would repay the loan. Like most other firms, the banker wanted his twenty percent investor share separate from the repayment of the loan.

"How about this," Harkaman said after several back and forth offers. "An average Space Viking raid will net about thirty million stellars. What if you get your typical twenty percent share of profit up to thirty five million stellars; above that one fifth of the owner's share goes to pay off the loan and interest, with a cap agreed to by both parties."

The banker countered back. "Thirty million stellars is just an average. That includes dozens of raids that aren't much more than chicken stealing set off against a few bonanzas like the *Black Hawk* achieved on Susano."

They were impressed; this banker knew more about Space Viking business than anyone else—other than Viktor—they'd talked with.

"All right," Harkaman countered. "How about everything up to net fifty million stellars is subject to your twenty-percent owner's share? Above that amount, one half of the owner's share goes to pay off the loan, subject to a formula and cap we both agree to."

The banker didn't spend much time thinking the offer over. "It's a deal," he said. "I'll draw up an agreement and set up an inspection for you and your crew." He stood up and extended his hand. "Hopefully tomorrow we can sign our agreement and you'll be owners of the *Corisande*."

They stood and shook hands with him, giving him their hotel location so that he could contact them. Harkaman held his tongue until they had left the building.

"Alvyn, you continue to impress me," Otto Harkaman said, clapping him on the shoulder. "How'd you know how old the *Corisande* was?"

Karffard laughed. "I didn't. I just took a shot in the dark. And he bought it."

Harkaman choked, then almost fell over laughing. When he was done, he stopped and looked at Karffard. "Alvyn, you were the first one to believe in me. Thanks," he said, a little embarrassed by his solemnity.

Alvyn grinned and extended his hand. "I always knew we could do it," he said as they shook. "Now," he added. "Don't screw it up."

He laughed and clapped Alvyn on the shoulder again. They set off, anxious to share the good news with their comrades. At last, they had their own ship.

III

When the ship inspection didn't reveal any significant problems, they concluded their deal. After signing the ownership papers and transferring funds, they received the keys, access codes and ship's papers to the *Corisande*. Harkaman spent the evening celebrating with his partners, and later a girl he'd met at the hotel bar. He was awakened back at his hotel room by the chime of the bedroom viewphone at the break of dawn.

He noticed the girl was gone; he'd have to check his pants in case she'd taken off with his credit chit. If she tried to use it she wouldn't get anywhere, but he'd have to return to the bank to get a new chit, which would cost time he didn't want to waste.

Harkaman leaned over and pressed the welcome button. The viewscreen came to life displaying a wavy, fuzzy gray background. It was obviously a clandestine call. He pondered whether or not to accept, and then decided—*What the Hell?* He had nothing to lose.

"Who is this?" he demanded.

"A friend, with important information."

"Hmm..."

"I can tell you things you need to know, if you're going to buy the *Corisande*."

That did it. "When and where do you want to meet?"

"Go to Icacan Spaceport, Dock #6. Leave now. Somebody there will give you a message."

The screen went dark. *Curse and blast it,* thought Harkaman. He hated mysteries and unknown callers even more. *The caller probably doesn't even know we've already bought the* Corisande, he thought. *It might be worthwhile to find out what he does know, though.*

After checking to see that his credit chit hadn't been stolen—it hadn't, but his pocket money had been—he got up and showered. Feeling better, he took a robocab to Icacan Port. This early in the morning, there were few people around the spaceport and they were outnumbered by the robot cleaners and maintenance people. He made his way to Dock #6, which was empty, and waited. After a few minutes a young boy, a local dressed in ragged clothes and wearing a scruffy pointed cap, ran up to him and passed him a note.

Harkaman gave the boy a silver centistellar coin and he ran away.

The note read: **Meet me at the Beat to Quarters in half an hour.** There was no name or signature.

Beat to Quarters was the Xochitl port of call and he'd meant to go there anyway to start his search for a crew for the *Corisande*. He hoped this didn't end up being a case of 'Run the Dummy Around the Block.'

The bar was next to the spaceport, so he walked there. Beat to Quarters was a ramshackle spaceport tavern with corner booths, a dozen small tables and a long bar with about half the seats already filled. At the far end of the building, opposite the bar, was a large bulletin board affixed to the wall where ships could post openings for applicants. He went over to the board and posted all of the crew openings for *Corisande* he'd stashed in a pocket before sitting down. Several of the drunks at the bar, looking the worse for wear, appeared as if they'd been there all night including two who were asleep or passed out.

Harkaman ordered bourbon, one of the specialties of Xochitl, and waited. He figured he'd give his caller about fifteen minutes, then—if he didn't show—he'd head back to his hotel room.

A few minutes later, another disheveled local boy came into the tavern and headed straight to where he was seated.

Several of the patrons wrinkled their noses and gave him a look of disdain. He suspected they thought he was setting up an assignation with the young boy. *To Nifflheim with 'em!*

The slender boy handed him another slip of paper. Harkaman sighed and gave the kid a silver coin. He read the note: *Meet me at the Trade Winds motel, Room 214; it's on Fourth and Main. A friend.* He looked up to ask the boy a question, but all he saw was the back of his torn shirt as he hurried out the door.

What in the Hell have I got myself into? he asked himself.

Before he'd left the Beat to Quarters, Harkaman posted his crew requests on the bulletin board. After a brisk twenty-minute walk, pausing every half block or so to peer in store windows to see if he was being followed, he found the hotel. Of course, he knew that if whoever was tailing him were professionals and had a team, he'd never notice anything.

The Trade Winds motel, like most buildings in Icacan, was an ancient ground-hugging structure in bad repair. It appeared the Liebigs didn't spend much on local upkeep. He carefully walked up the cracked stairs to the second floor, pausing when he reached 214.

After loosening the flap of his holster, he knocked on the door.

"Come in."

The inside was your typical low-rent motel room, with a weathered bed and a patched bedspread. A tall man, almost as gray and anonymous as the room itself, sat hunched over in one of the two chairs. He was nursing a bottle of Colada rum.

"What's this all about?" Harkaman demanded.

"Shush is the word. In Icacan, even the walls have ears."

He took him at his word. "Is it safe to talk here?"

The man nodded. "I've debugged the room. It only had a simple telltale. The room's too cheap for anything sophisticated."

A look of comprehension came over Harkaman's face. "So I can assume that all my calls and conversations in my hotel room are being recorded."

"Yes. King Thom keeps a close ear on his subjects. His son, Viktor, is even worse. Although they ignore the ginks, which is why I felt free to use the boys as messengers."

Gink was a term of derision many Space Vikings used for Neobarbarians. It was an acronym for "Grounder ignorant of normal knowledge," or "not knowing shit," as the less polite put it.

He nodded, "Good idea. One of these days the locals are going to get tired of the Liebigs' misrule and cut all their throats."

"Couldn't happen to a nicer bunch."

"So who are you and what's all the hush-hush about?"

"I'm Captain Jorgen Trevithick. Prince Viktor has plans for you and your friends."

"What do mean?"

"He wants control of your ship. If you make any deal with Viktor, he'll end up owning you and your crew. I know, because he owns me lock, stock and collapsium. You're familiar with the ship, the *Jolly Roger*."

Harkaman felt his hackles rise and he stood up suddenly, his hand dropping to his pistol grip. "What do you know about the *Jolly Roger*?"

"I'm her captain, or was." He held his hands out to placate Harkaman. "Over half a dozen standard years ago, I arrived on Xochitl with a damaged ship, the *Joy Rider*. Our last raid was on Ashur, a semi-civilized Neobarb world which, unfortunately for us, had atomic missiles. We took a couple of bad hits and needed to go to the nearest spaceyard for repairs, which happened to be here on Xochitl. It was a most unprofitable voyage and the port officials refused to make the necessary repairs because I lacked the necessary funds. I was on the verge of disbanding the crew and selling the ship for scrap, when Crown Prince Viktor arrived and offered me a *deal*."

"What kind of deal?"

"He would pay for my ship repairs out of his own pocket; in return, I'd do certain favors for him. Raid the planets of his competitors and punish his enemies, or so he told me at the time. Unbeknownst to me, Viktor had a much deeper plot in mind. Of course, I didn't know that at the time; I was desperate and figured: what have I got to lose? Well, for starters, my self-respect."

Raid the worlds of his competitors…? That must mean the other Sword-World base worlds of Jagannath, Nergal, Hoth and Dagon, Harkaman reasoned. While no one raided those worlds directly, most of them had a few nearby Neobarbarian worlds that they traded with and considered their own. Most Space Vikings wouldn't raid those worlds because it wasn't worth antagonizing a base world. They wouldn't let you sell your loot there; some might even bother to send a ship or two after you to destroy your ship. But, if someone from another base world wanted to disrupt their trading partners, it wasn't a bad plan.

"Once the ship was repaired and after I'd run a few errands," he continued, "Viktor told me he wanted me to run under a false flag. He ordered me to attack the ships of Space Vikings who had full holds and could give a good possible return. All based on information his spies picked up at the Icacan local watering holes for off-worlders. That's why every room, bar, tap room, sports center, whore house and entertainment offering in the city is wired tight for sight and sound. He has his agents on Hoth, Dagon and Jagannath, too."

Harkaman whistled. "He is an evil little shit."

"You don't know the half of it. Viktor told me that if I didn't do everything he asked, he'd inform everyone that I was the one who came up with the idea for using the *Jolly Roger* to put his competitors out of business! I've been doing his work for a number of years and now.... Well, after the beating I took from you on Junrojin, I came back to Xochitl to find Viktor very unhappy with my performance. My guess is he wants to use you and your ship in my place."

Harkaman sucked in his breath. He had wondered why they hadn't heard anything about the *Jolly Roger* lately. "That almost makes a perverted sort of sense. If he's lost faith in you, he wants the crew who'd almost put you out of business to take your place. Right?"

"Yep. Otherwise, why does he want you to cut a deal with him so badly?"

"How do you know about that?"

"People talk. They don't know what's really going on, but one thing's for sure: they don't want some outsiders—like you and your friends—horning in on their turf. So, I'm warning you, be very careful of any deal you cut with Viktor."

Harkaman was very glad they'd made a deal with the Royal Bank rather than Viktor; however, even with the confidential information Trevithick was sharing, he wasn't going to tell him that. "What about you?"

"Ha! I'm stuck. A wrecked ship, little cash and all my crew are Prince Viktor's men, now. I'll do whatever Viktor tells me"—he paused to pull a pistol out of his belt—"or, I'll end it right here."

"You'd do better to plug Viktor."

"He'd never let me get that close with a gun, not in this lifetime."

IV

Prince Viktor was pacing back and forth in his private office. His top agent had sent him a message flagged in red about a call made to Otto Harkaman. When he got the buzzer informing him that Beazley was on his way up, he took his usual seat. Agent Beazley showed up promptly and sat across from him, looking up.

"What's going on with Harkaman? And who made the call?"

"I'm not sure, Your Highness. Our tap on Harkaman's viewphone shows an unknown screen call arriving at 0534 this morning."

"Why wasn't I notified earlier?" Viktor demanded.

Beazley winced. The Crown Prince had been in a bad mood ever since he'd received Harkaman's message yesterday that he had come to terms with the Royal Bank of Excalibur and was purchasing the hypership *Corisande*. He hadn't even known the *Corisande* was for sale. Viktor had already been upset that Harkaman had dared to counter what he felt was a generous offer to finance a ship for him and his partners. He believed Harkaman was going to become a very successful Space Viking captain and wanted him working for him. By happenstance Harkaman and his partners had eaten yesterday at an outside plaza where they didn't have a nearby bug planted, so Viktor hadn't known the counter-offer was coming, which made him even angrier. "The agent covering the hotel board fell asleep and missed the call until three hours later."

Viktor's face turned beet red. "I want his head!!! Damn him!"

"He's been reprimanded and put in a cell, awaiting your pleasure, Your Highness."

"Good. I'll deal with him later. Have my usual team put on notice."

"Of course, Your Highness."

"Did you trace Harkaman's movements?"

"Yes, we traced him as far as the spaceport. He stayed there for about fifteen minutes, inspecting the *Corisande*, I suspect. From there he went to the tavern, Beat to Quarters—nothing unusual there. He has a habit of frequenting taverns and questioning other captains and astrogators. Black Bart, the morning bartender, said Harkaman posted crew vacancies on the hiring board and sat by himself, only leaving when he was approached by a gink."

"Who was the gink?"

"Some ragged-ass boy. No one we know; probably selected for being anonymous and too young and stupid to ask any questions."

"Did you question him?"

"Yes, Your Highness. He knew nothing except that a man in a funny hat gave him a message to give to the spaceman. We made it hurt a bit, but the boy didn't change his story."

"So you have no idea what Harkaman was doing after he left the tavern."

"No, Your Highness. Only that he was gone and out of our sight for roughly an hour. Not enough time to get into any trouble, in my opinion."

Viktor slammed his fist on the table. "I don't want your damn opinions! I want facts. Keep two teams on Harkaman at all time, especially when he's out of the hotel."

"Yes, sir!"

V

Harkaman needed to inform his crewmates of his latest discoveries about Viktor and the *Jolly Roger*. The only truly safe place to do it was on the *Corisande*. He went through one of the smaller staff cabins with a fine-tooth comb before everyone else arrived. *I may be paranoid*, he thought, *but I'm going to have the rest of the ship checked for bugs after we leave.*

Everyone sobered right up after he filled them in on everything he'd learned from Captain Jorgen Trevithick.

"Even for a Space Viking, this Viktor is one nasty character," Alvyn Karffard said. "We've got to be very careful."

"I agree," he replied. "I wouldn't put it past him to have us all murdered, if he thought he could get away with it. Captain Trevithick is absolutely terrified of him."

"We've been too visible for that," Karffard offered. "Killing us would create more problems than it would solve. People would wonder what happened to us. A story like that could cause people to pick another base world to trade on. He wouldn't like that. I don't believe Viktor's a complete monster, like Drago of Tizona or the Butcher of Skathi; instead, he sees himself as an efficient ruler who, on occasion, doesn't mind dirtying his hands."

"Well, let him dirty them on someone else!" Guatt Kirbey declared.

That brought forth a gale of laughter.

"So what do you suggest we do, Otto?" Paul Koreff asked.

"First, I want Sharll and Guatt to take the hyperyacht for a little trip," he paused for a moment, "to Jagannath for a visit with Trevor Mavuso."

Renner looked puzzled. "Why? What can he do?"

"After my talk with Captain Trevithick, I wrote down everything he said as well as my own observations. I want Trevor to keep a copy and send another copy to a law firm I've used in the past, Vance, Jerningham and Volgarth in Camelot on Excalibur. I want a safe record of everything the Crown Prince has been up to in case Viktor has something unpleasant in mind for all of us. If we die or disappear, one or both of them can release the information. I know we can trust Trevor to help us."

"That's a good idea," Karffard said. "I know Viktor has his own hyperyacht but it would probably take him a day or two to fit it out. So, unless, they're detained at the spaceport, they should have a safe flight."

"Is it wise to send just Sharll and Guatt?" Ranjit Chaudry asked worriedly.

He knew what he meant. Neither of them had participated in raids and weren't used to protecting themselves. And neither was a particularly good shot. "We can't spare anyone else," he said. "Ranjit, you're needed to interview all the ground troop applicants. Alvyn and I will be interviewing the junior officer candidates and the crew chiefs, while Vann and Paul will be interviewing for the rest of the crew."

He hoped he'd have time to interview as many of the crew as possible. He believed it was a good policy that everyone on the ship should be familiar with their captain and vice versa.

"When do you want us to leave?" Renner asked.

Harkaman opened his jacket and pulled out a parcel which he handed to him. "I think you and Guatt should grab what you need and leave immediately." Seeing the look on their faces, he said, "I know, I sound paranoid, but better safe than sorry. Give me your room keys and we'll pick up your things from your hotel rooms. And remember that Viktor has agents on Jagannath, so be careful what you say to anyone other than Trevor."

"I noticed that when Captain Trevithick mentioned Viktor's spies, he didn't mention Nergal," Vann Larch noted.

"I suspect it's because the locals look so unique," Karffard noted. "Off-worlders would stand out more on Nergal than anywhere else."

"We might just have to make Nergal the first world we visit when we want to sell loot," Otto said. The others nodded in agreement.

"After our visit to Jagannath, where shall we meet the rest of you?" Kirbey asked.

"Return here. Jagannath is about four hundred hours away so the round trip should take you a month. It should take us close to that to hire a crew, stock supplies and fix up the *Corisande*." He didn't say so but he intended that no work crew would enter the ship without one of them present so that Crown Prince Viktor wouldn't have the opportunity to pull a fast one.

"Remember the Royal Bank of Excalibur is paying all our costs for hiring, restocking and updating the ship." Otto grinned. "I want to get our money's worth."

PART THREE

Captain

tanith

I

1710 A.E.

Guatt Kirbey muttered disapprovingly while looking at his readings. The others were used to his grumping since no matter what he did, he always thought he could do better so they waited patiently. After pushing a few more buttons, he indicated he was ready.

"All right," he said. "Jumping."

He twisted the red handle on his board to the right and shoved it in. Since this jump was only twenty-five light-hours rather than the thousand light-years they had traveled from Xochitl, the outside viewscreen barely had time to change from the colored turbulence of an initializing hyperspace jump to the featureless grey of hyperspace before it changed back to a burst of color, and then the black void of regular space. There on the viewscreen was Ertado's Star and the seven planets of its system. The third, Tanith, was their destination and it was only ten light-minutes away.

Tanith had been chosen as the destination for the first raid of the *Corisande* for two reasons. First, Captain Harkaman wanted an easy test for all the ground troops they had hired on Xochitl. This chicken-stealing raid would allow the section leaders to get to know their troops, the squad leaders get to know their sections and Ranjit Chaudry, as raid commander, get to know all of the squads. Tanith should provide a low stress opportunity to do that. Second, it was supposed to have a large intact spaceport and he wanted to check it out, especially because Tanith was located in an area of the Old Federation where he thought a new base world might be successfully established.

Kirbey continued his calculations for his next microjump, which would be his final jump since reaching the Tanith system. Sharll Renner joined him since he'd soon be taking over normal-space astrogation.

"All right," Kirbey said, "Jumping." This time the microjump seemed almost simultaneous; one moment they were looking at a dim star, the next they were looking at a sunlit planet. After checking his instruments for a few moments, he seemed pretty satisfied. "We're about three-hundred thousand miles from the planet," he announced.

He turned to Renner, "All yours, Sharll." With that he locked his instrument console and left the bridge.

"We're about eight to nine hours from the planet, Captain," Renner noted. "Do you want me to go into orbit or straight down to the surface?"

Harkaman wanted to take a thorough look at the planet. "Let's go into orbit." He got up from his chair. "Give me a call in about eight hours."

He always liked to be on the bridge when any ship he was on came out of hyperspace. If there were going to be any problems, he wanted to know about them right away. Now that he was on his first trip as captain, he felt convinced that he had to be present. However, it was after midnight ship time and he needed to catch up on his sleep.

They hadn't had any problems recruiting a full crew on Xochitl. Nor had they heard anything further from Crown Prince Viktor, other than a terse message congratulating them on the purchase of the *Corisande*. Recruiting was easy, because there were always a few thousand experienced Space Vikings on Xochitl at any one moment relaxing, raising hell or just enjoying being groundside. Many were open to new berths. The banker had provided the requested several million stellars for recruiting a crew, which was much more than he had expected he would need. He'd even hired some extra engineers and machinists.

He had met with his officers for a final review when the crew was all aboard ship just before they were ready to take off.

"Are you going to return the remaining bonus money, Otto?" Renner asked with a smirk, to general laughter.

"What remaining bonus money?" Harkaman said, seriously. "I had to pay what was necessary to get a good crew." With that he reached into his pocket and handed envelopes to each of them. "See," he said, with a grin, "I had to spend it all."

They all shared another laugh. It nice to have some extra stellars in case their first voyage was not very successful. Nor had the banker balked at paying any and all costs for refitting the *Corisande*. They had found that everything was generally in good order, aside from some minor structural problems and hull damage which was easily fixed. Using the bank's funds, they had updated every piece of equipment that they could. Based on past experience, he had made certain there were plenty of power units and robo-equipment on board. One never knew when he might discover another Old Federation installation that they could profitably repair and operate.

Harkaman had also reconfigured part of the *Corisande* to store more small arms and ammunition in the outer part of the ship. He also had additional missiles stored there, protected by an extra layer of collapsium. Typically, nothing was stored in the outer layers of the hull in case they were breached by artillery or missiles during a raid. He figured there might be times when they could use something extra in the weapons department. He was still thinking of all the possibilities they might run into when he entered his cabin, which was several orders of magnitude larger than any cabin he'd shared or occupied in the past—another fringe benefit which came with his new rank.

II

Harkaman woke up much refreshed. He was taking a sonic shower when the bridge called to say the *Corisande* was just about to enter orbit. He quickly got dressed, took a cup of hot coffee from the mess-robot and made his way to the bridge.

"Anything unusual detected, Paul?" he asked Koreff, his signals and detection officer. He was the only senior officer present. Sharll had gone to bed once they had attained orbit, while the others were apparently still waking up realizing they're now in orbit.

"A little radiation in one spot," he replied. "Other than that, nothing to report, Captain."

"Radiation. Could it be from an old industrial site?" he asked, perking up.

"No such luck, I'm afraid," Koreff reported. "It's not that concentrated, more diffuse. Probably a site that was nuked a long time ago."

That was just what it turned out to be. Tanith had five continents. One was almost entirely within the Arctic Circle; icy and uninhabited. Two others were inhabited at what appeared to be the small village, peasant level. On one continent, the population was mainly concentrated on the coastlines and along rivers; it had probably been settled after the Federation collapsed. The largest continent was mainly in the temperate zone and was where the spaceport was located. The radiation came from the city where old spaceport resided.

By the time they reached the spaceport, all of the normal bridge crew had assembled and were in various stages of wakefulness, depending on the amount of coffee they had consumed. The spaceport was designed like an eight-pointed star. The center of the star was a mass of buildings. The ship-berths were circular pits between the octagon mass of buildings, and the triangular airship docks and warehouses.

"Standard Old Federation spaceport design, just like Xochitl or Nergal," Karffard noted. The city was adjacent to the spaceport and covered four or five square miles, dominated by two large towers, one which was broken at the top. There were many open areas between the buildings, typical of a contragravity civilization. The city had been built in the middle of the continent next to a large river.

As they descended they saw that much of the city was choked with brush and trees; there were a few small clearings with crops growing. One of the eight ship berths had been nuked and was a pile of slag. There had also been a third large tower. It looked like a missile had hit right at the base of it as there was a pile of rubble spread out in a long ridge running away from it. The radiation was coming from those two areas.

"There's not enough to worry about," Koreff noted, speaking of the radiation.

"Do you want us to land in one of the ship's berths, Captain?" Renner asked.

"If you can find one in the spaceport that's clear of debris, go ahead," he replied.

They were able to do so without much trouble. Swinging the outside screen pickup around showed an area without many people. Here and there some smoke rose from individual fires but there appeared to be no inhabited area of more than a dozen homes in any one place. It was late afternoon local time.

"Let's break out an aircar and start exploring," Harkaman said.

"The population of the city is probably around fifteen hundred people," he said later as he met with Chaudry and the troop squad leaders to review information and determine their next step. There was one city of about twenty thousand or so population at the forks of a river a few hundred miles away with scattered small villages between them and the old Federation city. Most of the rest of the population was found along rivers and at various points along the coast.

"On this raid, we'll raid the other continents." He paused to pass out the pictures of some of the cities. "If we ever establish a base here we'll want to have good relations with that big city because that's where we'll recruit our workers."

Based on their initial planetary observations of Tanith, targets of opportunity were limited. So they needed to do a more detailed study. Alvyn Karffard volunteered to contact the spaceport locals and try to see what they had to offer. Chaudry volunteered to take one of the pinnaces and a squad of fighters and visit the city on the forks of the river to see if they knew of any promising avenues. He took along some few trade goods along to open negotiations.

Harkaman and Vann Larch decided to take a combat car and visit the other continents. The only data he'd been able to find about the planet from his Old Federation microbooks and journals informed him that the first wave of Tanith settlers had been a pacifist group which had called themselves the Transvisionists. They were dedicated to doing no wrong in this life as preparation for the next cycle of existence. From what he read, Harkaman learned that they believed in some sort of reincarnation, but their rationale seemed oblivious to logic. Like most religions, it had to be taken on faith. The Transvisionists had moved as far away from the center of the Federation as they could go in search of a world where they could live unmolested and free of the taint of modern life and civilization.

He wondered how that had worked out for them.

The next wave of settlers was part of a company anxious to find a Terra-like world with resources to export. They had been the ones who had built the spaceport and the three tall buildings. Those looking for radioactive ores and rare earth elements had been disappointed according to the records. True, there were a few small and isolated pockets of pitchblende, but nobody was going to get rich exploiting them. Meanwhile, all this hustle and bustle had caused the Transvisionists to leave the more habitable central continent for the smaller northern continent which they named Joftland after their founder, Rylar Joft.

Harkaman decided that their first visit would be to Joftland. He was curious as to how well their pacifism had held up after almost a thousand years living on Tanith. He discussed this with Larch as they flew over the mainland toward the smaller continent. One of the reasons he was so interested in history was that he found the variety of governments and how they changed over time fascinating.

"It all depends on how isolated they've been able to remain, would be my guess," Larch opined.

"I'm sure whatever they've come up with will mirror some type of government from Terra's Pre-Atomic era history," Harkaman replied.

Vann Larch nodded agreement. He'd heard Harkaman expound on this theory enough times, during the many discussions the partners engaged in, throughout the long hyperspace journeys between worlds. He believed that every form of government that they ran across on the worlds of the Old Federation had its equivalent back on Pre-Atomic Terra. In most cases, Harkaman was even able to provide the names of long-deceased societies and civilizations, taken from his personal historical archives, to back up his assertions. Larch didn't need any more convincing; he was tired of hearing the same old argument.

However, he thought it was a small price to pay for working with such a successful captain. Otto Harkaman had already helped him make more money than he'd ever believed possible for a man with his limited education and common birth to earn. And, thanks to Otto, he was fulfilling his lifelong dream, which was to be part of a successful Space Viking crew. In addition, Vann was one of the officers—life didn't get much better.

A few hours later, they found themselves cruising over Joftland. From quick observation, it appeared to be well inhabited. There were a few small hills and occasional copses of trees, but the majority of the continent consisted of a huge prairie that went on for several thousand miles until it reached the glacial ridge in the far north. Thousands of small farming villages crisscrossed the steppes; they were geometrically placed in such a manner that it was obvious that they'd been planted by some earlier and more advanced civilization.

Using the telescopic screen, they saw dozens of yurts in small caravans moving across the plains. They were herding what appeared to be sheep or their local equivalent. They were almost mid-continent when Larch pointed downward to the surface. "Look, one of the caravans is stopping at one of the small villages."

Harkaman lowered the combat car and increased the viewscreen magnifier. "Yes, and it appears the nomads are attacking the villagers."

He watched as some of the nomads, brandishing long spears, herded the villagers onto the commons open area. Others appeared to be sorting the villagers, taking some of the younger men and woman and putting them aside. The villagers were offering no resistance to the nomads. He was intrigued.

"I'm going to land and find out what's going on," he said.

Larch nodded agreement.

As they approached the ground, several of the nomads pointed up at the combat car which was hovering above the village. They began shaking their spears and making gestures, probably to ward off witchcraft or sorcery. They didn't appear frightened so it was unlikely that previous Space Viking raiders had bothered with these obviously poor pickings.

Suddenly the mounted archers began to fire at their vehicle. The sound of striking arrows reminded him of falling hail beating against the hull. Harkaman, who normally would have continued observing, decided to take offense. "Vann, give them a blast of cannon fire!"

The explosion hit the middle of the train of yurts, demolishing several and causing fires that quickly spread to the others. Suddenly, the nomads began to flee as they abandoned the fight and their yurts; some on their horses, the others running through the tall grass, their prisoners forgotten.

"Let's land and see what these villagers have to say," Harkaman ordered.

They put the combat car down on the commons at the side of the village, being careful to avoid landing on any of the small vegetable plots. They left the car with weapons in hand and waited for the villagers to gather.

An older man, maybe a priest or local headman, was the first to approach. He had a long flowing gray beard that reached his belt and was the only one wearing a tall hat. The leader was followed by two big farmers wearing rough woolen garments dyed in earth colors; they all had pale skin and blonde or light brown hair. By pure chance Harkaman and Larch were the two members of the bridge crew most like these people in terms of skin and hair color, which might help them in establishing relations. The leader's face was cherry red and he was shaking his hands. It was obvious that he was very angry.

"What have you done?" he demanded. The local leader spoke a rough form of Terra Lingua, but it was understandable.

"We have delivered you from the hands of those slavers," Harkaman answered.

The headman pointed to the dead nomads and shook his head. "You, arrogant sky people, have murdered our friends! They come at our invitation. They only take what we give. You have gone against the Way!"

Now Harkaman was perplexed. This was not how things like this were supposed to turn out; they were supposed to be grateful, not hostile, after their deliverance from the nomads.

"I don't understand," he said. "From our sky car we saw these nomads taking your people. We thought they were slavers."

"They are. The Hagachi are part of the Way." He looked at Harkaman as a parent might look at a child who makes a stupid observation.

Vann Larch, who had gone over to one of the dead nomads to examine him, returned and reported in a low voice, "The nomads share the same features and lighter skin and hair color as the villagers do. Maybe they're related or have some sort of reciprocal deal going on." The next part he whispered. "The dead nomad in the fancy dress wears a torc that appears to be solid gold. It must weight over a pound."

"I apologize," Harkaman offered. "We come from far away and live a different kind of life. Please explain the Way."

"It would take a decade of study for you to thoroughly understand the Way, but I will tell you this much. We live this life in peace so that we can pass into the next cycle in a higher place. Once we have completely left this world's cares and troubles behind, we ascend to join the Sun God and become a part of his majesty."

Harkaman nodded, as if he understood. Somehow the locals had blended their original Transvisionist beliefs into sun worship, not uncommon among decivilized barbarians. The man with the hat was most likely their priest or shaman. He was better dressed and had more body fat than the other villagers.

"However," the priest continued, "not all our young people are ready to prepare for the next cycle; many show rebelliousness and question our faith. Some even conduct unwed conjugation and talk back to their elders. This is why the Hagachi visit every three cycles."

Harkaman figured the headman was talking about planetary rotations or local years. The local year ran about one and a third Galactic Standard years, which meant the nomad slavers took away the village's troublesome youth every four years. No wonder their society was so static; it probably hadn't changed in centuries.

While they were talking, Larch went over to examine more of the dead nomads. He even went inside one of the less damaged yurts. The villagers paid him no attention; their eyes all looked upon the priest as if he were a transcendent being.

"We welcome the Hagachi," continued the priest. "They bring us the wool that we use to make our garments and fresh meat for a feast to celebrate their arrival. By your violence, you have disrupted their Cycle and the Hagachi you have murdered will have to start at the beginning again."

"What do they do with your young people?" Harkaman asked.

The priest shrugged as if he didn't care. "They use them to work the mines and care for the elderly. We only know what they tell us. Whatever they do, it will prepare them for the next Cycle. It is the Way.

"What about these youngsters?" he asked.

"There is no place for their kind in our village."

Harkaman would have offered to take the youngsters with him, but there was no room for them in the combat car. They would have to abide by their culture's strictures. He suspected there were other outcasts they might join.

He wondered if some of the more rebellious ran away from the village before the Hagachi caravans came to round them up. He would have. If they ever were to put a Sword-World base on this world, this would be a fertile area to recruit workers. He bet that a lot of young people would like to leave their villages for a better life, rather than be given away to slavery.

There was nothing more to discuss, since they couldn't bring the dead back to life. They got back into the combat car and flew north toward the mountains.

"Most of those nomads had gold rings and bands," Larch said, showing a handful taken from one of his jacket pockets. "I think we need to give them a visit."

They passed over thousands of villages and the occasional nomad party. It took them half an hour to reach the first mountain range. There were several good-sized cities nestled amongst the hills leading to the mountains. They stayed high enough so that the Hagachi wouldn't notice them. There were five cities, each of them big enough to hold eighty to a hundred thousand inhabitants. The cities themselves were built of stone and blended into the mountainscape. It was no surprise that they'd remained unobserved by previous raiders.

"I think this might be a good place to give our troops some practice," Harkaman said. Larch grinned in agreement. After long months of preparation and travel, the first raid of the *Corisande* was about to begin.

III

The round of toasts continued until everyone's glass was empty. The officers were celebrating in a conference room while the crew held a series of parties throughout the *Corisande*. Soon they'd go circulate and have a drink at every party. They had just completed a four-day raid on Ganpat. After practicing several different raiding operations on various parts of Tanith, Harkaman had decided the ground troops were ready. He had already picked out Ganpat because it was a nearby world with a technological level of about two centuries Pre-Atomic and would be a good test of their ground troops. They hit several cities and after four days Ranjit Chaudry was satisfied with his ground troops' performance. They had estimated their loot at about twenty to twenty-five million stellars.

While they were waiting for the bartending robot to refill everyone's glasses, Larch continued his argument with Karffard. They were the two officers who most liked to discuss subjects thoroughly, occasionally to the point of boredom to the other senior officers. Given the long trips between worlds, there was plenty of time for talk.

"That spaceport is in fine shape, Alvyn. We could make a good base world out of Tanith right now," Larch said.

"We'd have to clean it up first," Karffard observed.

Larch laughed. "We'll conscript some of the locals to do that. They can learn how to use contragravity and other Sword-World equipment as part of their efforts."

"But where would we get the financial support, Vann?" Karffard asked. "We spent almost all of our available funds to buy the *Corisande*. We'd need a lot of equipment and personnel to make a base work. And where's that going to come from?"

Harkaman grinned to himself. He could see that Alvyn had come to agree with him on the most important consideration for a base world.

"Good point," Larch replied. "I wonder if we could partner with someone. Maybe Stafan Mavuso would be interested."

"Where's Guatt?" one of the junior officers asked.

Harkaman drained his glass. "He's calculating the jump to Urun."

When the fighting ceased on Ganpat, some troop sections had been sent to explore various buildings to see if there was anything more valuable to loot. One of the troopers had come across a reference to a library on the top of an old building. Harkaman had investigated and, along with his usual pickings from history section, he'd found a chart of nearby worlds and what was traded back and forth. Urun was a world that was not on their charts and apparently had been a source of a flourishing metals trade. This must have been what drew the original settlers to it since it orbited an M5 red dwarf sun.

"It's supposed to be in the middle of an ice age," Harkaman noted. "There probably aren't many people living there, but there might be something to salvage from the old mines and industrial sites. Let's let the men have a couple of days off to celebrate, then we'll go and see what Urun has to offer."

URUN

1710 A.E.

In the middle of an ice age turned out to be an understatement. Like all habitable worlds around red dwarf suns, Urun was close enough to the star that it was tidally locked, with one side always facing the sun. Much of the planet, including almost all of the night side, was covered in ice. The planet was large and dense enough that the gravity was twenty percent over Galactic Standard gravity.

"It doesn't look like much has survived," said Paul Koreff. "Most of the old cities and industrial sites have been nuked or are covered by ice."

"The ice covers much more of the planet than it did in the pictures we saw," someone said.

"The nukes here may have pushed enough dust and pollution into the atmosphere that it blocked the sun for a while and tipped the balance," Harkaman said. "Well, there doesn't appear to be anything viable in the twilight zone. Let's head out into the day side."

Even the day side didn't appear to be much more welcoming. The major body of water was in the equatorial zone; it was more of an inland sea than an ocean. The only area that seemed to have any people was right on the equator and it only held about a dozen or so small villages that were hardly worth raiding. There was a large mountain chain north of the inhabited area that probably kept some of the cold from penetrating further south.

"I'm getting something," Koreff announced. "There's an industrial facility on that large island ahead." He adjusted his instruments to take some more readings. "There's only minor radiation but the installation appears intact."

A pinnace with a squad of troopers was sent down first. When they reported that the site was clear, Harkaman followed along with most of the engineering staff.

"Whew," said Engineering Chief Marc Van de Brost, as they left the pinnace, shortening his stride to deal with the heavy gravity. "Just walking around on this world is quite a workout."

He thought the same thing. The weather was cool, even with the sun covering a good portion of the sky. He told everyone to take it easy as they went about examining the installation. The large number of slag piles showed that it had been an active facility. They very quickly ascertained that it was an aluminum smelting plant; however, there was no finished product in any of the warehouses.

"It looks as if they had a chance to haul everything away before they closed it down," Van de Brost said disappointedly. "There's no bauxite ore ready to be processed either. You'd have to mine it and haul it here."

"Let's look around some more," Harkaman said. "Send a couple men into the mines. Have a few others check out those buildings over there," pointing to several buildings half a mile away. Then he sat down on a nearby rock and pulled his pipe out of his pocket to wait.

There turned out to be a couple of neatly stacked piles of aluminum sheets in one of the buildings. Whoever had closed down the facility hadn't been able to haul everything away. An even bigger discovery was made in the mine.

"Captain, there's a huge pile of ingots in the back of the mine," a trooper reported with a big smile on his face. "It looks like they hauled everything in here hoping no one would find it until they could return."

Removing the ingots required numerous trips, one landing-craft at a time, because the mine entrance was so narrow. It wasn't until later the next day before had they finished loading everything into the last pinnace.

In the meantime, Harkaman took the *Corisande* to explore the rest of the day side for any other installations they could find. They found two pinnace loads of copper at one of them and some pitchblende, but not a lot of it. It was another good reminder that every world was worth checking out. It also meant he was going to end his initial voyage as Captain with enough funds to make a first payment towards permanent ownership of the *Corisande*.

Jagannath

1712 A.E.

"Tanith, Urun, Lakshmi, Chantico, Ganpat, Irminsul, Paktai, Telepinu, Lioth and Hathor," Trevor Mavuso named them aloud, as he listed all of the worlds Harkaman and the *Corisande* had raided in the last few years. "An impressive list Otto," he said. "How close are you to paying off your loan?"

They were sitting on the deck of Mavuso's home outside of Craigstown on Jagannath, enjoying after-dinner drinks. It was a cool fall evening and Harkaman was feeling contented, due to the drinks and the good company of his old friend and mentor. They'd been talking about his experiences as captain of the *Corisande*, as well as sharing the usual gossip about the goings on in the Space Viking worlds.

"Close to the halfway point," he answered. "I'll know more precisely once we sell the remaining vanadium that we picked up on Hathor," he said. "We sold some on Nergal but there wasn't enough demand for all of it. We have a few hundred pounds of amber left over from Irminsul as well. Everything we picked up on Lioth and Telepinu, we'll be able to move easily."

All of the *Corisande's* voyages had been profitable and after each of them they had been able to pare down their loan a little more. The crew was running like a well-oiled machine and morale was high. Typically, they had to replace some of forty to fifty crewmen, primarily ground fighters, after each voyage, although the vast majority of those were men who left the ship rather than those killed in action. The *Corisande's* reputation as a successful ship had grown to the point where they didn't have any trouble recruiting replacements.

"Are you ever going to return to Xochitl?" Mavuso asked, changing the subject after his young wife refilled their drinks. No robots allowed in his household.

He chuckled. "Our next raid will be closer to Xochitl than any of the other base worlds, so the answer is yes. Prince Viktor should have cooled his jets down by now; besides, with his father not long in the grave, he should be very busy ruling his new realm."

Crown Prince Viktor had become Prince Viktor upon the death of his father about ten months ago. Trevor Mavuso had told him about all the suspicions regarding Prince Thom's death; Thom hadn't even reached sixty years of age when he died of a sudden stomach ailment. Many believed Viktor had his father poisoned. From what he knew of Viktor, it wasn't unlikely. He had heard similar speculation on Nergal. Viktor was feared, but not well-loved—even by his own subjects.

"Where are you going next," Mavuso asked.

He swallowed the remainder of his drink. Rather than ask for more he got his pipe out, recharged it, and then lit it. "We're going to raid Cernunnos."

"Cernunnos!" Mavuso exclaimed. "Why there? You've had nothing but successful voyages so far. Why take the risk?"

Cernunnos was known as one of the toughest Neobarb worlds to raid in the Old Federation. It wasn't considered a civilized world, as it didn't have contragravity or hyperspace capability, but it had everything else, including atomic energy and nuclear missiles. It was last raided fifteen years ago by Rance Diaz and the *Doombringer*. The *Doombringer* had been heavily damaged during the raid and didn't get away with much plunder, increasing the planet's tough reputation. No Space Viking had raided it since.

Harkaman discussed all of that with Mavuso, ending with: "If we're successful, we should be able to bring home enough booty to pay off the *Corisande*. If it gets too hot, we have enough financial reserves that we can handle any repairs, even if we're forced to leave with empty pockets."

Mavuso refilled both their glasses and raised his. "To Otto Harkaman, Captain of the *Corisande*. May he return safe and sound with holds full of loot!"

They drained their glasses, rose and bumped fists. Then Otto strode over to his rented aircar and left for the biggest raid of his tenure as Captain.

Cernunnos

I

1713 A.E.

Everyone looked around expectantly as they entered the largest staff hall on the *Corisande*. It was a large circular room with chairs facing the podium. Although the furniture, bulletin boards and everything else was the same, there was none of the other paraphernalia which accompanied a regular raid planning meeting. There were no maps, no charts, nothing to write down the assignment of various troop sections and squads to particular tasks. They expected to come out of hyperspace in twenty-four hours and typically that was the point at which the final raid planning was done.

"Aren't we meeting to discuss the raid, Otto?" Ranjit Chaudry asked. Accompanying Ranjit were all of his squad leaders, plus Alvyn Karffard, Paul Koreff and Sharll Renner, who he had invited to the meeting with their junior officers. There were fifty-two crewmembers in attendance.

"No," he said, "we'll have plenty of time to do that. I'm proposing we do things a little differently this time."

They glanced at each other, with questioning looks.

"What do you mean?" Ranjit asked.

""I intend to orbit the planet for several days before we strike," he said. The others were nonplussed. Space Vikings typically attacked as quickly as possible, before any local opposition could be fully organized.

Harkaman continued, "Based on the records I've read and everyone I've talked to who was involved in the *Doombringer's* raid, we're not going to catch anybody on Cernunnos by surprise. They're going to be ready for us before we're within twenty hours of the planet's surface. So we'll take our time."

They all sat there quietly, digesting this information. It was Sharll Renner who got it first. "You're going to try to wear them out," he said. "Keep them on continuous alert until they become fatigued."

"Exactly," Harkaman replied. "Based on what we know about this world, I think we're going to have to hit multiple cities to get all the loot we want. I want each country and state's military waiting on tenterhooks, wondering when and where we're going to strike."

Ranjit nodded. "I get it. We might also pick up more information on where to target our raids."

Koreff gave a wolfish grin, then turned to Harkaman. "So you'll want me and my boys to monitor everything the locals have to say."

He grinned back. "I talked to an old friend, one of the *Doombringer's* guns-and-missiles officers. He remembered hearing someone say that Cernunnos was advanced enough to have communication satellites in orbit.

Koreff, the signals-and-detection officer, nodded. "Already noted and identified, Captain."

"Good. We'll tap into them and see what information we can pick up."

He turned to Renner. "Sharll, I'm going to ask you to do a lot of atmospheric work. We're going to make a series of maneuvers so that it looks like we're attacking particular cities, then we're going to veer off and change course at the last minute."

Renner grinned, saying, "I understand, Otto, just like we did on Epona. Get everyone thinking they're the next target."

"Right," Harkaman said, then turned to face the rest of the group. "So we'll save the final few days of raid planning for when we're in the atmosphere. That will give us something to do while Sharll's doing his best to scare the crap out of everyone on the surface."

They all chuckled.

"And," he added, "that'll give us something to occupy our time so we won't get anxious and attack too early."

This time they laughed out loud. After their long hyperspace trips between worlds, most Space Viking crews were dying for action and typically attacked the moment they came out of their last microjump. The chicken-thief raiders would usually attack the first city they saw on the dayside of a planet without bothering to do any scouting. There were far too many stories of Space Vikings precipitously looting lesser-value cities, while giving more profitable targets time to hide their valuables or prepare a strong counterattack.

Before he dismissed his crew, Harkaman ordered them to inform all their people about what had been discussed so that everyone would be on board. As his officers filed out of the room, Alvyn Karffard waited.

He looked curiously at him as he hadn't said anything during the meeting.

"Sometimes I think that you just like to do things differently, Otto," Alvyn said. "But, in this case, your plans make sense."

He clapped Alvyn heartily on the back. "I hope so. We'll find out, shortly."

II

The scene at the *Corisande's* loading dock was very different than what they were used to. Normally the last hour before a raid was, at best, controlled chaos, everyone rushing to get equipment aligned and all the ground troops into their proper positions. All the work that you couldn't do in advance, but had to complete before you sent out your attacking force.

This was completely different. They had been cruising at forty thousand feet above the surface of Cernunnos for four days, periodically descending toward a city before changing course. High enough so that jet planes couldn't attack them and missiles couldn't reach them without a lot of warning, though a few dozen had been fired at them until the locals figured out that it was a waste of good weapons. They could tell from the radio chatter that everyone on the planet was becoming increasing frazzled, wondering what game they were playing and when they were going to strike. In fact, the *Corisande* was about to change course in less than half an hour to launch their first attack.

The final hyperspace jump had put them into the shadow of the largest of Cernunnos' four moons. Several days of listening to various radio broadcasts and phone calls had allowed them time for some precise targeting. The knowledge that a large gold shipment had recently arrived at New Falkland meant it was their first target.

"Everything's been loaded, Captain," the deck chief's statement interrupted his thoughts. "The men are ready to go."

"All right, Chief," he replied. Harkaman used his handheld communicator and called the bridge. It was answered promptly; everyone was ready. "Alvyn, tell Sharll to hairpin it and head for New Falkland." The raid of Cernunnos had begun.

"Where do we go next Otto?"

They were gathered in the staff theater to plan their next step. The

New Falkland raid had gone off like clockwork. Three pinnaces had come and gone several times with cargo filled to the gunwales. There had been minimal problems, since the island was not affiliated with any other nation and hadn't had much in the way of military forces. New Falkland was a banking and trading center so there had been a lot of wealth there. They had spent over two days looting the banks and stores in the major city. Other nations had dallied in sending help. It was only in the final hours that they had to fight off a variety of air attacks; those had ceased when they destroyed the aircraft carriers that had brought the planes.

They had continued their psychological warfare by taking the *Corisande* up into orbit as if they were leaving; then, after a few hours in orbit, they had abruptly turned around and started descending earthward again. They had spent the last day traveling around the world, again at the forty-thousand foot elevation. This had given the *Corisande's* ground troops a chance to get some rest. They had changed direction several times, created panic in various cities when they thought they were being targeted. Meanwhile, they shot down any aircraft that dared to come within missile range. While they'd talked about several cities as their next target, there were really only two under final consideration.

"Recoleta is the largest city on the planet," Koreff said. "We estimate it at about nine to ten million people. There's a large commercial area that should provide plenty of goods to steal."

"We already got a lot of gold, silver and jewels at New Falkland," Chaudry countered. "Barraba is adjacent to a large mining area. It's supposed to be full of valuable metals. They're probably not going to have any gadolinium or neodymium, but there should be platinum, palladium and other precious metals."

They had limited the ground troops to looting only monetary metals and jewels at New Falkland. He hadn't even landed to check out libraries or museums. He wanted to leave plenty of room for additional loot.

"Regardless, both cities are going to be harder targets," Larch said. "Both of them show plenty of air and ground support. Either way, it's not going to be an easy raid."

Fortunately, the *Corisande* hadn't taken any more damage than a few scratches; the New Falkland military hadn't had anything stronger than chemical-explosive artillery. "Chief Akers says the equipment will be loaded in two hours," Harkaman added. "The boys will have all finished breakfast by now and should be ready to go by then. Paul," he said, turning to the signals and detection officer, "what will the local times at Recoleta and Barraba be then?"

Koreff checked the screen in from of him. "Early evening in Recoleta." He made an adjustment. "And some three hours before dawn in Barraba."

He smiled. "Then let's give the Barrabans a wakeup call. We'll visit Recoleta later."

III

Koreff had forgotten to mention one thing: it was pouring rain in Barraba. The flashes of explosive shells provided momentary bursts of illumination which were quickly swallowed up by the downpour. They hadn't caught the Barrabans totally by surprise, but their response was erratic. Some of the troops fighting them were only half-dressed. Most of their artillery was concentrated around and in the city. They found the various mines outside the city to be lightly defended.

The *Corisande,* hovering a mile above the city, was able to take out most of the missile launchers, especially those coming from what appeared to be a military installation just outside the city. An nuclear missile from the ship had put the place out of commission. However, there were a variety of artillery pieces scattered around the city, many emplaced on building tops. Since those buildings often were worth looting or adjacent to buildings being looted by their troops, they didn't dare use heavy weapons against them for fear they'd collapse; consequently, they had to be cleared one by one, by combat cars and one-man air-cavalry mounts, before the landing-vehicles could be brought in to be loaded. The

Corisande took a few missile hits during this time but none of them caused any serious damage. The Damage Control crews and robots sealed off all of the breaches, most of which did not penetrate more than a deck or two.

Two of the pinnaces went down to the mines. Landing-vehicles swooped between the warehouses by the mines and the pinnaces, loading various metals. They could hear a variety of chatter as Ranjit Chaudry and the various squad leaders directed the troops from one mine to another. Harkaman also heard a lot of complaining about the rain, which he ignored.

Once artillery was eliminated, the action in the city became concentrated in three areas: a bank with spacious vaults full of gold, a string of warehouses on the edge of town and a couple of department stores in the main shopping area.

"Ranjit," Karffard called out. "We're getting requests for more men in the city. Can you spare any?"

Chaudry said he could, and directed one of the squads at the mines to take one of the pinnaces to support the troops in the city. After another hour, Harkaman ordered the other pinnace from the mining area to provide more support to the troops in the city. They could respond to the small arms attacks much better than the *Corisande* could. That allowed one pinnace to hover above each of the areas being looted while the other one swooped between areas to provide additional fire support where needed. He brought the *Corisande* down to the mining area where it could be easily loaded by the landing vehicles. Combat cars, aircars and one-man air-cavalry mounts mingled with the off-loading landing-vehicles as they returned to the ship for more missiles and ammunition.

The sky began to lighten slightly as dawn advanced, although the rain didn't slacken one bit. When the downtown fighting started to die down, Harkaman called one of the pinnaces back to the mining area to finish up the loading operation. Since they had been raiding over eight hours, he wanted to rise up and take a look around to see how the rest of the world was reacting. It was fortunate that they did. As the *Corisande* was rising into the sky Koreff called out "A large group of air craft headed this way. They're about twenty miles to the west."

Harkaman grinned wolfishly. "Let's give them something to shoot at," directing Renner to send the ship at them full speed. His tactic caused the aircraft to attempt to scatter while firing their missiles at the *Corisande*. The wind-shear factor alone caused a number of severe crashes among those planes traveling too close together, and sent several others to the ground where they exploded in fiery crashes.

Missiles and counter-missiles threw up flares and light bursts as they tore past the enemy planes. The damage board on the bridge showed those missiles that did hit caused only light damage. They weren't any more powerful than the city's atomic missiles. The inhabitants of Cernunnos clearly hadn't developed nuclear bomb technology. When the enemy planes were within range, their short-range guns let loose and raked the enemy craft. As the *Corisande* turned around to return to the city, the few fighters left in sky were hastily retreating.

"Anything else visible, Paul?" Harkaman asked.

After some moments, Koreff shook his head. "Nothing within a hundred miles."

By the time they reached the city proper, the fighting had ceased except for some scattered small arms fire. All large concentrations of troops had either been killed or were in full retreat.

The *Corisande* flew down to just a few hundred yards above Barraba to facilitate loading and unloading. Harkaman sent Guatt Kirbey and all of the bridge crew that were not needed to assist with storing the loot in the various holds of the ship to make room for what was still on its way. This went on well into the evening. By then, the bank vaults and department stores were empty, and all of the metals worth stealing had been removed from the mines. He ordered Karffard to fire the red flares, while all the radios signaled recall.

After a few minutes, he screened Chaudry.

"How about it, Ranjit," he said when he got him on a screen. "Do we have everybody?"

His ground force commander checked the screens in front of him.

"All the men are loaded aboard the pinnace. Wait a moment, Captain. I show one man missing."

Someone off screen said something he couldn't make out.

Ranjit chuckled. "He was last seen with a bottle in one hand, chasing after some girl."

Harkaman snorted. "Well, I hope he had fun. Leave him for the locals." He knew they'd make brisk business of him.

Ranjit nodded. "Everyone alive accounted for, then. We'll be back aboard on the ship in ten minutes."

IV

Recoleta was not easy. They had debated whether they should even try for another city. "The troops are pretty worn out, Captain," Ranjit had told him.

"Once we're back in hyperspace, they'll get all the rest they need," Harkaman replied, although he suspected the real issue was that many of the troops wanted to start drinking and celebrating. The *Corisande* once again left the surface as if it was leaving the planet. This time they left orbit and accelerated away. He had Renner circle back into the shadow of the largest moon while they debated what to do.

It was ultimately one of their newest crew members who decided the issue. He'd hired Johann Carvsan on Jagannath. He'd been an assayist on a number of Space Viking vessels, although he liked to use the old title of Supercargo. He was also an expert metallurgist. He was responsible for estimating the value of any loot and loading it into the holds of the *Corisande*. He had hired him mainly for his knowledge of past Space Viking raids, but had been pleasantly surprised by his skills and knowledge.

Carvsan was by far the oldest member of the crew. He had long white hair which he tied in a ponytail and a full white beard which looked as if he trimmed it about once or twice a year. He had demonstrated an ability to pack the holds tighter with loot than anyone Harkaman had ever worked with. He said there was plenty of room for more, which decided the issue. After over a day in the shadow of the moon, they started to descend again to the surface. This time they dispensed with the maneuvering and headed straight for Recoleta.

The air seemed to be full of missiles; besides the planes that were firing at them there were numerous missile stations on the ground. Recoleta was also a major sea port and there were a lot war ships in port. Their guns and missiles only added to the amount of firepower directed at them. And they were determined. One of the planes, its missiles exhausted, evaded their counter-missile fire and crashed into the *Corisande*. Fortunately, the plane's impact wasn't powerful enough to do more than pucker the collapsium skin of the ship.

"That'll create a nice scar," Vann Larch said to no one in particular.

Ranjit Chaudhry's face appeared on the main viewscreen. "Otto, we've just lost a third air-cavalry mount and a landing-craft!"

Harkaman swore. "Pull them back," he said. "We've got to take out their firepower before we lose all our small craft."

If they'd worn out the Recoleta troops or taken them by surprise with all their maneuvering, it was not apparent. They'd been hit by a variety of fire once they were within fifty miles of the city. He was glad he had stocked extra missiles on the *Corisande* before the trip. He had ordered all the missile batteries refilled while they were in the moon's shadow. It was looking like they might need them.

"Otto, permission to use a subcrit above the port?" Larch asked.

He hesitated for few seconds. Ports were typically lined with warehouses full of valuables. A subcritical missile would probably flatten some of them, denying them access to any loot. But they had to take out the missile batteries and other artillery being directed at them if their troops were to have any chance to land and do any looting.

"Go ahead," he said.

A few seconds later the viewscreens went white and the ship rocked from the blast. When the filters kicked in and the screens cleared, it looked as if a large meteor had hit the harbor; all the ships were capsized or in pieces and many of the buildings were piles of rubble.

"All right," he said with a grin. "Now let's get the rest of the missile sites."

The damage-board showed a lot of red lights, but only a few were blinking; illustrating that the locals' missiles had only penetrated one or two decks and that those openings were rapidly being sealed off by Damage Control personnel and robots. The boards showing the condition of the pinnaces showed similar damage, except for Pinnace Four. Just as he was about to say something, he heard Alvyn order Pinnace Four to get underneath the *Corisande* where she would be more protected from missile fire.

After what felt like hours, the missile fire started to slacken and then fizzled out. He heard Alvyn confirm with the deck chiefs that all aircars and air-cavalry mounts had their ammunition restocked. When Alvyn turned to him, he nodded.

"Send them back out," Harkaman ordered.

The problem, as Ranjit said later, was that there were so many good targets it was hard to pick the best ones. There were numerous banks, jewelry stores and department stores. One troop section found a store selling rare gems, another a rare metals shop, a third found a warehouse full of high quality machine tools. They all wanted landing-craft immediately, while the metals and machine tool groups needed heavy-duty lifters due to the weight of their loot. And they all needed troop support to protect them from small arms fire while loading the landing-craft.

A steady stream of orders and requests flowed from the *Corisande* to Chaudry, and then from him to the squads and ground troops sections. By nightfall he could tell that the troops were getting tired from the number of times Ranjit had to tell the laggards to pick up the pace. They started taking troop sections back to the ship with the aircars and landing-craft to either unload or pick up more ammunition. At least that gave them fifteen to twenty minutes to stretch out with their eyes closed during the trip. That seemed to help.

As morning broke the next day, Carvsan reported that the holds were finally full and they fired red flares and announced recall on all radios. Everyone alive, including the thirty plus who were wounded, made it back to the ship. As the *Corisande* rose into the air, Carvsan entered the bridge and reported to him with a tired but happy expression on his face.

He looked around at his top officers and said, "Gentlemen, I think I can assure you, that after this trip, we now own the *Corisande* free and clear."

Xochitl

I

1713 A.E.

They had not even made their final hyperspace microjump to Xochitl, the *Corisande* still being four light-minutes away, when the call came in over the radio. "Prince Viktor requests the presence of Captain Harkaman as soon as possible after landing."

The bridge officers turned and looked at him, wondering how he was going to respond. Based on what he knew about the Prince, the last thing he wanted to do was enter Viktor's palace alone. There was no telling what might happen to him in those circumstances. However, he couldn't afford to turn down the invitation. Besides making Viktor angry, it might make him suspicious of how much he knew. And he wanted to keep him from thinking along those lines.

"Paul," he said, "what time will it be in Icacan when we land?" Koreff turned and checked the instruments on his panel.

"About mid-afternoon."

Harkaman pressed a button, re-opening communication with Xochitl. "Please extend my complements to Prince Viktor. My officers and I would be happy to host him and his party for dinner this evening." He gave the name of the restaurant they had enjoyed during their last visit to Xochitl.

"I will leave it to Prince Viktor to book the private room in the back."

He was certain that the restaurant would jump through hoops to allow its Prince to use any room he desired. That would also give Viktor a chance to bug the room thoroughly. As the conversation ended, he grimaced. Now, when they should be thrilled over landing with the largest amount of loot the *Corisande* had ever accumulated—the initial estimate was close to half a billion stellars—they had to be both physically and metaphorically prepared for a knife in the back. Who knew what treachery or vile deeds Prince Viktor was capable of?

There was a lot of discussion among his officers over who should and should not attend the meeting with Prince Viktor.

"We should take a squad of troops," Ranjit Chaudry insisted.

"No, we'd never get away with that," he replied. "Pick two of your men who are good shots and reliable but don't look liked hired gunmen. That will have to be enough."

"Alvyn and myself, for the officers," Larch offered.

He knew what he meant. Larch was the best shot among the officers and had been in a few gun fights, while his exec was no slouch either. If the dinner party went south, they would be good men to have around, as would Ranjit and the two men he brought.

"Yes," he replied. "And Guatt, too."

Kirbey looked at him in surprise. "Me, I'm not a good shot! And what would I have in common with Prince Viktor, or his men?"

"We have to show them we're cultured, Guatt," Harkaman replied, ingratiatingly. "Talk to them about your music."

Kirbey smiled happily; he loved to talk about his hobby. Fortunately, he didn't notice the rest of the bridge crew who were barely smothering smiles. They'd figured out why the Captain wanted Guatt along. His job was to be non-threatening and bore the hell out of anyone he talked to.

The seven of them assembled in the plaza outside the restaurant. The Prince had turned out to be busy the evening they arrived and so it had taken three days to set up this dinner. "All right," Harkaman said. "Remember, no one gets drunk. And, if you have to use the facilities—don't go alone."

They nodded. They'd heard his instructions before but it didn't hurt to repeat them. There would be hell to pay if one of the men were kidnapped, questioned under a veridicator and then spilt all he knew.

The two men Ranjit had selected, Costigan and Khumalo, were good choices. Costigan was of average height and had a bland face, the kind no one would ever notice in a crowd. Yet he was both very observant and the fastest gun on the ship; he'd won every shooting contest they'd held. Khumalo was good natured and friendly; yet he was also a good shot and had been promoted to squad leader due to his good judgment and leadership.

Prince Viktor was already seated when they entered the back room. Harkaman relaxed a little when he saw that Viktor had only eight men with him. He'd have brought a lot more if he was going to pull something. Two of the men were clearly advisors of some type; the others were probably gunmen, but didn't look like it any more than his men did. He relaxed further when he saw that the table had been set up so Viktor could sit at the head of it. He'd also brought a special chair that raised him up to look taller. Hopefully, this was just to be a normal political meeting and not a possible interrogation.

The conversation was innocuous enough during drinks and dinner. Viktor and his two aides asked about the *Corisande's* recent voyages and actions they had taken to obtain their loot. Harkaman shared his thoughts on how the past history of Terra applied to its many colony worlds and the type of governments they had developed. They discussed the usual Space

Viking gossip about different ships, captains and recent raids. No one batted an eye when Karffard asked innocently if anyone had heard of any other attacks by the *Jolly Roger*, replying in the negative.

He was happy to see that Ranjit, Costigan and Khumalo had managed to seat themselves in three corners of the room where they could monitor everyone in the room, as well as anyone who came and went. It was when the after dinner drinks arrived that Viktor steered the conversation to what he really wanted to talk about.

"Congratulations, I understand you made enough on your last raid to pay off the *Corisande*, Captain Harkaman."

"Thank you, Prince," he replied. "We are very happy with the prices we've found here on Xochitl." That was an understatement. Prince Viktor had reduced the port landing fees by ten percent, which had increased the traffic at Xochitl. There were now eight merchant vessels in orbit along with four other Space Vikings. There were two independent traders along with ships from Morglay, Tizona, Haulteclere and Gram. There were even two Gilgamesher ships; no one had ever seen more than one Gilgamesher hypership in any one place before. The natives of Gilgamesh were the itinerant traders of the galaxy. Their religion did not allow them to interact with outsiders other than to trade. They traveled throughout the known worlds and it was rumored that they knew of worlds that no one else did. They also tended to establish small trading colonies on major worlds and there was one on Xochitl adjacent to the space port.

The large number of ships had generated a big demand for monetary metals like gold and silver. The machine tools were receiving a lot of interest with ever increasing bids. Carvsan had already told him they were going to do very well on the sale of their remaining loot.

One of the Prince's aides, Beazley was his name, asked why they didn't do all their trading on Xochitl. Beazley was shorter than average with close cropped hair and a tightly-trimmed beard. He wondered if everyone who worked closely with Prince Viktor was short, noticing his other aide was too.

Assuming he was told by Viktor to ask the question, Harkaman repeated the story of the *Black Hawks'* journey through five worlds before they finally found enough demand to sell their silver at a decent price. He hadn't heard any title for Beazley so he settled on the most basic one. "So you see Lord Beazley, as a Space Viking, you never know how your luck is going to run," he concluded.

"Given the uncertainties of the Space Viking life," replied Beazley. "Would you like some more certainty?"

Harkaman exchanged puzzled looks with his officers. "What do you mean, Lord Beazley?"

"If you would be willing to undertake some special voyages for us, it could be very worth your while."

He realized that Beazley had been familiar with the *Black Hawk's* struggle to sell its silver and had intended to lead the conversation in this direction. He decided to play dumb.

"Do you mean trading voyages, Lord Beazley? I would assume that Prince Viktor would have plenty of independent traders anxious for his business."

Prince Viktor spoke up at this point. "Some of the voyages we have in mind might require a ship with more firepower than a trading vessel." While he was digesting that statement, Viktor continued. "And they might also require a skilled leader such as yourself, Captain Harkaman."

While he expressed how flattered he was by Viktor's praise, he came up with the perfect answer to the Prince's request.

"We're always ready to consider propositions that would be profitable, Your Highness. I have been asked several times by Sword-World nobles looking to hire ships for a rebellion against their king. I always reply the same way."

Prince Viktor leaned forward. "How's that?

"We would need to be paid twenty-five million stellars in gold up front to consider it."

It was a good thing that Prince Viktor was not drinking at the moment, as he probably would have spit it out. "Twenty-five million! That's ridiculous!"

Harkaman grinned. "That's the response I've received from everyone else. That's why we've never hired out to any Sword-World faction."

Beazley looked just as upset as his sovereign. "Why twenty-five million, aren't you willing to take a risk?"

Harkaman laughed at that. "We take risks every time we raid a world, Lord Beazley. But I can tell you that I wouldn't take those risks if I didn't think we could at least make twenty-five million stellars. I leave the lesser worlds for the chicken-thieves."

Beazley paused, uncertain how to respond to that. At that point there was a little bit of a commotion at the door. Someone was coming in and had been stopped by two of Prince Viktor's men. Ranjit Chaudry stood up. "That's all right; he's one of our crew."

The men turned and looked at Prince Viktor. There was only one man.

Viktor nodded.

As the man came into the room, Harkaman recognized him. He was the trooper who had been piloting his aircar when they were shot down on Susano as part of the *Black Hawk's* raid. When he'd been free a few years later on Nergal, he'd signed up with the *Corisande*. He struggled mentally for a moment and then came up with his name and stood up.

"What is it, Trooper Gomez?"

Gomez looked a little embarrassed. "Captain I'm sorry to interrupt but I wanted to speak to you before I left."

"Left," Ranjit asked. "Where are you going?"

"When I picked up my messages, I found out that my father's died and my mother and older brother need me to help with the family business on Curtana," he replied. "One of the merchant ships is going to be stopping there, but they're leaving in a few hours. I wanted to thank you before our departure."

There were a variety of ways to send messages between worlds. Harkaman had his routed to his account at the Trans-World Bank. His only message this trip had been from his sister, Marta, thanking him for the recent money he had sent her and updating him on family news.

"Since I'm going to get about a hundred and thirty-five thousand stellars from this voyage," Gomez paused, and smiled at the thought. "I'll really be able to help them. I can pay off the mortgages on our home and business, and still have plenty left over."

Harkaman didn't miss the reaction from some of Viktor's men. It was clear a hundred and thirty-fifty thousand stellars was a lot more than Viktor was paying them.

"I'm sorry to hear about your father, but I'll be sorry to lose you, Gomez," Harkaman replied. Chaudry echoed his comments. "I might not be alive if it weren't for your actions on Susano."

"Oh please, sir," Gomez said, embarrassed. "It was you who saved me. I want to thank you for that, and for making me so much money."

He extended his hand and they shook. He turned and shook hands in turn with Chaudry, Costigan and Khumalo, telling them it was an honor to serve with them. He waved to the rest of the officers as he left the room.

Harkaman decided to take advantage of the break given by Trooper Gomez, former Trooper Gomez he corrected himself, and end the evening. "Thank you for joining us Prince Viktor," he said, walking over to him and extending his hand. "While it is early evening, Xochitl time, I'm afraid it's after midnight ship time and I need to retire."

Viktor rose. "Are you sure you won't stay for another drink?" He gestured to the rest of the officers. "You are all welcome, drinks on me."

They all thanked him but said no. Viktor didn't look like this refusal bothered him. As Viktor shook his hand, he said, "I hope we will see each other again, Captain Harkaman."

He assured him that they would.

II

Once Harkaman and his crew had left, Prince Viktor grimaced. Harkaman wanted twenty-five million stellars upfront for any risky voyage. He couldn't decide whether to be insulted or to admire him for having the guts of a stick-up man.

Beazley had no problem deciding. "The nerve of him. Twenty-five million up front," he fumed.

Viktor waved his hand dismissively and turned to the rest of his men. "What did you find out?"

It turned out not much. "That astrogator has to be the dullest man I've ever listened to," one of his aides, said. "All he talked about was his weird music."

The others reported similarly. It seemed that the *Corisande's* officers were not great conversationalists about anything but raiding and space travel. One thing they all had heard: "They think they've got the greatest Space Viking captain around."

Viktor gestured for everyone but Beazley to leave. "Listen carefully to what the bugs picked up, although, I doubt we're going to learn anything new."

Beazley nodded.

Damn, but I was right, Viktor thought. *Harkaman is one fine captain. But how am I to get him to work for me? He's not likely to show up on Xochitl broke like Captain Trevithick did.*

He grimaced at the thought of Trevithick. He would have removed him as captain of the *Jolly Roger* for his failure long ago if he'd had any better alternative. Instead he had the ship's blazonry changed back to the *Joy Rider* on the small secret base he maintained on one of the moons of the outer planets in the Xochitl system. Now he just used the ship for ordinary trading voyages. Maybe now that the *Jolly Roger* hadn't been seen for a number of years the other Space Vikings might relax their vigilance and he could steal some cargos again. At a minimum, he should have them raid some of his competitor's trade planets. He resolved to think more about that.

He turned to Beazley, who had been patiently waiting. "Do you have the girls set up for their hotel?"

"Yes sir," Beazley replied. "I've got a dozen of all types and descriptions, so there should be at least one girl to appeal to each and every one of them. They've been provided with the tell-tales. And they have the micro-dot listening bugs to attach to their clothing."

"It's a long shot," Viktor acknowledged, "but, it's worth a try."

He certainly hadn't received any worthwhile information from the five men he'd been able to plant on the *Corisande* three years ago. Two had managed to get themselves killed during raids. One had deserted when the ship stopped at Nergal to sell loot.

Nergal, blast and curse that damnable world, he thought. It was the one base world where he hadn't been able to establish a spy network. Nergal's natives looked so unique that off-worlders immediately stood out. Visiting Space Vikings pretty much kept to the port area so anyone leaving the spaceport was heavily scrutinized. He sighed mentally. The remaining two men he'd planted on the *Corisande* hadn't told him anything he hadn't found out from other sources. Harkaman was a daring and successful Captain with a loyal crew. Many men competed to serve under him.

Maybe that was all there was to Harkaman, but somehow he thought there was more. He always seemed a little too guarded during their talks. *One way or another*, he resolved, *I'm going to get that man to work for me.*

JOYEUSE

1713 A.E.

After leaving Xochitl, Harkaman decided to make one last foray since they had a ways to go before they reached the edge of Federation space. He had decided to hit Coventina, another world with radar, radio, atomic power and rudimentary atomic weapons, for its fissionables along with the usual precious metals, jewelry, fine art and all the other odds and ends that made for a successful raid. Everything went well until the very end. Up until then they only had been hit by a lot of artillery and rockets, but for the most part they had done little damage. Some of the depleted uranium rounds had dented the hull, but only a few had penetrated through the ship's collapsium armor—but only by one deck.

As the *Corisande* was withdrawing from the port city of Hadrian several submarines entered the bay and launched dozens of atomic tipped missiles at them. Almost all had been shot down by the *Corisande's* anti-missile missiles. Due to the rudimentary nature of their warheads, even those that had scored direct hits had not penetrated the ship's collapsium skin. However one missile, by pure chance, had hit one of the openings made by an earlier strike. It had destroyed several decks, some bulkheads and killed a number of personnel, including a pinnace full of ground troopers that had just docked. *Just bad luck*, thought Harkaman, although he still found himself brooding, wondering what he could have done differently.

He was troubled by the thought he was taking too many chances, maybe even using up his luck. He began to question whether he'd made a good decision to raid another semi-civilized world so soon after the drubbing they'd taken on Cernunnos.

With the *Corisande* having taken significant battle damage and losing a lot of ground fighters, he decided it was time for a thorough repair and overhaul of his ship. He had initially thought of returning to Xochitl, but there were too many Space Viking ships under repair in their dockyards. During their earlier visit, the Xochitl Spaceport Dockmaster had told them they would have had to wait several months before he could fit them into the repair yards. In addition, high demand had caused Xochitl to raise their docking fees substantially. Consequently, Harkaman decided to return to the Sword-Worlds for the first time in almost a decade.

He had picked Joyeuse for his Sword-World stop. It was one of the more advanced Sword-Worlds. It also had the advantage that repairs and parts were less expensive than on Excalibur, nor was the spaceyard as busy. After landing at Bevis Spaceport and paying the docking fees, he met with the Master Shipwright to discuss necessary repairs to the hull and drives. There was significant structural damage to the *Corisande*; the Shipwright estimated the work would take over two thousand hours.

Harkaman's next visit was to the local port of call tavern, the Bucket of Blood, where he posted a notice for ground fighters. While taking a seat at one of the open tables, he saw a familiar face. It was Captain Morley Sopwirth, an old acquaintance.

"Hi, Sop," he said as he took his seat.

Sopwirth, a tall lanky figure with a long horse face and a forehead etched with furrows, turned toward Harkaman. "Long time, no see," Sopwirth said. "What are you up to these days, Otto?"

"I left my ship at the spaceport for repairs. We had a helluva tough fight on Coventina."

"Coventina—I haven't heard of it."

The world wasn't known to many Space Vikings, although it was well known on Harkaman's home world of Colada. Captain Endymion Rodriguez had been one of the few Space Vikings who was married with children. He returned to Colada from each raid to visit his family along with selling loot and making repairs to his ship. His final raid had been on Coventina over forty years ago; while he had returned with a great deal of plunder. His ship had been so damaged that he sold it for scrap and promptly retired, so his raid became a local legend.

"It's a semi-civilized world with atomic power and a good missile defense. We had our job cut out for us."

"What ship were you on?"

"I have my own ship; well, my partners and I do. She's the *Corisande*."

"I'd heard you made captain—the words gotten around. Congratulations, Otto. The name's familiar, but I can't remember her former skipper."

"We bought the *Corisande* from one of the Excalibur banks. I later learned she'd been a loan foreclosure on Captain Alden Bartley, who was down on his luck."

"Wasn't he always?" Sopwirth laughed. "He was a gambling fool, as well."

"We who hunt through the graveyard of the Old Federation are all gamblers," Harkaman stated.

"True, but Bartley toyed with games of chance and cards as well," Sopwirth said, shaking his head in disgust. "The *Corisande* is a fine ship, and much bigger than my own."

"Are you still captain of the *Hellmouth*?" As he recalled, the *Hellmouth* was one of the oldest Space Viking vessels around; over two hundred years old, if you could believe the stories told about her. It was twelve hundred feet in size which was the size of most of the original Sword-World ships. Space Vikings had started using fifteen-hundred-foot ships over a hundred and fifty years ago. In the last generation two-thousand-foot vessels had become the spaceship of choice, assuming one could afford them. *Where will it end?*

"Yes, we're just undergoing a final refitting before we space out. "If you're looking for work, I've got a good deal for ya."

"What's that?" he answered carefully. He didn't completely trust Sopwirth; he was known to cut corners and take what he thought were unnecessary risks.

"I've got a raid in mind and multiple ships are always better than one."

"If you can afford to wait while I get her repairs done and reinforcements for my ground units, I'll give it consideration."

"Ground fighters, you can get them easily. The *Black Imp* recently decommissioned here, and there are a lot of unemployed spacers and ground fighters."

"That's good to know," he said, thinking he'd be happy not to have to pay any bonuses to get an experienced crew. "What's the plan?"

"A few days ago, I was approached by Big Jim about getting some neodymium for the Bevis repair dock. They're running low. He usually gets supplies from Lugaluru, but a ship recently tried to raid their mines and got into a dog eat dog fight with the locals and their Mardukan overlords and seriously damaged their mining operations."

Harkaman shook his head. "Now, that wasn't too smart. Marduk has controlled the neodymium supply in this sector of the Old Federation for centuries. They should have known it would be protected. They also control the other major source on Ithavoll."

Sopwirth nodded in agreement. "It could take years to get the mines back into operation or start a new mine on another world. Since then the price for neodymium has quadrupled, and every repair yard from here to

Hoth is looking for resupply."

He paused to comb through his memory, then shook his head. "I can't think of any other nearby planetary source. Though you could find it in small amounts on many worlds, large deposits of monazite that are worth mining are rare."

Sopwirth made a wry smile, saying, "There is one Old Federation source I'm aware of, the planet Midgard."

"Midgard! That's in the heart of the Old Federation. It's got to be over five-thousand hours from Joyeuse!"

"I didn't say it would be quick or easy. However, every Space Viking world and base, from Joyeuse to Jagannath, will soon be begging for neodymium. Without it there can be no new drives built, nor repair of older ones. It's a once in a lifetime opportunity to strike it rich!" Sopwirth was all but salivating. "I would do it alone, but I'm sure we won't be the only ones looking for it."

He shook his head. "You're right. Just ships from most of the civilized words! We would need more than two ships."

Captain Sopwirth smiled. Now, he thought Harkaman was hooked. "I've already lined up Boake Valkanhayn of the *Space Scourge* as well as Poul Mangus of *Thor's Hammer*.

"I've never met either of them. Are they reliable?"

"They're both good in a fight and neither one is a back-stabber," Sopwirth replied. "I worked with Valkanhayn for a raid on Shango. We made a fair profit. Captain Mangus is new to me, but Gunnar Sorenssan, the proprietor of the Bucket of Blood, recommended him."

Harkaman paused to knock the dottle out of his pipe and refill it with fresh leaf while he thought. After relighting it, he said, "Since Midgard isn't a civilized world, four ships should be more than enough. Plus, we can raid any major cities with the extra ships, while we strip the processing plants of neodymium." He paused. "We'll need good industrial engineers if we have to repair and restart the plants," he said, thinking of his past experience on Ereshkigal. "I've got a couple of engineers, but we could use a couple more and some additional machinists."

"I've got a dozen signed up and ready to go, Otto," Sopwirth said. "We'll have our own fleet. The first out of the Sword-Worlds in over a hundred years," he enthused.

He shook his head. "Four ships do not make a fleet, more like a small flotilla."

"Still, it will be a doughty force, one to be reckoned with."

He hoped so. It had been a long time since any Space Viking ships had ventured that far into the heart of the Old Federation; over half a year's travel. He had no idea of how well-protected Midgard might prove to be. He did see one possible problem he wanted to head off: "We'll need to have one captain in charge of the raid, or there's going to be problems."

"You've got the best rep and the biggest ship, Otto. In my book, that puts you in charge."

Harkaman nodded. He wouldn't have accepted anything less. Sopwirth was reliable and a reasonably successful ship captain, but leading a fleet action was way beyond his pay level. Of course, he hadn't led one either but he trusted himself a lot more than he trusted Sopwirth.

Space Viking shares were different in multiple-ship actions, the split was one half share for the man in charge, a three-share split between all the captains, one and a half shares to the officers with the remaining five shares going to the crews. A captain had to take care of his investors out of his own share. Depending on what he owed the investors, a captain might spend the bulk of his share paying interest or principal on loans. Since he and his crew owned the *Corisande* outright, they'd all come out very well if they were successful.

"There's only one problem."

"What's that," Sopwirth asked

"According to the local shipwright, it could be up to two thousand hours before our repairs are complete."

"We can wait. For a score this big, that's not a problem."

"Good," Harkaman replied. "Now that that's settled, I'm going to check the local library to see what they have on Midgard." He knew his own personal ship-board library was probably superior to most of those found on the Sword-Worlds, but he was unfamiliar with the Joyeuse Royal Library. Now that he was stuck on Joyeuse, he would have time for a thorough examination of the library. He smiled in anticipation.

MIDGARD

I

1714 A.E.

The four ships spaced out two thousand hours later, after getting a detailed briefing from Otto Harkaman. There was very little recent information on Midgard, nothing since the end of the Interstellar Wars. It was the third planet of Rheingold's Star, a G7 yellow sun, and there was minimal local flora and fauna; most of what lived there had been brought from Terra and other nearby planets.

During the early Federation Era, Midgard had been a major hub, supplying neodymium, other rare earths, heavy metals and fissionables in trade. It was an old world, theorized to be the remains of a planetary core of a larger planet from a system whose sun went nova, then captured eons later by the local star. The only reason

Midgard never became fully civilized was due to its heavy gravitational pull, 1.4 Gs, and because much of the planet was too hot for comfortable human habitation. There were only two small oceans with very little water; the planet was almost eighty percent land. Most of what fresh water the planet had held was derived from intermittent streams of rainwater. In the Federation era, several comets had been captured and crashed into the Great Northern Desert forming a small lake.

It had been almost a thousand years since the Big Breakup and Harkaman wondered if the Miracle Sea, as it was named, had any remaining water. It would be a terrible waste of time to arrive only to find that the world was uninhabitable with only ruins left behind. The other captains had been dispirited by his news of Midgard. However, he informed them that he had made a list of possible nearby targets for them to raid, if Midgard turned out to be a lost cause. The heart of the Old Federation hadn't really been raided much by Space Vikings due to its distance since the days of Erlic Sanchez the Planet-Buster, well over a hundred years ago, and there were lots of possible targets. Of course, they would steer clear of Aton, Isis, Odin and any of the other civilized worlds.

Harkaman thought the neodymium deposits seemed too large and too rare to have remained unmolested. He suspected that at least one, if not more, of the civilized worlds might have mining operations there. The flotilla would have to be very careful in their approach, he decided. Before they committed themselves, they would make a site-stop at the outer edge of the Rheingold system and do some scouting.

The biggest astronomical problem Space Viking ships faced, when arriving at a star system that hadn't been visited for a long time, was that they were basing the star's position on either old Space Viking pilots' notes, former captains' logs or the *Astrogator's Guide to the Worlds of the Federation*, which was close to a thousand years old.

It was a long journey and he had lots of time to mull over possible problems and solutions and discuss them with his officers. He read and re-read everything in his large library regarding Midgard. It was one of the earliest Terran colonies, founded in the Third Century Atomic Era. For the first fifty years after discovery, it had been left alone until a prospecting expedition had found large deposits of both fissionable ores and rare earths, including neodymium. This had led to a short Gold Rush of sorts and the Federation had found Midgard valuable enough to spend the time and money to locate and send several large comets crashing into the northern desert to increase the water supply. Over two centuries later, a brief war had broken out between Aton and Odin over their trading companies' mining rights. The Federation had stepped in and ordered both parties to leave and not return. After that fracas, the Federation had put a small naval base on its single moon. The planetary population had never been higher than half a million and Harkaman wondered how many had survived to the present day. Midgard would not be a world for the weak and diffident.

As the vacant grey of hyperspace changed into the indescribable color of a collapsing hyperspatial field, they found themselves an unknown number of light-years from the edge of the Rheingold system. As Guatt Kirbey checked all the star references, Harkaman reviewed his plans. He decided that once they reached the edge of the Rheingold's Star's magnetic fields, or heliosphere, he would send a pinnace to search for other visitors and ships that might be lurking in Midgard system. The last thing he wanted was to come out of a hyperspace microjump and find the *Corisande* surrounded by hostile ships.

"Everything is good," Kirbey reported, after checking with his detection screens, "I've confirmed the location and shared that data with the other ships. Ready to jump upon your order."

Normally, Kirbey would handle the microjumps all the way to the planet without any feedback. With a four-ship flotilla, that necessarily became a little more complicated. He turned and looked at Paul Koreff.

"Nothing," said Koreff, shaking his head. "I'm not getting any read off the sensors."

That wasn't surprising. It would be a miraculous occurrence if anything as small as a hypership could be detected from one or two light-years away.

"All right, jump," He ordered.

Once their location was confirmed at the edge of the Rheingold system's heliosphere, Alvyn Karffard and Paul Koreff boarded one of the pinnaces to reconnoiter the system.

Alvyn was glad for any excuse to leave the *Corisande*, as was Koreff. After over five thousand hours of hyperspace travel, even his hobby of model making hadn't keep him distracted enough from catching a case of cabin-fever. They made six microjumps of about thirty light-minutes apiece. At each stop Koreff used his detection equipment to search for any nearby hyperships.

"There's a ship just outside the fifth planet," Koreff noted, after their last stop. "It's large enough to be a warship, but it's not radiating enough juice. But there's too much for a freighter or tramp ship. If I had to guess, I'd say it's a Gilgamesh freighter."

"Can they detect us?" he asked.

"Not likely unless they were looking for us," said Koreff. "We're at the extreme range of detection and a pinnace radiates a lot less energy than a big ship." What Koreff didn't say because he wasn't a braggart was that his skills with his instruments were much better than the average signals-and-detection officer.

"I want to check out the rest of the system before I report back," Alvyn said. "Let's take another jump. Put us on the opposite side of the sun from the fifth planet and the Gilgamesher."

Koreff looked at him closely. "I'm not Guatt; that's a different kind of microjump than just going thirty light-minutes per jump into a system."

He grinned back at him. "Take your time on the calculations. I know you can do it."

After about twenty minutes, Koreff was ready and they jumped.

"Nothing to report from either of the third or fourth planets," Koreff said after carefully reviewing all of his equipment. "Or anywhere else."

They jumped back to the four-ship flotilla to report. Alvyn called Harkaman, then patched-in the other captains on the viewscreen and made his report.

"A Gilgamesher. What in Satan's name are they doing here?" Harkaman asked.

"They could just be mining the fifth planet for chemicals, or scooping up deuterium. It is a gas giant. We didn't get close enough to measure its composition for fear of detection but what else could they be doing?" Alvyn conjectured. "I've never heard of a Gilgamesher mining outpost, but—if there's a stellar to be squeezed or profit to be made in the Old Federation—you can be sure a Gilgie is nearby!"

Harkaman nodded. "What about Midgard's moon? According to the *Astrogator's Guide* it used to be the site of a Federation Navy base."

"The moon's dead, and we didn't detect anything on the third and fourth planets," said Koreff. "That includes their moons, as well."

"What are we gonna do about the Gilgamesher?" Captain Sopwirth asked, frowning.

"We came here for the neodymium," Harkaman replied. "So, we'll continue on to Midgard and ignore the Gilgie."

II

Trouble started soon after they entered the atmosphere. Guatt Kirbey had calculated several microjumps, all of them taking place on the opposite side of the Rheingold system from where the Gilgamesh ship was located. The last jump had put them less than a light-second and a half away from Midgard.

"Otto," Koreff reported, "message coming in."

The communication-screen remained blank. The message was voice only. "This is the *Fairtrader*. What is your business here?"

"*Fairtrader*," Karffard said. "I've seen that ship before. It's a Gilgamesher hypership."

Harkaman thought for a few seconds before replying. It was very unusual for a Gilgamesher to contact another ship that was not from its world. They were a highly clannish group that typically wanted no contact with others except to trade. Most trading was done at selected worlds following long-established routes.

"*Fairtrader*, this is Otto Harkaman, Captain of the Sword-World ship *Corisande*. With me are the Sword-World hyperships *Hellmouth*, *Thor's Hammer* and *Space Scourge*. We are here to raid the neodymium mines. If you do not interfere with us, we will not bother you."

The reply was swift and shocking. "*Corisande*, this is Captain Salmesh. The neodymium mines are part of a Gilgamesh colony. Any attempt at raiding them will be met with all necessary force until your ships are destroyed."

He was astonished, and as he looked around, he could see that his bridge crew was as well. Gilgamesh ships typically stood aside when a Space Viking ship raided a planet or city they happened to be visiting. As long as they were not directly attacked, they avoided confrontation. And he'd never heard of a Gilgamesh mining colony before. Their colonies were typically small trading settlements established in the capital cities of major planets such as Odin, Marduk, Baldur or Vishnu.

Sopwirth's face appeared on a separate panel on his communication screen. "We've caught them with their pants down!" he cried. "Let's blow the damn Gilgies to Em-See-Square!"

"Are you nuts, Sopwirth?" Harkaman replied. "Anyone who attacks a Gilgamesh ship or colony will face retaliation from Gilgamesh."

That had been proven many times in the past. Though the retaliation might take years, Gilgameshers would eventually destroy any ship that attacked them and ruined one of their vessels. This would happen even if the ship were sold and renamed. They would go so far as to hunt down and kill the captain of the ship, even if he had retired. The Gilgameshers might be clannish, but they had excellent intel.

Mangus's face appeared on his screen, echoing Sopwirth's suggestion. Harkaman's description of past Gilgamesher responses to attacks against their ships had no visible effect on either captain.

"With four ships, we've got the firepower to wipe them all out," Magnus crowed. "Then we can clean up!"

"And, we've got the drop on them!" cried Sopwirth, with an almost fanatical gleam in his eye. "No one will ever know we did it."

"And how are you going to keep our crews from talking," Harkaman asked, trying to reason with them. "Word will inevitably leak back to Gilgamesh about who destroyed their ship and sacked their outpost. And then watch out!"

As Sopwirth continued to argue, all of a sudden it hit him. "Sopwirth you son of a bitch! You knew this was a Gilgamesher colony all along, didn't you?"

Sopwirth's face contorted with rage. "So what! Those damn Gilgies need to be taken down a few pegs. And we're the ones to do it!"

Harkaman shook his head. "You can count me out. I'm not getting into some vendetta with Gilgameshers, even if you want to. You're on your own."

Sopwirth looked even more enraged. "You yellow-backed skunk!" he screamed. "I should have known you didn't have the guts. We'll take 'em out, even without you."

Valkanhayn's face appeared on the communication screen. He'd been silent during the entire discussion. "I'm with Otto," he said. "I'm not getting into a fight with Gilgameshers, no matter how much loot is involved. They don't forgive, and—as sure as Loki's Scepter—they don't forget!"

Boake Valkanhayn was promptly called every name in the book by Sopwirth. "Go ahead, you cowards," Sopwirth finished. "Boake, we can do it without you and Harkaman."

He was probably right there, Harkaman thought. They had found out from their crews mingling on Joyeuse that the *Space Scourge* was severely underpowered. It also had less than half of its complement of missiles. The problem was Valkanhayn hadn't made enough profit on his last few garbage runs to keep the ship up. The *Space Scourge* looked fine from the outside, but only because they had repaired any breaks to the outer skin.

However, Valkanhayn had not repaired the underlying structural damage. Even though the *Space Scourge* was larger at fifteen-hundred feet than the *Hellmouth's* twelve-hundred feet, she would not be as good in a fight as the *Hellmouth*. As for the *Hellmouth* and *Thor's Hammer*, they would have their hands full against the *Fairtrader*, which their detection sensors showed was a fifteen-hundred foot diameter ship.

"The *Space Scourge* is breaking away and heading out of the atmosphere," Koreff announced.

Harkaman punched a few buttons and Sopwirth and Mangus's faces and voices vanished from his communication-screens. "Valkanhayn," he said. "I'm going to see if the rest of the world has anything worth raiding. Do you want to join us?"

Valkanhayn's face appeared in the screen. As he was the only one on the screen, the picture expanded, showing that the *Space Scourge's* bridge was old and poorly maintained, which reflected the condition of the entire ship.

"No," he replied. "I've had enough of this ill-fated adventure. Good luck to you." With that the screen blanked out.

He turned to Sharll Renner. "Make for the Miracle Sea. We'll see if there's anything else worth stealing on this gods-forsaken planet." Though he didn't expect much in the way of likely targets, he had to admit that, after all the time it took to get to this world, he wanted to find out what had happened on Midgard and see for himself if the Miracle Sea still existed.

III

The Miracle Sea not only existed but it appeared larger than the photos taken a thousand years ago. There was an extensive network of canals in the area and a variety of cities, the largest of which held about forty thousand people. They could see small ships on the canals which appeared to be driven by steam power from the smoke rising from them.

"There were a couple of mines in this area, weren't there?" Vann Larch asked.

Harkaman consulted his notes. "Yes. There were two platinum mines. He thought a moment.

"Inform Ranjit that we will send one pinnace to each mine, while the other two go the largest city. Let him know we'll be approaching the targets in"—he paused and looked at Koreff who held up two fingers—"two hours. That should give him enough time to get ready."

"Captain," announced Karffard, "the *Fairtrader* has left the ground and is moving to engage the *Thor's Hammer* and *Hellmouth*."

"How long before they meet?" he asked.

"It should be about two and a half hours," he estimated.

One of the mines turned out to be abandoned but the other was in use and had a processing planet and a warehouse full of ingots next to it. There was no opposition as the workers ran away at the first shot; they began loading the ingots right away. The other pinnace joined the two that were looting the city. Harkaman debated sending them to another city but decided to wait. They'd see what this city had before they attacked any others. The initial reports were positive. At least they'd come away with something from Midgard, even if it wasn't much more than ship expenses.

"The *Fairtrader* has approached the other ships," Karffard announced.

"Keep us informed," Harkaman replied.

The ship battle was probably going to be more interesting than the raid. Koreff used one of his channels for both the *Hellmouth* and *Thor's Hammer* so they could hear the running commentary of the battle. Sopwirth's excited comments contrasted with Ranjits' relaxed voice as he directed his people between various targets.

"Pinnace Two is full. Pinnace Four relieve them at the mine. There're still a lot of ingots left."

"Mangus, move to your left. We'll box 'em between us and hit 'em with our short-range guns simultaneously!"

"Aircars Four and Five, assist with loading Pinnace Three at that bank."

"Those imps of Satan took out missile rooms six and eight!"

"Pinnace Three full and returning. Send Pinnace Two to the main bank when unloaded."

"By Satan, they got *Thor's Hammer*. Launch a Planetbuster at 'em."

Everyone on the bridge swore. Detonating a Planetbuster in the atmosphere was going to wreak havoc everywhere.

"How far away is that Planetbuster?" he asked Koreff.

He overheard Alvyn warning Ranjit to get the troops out of any building that didn't appear sturdy enough to survive an earthquake.

"They're about two thousand miles away," Koreff said.

"Did he get the Gilgie?" Renner asked.

"Not yet," said Karffard after a few moments. "She's still intact. They're both too far away to tell how badly either ship is hurt."

Unless the Fairtrader *is on its last legs, the* Hellmouth *is in serious trouble*, Harkaman thought. They don't have the firepower to stay with the larger ship. If he were Sopwirth, he'd be running as fast as he could.

Suddenly Koreff swore, as the shock wave from the Planetbuster hit. The *Corisande* rocked slightly as if it had been hit by a few missiles.

Harkaman looked at the screens showing the town below. Some of the larger buildings below them had toppled, but about half of them appeared intact. Hopefully their troops hadn't been in or near any of the buildings that had been destroyed.

"Otto," Koreff cried. "A second Gilgamesher has just entered the atmosphere. It must have been the one sitting at their mining colony."

Unless he could get away quickly, the Hellmouth *was doomed*, he decided. He couldn't muster any sympathy for Sopwirth, who'd recruited them on what appeared to be a fruitless mission. *And I agreed to it*, he thought sadly. *I'd have never come, if I'd known it was a Gilgamesher mining base.*

Karffard reported that they hadn't lost any troops planetside. The shock wave had dissipated enough so that it only had the impact of a minor earthquake. "Pinnace Two is unloaded and returning to the surface. Pinnace Three docking now."

About ten minutes Karffard announced "*Hellmouth* destroyed." That drew a few grim chuckles around the bridge. Apparently the rest of the officers felt the way he did about Sopwirth.

Then Koreff turned toward him, consternation on his face. "Captain, both Gilgameshers are heading our way at top speed."

Harkaman swore, then punched up his communication-screen. "Captain Salmesh, why are you heading toward us? We have complied with your request not to loot the Gilgamesh colony."

"This whole world belongs to Yah the Almighty!"

Harkaman swore, then came to a decision. "Alvyn, order the rest of the ground fighters to return to the *Corisande*. Paul, how soon can we get those pinnaces get back?"

"Fifteen minutes is my guess."

Everyone on the bridge was staring at him, wondering what he would do. He did his best to remain calm. "Battle stations."

Sirens began blaring throughout the ship. He heard Vann Larch calling all the missile control rooms to check their status.

"What's the status of the troops? Can they make it back in time?" He knew the answer but wanted everyone to hear it.

"No," Karffard replied. "Pinnace Three will be back here in five minutes but the others won't even be off the ground by then."

"Call Ranjit," he ordered.

When Chaudry was on screen, he asked how soon all the troops could be loaded.

"My troops are scattered all over, Captain," Chaudry replied, looking at his screens. "It'll be twenty-five minutes at best."

As he hesitated Ranjit continued. "I've been following what's going on. Take the ship up and protect us. We can always jump separately from you in the pinnaces."

He nodded his approval. After a few minutes, Larch reported that all missile stations were ready. Karffard indicated that Pinnace Three was aboard and secured.

"All right," he said. "Take us up, Sharll."

IV

The *Corisande* ascended high enough so that the *Fairtrader* and the other ship, which was now identified as the *Golden Trumpet*, couldn't pin them against the ground. After about five minutes, the two Gilgameshers separated, the *Fairtrader* heading straight for them while the other ship rose higher in the atmosphere. *That's peculiar*, Harkaman thought, *you'd think they'd both want to engage us at the same time.*

"Vann," he said. "Until I say so, use defensive missiles only. If we can get out of this alive, I want to give the Gilgameshers as little excuse as possible to come after us."

Larch nodded.

At extreme range, the *Fairtrader* started firing missiles. Their initial salvo was easily picked off by the *Corisande's* counter-missiles.

"The *Fairtrader* has been hit in eight places but none of the impacts appear to be serious. There's a big dent and some kind of rip in the hull on the north side of the ship; that must be from the planetbuster," Karffard announced.

"The *Golden Trumpet* has turned and is coming at us," Koreff reported.

Missiles and counter-missiles fired and flared all around. After a minute, it sounded as if a giant fist was beating against the hull, as a few missiles struck the outer shell near simultaneously.

He heard Larch telling the missile rooms to load the replacement anti-missile counter missiles as fast as they were fired.

"The *Fairtrader* is descending below us," Koreff noted, puzzled. Suddenly he turned, alarmed. "She's heading for the city!"

Harkaman ran of a string of curses. Now he understood their strategy. "Stay between the *Fairtrader* and the city," he ordered. The Gilgameshers hoped to distract them with the air attack, while keeping the *Corisande's* close to the surface by threatening their troops in the city.

That's a good strategy, he thought. Meanwhile, missiles continued to spew from the *Fairtrader* straight towards them. Most were intercepted but a few got through, causing light jolts. He pressed a button.

"*Fairtrader*, break off your attacks and let us recover our men and we will leave Midgard," he said. "Otherwise we will use whatever force is necessary to defeat you."

There was no change in the *Fairtrader's* course.

Ranjit announced that it would be at least six more minutes before all troops were loaded.

"The *Golden Trumpet's* reached extreme firing range," Koreff announced. "The bastard's firing missiles at us, Captain!" he said a few moments later.

"Vann," he said. "Fire offensive missiles!"

Larch began pressing buttons. Missiles went out towards both Gilgamesher ships. "We hit him a few times, but he's still coming," he reported.

Then a thought occurred to him. "Sharll, head straight at the *Fairtrader* as fast as possible at an angle that forces him to either turn away from the city or come within reach of our short-range guns."

Renner grinned and began punching buttons.

He's taking me literally, Harkaman thought as items began sliding around the control room from the sudden acceleration. They appeared to have surprised the *Fairtrader*, which did not initially react to their course change. Then she began to turn, but it was too late; the *Corisande's* short-range guns cut loose, raking the *Fairtrader* and ripping holes in the collapsium-plated hull with depleted-uranium slugs as they passed within a few thousand feet.

"Turn back to the city, now," he ordered.

"We got them good," Karffard yelled triumphantly. "She's badly hurt; the *Fairtrader's* turning away."

Harkaman grinned. It had occurred to him he'd never heard of a

Gilgamesher having short-range guns. The *Fairtrader* had been at a major disadvantage when the ships had passed each other so closely.

"Pinnace One is off the ground," Karffard announced.

"Keep between the Gilgie and the pinnaces, Sharll," he ordered.

The *Golden Trumpet* paused for a few moments, when the *Fairtrader* sheared off. Now it pressed its attack again; another round of missile fire was exchanged between them. He could feel the shocks as they hit the ship. However, the Gilgamesher ship made certain to pass far enough away so that they were out of range of the *Corisande's* short-range guns.

Klaxons were screeching and the bridge was haloed in red; he looked at the damage-control board and felt his stomach drop. *Damn it, didn't I just refit this ship!*

Several lights ceased to blink as repair crews sealed the openings up. There was one light blinking rapidly; there must have been several impacts in the same area as the break in the ship was twelve decks deep rather than the usual five to eight decks. He heard Alvyn discussing the breach with a repair crew.

Someone yelled, "Get some more damn robots down here!"

"Pinnace Four has left the ground."

"The other Gilgie's coming back again," Koreff announced. A wave of missiles shot out from the *Golden Trumpet*. The *Corisande* fired a return volley. There were bumps and screeches as the ship took more hits.

A moment later; Paul shouted, "Hey, she's turning off."

Maybe they're finally giving up, Harkaman thought. He was just about to ask how fast they could get the last pinnace off the ground when Karffard cried.

"The *Fairtrader's* returning! She's headed for the pinnace!"

"Pinnace Two get the damn-hell out of there!" Harkaman bellowed in alarm, as if yelling could get them to move faster.

"How long until we're within range?" he asked.

Koreff shook his head, holding up two fingers. Renner accelerated as fast as the *Corisande* could but it was too late. They watched a series of missiles slam into the pinnace. While they were still a minute away

Pinnace Two blew up in a ball of orange fire. The *Fairtrader* immediately turned away and accelerated as fast as she could. The *Corisande* rocked gently when the shock wave reached them.

Harkaman shouted, "Break off and head off-world!" The Gilgies had played him for a chump. The *Golden Trumpet's* change of course had distracted him and he had forgotten about the *Fairtrader*. It had cost them; he looked at the personnel-board—a hundred and two troopers and four crewmen. He felt equal parts sick and angry.

The rest of the crew looked as if they felt the same way. "Where are Pinnaces One and Four?" he asked.

"Ranjit is accelerating. Pinnace One will be out of the atmosphere in a half an hour. Pinnace Four is about ten minutes behind him. Neither of the Gilgies are anywhere near them," Karffard announced.

"Where are the Gilgameshers?" he asked grimly.

"Koreff examined his instruments. "The *Fairtrader* is wobbling badly. It looks like she's hurt: I don't know how bad… Her current course will take her back to their mining base. The *Golden Trumpet* is heading toward orbit." He turned toward Harkaman. "It looks like they want to meet us at the edge of the exosphere."

Harkaman smiled tightly. "That'll be fine with me."

Guatt Kirbey arrived on the bridge at that moment. He took his station and unlocked his console. "Captain, I assume, that once we get past them, you want to jump as soon as possible."

He nodded. He looked at the damage-control board. The damage in the one area of the hull was extensive enough that it would be dangerous to risk any more raiding this voyage. Someone might get in a lucky shot. They might as well head straight to a base world and he said so to Kirbey.

Koreff turned to him. "Five minutes until the Gilgamesher is at maximum range."

Harkaman wondered again why the Gilgamesher was so intent on fighting him. *We followed their request not to raid their colony*, he thought. *Of course, at the time we didn't know they claimed the whole damn world.*

Harkaman turned his attention to the upcoming battle.

"Any chance we can maneuver and get past them without fighting, Sharll?" he asked.

Renner shook his head. "Only if they don't change course, Captain. They're already in orbit so it's pretty easy to match velocity and course with us."

He looked at Vann Larch. He indicated with a nod of his head that everything was ready with their weapons systems. "Very well. Change course half a minute before we reach maximum range. We'll see how tightly they can maneuver with us."

He turned to Karffard. "Tell Ranjit to jump with both pinnaces as soon as he can. He can meet us at Jagannath."

"Why, Captain? According to Kirbey, Dagon is the closest base world."

"I don't want to put all our eggs in one basket."

Karffard nodded.

"What if the *Golden Trumpet* follows us?" Vann asked.

"**I'LL SEND THEM TO EM-SEE-SQUARE**!" Harkaman bellowed.

A few seconds after their change of course, the Gilgamesher began to shadow them. Missiles fired from both ships; fires blossoming between each ship as most were intercepted and blown up. He felt a few jolts, but the damage-control board showed that Renner had done a good job keeping the most damaged part of the ship away from their missiles.

"The Gilgie's launched a pinnace," Karffard yelled.

Harkaman furrowed his brows in concentration. They were trying to get the pinnace on the other side of them to target their damaged section. Two could play at that game.

"Turn toward the pinnace," he ordered. "Target them the minute they're in range. Hit them with everything we've got!" That should drive them away or force the *Golden Trumpet* to turn and protect them.

"Pinnaces One and Four have jumped," Karffard announced.

Moments later, missiles began going out. The Gilgie pinnace began firing defensive missiles but couldn't keep up with the *Corisande's* fire, taking several hits. But they didn't turn away, instead, increased speed and headed directly for them on a kamikaze run.

"Son of a bitch, they're sacrificing the pinnace," he yelled. "Vann, give them everything we've got!"

Larch began pressing buttons and yelling orders into his communication screen. Their screens showed both Gilgie ships taking plenty of hits, then the short range guns went into action. A few seconds flew by, and they had the pleasure of watching the pinnace blow up with a blinding flash.

Unfortunately, there were some new blinking lights on the *Corisande's* damage-control board.

"Turn us toward the *Golden Trumpet*, Sharll," he ordered. They'd either get a crack at them with their short-range guns or make them shear away far enough to get past them to climb out of Midgard's atmosphere.

The *Golden Trumpet* didn't turn and kept coming toward them, missiles spewing rapidly. The short-range guns cut loose as they passed, pounding the ship.

"We got them good!" Karffard announced.

Then he felt a terrific jolt and lights started blinking all over the board.

"What the hell?" he exclaimed. Red lights blazed: the damage-control board showed extensive engine damage. Without being ordered, Renner accelerated away as fast as he could.

"Can we jump, Guatt?" he asked.

Kirbey looked confused. "The hyperspace engine lights are blinking on and off," he said. "Captain, I've never seen anything like it! It's as if one moment we can jump and the next we can't."

He started punching his communication-screen key with the Engineering department code. Koreff had anticipated him and put it up on the main viewer. Chief Van de Brost appeared on screen. The background behind him was chaotic, showing flames and some equipment sparking with crewmembers in the background frantically trying to put out fires.

"Chief, what's wrong?" he asked.

More klaxons went off, making it almost impossible to hear.

Van de Brost looked at the screens before him. "Captain, the hyperspace engines are damaged!" he cried. "I don't know if we can jump at all."

Karffard yelled "That damn Gilgie's still coming after us!"

He turned back to Van de Brost. "Chief, can you get it fixed so we can jump?"

"Working on it," was all he said, frowning as his screen winked out.

"How far away is the Gilgie?"

"They're just over two thousand miles away," Koreff said.

Harkaman looked worriedly at his instruments again. "But they're gaining on us. Can we go any faster, Sharll?"

Renner shook his head. "We're at maximum; whatever damaged the drive engines has slowed us down."

He turned to the navigator. "Guatt, prepare to jump."

Kirbey turned back to his board and continued his calculations.

Anticipating his question Koreff spoke. "We've got about four minutes before the Gilgie's in range again."

He turned to Larch, who also anticipated his question. "We'll hit them with everything we have."

"They're as damaged as we are," Karffard noted. "We could end up taking each other out at the same time."

He shook his head. Most rational men would not engage in a ship-to-ship duel that promised mutual destruction. But the Gilgamesher captain had not been acting rationally, and seemed determined to destroy them—no matter the cost. *What was going on down there?*

Just then a couple lights stopped blinking on Kirbey's board. "We're jump ready," he said, starting to press buttons, then reached for the red lever. A second later he swore as the lights started blinking again.

"Guatt, be ready to jump the second it stabilizes, again," Harkaman ordered. *If it ever does!*

Kirbey nodded and continued press buttons. After a minute or so he indicated he was ready.

"What happens if the engines go out in the middle of a jump?" Karffard asked.

Kirbey shook his head, a worried expression on his face. "I don't know. I've never heard of anything like that."

"They've reached maximum range," Karffard announced.

"Oh, Hell! Two dozen missiles headed our way!" Koreff announced a second later. "That damn Gilgamesher must have sent everything in his tubes against us!"

All of sudden the lights on Kirbey's board stopped blinking. Before anyone could say anything, he grabbed the jump handle, twisted it to the right and shoved it in as fast as he could. The outside screen turned a featureless grey. They'd made it into hyperspace.

V

In meetings with the engineering staff after the hyperspace jump, they had found that it was not the jump engines themselves that had been damaged but all of the power connections to the engines. Harkaman had been relieved; replacing a jump engine would have been very expensive.

"Can't you repair the connections, Chief?" someone asked.

"To do that we would have to turn off the jump engines," Chief Van de Brost said. "That's never been done in the middle of a hyperspace voyage, at least to my knowledge."

"What if the engines just quit all on their own?" Karffard asked. All of the bridge staff had been very concerned about the blinking lights on the engineering board, wondering what they meant and what might happen. It was a good thing that Kirbey had closed his console. They'd opened it once to look at it again, and had promptly closed it, as all the lights continued to blink on and off. There were already rumors flying around the ship that they were lost in hyperspace and would never come out of it.

"No one knows what might happen," Van de Brost said. Aa a sign of how puzzled and concerned he was, Van de Brost turned and asked the two youngest members of his staff what they thought. Both were recent engineering graduates of Joyeuse University and new additions to the crew. Van de Brost, who had learned his skills starting as a teenager in engine rooms over forty-five years ago, often kidded them about their book learning, as opposed to his practical knowledge. Now, he wanted their opinion. They both shook their heads.

"This was never discussed in class," one of them replied. "But, it seems to me that if the jump engines failed in mid-jump, it would be like turning off your aircar's contragravity in mid-air. Nothing good could come of it."

"What should we do?" Harkaman asked.

"Wait until the jump is complete, Captain," Van de Brost advised. "If we don't come out of hyperspace when scheduled, then we can start worrying."

The next four hundred hours were the longest of Harkaman's life. He was so wound up he couldn't concentrate on reading and found he could barely sleep or eat. He couldn't do anything but worry. He finally passed out for twenty-four hours and woke up famished.

After a quick meal, he was sitting by himself in the officer's mess, fidgeting with his pipe, when Alvyn Karffard came in.

"Hi, Otto. Did you finally get a good sleep?"

He shook his head wearily. "No, too many dreams, make that nightmares. My mind kept replaying that Gilgamesh attack over and over...."

"You can't hold yourself responsible for that debacle!" Karffard told him. "You can lay that right in Sopwirth's lap. He knew all along that Midgard was a Gilgamesh colony, but never told anyone else. He got his."

"Yes, and so did over a hundred of our boys," He said, grimacing. "I'm sure the crew blames me for this whole thing...."

"You're wrong, Otto. The crew knows damn well just how lucky they were to get off Midgard with their lives and the ship intact. They'll be bragging about it at the next port. You'll see."

"I don't see how, Alvyn," he said with a sigh. "We lost Pinnace Two and her entire crew! Plus, we're flying blind; unless you know something I don't."

"If anyone can get us to Dagon, Guatt's the man to do it." Kirbey had told them after the jump that he had set the coordinates for Dagon as that was the closest base world. As Kirbey had explained, if the jump engines were going to fail, they wanted to be as close to a base world as possible.

"Otto, there are not many captains that could have outfought two Gilgameshers and come back to talk about it."

"Maybe, so. But I still feel like a failure. Only Satan knows just how much it's going to cost to repair our ship—again!"

Everyone was trying not to hold their breath as the *Corisande* reached the scheduled time to come out of hyperspace. Suddenly the screen changed from the grey of hyperspace to a twisting swirl of colors, then to the black of regular space. There were more than a few breaths let out along with some muted cheers. Harkaman saw Guatt Kirbey's back relax.

That changed a few seconds later when a there was a shrill warning of an alarm. The lights on the engine board started to blink and then suddenly—they all turned solid red. He'd never seen that before: it indicated total engine failure.

Harkaman felt as if his heart had jumped up into his throat. While Karffard started talking to Engineering to find out what happened, he turned to Kirbey. "Did we make it, Guatt?"

Kirbey refused to be rushed. "I'll find out. Just don't bother me for a while."

So they all had to sit and wait. After a few minutes, he said "I'm still checking references but everything looks good."

For Kirbey, that was the same as saying yes.

"I'll give you a precise measurement in few minutes," Kirbey replied. "But from what I can see, we're at the edge of the Dagon system, somewhere in their Oort cloud."

Everyone on the bridge signed in relief. The comm officer reported Kirbey's finding throughout the ship.

That takes care of one problem, he thought. *Now, on to the next.*

The officers were gathered together, sitting around a conference table, reviewing their situation. Van de Brost described the damage and what needed to be done to fix it.

"How soon can everything be fixed, Chief?" Harkaman asked.

Van de Brost snorted. "Hanging here in space, forever! We need a regular shipyard to do the repairs, Captain."

"Then we're stuck here?" someone wailed.

"Not at all," Van de Brost said. "The lift-and-drive engines are fine. We just can't jump—not even a microjump."

"How long will it take to reach Dagon?" Larch asked.

"We'll have to set a course," Van de Brost said, indicating Renner with a nod of his head. "I would think we can manage to get there in five to six months."

"That's about right," the normal-space astrogator verified.

"Five to six months!" Vann Larch exclaimed. "If we can get there that fast, how come it takes so long to travel by our normal space drive from our last in-system microjump to a planet's surface?"

Harkaman could tell that Van de Brost, who was normally very patient about explaining engineering matters to non-engineers, was feeling stressed, by the fact he looked ready to explode.

"Acceleration, right, Chief?" Harkaman quickly interjected, trying to calm the situation. Vann was a weapons guy and not a navigator or engineer.

"Yes," the Chief replied, relaxing a little. "We'll probably cover most of the trip in just a month or two once we've accelerated to our top speed based on fuel consumption. But it can take as long as two or three weeks to reach maximum acceleration. At that point, we shut down the drives to conserve fuel."

Vann Larch nodded. No one wanted to run out of fuel before

reaching their destination.

"All right, everybody," Harkaman said. "Pass the information on to the rest of crew," he indicated with nods to the various department heads in the meeting. "I'm sure that people will be relieved to know that we're not—" he paused dramatically, "trapped in hyperspace forever!"

That drew nervous laughter from everyone; some were clearly very relieved, as if they'd expected to be stranded for life. He stood up, figuring that it was good to end the meeting on an humorous, albeit nervous note. They'd have plenty of time to review any other problems on the way to Dagon.

Dagon

I

1715 A.E.

Alvyn Karffard moved restlessly in his chair, trying to quell his impatience. He'd been sitting in this anteroom for almost three hours. He had no idea why he'd been summoned here. The Master Shipwright at Dagon Spaceport had sat on their request for the cost estimate to repair the *Corisande* for two days. Then he told them they had to speak to someone at the palace.

Since Captain Harkaman already had a conference scheduled with someone who wanted to discuss a special cargo, he had asked Alvyn to attend the meeting. "Probably some palace functionary who wants a bribe," he'd said. "Find out what they want and, if it's a small amount—just pay it."

While there had been several other Space Viking captains present in the waiting room, they had at least been able to exchange some gossip, though he hadn't heard anything particularly earth-shattering. However, everyone found their battle and escape from Midgard fascinating, especially their hyperspace adventure. *They wouldn't find it so damn fascinating, if they'd just gone through it!*

But, for the last hour, he'd been sitting here all by himself. He just got up to stretch his legs for the umpteenth time, when a secretary entered, saying, "You may go in now."

Finally, he fumed, forcing himself to hold down his impatience. It had taken them close to four thousand hours to make the voyage from the edge of the solar system to Dagon. After the long journey from Joyeuse to Midgard, and then their journey to Dagon; well, everyone aboard the *Corisande* was more than a little stir crazy, himself included.

Alvyn actually wouldn't mind spending a month or so on Dagon. It was a pleasant enough world, the second planet of a K5 sun. He'd already heard of a couple places where he could go fishing, which was something he liked to do when he was groundside. It was also nice to look up and see a sky.

Once he got through the door, he found himself in another waiting room with the secretary seated behind a desk. This room was much more elegant than the previous one. Without a word, the secretary directed him to the door furthest on the right. As he entered, he wondered why there was a smirk on the secretary's face.

The room he entered was richly appointed but that wasn't what caught his immediate attention. Sitting behind a raised desk was Fedrig Barragon, the Lord Protector and ruler of Dagon. He paused, surprised.

"Lord Protector," he said, bowing from the waist. He didn't know what court procedures royalty followed here on Dagon, but typically a bow was pretty safe response. Barragon had been a successful Space Viking from Joyeuse when he started a base on Dagon twenty-five years ago. It was probably the least successful of the Space Viking bases, mainly due to Barragon's reputation for sharp trading, and the fact it was in a part of the galaxy where there weren't that many good worlds to raid.

Barragon pointed to a chair in front of the desk and told him to be seated. He was a fat, round-faced bald man, who appeared to be in his sixties. There were two other men in the room. One was in his early twenties and looked enough like Barragon that he had to be one of his two sons. He wasn't bald yet, but was packing on the weight. The other man held a tablet and had the look of a secretary. All of them were clean shaven.

No one said anything after he was seated. They just kept staring at him. He started to get uncomfortable and then realized that's why they were doing it. He schooled himself into holding the same bland expression that he used whenever he played poker on the *Corisande*. Finally the Lord Protector spoke, "I understand you are looking to do some repairs for your ship."

"Yes, sire."

Everyone in the room looked slightly annoyed, as if he had milk in his mustache. *I wonder if I'm supposed to use a different title… Just what is the correct address for a Lord Protector? I'll say your lordship from here on out.*

"We took some heavy damage on Midgard, Your Lordship," he added. They all looked a little less intense, so he concluded that must the proper title.

"Yes. Fighting Gilgameshers, I understand." Barragon's face had a bland expression but there was a hard look in his eyes that Alvyn didn't like. He agreed with his statement and waited.

There was another long silence until Barragon continued. "I have an estimate for your repairs." He held out his hand and the secretary handed him a document. He glanced at the document, then suddenly smiled. It was the smile of a predator which has its prey backed into a corner.

"The cost will be just short of thirty million stellars," he announced.

"What!" exclaimed Karffard. It was all he could do to keep from jumping out of his chair. The repairs should cost around eight million stellars, nine at most. "That's ridiculous," he said. "Your Lordship," he added carefully. Apparently that was the wrong thing to say.

"With that remark, the cost is now thirty-one million stellars," interjected Barragon's son, with a sneer.

"But, Your Lordship," he sputtered. "Those prices are…." he stopped himself. He was going to say outrageous, highway robbery!—but that would not have been diplomatic and might have cost them another million. "Sire, those prices are much higher than any other base world," he said as politely as he could.

Barragon leaned forward in his seat. He looked as if he was enjoying himself immensely. "Well, if you're unhappy with what we're charging, you can always go elsewhere."

But we can't, he almost spouted, *we don't have a working hyperdrive*, but restrained himself at the last moment, choking instead.

Suddenly, he understood why he'd been summoned and made to wait for hours; Barragon wanted to rub it in his face. The Lord Protector had them over a barrel. They were stuck here on Dagon with no alternative course of action except to pay whatever amount he determined to get their ship fixed. Taking a deep breath, Alvyn decided that it would be smartest to give Barragon what he wanted and crawl a little bit.

"Yes, Your Lordship," he said meekly. "Do you need me to sign the estimate? When can the repairs begin?"

"Oh, I don't think a signature is necessary," Fedrig Barragon said, a broad smile on his face. It was all Karffard could do not to leap to his feet and wipe that smile off his fat face with his fist. However, he didn't want to spend the rest of his life in jail or die slowly hanging from the end of a rope.

Barragon nodded to his secretary who said, "I believe that the repairs can begin as soon as you transfer the money to our account."

He swallowed hard; not only would the cost wipe out what little profit they'd made on the Midgard raid, but would clean out their Trans-World account as well. "We will make the transfer tomorrow, Your Lordship."

"Excellent," Lord Protector Barragon replied, continuing to smile broadly. "We look forward to a good relationship with you and the *Corisande*." He waved his hand in dismissal and turned to his secretary, starting to discuss another matter.

Karffard rose slowly from his chair and left the audience chamber in a state of shock. He was not looking forward to sharing this news with his shipmates.

II

To say that his shipmates didn't take the news well would be an understatement. There were loud cries of outrage.

"I'd like to hang that fat slob up by his toes!" exclaimed Vann Larch.

Harkaman was so agitated that he shot up out of his chair and stalked around the conference room of the *Corisande*, muttering to himself.

"Are all of the base world rulers crooks?" Sharll Renner asked. "We know Prince Viktor's a robber, Nikky Gratham's a liar and Barragon's a chiseler. The only straight-shooter has been Rolf Everrard on Jagannath. And maybe that's only because he hasn't screwed us yet!"

Karffard got tired of their complaints and told them to stop shooting the messenger. That calmed everyone down. By this point, they were enough of a team to know they had to work together. By unspoken consent, they all paused to refresh their drinks from the bartending robot.

"Where did he get the thirty million stellars figure from?" Vann Larch asked.

Karffard shook his head. He didn't know.

"Wait a minute," Harkaman said, who'd finally stopped prowling around the room. "I don't believe he chose that figure at random."

"What do you mean, Captain?" Ranjit Chaudry asked.

Harkaman resumed walking around the room, but this time he was deep in thought rather than just working off steam. He stopped suddenly and turned to Kirbey.

"Guatt, approximately how much do we have in spare funds, including what little our Midgard cargo brought in?"

They divided up their funds after each voyage like all Space Vikings. Unlike most crews, the partners kept their ownership funds in a separate account from their personal funds. Anyone else would have had to look up the numbers but Guatt Kirbey's facility with numbers allowed him to keep them all in his head.

"Roughly, a little over twenty million," he replied. "The repairs we underwent on Joyeuse burnt up a lot of our savings. Why?"

"What about personal funds?" Harkaman continued.

"Well, I don't know precisely how the rest of you spend your money," Kirbey said, sarcastically. Since Guatt only spent his money on music, and that infrequently, he would often kid the others about their spending habits. Particularly Vann Larch, who usually returned from any base world laden with canvasses and paints. Seeing from the look on his face that Harkaman was serious, he replied, "Probably ten to eleven million, depending on what you send back to the Sword-Worlds."

"Great Gehenna!" Karffard cried. "The bastard knew how much money we had, almost to the last centistellar. But how?"

"There's only one way he could know," Kirbey replied. "He's bribed the Trans-World banker!"

"Precisely," Harkaman replied.

"Yes, but the regional bankers are supposed to be paid so well that they're above bribery," Renner said.

"So they say," Harkaman offered. "But most people can be tempted; particularly a banker, who measures success in terms of how much money he acquires."

They all got his point. Although, they enjoyed having money in the bank, to them success meant having their own ship and being a successful Space Viking. The respect for achieving that, both personal and what they received from other Space Vikings, was worth more than money. They digested that for a few moments and then Renner spoke:

"This adds another complaint to our list," he said with a grimace.

Harkaman had already been to the local Gilgamesh colony. He had filed a complaint about the attack by the Gilgamesher ships on Midgard, along with a bridge recording of their battle. He had paid the local head of the colony five thousand stellars to transmit the complaint to Gilgamesh. They didn't know if anything would come of it. He had asked for compensation for the pinnace and the hundred and two lives lost, figuring that the Gilgameshers might take the complaint more seriously with a monetary claim included. The main reason of course was to try and prevent any future vendetta from Gilgamesh.

"Who can we complain to?" Kirbey asked. "It would have to be the local Trans-World banker who was bribed, curse him! He won't do a damn thing about it!"

Karffard nodded in agreement. "We'll have to send the complaint back to their headquarters on Excalibur."

He looked around the room and everyone slowly nodded in agreement.

"We'll have to visit Excalibur and make our complaint in person," Harkaman said. "If we try to do it here, Barragon will do his best to stop us. Maybe even lock us up." That was the problem with Space Viking base worlds, the rulers made up all the laws, then changed them whenever it suited them. Word of mouth, about this holdup, might well hurt Dagon in the long run, but Fedrig Barragon didn't seem too worried about it.

"If we're through with lamenting our current misery," said Paul Koreff, who had been silent during the discussion, "I have some interesting news."

"More gossip from the *Lamia*?" snorted Larch. The only other Space Viking ship currently on Dagon was the *Lamia*, with a blazon of a coiled snake with the head, bust and arms of a woman. The *Lamia* wasn't in the *Corisande's* class, either as a ship or as a crew. She was an old, fifteen-hundred foot diameter vessel. Poorly run, she was so well-known as a chicken-thief that the *Corisande's* crew had been deluged with requests from her people to join their crew.

He shook his head. "No, this news comes from a trader just come back from Jagannath. He picked it up from a fellow merchant ship. Our old friend the *Jolly Roger* is back in business."

That news got everyone riled up all over again. They had all wondered what Prince Viktor had done with the ship and whether or not he'd changed the name, since it had taken significant damage on Junrojin. However, the Xochitl repair docks could fix even the most serious damage and have the ship repaired almost as good as new.

Koreff had all of their attention. "The *Jolly Roger* recently raided the worlds of Maitreya and Kuanti. Did pretty well from what the trader said, though of course he hadn't heard of her selling the loot anywhere."

That was another puzzle they had pondered; where and how did the *Jolly Roger* dispose of her loot? Their best conclusion, after several brain-storming sessions, was that Prince Viktor must have a secret base somewhere that he used to transship the plunder to other ships.

"Maitreya is a trade world of Jagannath, while Kuanti is a trade world of Nergal," said Harkaman. "That fits Viktor's profile; it looks like he's back to attacking his competitors."

"That's not all," Koreff clearly relished being the possessor of the news. "She's also attacked two traders. One was from Hoth and the other," he paused dramatically, "was a Gilgamesher."

There were a variety of exclamations at that news. Once everyone calmed down he continued.

"Both attacks occurred on Kybele." That also made sense. Kybele was one of Hoth's trade worlds. It was also a planet that Space Vikings would occasionally stop at for a little R&R, since it was a lot cheaper than a base world and was known for good booze. That provided an incentive for traders to stop there, both to relax and to see if anyone had anything worth trading for. There was a Gilgamesh colony on the world for the same reason.

"The *Jolly Roger* caught the trader on the ground so there was nothing they could do but surrender and give up whatever they had in their hold," said Koreff. He paused to take a sip of his drink and a drag of his cigarette.

"And the Gilgies?" Chaudry asked.

"The Gilgamesher was a few dozen miles away at their colony next to the port city. They didn't take any action while they were looting the trader."

That wasn't unusual. Gilgameshers, typically, didn't intervene in the affairs of others.

"When the *Jolly Roger* was finished looting the trader, they rose up in the air, as if they were leaving. Then they suddenly swerved until they were right just above the Gilgamesher."

"Great Satan!" Renner exclaimed. "What do you bet that Viktor heard about that misdirection tactic when we had dinner with him on Xochitl?"

"Never mind that," said Harkaman impatiently. "What happened next?"

"Obviously no one knows what passed between the *Jolly Roger* and the Gilgie. But the Gilgamesher apparently refused to surrender. They tried to take off. The *Jolly Roger* fired on them but they didn't back off. Trapped on the ground they didn't have a chance," he finished. "So they were destroyed."

While everyone was digesting this information, Karffard asked, "When did this happen?"

"Almost two years ago," Koreff said significantly. "The way I figure it, it was when we were raiding Coventina or right afterward."

"But why didn't we hear about it before now?" Vann Larch asked.

Harkaman drew heavily on his pipe. "I'll bet we stayed just ahead of the news. Remember we didn't land on Xochitl because they were backed up on ship repairs, so we didn't pick up any gossip there. We most certainly beat the news to Joyeuse. Then we spent the last year traveling, mostly in hyperspace."

"Maybe that explains why the Gilgameshers on Midgard were so hostile," Kirbey offered. "They may have thought after the *Hellmouth* and *Thor's Hammer* attacked them that we were going to do the same thing the *Jolly Roger* did once we were done raiding."

That gave everyone something to think about. They had all wondered why the Gilgamesher ships had been so adamant about attacking them, pressing the attack even when the *Fairtrader* had been in bad shape. To defend their mining colony was one thing; to attack the *Corisande* when they were raiding people who didn't have anything to do with them was totally out of character.

Speculation continued, until Harkaman said he had something to talk about.

"Are you going to post the job openings at the tavern?" Larch asked, referring to the Swaggering Corsair, the local Space Viking port of call. "It would be nice to go out and have a drink without all the boys from the *Lamia* bugging us to join the ship. We could at least direct them to the list."

"No," Harkaman said. "Based on an offer I just received, I don't think we need to hire any more ground troopers here."

They all looked at him in surprise, waiting for him to explain.

"I met with someone who wants us for a special mission, an associate of Prince Hareld Elmersan of Durendal," Harkaman said. "He was looking for a ship to aid in the Prince's fight to take the throne from his cousin King Olaff Oskarsan. He's even agreed to our price, twenty-five million stellars in gold upfront."

There were a few gasps at that. Frankly, his partners had never expected any rebel faction to meet their demands. They had regarded their high price as a way to fend off the various rebel groups and dissatisfied nobles, who were always lurking on one of the Space Viking base worlds, looking for help to depose their king—usually on the cheap.

"They also agreed to let the *Corisande* loot some of the cities held by the Oskarsans after the battle. I've agreed to their offer."

"What!" Karffard exclaimed. Some of the others were just as surprised.

Renner jumped to his feet, his face showing his concern. "Otto, you should have consulted us before committing our ship," he shouted.

"You all agreed to follow me as captain," Harkaman put forth, his face coloring.

"During raids, yes," Larch said. "But we've always picked our targets together."

Before anyone could say anything else, Koreff interrupted, which was totally unlike him. "Perhaps you should tell us why you think this is a good idea, Otto."

Everyone calmed down a little and looked at Harkaman expectantly.

"I thought it was a good chance to rebuild our funds," he said. "Especially, after the robbery we just experienced here on Dagon. In addition, we're not going to be the only Space Viking involved. They said that they've signed up Sten Patel."

"Patel," said Karffard. "I thought I heard he'd retired and sold the *Widow Maker*."

Harkaman nodded. "He has. I don't know what ship he'll captain but that gives us another experienced captain."

"What else are they promising?" Larch asked.

"They claim they'll have a few armed merchant ships," he said. Everyone snorted at that. Freighters weren't typically built to fight. Most might have one missile control room armed with primarily defensive weapons. To give them offensive capacity, it typically required snaking a few missile tubes through a number of decks. Those jury-rigged systems were notorious for not working when they were most needed, which was why merchant ships usually dealt with armed opposition by running away.

"I agree," Harkaman said hastily. "But armed merchantmen are what we're likely to face. So having one or two of them on our side won't hurt."

"How do we know that the Oskarsans don't have any real ships that we'll have to fight?" Kirbey asked.

"Supposedly, they don't," Harkaman answered. "Look, I understand your concerns," he continued. "What I agreed to is that we'll meet with all the ships they have at Excalibur. If we don't like what we see, we can back out of the deal."

That mollified some of them, but not Karffard. "What if we find out when we reach Durendal that Olaff Oskarsan has half a dozen real ships. Will you back out after we've taken their gold?"

"Yes. If the opposition is greater than what they've told us, we'll leave. We can return the gold—to their heirs if necessary."

They all laughed at that. If a rebellion didn't succeed, there was only one end for the rebels, unless they could somehow get off-world. Kings did not tend to be forgiving.

"Why do you say we won't need ground troops?" Karffard asked. "If we're successful, don't we need some for looting?"

Harkaman nodded his head. "Yes. We've got about ninety ground troops left. I plan to jump to Jagannath to pick up Ranjit and however many of our troops remain. That should be enough."

Karffard looked like he wasn't convinced. But all he said was, "Let's see what we find out on Excalibur."

EXCALIBUR

I

1715 A.E.

Camelot Spaceport was full when they arrived at Excalibur and there was a four-day wait period before the next dock would be vacated. Otto Harkaman decided to go planetside with Sharll Renner in one of the *Corisande's* pinnaces along with those crewmembers who had family or friends living on Excalibur. He hadn't been there since that night many years ago when he and Alvyn had pledged themselves to one another. He took a moment to marvel at all that had happened since then and how they had managed to achieve their dreams. Then he returned to the task at hand.

The Trans-World Bank of Excalibur's headquarters was located in the tallest tower in Camelot City. The building was built out of faceted diamond glass and rose above the surrounding towers and spires like a giant scepter rising high above the city. It was the tallest and most expensive building on any of the Sword-Worlds and rivaled the legendary buildings of Montevideo and Sydney on Terra during the height of the Terran Federation.

At the main desk, they gave their names and said they had a serious complaint that needed the attention of the bank manager. The receptionist directed them to wait in a nearby lounge. After only a few minutes, much sooner than expected, she told them to proceed to the manager's office and directed them to the proper contragravity lift. The bank's main office was in the penthouse, at the twelfth-hundredth floor; the trip up the building in the lifter tube seemed to go on for ages, leaving Renner looking pale and sweating.

"We'll be there in a few minutes, Sharll," Harkaman reassured him.

Renner gulped. "I get a bit of claustrophobia when I'm in a small enclosed space for over a minute or two."

He thought that was a little strange for someone who spent most of their life in an enclosed artificial environment. On the other hand, there were rooms inside a two-thousand foot hypership that rivaled amphitheaters for size and spaciousness. Finally, the lift came to a smooth stop and the doors opened. Renner gulped and said, "I'll be fine. I just need a moment to catch my breath."

They waited for a few minutes before walking into a large anteroom, filled with framed artwork and statues, where a gorgeous receptionist, seated at a jet black desk, asked their names.

"Otto Harkaman, Captain of the *Corisande*, and Sharll Renner, Normal-Space Astrogator, to see Director Lawery." Lawery was the Trans-World Bank Manager of the bank as well as head of the Board of Directors.

She quickly typed something into her handheld. A few moments later, a chime rang out.

"You can see Director Lawery, now."

They heard the whoosh of a door and she personally escorted them into the Director's office. It was a large room done all in white; noticeable by their absence, there were no paintings, objects d'art, books or rare wall hangings. It was quite austere and the gray-haired man behind the large teak desk that dominated the room was almost as bleak. This was a place of business and nothing else: that was what the room and the Director himself declared before a single word was spoken.

They introduced themselves again, and the Director asked them to sit down. The first thing he noticed was that the wing-back chair was hard and uncomfortable; probably to discourage lingering.

"Gentlemen, I'm only seeing you now because in the past you've been major depositors," the Director Lawery said, with the wave of a hand, as though he were granting them a favor. "I've been informed, Captain Harkaman, that you and your crew have recently emptied your accounts and that you have a complaint you wish to discuss. Were you dissatisfied in any way with our service?" He made that question sound as if it were an improbability, at best.

"Not in general, Director," he replied. "However, we do have a complaint about your staff." He spent the next ten minutes outlining exactly what had happened on Dagon and how the Lord Protector had known the full amount of their joint deposits almost to the last centistellar. Then, knowing their vessel was disabled, he'd charged them many times the going rate for repairs. He finished with, "There is only one way that Lord Protector Barragon could have known the full size of our accounts would be with inside information. I suspect there's a leak—most likely at the top—within your Dagon branch."

The Director appeared shocked, almost as if Harkaman had removed his dirk and placed it at the Director's throat—which he was tempted to do.

"Our branch offices are manned with only the highest-caliber of professional bankers available in the Sword-Worlds and beyond. Our reputation is beyond reproach. Only the bank manager has access to the information contained the locked-account files, as you know. There has to have been some sort of mistake or misunderstanding."

Lawery actually looked worried, and Harkaman was certain he saw sweat beading on the Director's forehead.

"If you wish to hook me up to a polyencephalographic veridicator and take a veridicated statement from me I'd be happy to provide one," he said. "If I had thought we could have gotten a fair hearing on Dagon, I would have had your branch manager brought into court and hooked to a veridicator. However, due to the personal involvement of the planetary ruler, I assumed a fair trial would be impossible. If necessary, I will submit such a claim to the judiciary here in Camelot and they will subpoena your manager."

"These are very serious charges," the Director said, frowning. "However, there is no need for you to take any action here. I will personally send a representative to Dagon to put the bank manager under veridication—with you or your representative in attendance, of course. If the bank manager is not the guilty party, we will go down the chain of command until we find the party responsible. If we find you are correct, we will, of course, be grateful for your information and"—he paused—"your discretion."

'Excellent," he said. "I would have expected nothing less from your firm, which I have always held in the highest esteem, along with my Space Viking comrades. If any malfeasance is determined, I'm sure we can work something out."

"Of course, if your case is proven, we will reimburse your losses." the Director was smart enough to know that a captain of Harkaman's standing—Harkaman was certain that he'd been investigated thoroughly from the moment he'd given his name to the receptionist—could cause serious problems, maybe even damage the bank's reputation, if this issue were not cleared to everyone's satisfaction.

"We will be leaving for Durendal shortly and I know that it will take some time for your representative to reach Dagon"—almost half a year, since it was four thousand, two hundred light-years from Excalibur—"and an equal amount of time for your him to return. Since it is highly unlikely that either I or my officers will be on Excalibur, I will give directions to my local representatives, the legal firm of Vance, Jerningham and Volgarth to represent me and my partners.

The Director nodded with a satisfied look; he obviously was acquainted with the firm and approved of his choice. "Thank you, Gentlemen. I'm certain that in good time we can get to the bottom of this unpleasant matter and clear my firm's good name."

They didn't speak until after they left the Diamond Tower, since both men were convinced there were listening devices throughout the Tower. After all, it was only prudent.

Renner said, "Well, that went better than I suspected."

He nodded. "They have a lot to lose, a dissatisfied customer could cause them no end of grief."

Renner laughed. "Especially, one who's a noted and successful Space Viking captain!"

II

They waited at Excalibur for another ten days before the *Star Wanderer*, a merchant ship, from Durendal docked at Camelot Spaceport. Less than an hour after it arrived, the *Corisande* received an urgent message, calling for a captains' meeting aboard the newly arrived spaceship. Harkaman and Karffard left for the meet with numerous questions on their mind.

After boarding the merchant vessel, they were taken immediately to Count Rafael Pienaar's richly appointed cabin. Pienaar was a long-headed man with a large hawk nose and the air of a pampered aristocrat. Seated next to him was an older man wearing a captain's braid. The Count introduced him as Sten Patel.

A down-in-the-mouth old servant, with slopping shoulders, served them goblets of Curtana champagne, then quickly sat out of sight in a small alcove, patiently awaiting his master's beck and call.

After introductions and a quick exchange of background were completed, Harkaman asked, "My Lord, I was wondering just how many ships will be supporting our venture when we reach Durendal and how many will be opposing us?"

The Count's face expressed complete shock. "Why would you want to know that, Captain Harkaman?"

"Because Count," he replied grimly. "If we find out when we reach Durendal that the opposition is greater than you've told us, we're not going through with the deal." Ignoring the Count's outraged expression, he continued. "I would not take your money under those conditions. And if you continue the rebellion without me and fail, I would need to know your next of kin so I can return the money to them."

As Count Rafael Pienaar continued to sputter, the other man at the table spoke up. "Don't worry, Captain, I checked out the opposition. The Oaskarsans' have nothing but modified freighters. There're four of them. A fifth one is supposed to be back soon from a trading voyage."

Harkaman had never met Captain Patel but so far he had lived up to his reputation. He was a tall man with dark olive skin and a sparse white beard. What little hair he had left had gone white as well. His knowledge and credibility had been obvious as they talked and their conversation was easing some of his concerns.

"It's Prince Hareld's money, not mine," Count Pienaar announced, when he finally regained his composure.

Well, at least he's honest, he thought. The Count seemed to be a loyal supporter of the Prince, he'd probably been promised a dukedom or some such thing if the rebellion succeeded. He told him they'd deal with the issue if they needed to when they reached Durendal.

"I've put the freighter they gave me through some training along with Prince Hareld's other ship. They're about as good as they can be," Patel said. "But I'm not pretending they're anywhere near a regular Space Viking ship. That's why you're going to be in command."

Count Pienaar had objected to that; however, he'd backed down when Patel had told the Count that the best ship should lead.

"And the other ship's Captain?" Harkaman had asked.

"He's reliable," replied Patel. "He's a nephew of Prince Hareld. And he's captained a merchantman so he knows his way around a ship. But he's never had to do any fighting and he doesn't have any illusions about that. He'll do what you tell him to."

The Count returned to his discussion with Patel about how soon they should leave for Durendal. "Both King Svenn of Joyeuse and King Napolyon of Flamberge have said they'd support us," the Count said. "We should wait for their ships."

"The deadline for any ships to be here was yesterday and no one's come," Captain Patel stated. "The Prince asked me to bring the ships to Durendal as soon as Captain Harkaman arrived. King Olaff has sought help as well and he'd like us to get there before anyone else can."

While they argued, Harkaman thought about all the other changes he had noticed on Excalibur. While the spaceport was busy, he had counted only four Space Viking ships in orbit or on the surface. The last time he'd been to Excalibur there had been over three times that many. It looked as if his prediction that the Sword-World bases in the Old Federation would begin to dominate Space Viking commerce was coming true. However, the reduced Space Viking trade did not appear to have obviously affected Excalibur; there were over a score of merchant ships in orbit or docked in the spaceport.

As Patel and Pienaar wrapped up their argument by agreeing to stay another week, he brought up something that had concerned him more and more during their discussions. "It seems as if Prince Hareld's intention to rebel is widely known," he said. "Why hasn't King Olaff launched a preventive attack on him?"

Count Pienaar started to embark on a description of the politics of Durendal and the constraints on King Olaff, but Patel interrupted him. He knew what Harkaman was getting at.

"You'll see why when we reach Durendal," he said with a big grin. "Now let's have a drink."

Durendal

I

1715 A.E.

Captain Patel's meaning became clear when they reached Prince Hareld's city on Durendal. Durendal had four continents. One of them, stretching from almost the South Pole up to the northern temperate zone, was the largest continent Otto Harkaman had ever seen. It held the capital city of Roland, the seat of King Olaff Oaskarsan.

Prince Hareld was located on one of the other continents. In fact the entire continent was under his control. His principal city of Westport was ringed with dozens of missile launchers. Harkaman understood what Patel meant; no ships could attack the city without being overwhelmed by too many missiles to shoot down.

Their ships landed at the spaceport and later Harkaman joined Captain Patel and Count Pienaar in an aircar to the Prince's palace. They were quickly ushered in to see Prince Hareld Elmersan, who greeted them warmly. Hareld was a man of slightly above average height with dark skin and straight brown hair that reached his shoulders. He wore a van dyke beard that was just beginning to turn grey. As they talked Harkaman could see why the Prince had followers that were willing to support him in a dangerous rebellion. He had an easy charisma that made you like him. He had none of the arrogance that Prince Viktor had displayed.

"Count Pienaar tells me you are only interested in loot," Prince Hareld said after greetings had been exchanged and everyone had a drink in hand. "Are you sure you would not like a barony after Olaff is deposed?"

Harkaman thanked him but declined. The last thing he wanted to do was be subject to a king's whims. While Prince Hareld seemed to be a reasonable sort, he knew that could change in a moment. Instead, he directed the conversation to the topics he was concerned about.

"What do you know about the opposition we will face?"

One of Prince Hareld's advisors started to speak but the Prince gestured and he stopped.

"You will face two old twelve-hundred-foot freighters, the *Incitatus* and the *Elektra*, and two fifteen-hundred-foot freighters, the *Rozinante* and the *Invasor*. They also have a two-thousand-foot merchantman they've renamed *Olaff's Sword*. My spies tell me she's the best armed of the lot."

The advisor spoke up to give them the specifics of what they knew about the armament on all five ships. All were freighters that had been refitted with offensive missile capacity.

Harkaman wasn't particularly worried about their armament. Under most circumstances he would have felt the *Corisande* was the equal of at least three or four of them. His biggest worry was that one or more of them might turn out to be better armed than they thought, like the Gilgameshers had been on Midgard. However, the Prince's assistant was pretty specific about what they knew for each of the ships, which eased his mind. With the two armed merchantmen supporting the *Corisande*, he felt pretty certain they would have a substantial advantage in firepower.

"Do you know who their commanders are?" he asked, wondering if they had any command or battle experience. What he heard pleased him.

"Duke Salazar is in overall command and will be in *Olaff's Sword*," Hareld's advisor said. "Count Rudhall and Baron Kaungana command the *Invasor* and the *Rozinante*. I don't know who's commanding the smaller freighters."

When he asked if the captains had any combat experience, the advisor didn't seem to know and acted surprised that he'd asked. Maybe he considered being a noble experience enough. Sten Patel caught his eye and shook his head with a grin.

He then brought up his other concern. "I saw a number of ships in orbit. How do we know none of them are supporters of King Olaff?"

The Prince looked at his assistant. "We have checked them out," the advisor said. "They are all freighters, most from other Sword-Worlds along with two independents." He listed their names from memory.

Harkaman looked skeptical. "Did you actually send a ship to check them out or just take their word for it?"

The advisor looked insulted. "That's ridiculous," he said. "Our agents-inquisitory are the best in the Sword-Worlds."

Harkaman started to argue that it was well worth getting a second opinion, when the Prince intervened. "I think it's best if we focus on the attack," he stated firmly. Seeing he wasn't going to get anywhere, he acquiesced.

"My thinking on the attack route," Prince Hareld said, "is that you would head southeast, then go around the Boesak Mountains and approach Roland from the south."

Great, Harkaman thought, *another noble who wants to tell me my business.*

"But, My Lord," interjected Captain Patel, who had been quiet during all of the discussion. "That would add several hours to our trip and give Olaff more time to prepare."

"He's already prepared," Prince Hareld replied, impatiently. "We're not going to surprise him. If you head straight to Roland City, Olaff's forces will most likely meet you over the mountains. If you approach from the south, you'll be over heavily occupied territory for most of the journey. He'd never use a Hellburner there."

That actually makes sense, Harkaman thought, revising his opinion of the Prince upward.

Captain Patel wasn't so sure. "That will turn a four-hour journey into an almost seven-hour one."

"I've made my decision," the Prince said. That ended the discussion.

"If there are no other items to discuss, I'd like to attack tomorrow," Harkaman said. "I don't believe we should give your cousin any more time to get reinforcements."

The Prince seemed surprised by this. "But I would like you to meet some of my nobles, Captain Harkaman. They should know the men who are going to lead us to victory," he said, waving his hand and throwing his head back to add a rhetorical finish to his statement.

That's all I need, Harkaman thought. *Another time wasting meeting with men who think that because they're nobility, they know my profession better than I do.* He was tired of all the waiting around they'd done on Excalibur; he certainly didn't want to spend any more time on Durendal than was absolutely necessary. He wanted nothing more than to get the battle over, load the plunder into the *Corisande's* holds, and then leave the Sword-Worlds far behind.

Maybe I'm just uneasy because the Sword-Worlds seem so backward, he thought. *Or is it me who's changed?*

However, he reined in his impatience, making a more diplomatic statement. "We don't want to give"—he caught himself just before he said King Olaff—"Olaff a chance to get any more support. I can meet with whomever you like once you're seated as King of Durendal."

Prince Hareld smiled at the thought, swelling a little with importance and promptly agreed with him. They decided to leave a few hours before dawn so that they would reach Olaff's base early in the morning and have most of the day available for the attack. Captain Patel said he'd make certain that the other ships and their troops were ready. Those ships were carrying about eighteen-hundred ground troops; their job would be to conquer Roland after the ships defending it were destroyed or crippled.

Harkaman had made it very clear that his ground troops would not assist in taking Roland. When they had reconnected with Ranjit Chaudry on Jagannath, they had learned that less than a hundred of their ground troops had waited for them to return. The rest had gotten bored and found other berths. Ranjit had sold the loot and one of the pinnaces, with Trevor Mavuso's help, to cover expenses for the fighters who'd remained. They had hired a few more men on Jagannath before they spaced out, but the *Corisande* still had less than half of her normal compliment of ground troops. He remained convinced that they would have enough ground fighters to loot the larger cities, since they weren't expecting much opposition once King Olaff's navy was destroyed. Most of the King's troops would undoubtedly be concentrated at Roland, his capital and largest City on Durendal, leaving the planet's other cities woefully unmanned.

When Captain Patel stood to depart, he seized the chance to take his leave as well, draining his drink and telling the Prince that he had to get his ship prepared for the attack. Of course, the *Corisande* had been ready since she arrived. Nor had he any intention of sticking around after the battle. The moment the *Corisande's* hull was full of plunder, he planned to put the Sword-Worlds and its politics behind him.

II

"Ships taking off from Rocamadour Spaceport," Paul Koreff reported. "Two, Three, Four, Five."

They'd been underway for several hours and had just entered the airspace over the main continent. "That's it," he finished. "No other ships. If they come straight at us we should meet them in a little less than two hours."

Otto Harkaman nodded. Every system console on the bridge showed full readiness. Captain Patel's ship, the *King Hareld—presumptuous of the prince*, he thought—and the other ship, the *City of Westport* were on either side of them.

"Any change in course with the ships in low orbit?" he asked.

Paul Koreff didn't even need to glance at his instruments, showing that he was maintaining a continuous check on them. "No. Four of them are still in low orbit and the other six are in orbit between the planet and the largest moon."

He wasn't worried about the ships above the atmosphere. It would take them a few hours or more to reach the surface. The four in low orbit could get here in less than an hour, though. The fact that ships were parked in low orbit was not unusual but he still worried about them.

"Keep me informed," he said, settling back with his journal of notes on the worlds of the Old Federation. He had some updates to make to it based on his visits to the Royal Library on Excalibur. He'd also managed to squeeze in a visit to the local Westport library after the meeting with Prince Hareld and a final drink with Sten Patel. He'd just about finished all his updates when there was an announcement.

"Passing over New Falcon," Karffard said. New Falcon was one of the cities they had discussed looting. There were a variety of mines nearby so they expected to find a lot of metals there. "Looks like a lively place," Karffard continued. Since it had a population base of about two hundred and fifty-thousand people that made sense.

"We'll be at maximum firing range in about twenty minutes," Koreff announced.

"Put them on the main screen," said Harkaman. He studied the ships' alignment. The four smaller freighters were in a line with about a half-mile gap between each ship; the largest one was in the middle of the formation just above the center of it. *A good formation for concentrating firepower on a single ship*, he thought. But he'd already thought of a way to use that against them. He'd discussed a variety of tactical possibilities with Captain Patel based on the number of ships and what formation they might assume. He was happy that he wasn't seeing anything they hadn't talked about.

"Send to the *King Hareld* and *City of Westport* to widen out a few miles," he ordered. The ships were about two miles apart from the *Corisande* and he wanted them further apart. After they had done so a few minutes later, the two ships on the edges of the Oaskarsan fleet also spread out a little more.

"Head for the center of the three ships in the middle of the formation, Sharll," he directed Renner. "When we reach about half a minute before maximum firing range, go to full speed."

He turned to Vann Larch.

"Everything's ready, Captain," Larch reported before he could ask, causing him to grin. "The short-range guns are locked and loaded."

That was one of the advantages the *Corisande* had in this battle. The armed merchantmen had no short-range guns and he was determined to use that to his benefit, just as he had against the Gilgameshers on Midgard.

The tension grew on the bridge as the enemy ships came closer. He puffed on his pipe and tried to look relaxed, knowing that would help his crew stay calmer. About fifteen minutes later, Renner announced "Going to maximum speed."

"Begin firing," he ordered a few seconds later.

On the screen he saw missiles leaving the *Corisande* for the three Oaskarsan ships. He was gratified to see that they did not respond immediately. Then there were flashes of brilliance as defensive missiles met the attacking missiles. He yelled involuntarily as he saw several hits on each of the three merchantmen. He felt a jolt as one of their missiles got through the *Corisande* anti-missile defense. Then the short-range guns began to go off, joining the missiles pounding the ships. The screen showed one of the smaller ships turning away from them.

"Hairpin it, Sharll," he ordered. He heard Alvyn announce the hairpin turn over the intercom, and he reached out to grab a solid hold on his chair. Some items began to slide around on the bridge as they came about. They had discussed this maneuver the night before. Both he and

Patel were positive the freighters did not have the ability to match it. As he watched them on the screen, it turned out they were right.

"*Rozinante* is breaking formation and fleeing, Captain," said Koreff. "She's badly damaged." He checked his instruments further. "Medium damage to *Olaff's Sword* and *Invasor*. Mild damage to the other two ships and to the *King Hareld* and *City of Westport*."

As he'd hoped, the freighters were not able to turn as fast as the *Corisande*. They were also unable to maintain formation and were all spread out. He could face each of them individually now. "Head straight for *Olaff's Sword*," he ordered.

At extreme range, missiles began going out. He noticed even fewer missiles coming from the *Olaff*. Suddenly they had closed, the short-range guns began to fire.

Olaff's Sword exploded into a fiery ball of energy, shaking the *Corisande* as gale force winds buffeted it.

The bridge crew let out a cheer.

"*Invasor's* coming up," Koreff announced. "*Elektra* has turned and is a minute behind her."

"The *King Hareld* and the *Incitatus* are engaged," Karffard announced. "The *King Hareld* seems to be getting the better of her."

"Accelerate toward the *Invasor*," Harkaman announced. He didn't want to give them a chance to slow down and combine forces with the *Elektra*. He wondered briefly where the *City of Westport* was but then the *Invasor* came into range. Once again their volume of missiles was considerably less than the *Corisande's*. They passed by too far apart for the short-range guns to reach her. *So someone's learning tactics*, he thought grimly.

The *Elektra* began to fill the screen. There were a series of explosions in between them and he felt a few more jolts. Then they were close enough for the short-range guns to cut loose.

"Got her," Vann Larch yelled. The bridge roared as the *Elektra* burst apart into flaming chunks of metal and fuel.

The *Corisande* rocked from the nearby explosion.

"The *Invasor* is changing course and making her way down to the surface," his exec cried. "She's badly damaged. It looks as if she lost her lift capability."

They watched on the screens as the *Invasor* tried to land. She must have had some lift capacity left as she slowed down but not enough for a good landing. As she hit the ground she crumpled slightly and rolled for about half a mile. *There's another ship we don't have to worry about,* Harkaman decided. *She'll never fly again.*

"How are our comrades doing?" he asked.

"The *King Hareld* is headed toward us," Koreff said. "I don't see any sign of the *Incitatus*. They must have sent her to Em-See-Square."

That was the story. A grinning Sten Patel appeared on the screen. He had his hands clasped above his head in the way people shook hands via screen communication.

"Well done, Otto," he said, grinning from ear to ear.

"And to you as well, Sten," Harkaman replied, copying his gesture. "Where's the *City of Westport*?"

"He's about twenty-five miles back," Captain Patel said with a smirk. "After the first exchange of missiles, he was happy to leave the rest of the fighting to us."

"All right," Harkaman said. "Let's head for Roland."

III

Unlike Westport, Roland City was only defended by five missile launchers. The *Corisande*, *King Hareld* and *City of Westport* stood off about forty miles firing missiles to take them out but without success. After five minutes of this, Sten Patel was on the communication screen.

"It's not working, Otto," he said worriedly. "We've got to get closer to have any chance of overwhelming their defenses."

"We may not have taken any of them out but we're causing them to use up their missiles," he replied. "They can't have an unlimited supply of them."

"They don't," said Patel, "but neither do we. I'm down to just over a hundred missiles. I can't imagine that you have much more."

Actually the *Corisande* had many more. After the battle with the Oaskarsan fleet he had ordered the missile control rooms restocked with all the extra missiles he had on the ship. But he liked holding a few hole cards.

"All right," he said, turning to Alvyn. "Pass the word that in thirty seconds we'll head at Roland full speed."

They didn't catch the Roland missile batteries by surprise with their attack; in fact their volume of missile fire increased. When they were within five miles, he gave the order to fire offensive missiles. At two miles the short-range guns joined in the attack. He felt a jerk again as a missile got through the *Corisande's* defenses; as they closed in he felt another. Several of the missile sites erupted in flames as they passed over the city.

"Swing around for another pass, Sharll," he ordered.

He took a quick glance at the damage-control board. There were several red lights but none were flashing, showing the damage wasn't too serious. "How are our comrades doing?" he asked.

"The *King Hareld* is with us, she's suffered some more damage," said Karffard. "The *City of Westport*," he paused, "is about twenty miles away."

Harkaman snorted. At least Sten Patel was willing to put his life and ship on the line. Prince Hareld's nephew didn't seem to share his enthusiasm.

"Only two of the sites are still functional," Koreff announced as they closed in.

Then the missile volume increased, filling the space between the *Corisande* and the city. He felt a couple more shocks as some of the missiles got through and then he saw the remaining two sites explode into large fireballs.

"Well done, Vann," he said, relaxing back into his chair. The tough part of the job was now over. He looked at the damage board and saw several lights blinking. As he watched, all but one steadied, showing that they'd been sealed off and were no longer a problem.

"What's the damage, Alvyn?" he asked his exec.

"A couple missiles hit next to an existing breach," Karffard said. "Fortunately they didn't hit the opening directly. But there's now an open scar about eighty yards wide. A nice big target for someone to shoot at."

"Keep the crews working on it," Harkaman replied. "But we shouldn't face any more missiles this trip."

The *King Hareld* and the *City of Westport* started to land in an open park area in Roland. They had about four hundred ground fighters each, whose job it was to seize the palace and capture King Olaff.

Once the troops had started toward the palace Karffard turned and grinned at him. "Where do we start then?" he asked. "New Falcon or Tarija?"

That was easy. Tarija was one of the other cities they had identified as a good target and it was less than thirty miles away. He directed Alvyn there and sat back in his chair, stretching his legs out. With the adrenalin of the battle fading he suddenly realized he was hungry. He also wanted a drink but that was best left until the looting was done. He ordered a mess robot sent to the bridge. If all went well, they'd be leaving Durendal within a day or two with the cargo holds full to bursting.

IV

Tarija was an industrial suburb of Roland. It was noted for its production of robots, contragravity engines and power units. Depending on how much plunder they could accumulate, they might not even have to raid New Falcon. Paul Koreff broadcast the *Corisande's* intention to loot the industrial sites as they approached the city. He warned everyone that if they resisted, they would be killed, but if they stayed out of the way they would not be harmed, giving the inhabitants fifteen minutes to flee. As they hovered over the city, they began discharging pinnaces, aircars, one man air-cavalry mounts, grapplers, as well as contragravity lifters and loading vehicles; all the things necessary for plundering a rich city in record time.

Thousands of aircars and a variety of contragravity vehicles were observed quickly fleeing the city.

"Just concentrate on the industrial sites," Harkaman ordered, as he gave final instructions to Ranjit Chaudry. "Leave the stores and other areas alone. The big industries aren't likely to have many defenders, people will certainly fight for their homes and businesses."

The raid had been underway for over an hour. Harkaman was listening to the radio chatter with one ear tuned to the *Corisande's* ground fighters and the other to the attack on King Olaff's palace. Suddenly Koreff exclaimed, "Captain, two ships have broken low orbit and are headed this way!"

"It's a total cockup!" Harkaman cried out. Everything had been going smoothly; apparently, their luck was too good to continue. "Send our screen combination and ask them their intentions."

After a few moments Koreff spoke, "No response."

Harkaman let off a string of curses. "If they are just going to aid King Olaff that's one thing; but if they are going to attack the *Corisande*, why hadn't they attacked earlier?" He hadn't realized that he'd spoken aloud until Alvyn replied, "If you were trying to catch a ship at its most vulnerable point in a raid, Otto, when would you attack?"

"Right now, an hour into a raid with all the ground troops spread out." He turned to Koreff. "Call Ranjit and tell him to abort the raid. Order him to get everybody back to the ship."

This was starting to feel like Midgard all over again to him, another screw up. He was determined not to be separated from his ground troops again. Once Koreff was done talking to Chaudry, he directed him to keep monitoring the approaching ships and let him know when he found out anything.

He turned to Larch, but once again he was anticipated. "All missile control stations have been re-stocked and every system is battle ready, Captain."

Harkaman grinned at Larch's response. There was nothing to do but wait and see what the approaching ships did. The pinnaces started to trickle in to the *Corisande* at the rate of about one every fifteen minutes. Koreff had determined that one of the ships was two thousand feet in diameter and the other was fifteen hundred. There continued to be no response from their communication attempts.

Then someone announced "I have visual, transferring it to the main screen."

The image flickered, then stabilized. A second later an explosion of swearing erupted from almost everyone on the bridge. One of the ships was the *Jolly Roger.*

"That damned Vik—" Renner started.

"Quiet!" Harkaman yelled out, before he could complete the name. They had kept the knowledge that Prince Viktor was behind the *Jolly Roger* to just the senior officers. None of the junior officers knew about Viktor's piracy and he wanted to keep it that way. The more people that knew about it, the greater chance of it leaking back to Xochitl. Renner turned to him, an apologetic look on his face.

"Let's focus on the battle," he said in a quieter voice. "Take us up as soon as the last pinnace docks, Sharll."

"The smaller ship is called *Star Stalker*," Karffard reported. "Has anyone heard of her?"

Everyone shook their heads. Koreff called out, "She's got to be a freighter; she's putting out a lot less juice than a Space Viking ship."

He wondered if this was a freighter from Xochitl that Viktor had modified and renamed. Before they could discuss the matter further, Koreff announced, "Signal coming in."

The communication screen lit up. Just as the last time they'd communicated with the *Jolly Roger* on Junrojin there was no video.

"*Corisande*," the voice said. It was distorted enough that Harkaman couldn't tell if it was Captain Trevithick or not. "If you surrender your ship, you will not be harmed. We know you are low on missiles and cannot survive a battle with us. All we want is your ship. You may leave the ship and go wherever you want and we will not interfere."

Harkaman laughed harshly. He was joined in that laughter by his senior officers while many of the others on the bridge looked on, amazed that the command crew could laugh in the face of disaster. The *Jolly Roger* couldn't know about all of the extra missiles they had on board. He had been careful to keep that a secret during any repairs and restocking of the ship. As for letting them go, they'd be left in the middle of a city they were looting and on a continent where they'd just led a rebellion against a seated king. He wouldn't give a single fig for any of them surviving.

"The last pinnace is aboard, Captain," Karffard said, staring at him expectantly.

"Go at full speed, Sharll," he said. "Head straight at the *Jolly Roger*."

As they approached the *Jolly Roger*, he wondered why they had waited an hour to attack. Were they here primarily to attack and try to capture the *Corisande*? That didn't seem likely. Though it was no secret on Excalibur that they were going to help Prince Hareld's rebellion, they had only been on the planet a few weeks. That wasn't enough time for a ship to travel to Xochitl, tell Prince Viktor the news, and return to Durendal with orders to attack the *Corisande*. No, most likely they were here because Viktor decided to help King Olaff. Perhaps he was getting the same twenty-five million stellars from Olaff that they had received from Count Pienaar.

But then why did they wait an hour to join battle? Was Prince Viktor playing more than one game here: Did he want to reduce King Olaff's navy so that he would be more dependent on him? Did Trevithick decide to improve his standing with Viktor by defeating or capturing the *Corisande*? Or had Olaff deliberately delayed them as a way to get rid of some ambitious nobles? By Satan's Black Heart, the political possibilities of all this could drive a man insane! He was happy to just be a ship captain.

Once they reached maximum range, the missiles started going out again. He noticed that Renner had turned the ship to keep the open scar on the side away from the *Jolly Roger*. The *Star Stalker* was headed for

Roland so they only had one ship to contend with. He heard one of the junior officers announce that the *King Hareld* was off the ground and heading to engage the *Star Stalker*.

The screen flickered from bursts of brilliance as both ships' missiles were met with counter-missiles. He felt a few jerks indicating some missiles had gotten through and then the ships were close enough to pound each other with their short-range guns.

As the *Corisande* slowed, he noticed that the *Jolly Roger* wasn't turning but was headed for Roland. Karffard and other bridge staff had turned and were looking at him for direction. "Orders, Otto?" asked Renner.

He found himself caught on the horns of a dilemma. They could keep going and probably escape Durendal without further problems. They would only have the small amount of loot in the pinnaces but there was twenty-five million stellars in gold in their vaults. He had not promised anything more than to defeat whatever navy King Olaff put together so that Prince Hareld could land troops on Roland. After that they were done.

At the same time Sten Patel had played fair with them. They owed him something. The *King Hareld* might be able to fight off the *Star Stalker*, but there was no way they could defeat the *Jolly Roger*. As for the *City of Westport*, he checked the screen, yes, they were already fleeing. Abandoning both the *King Hareld* and their troops in Roland. Then he realized, with a surge of emotion, they owed the *Jolly Roger*, and through her, Prince Viktor something as well.

"Top speed, Sharll," he ordered. "Head straight at them."

He saw Alvyn grin at him from the corner of his eye. Yes, they owed the *Jolly Roger* a pasting and they were about to pay off a long overdue bill.

Koreff said that the *King Hareld* had finished exchanging fire with the *Star Stalker*. He told him to contact Patel when he had a chance. In seconds a grim faced Sten Patel appeared on the screen.

"How are you doing, Sten?" Harkaman asked, as his face appeared on the main screen.

Captain Patel shook his head. "Not good, I'd feel a lot better if we had more missiles. I think I've only got enough left for one or two more attacks."

"Pull away from the *Jolly Roger* then," he replied. "Let us handle her."

Patel nodded and the screen went blank. He asked Koreff where everyone was at the moment.

"The *King Hareld* is a dozen miles away and is fleeing. The *Star Stalker* is after her. The *Jolly Roger* is firing on the troops in Roland." He waited a few seconds. "They must have detected us; they just turned and are now headed straight for us."

After a few moments, Koreff announced, "*Jolly Roger* is changing course. I think they've spotted that nice target on our side."

He started to direct Renner to keep the ship turned away from them, then realized he was already doing it. A few moments later they were in range and missiles began to spew from both ships. As they closed in, the *Jolly Roger* changed course again. They weren't successful in getting a shot at the vulnerable spot on the *Corisande* but the maneuver took them out of reach of their short-range guns.

If he thinks we're low on missiles, he wouldn't want to come near enough for our short-range guns to reach him, Harkaman thought. Then his thoughts were redirected.

"*Jolly Roger's* hair-pinned," yelled Karffard, with a few descriptive adjectives added.

"Sharll," he ordered. "Match his maneuvering so we can bring him in reach of our short-range guns."

Once again they were in range and missiles were exchanged. This time he felt a some jarring shocks from missiles they were unable to intercept. He also shifted involuntarily in his chair with everyone else on the bridge as Renner quickly changed course to stay with the *Jolly Roger*. Then their short-range guns hammered away at the *Jolly Roger*.

He's got to believe we're maneuvering close to him to use our short-range guns, he thought. *Maybe he'll become more reckless thinking we're running out of missiles.*

"Otto, *King Hareld* is approaching," Karffard said.

"Where's the *Star Stalker*?" he asked.

"She's about forty miles off but turning this way, Captain," Koreff reported.

"Captain Patel, what are you doing?" Harkaman asked as Patel's visage came on the communication screen.

"We ran off the *Star Stalker*," Patel said, with a grin. "We've got enough missiles left for one more go. I figured I'd lend you a hand."

He paused, not knowing what to say. He would have preferred that Patel keep the other ship out of the battle but it was too late for that.

"By Satan's horns, I've missed this," Patel replied, with a strange grin on his face. "See you on the other side Otto!" With that the screen went blank.

"Sharll, try and get the *Jolly Roger* between us and the *King Hareld*," said Harkaman.

As Renner acknowledged, he looked at the damage control board. The damage was extensive but nothing too serious. A look at the *Jolly Roger* showed her with as much or more damage.

"Vann," he said. "They'll try and maneuver to stay out of reach of our short-range guns. If you can anticipate where they'll go, see that our Hellburner is waiting there for them."

Larch smiled wolfishly and started speaking rapidly into his communicator. Then the three ships were within range. He saw the *Jolly Roger* veering off toward the *King Hareld* to stay away from the *Corisande* as missiles spewed out from all ships. On a separate screen, he watched the progress of the Hellburner as it approached the *Jolly Roger*, firing its own defensive missiles to intercept those coming at it. The ship loomed large in the screen then everything went white as the explosion overloaded the system.

"Did we get him?" he yelled. Then he saw an exploding ship on the screen and began to cheer. So did everyone else on the bridge, except one.

"That's not the *Jolly Roger*," said Koreff, disappointment on his features. "That's the *King Hareld*." The cheering changed abruptly to angry swearing.

Koreff checked his instruments. “But we’ve hurt the *Roger* bad,” he announced. The picture he put on the screen showed a huge gash on the north side of the *Jolly Roger*. They must have been able to detonate the Hellburner just a little ways away from the ship. He wondered how the crew on that side of the ship was doing.

“*Star Stalker’s* approaching fast!” yelled Karffard. As the two ships passed one another with missiles flashing between them Harkaman felt the short-range guns fire along with several more blows from missiles that got through. *How much more damage can we take?* He asked himself? Then he saw the *Star Stalker* come apart into numerous chunks of red and flaming metal.

“Missiles coming in from the *Jolly Roger*!” Karffard yelled.

“Let her have it, Vann,” Harkaman cried.

Once again he saw a series of flares on the screen as the ships approached. The *Jolly Roger* was desperately trying to turn away from them but appeared to have lost some maneuvering capability. The short-range guns fired again. Then there were some small jolts followed by a big one that rocked the ship. Klaxons were ringing and he smelled the astringent odor of burning metal and plastic. He swore as he saw several lights turn red on the board

“Captain, the bloody engines have been hit!” Karffard shouted.

“Missile rooms Two and Three are gone, Otto!” Larch yelled out.

Harkaman got out of his chair and headed toward Karffard. He felt the room sway slightly as he did. *That’s not good*, he thought.

“How bad is it Alvyn?”

Karffard was checking a variety of readings on his board. “The jump engines are fine,” he said. Harkaman sighed with relief.

“But the lift-and-drives are badly damaged, Captain. We might lose them.”

“*Jolly Roger* is badly hurt, but she’s coming back!” Koreff cried.

He turned to Larch. “Can we fire at her, Vann?”

Larch nodded.

“Then give her everything we’ve got. We can’t take much more!”

Larch began pressing a variety of buttons on his console. As Karffard discussed the situation urgently with Chief van de Brost in Engineering, Harkaman watched the main screen. As the *Corisande's* counter-missiles hit the incoming missiles he prayed none would get through and hit anything vulnerable. If they could finish off the *Jolly Roger* and get the *Corisande* back to Westport, they should be able to get repaired and safely off world.

His attention focused on screen showing one of their missiles approaching the *Jolly Roger*. This had to be their fifty-megaton missile, which would be the largest they had left. He watched as it approached closer and closer to the *Jolly Roger*. Then the screen went white with a blaze of energy. He didn't have time to cheer as he felt another jolt and started to float off the deck. The lift-and-drive engines had failed. They were in free fall.

He grabbed on to the back of Karffard's chair as his legs started to rise in the air. "Alvyn get the Chief on the line and find out how bad it is and whether or not he can fix it," he said.

Karffard turned with a stricken look on his face. "The engineering room's been destroyed. The Chief is dead."

Dead! How could an ageless wonder like Chief Van de Brost be dead? The answer came in a second. *Because I failed him. I failed them all.* Harkaman felt a moment of despair that he pushed away. He reached over and hit the ship wide intercom on his console.

"All hands, abandon ship! Repeat, this is the Captain, all hands abandon ship!"

The junior officers on the bridge immediately started heading toward the exits. They, and the rest of the crew, would be moving as fast as they could for the pinnaces and aircars. The senior officers, his friends and comrades through many a tough situation, were staring at him. Accusingly? No, they were waiting for further orders. He felt a surge of emotion. A man couldn't have any better friends than these.

"Guatt, get to the combat car and get it ready," he ordered. There was a combat aircar adjacent to the bridge for just this situation. He didn't know why none of the junior officers had gone there. Guatt could pilot the combat car and there wasn't anything left he could do on the bridge. Kirbey headed for the door leading to the combat car.

"How long do we have before we hit the ground?" he asked.

"Less than two minutes, Otto," Koreff replied

"The *Jolly Roger*?" he asked.

"Gone to Em-See Square." Karffard said, grimly. "At least we took that Satan spawned bastard with us."

They all grinned. He saw Renner was still pressing buttons futilely on his console.

"Sharll," he said, as gently as he could. "Give it up, head for the combat car." He turned to the rest of them. "The rest of you, as well. There's nothing else we can do."

They all stood up but no one moved toward the combat car. He looked at them puzzled. What were they waiting for?

Finally, Karffard looked him straight in the eyes. "Lead the way, Captain." he said formally.

Now he understood. They were afraid he might mirror the actions of some old sea captain and go down with the ship. Well, he wasn't ready to give up hope. He pushed himself over to the captain's chair, grabbed his recently updated journal and put his datapad away, then led the way to the aircar. Once there he crossed to the other side of the combat car and opened the door into the main corridor in case anyone was coming that way. He didn't see any of the crew; they were either loading on to one of the pinnaces, or dead. The rest of his friends seated themselves.

"Thirty seconds, Captain," Renner, who'd seated himself next to Kirbey inside the combat car, counted down.

Then he heard a yell. He looked down the corridor and saw Ranjit Chaudry and another man, pushing themselves as hard as they could.

"Come on, Ranjit" he yelled, waving to him.

Seconds later there was an explosion inside the ship. The combat car tilted under him, nearly pitching him out the open door. He slapped his hand against the wall to hold on but felt it starting to slide. Then his wrist was grabbed by Karffard, who reached over him and slammed the door shut. He looked up and saw the other man was down and Ranjit had grabbed him.

The ship twisted and the corridor collapsed on the two men. Karffard pushed him down toward the floor.

"Go, Guatt!" Karffard yelled.

The launch of the combat car and its sudden acceleration hurled Harkaman against the dashboard. As he sank into unconsciousness he had only one thought: *I've lost everything.*

V

Otto Harkaman was doing his best not to give in to complete and total despair. He'd not only lost the *Corisande*, he'd lost most of his crew and all of his funds when he'd picked the wrong side in the fratricidal civil war on Durendal. His insistence on getting the pinnaces back on the ship before engaging the *Jolly Roger* had cost him Ranjit Chaudry, a friend he'd known him for almost twenty years. Unfortunately, there was no time to mourn.

The only things he had been able to salvage were the clothes on his back, the weapons in his belt, his datapad, his log book and the emergency funds he kept in a money belt. Fortunately he was also able to save his precious journal, which he had been updating before the battle; it held most of his historical research into the worlds of the Old Federation and their value as raiding targets.

The winning cousin, King Olaff Oaskarsan, had put a price on his head but was too occupied in wrapping up the remnants of the battle with the Elmersans to enforce it. With Alvyn Karffard, Vann Larch, Guatt Kirbey, Sharll Renner and Paul Koreff, who fractured an ankle from a freefall impact. They had returned to Westport and hurriedly sold the combat car for what they could get, which wasn't much more than the cost of off-world passage and medical treatment for Koreff's badly injured leg.

They'd purchased passage on the *Endless Sea*, a freighter from Quernbiter, which had been on Durendal to deliver supplies to the Elmersans. Now that their employers were out of business—that is, having their necks stretched—the traders were as anxious to leave the war-torn world as Harkaman and his partners were. He didn't know what the rest of their crew—at least those who had survived the battle and left the *Corisande* by the surviving pinnaces—had gone after they landed. *They'll just have to wing it*, he decided.

With the destruction of the *Corisande*, he had lost the one thing he valued most in his life. Now, with more than two decades of hard work down the drain, he was in the unfortunate position of having to start all over again.

Quernbiter

I

1716 A.E.

Quernbiter was a Sword-World founded from Excalibur, four hundred years ago. It was not a wealthy world. The planet rested at the outer limit of the G4 sun's habitable zone and was a cold and dreary world. Most life resided in the equatorial zone and it depended upon Space Viking raids for economic survival. As a result, Quernbiter was a major launching pad for Space Viking expeditions. Over a fifth of the adult males were either actively serving on Space Viking ships, had served on ships at one point during their lives, or were part of the spaceport workers and industries that serviced, repaired and restocked the ships.

Without the money they brought in from raids in the Old Federation, life on Quernbiter would have been brutish and dismal indeed. This should have made it an ideal place for an unemployed Space Viking captain and his surviving officers to look for work. However, after several weeks of searching, Harkaman was growing disheartened; most of the employers and investors he talked with wanted crewmen, not a captain. And many captains were obviously hesitant to hire a successful former captain, especially one who'd lost his ship. He had no desire to go backwards and become someone else's executive officer or raid commander. If he did, it might take him another decade or so to earn enough money—if the ships he joined were profitable, and not every Space Viking ship was—to even begin to think of buying his own ship again.

The only solid offer he received was a promise of a ship from King Valgard if he returned to Durendal and supported Hareld Elmersan's continuing fight against his cousin. He was surprised to learn that Hareld had survived the blood-letting that had followed the failed uprising. He'd had more than enough of Durendal; however, he told the King that he would think it over in case he discovered they didn't have any other choice.

II

Rovard Grauffis was coming to the end of his tether. His friend and employer, Duke Angus had sent him to Quernbiter in search of a captain for the new hypership being built at the Wardshaven shipyard. He had known Angus all of his life; he had been his father's young squire who was assigned to take him to and from school. It had been a schoolyard tussle between Angus and his distant cousin Omfray that was the basis of their lifelong friendship. Angus was the bigger of the two boys, but Omfray had a crazy streak that erupted violently when he was angry. They boys had been playing kick the castle when one of Angus' feet had connected with Omfray's backside, which led to gales of laughter at the smaller boy's expense. Omfray cried, "Foul!" and began to beat Angus around the head and shoulders with a stick he'd picked up off the ground.

When Rovard saw Angus lose a tooth and get his eye almost poked out, he decided to intervene. Being much older and bigger he quickly made hash of little Omfray, busting his nose and giving him a black eye, thereby gaining his lifelong enmity in the process. But, at the same time, he had also gained the trust and friendship of Angus, who was now Duke of Wardshaven and Gram's richest and most important noble. He was the Duke's top aide, taking care of his problems and making sure things ran smoothly.

Now, Duke Angus wanted to become king of Gram, but that took lots of stellars, more than the Duke could squeeze out of his subjects. And the best way to get that kind of money was to steal it from somebody else who already had it; thus, Angus' plan was to launch his own Space Viking ships and plunder the Old Federation. And, the best way to do that was to establish a base world near the edge of the former Federation. Then his ships could raid constantly, thereby avoiding all the two- to three-thousand hour trips back and forth from the Old Federation to Gram to off-load cargo. Instead, Angus could use one of his freighters to run the plunder back and forth, saving the hypership for forays into the Old Federation.

It was an inspired plan, but, so far, it had been a bust. The first of Angus' ships, the *Enterprise*, was close to its launch date but needed a captain. There was no end of unemployed captains on Quernbiter, but they were an unimpressive lot. Most were out of work due to incompetence, drinking too much on the job, stealing from their employers or worse. During his visit with King Valgard, the king had mentioned hiring a down-on-his-luck Space Viking captain by the name of Otto Harkaman. That had sparked his interest and he'd asked around about Captain Harkaman.

Harkaman had recently arrived from Durendal, where he'd picked the wrong side in the long-running dynastic battle and lost his ship in the ensuing war. Every Space Viking he talked with at the Company of

Glory—the local spacer watering hole and port of call—had nothing but good things to say about the now shipless captain. He'd even encountered a former shipmate who knew him well.

"Yeah," replied Carlos Ericsan, "I knew Otto Harkaman. I spent thousands of hours with Otto on the ol' *Fortuna* and the *Manticore*. He was in command of the ground fighters and did a great job—too good of a job some might say."

"What do you mean by that?"

Ericsan looked around, as if to see if anyone nearby was listening, before continuing: "Sir Rovard, Harkaman was always suggesting ways to fight better, how to pick better target worlds and get more booty. The *Fortuna's* captain and his exec considered him to be a royal pain-in-the-ass. And, they let him know that in no uncertain terms, so he left the ship."

"Were his ideas bad ones?" Grauffis asked.

He shrugged. "Actually, Harkaman put some of his ideas to work when we were raiding. And they were damn successful, even if they occasionally went against the way Space Vikings normally do things. The captain didn't always like his independence, even when it made him money. But, yeah, he was full of good ideas."

"So would you recommend him as a possible captain, or not?"

"Oh, sure, I'd recommend him. Very few Space Viking crewmen ever earn or save enough money to buy their own ship, which, by the gods, Harkaman and his partners did. And none of them started at the bottom as he did. Plus, he was always studying."

"Studying? What do you mean?"

"Every time we landed on a Sword-World, or Viking base world, Harkaman would go to the nearest spaceport bars and dives and interview every spaceman he could find—especially the older and decrepit captains and supercargos. All for that bloody journal of his. He wanted to know about every raid or trip they'd made in the Old Federation, where the systems were and what kind of civilization they had. Liked to drive the rest of us nuts, when all we wanted was a quick drunk and a roll in the hay with some doxy.

"He also collected old logs and ship journals, some from the Federation days; if he could find them. Got to be if we couldn't find Harkaman, we'd search the local junk stores, emporiums and curio shops. He also spent a lot of time at libraries once our raids were wrapped up. By Satan's hooves, the man had more micro-books and journals than any man I've ever known! Some of us even called him Professor. Probably because he knew more about the history of the Old Federation than most history professors; after all, he'd visited a lot of those worlds, while most of them educators are just desk jockeys who've never even left their home system. Can't say that about Harkaman, he probably seen more of the Old Federation than any three captains combined."

III

Otto Harkaman had been nearing the end of his patience when he'd been contacted by Rovard Grauffis, who claimed he represented a duke on Gram who wanted to hire a hypership captain. He had offered to meet with Grauffis at the Company of Glory tavern. Sir Rovard was a small and unsmiling man with wide shoulders. It was quickly evident that Rovard was straightforward in his search for a captain who was both experienced and hardheaded enough to command the respect and loyalty of a top-notch Space Viking crew. It was clear he was impressed when Harkaman told him he had five top men, who had served as his officers and who had been with him for almost two decades.

After giving a brief rundown of his raiding experiences, Harkaman finished with, "Sir Rovard, I've got information covering almost all of the 'known' raid-worthy planets in the Old Federation. It's a project I've devoted my life to, something I've been working on for over twenty Galactic Standard years. The major problem facing Space Viking raiders, when going into the former Federation territory, is locating the right objectives, worlds that are both advanced enough to be profitable but not so advanced that their ship takes too much of a beating during the raid.

"I've spent years accumulating old ship logs, memoirs and astrographical ledgers, as well as interviewing experienced captains, so that I could learn which ones were the best target worlds and which ones are garbage worlds. This is why I was successful enough that I and my team were able to purchase our own ship."

"What happened on Durendal, then?" Rovard Grauffis asked.

Harkaman decided that the truth was probably the best answer to that question. "When Hareld Elmersan offered me a payout of twenty-five million stellars to support his side, kill his cousin and help him restore his family to the Royal Throne, I signed on. In addition, Hareld agreed that we could loot Olaff Oskarsan's cities as long as we were careful not to damage them too much. It had the makings of a good deal, but unfortunately we didn't know his cousin would have many more ships on his side than Hareld knew until it was too late."

"If you were such a successful raider, what did you need the twenty-five million stellars for?"

He sighed. "On Joyeuse, I joined up with three other ships to try and take advantage of the shortage of neodymium that occurred after the Lugaluru mine was destroyed. According to former Federation records, there were several neodymium mines on Midgard."

Grauffis frowned. "What shortage? I don't recall hearing of any."

"That was the ultimate irony," he relayed. "The neodymium shortage was already being remedied by the time we reached Midgard. It turned out there were several neodymium mines on other worlds that hadn't been profitable enough to operate at the going rates until word got out about the price increase, then these mines were suddenly put back into production. Even if we had returned from Midgard with holds full of neodymium it wouldn't have provided the financial windfall we had expected."

"Plain bad luck."

He briefly described the results of the raid and the battle with the two Gilgamesher ships. "Our jump engines were damaged so we didn't know how many hyperspace jumps we had left. We jumped to the nearest base world which was Dagon before the engines gave out. They knew they had us over a barrel and overcharged us everything they could. So the all the needed repairs wiped out all of our spare funds." Then his face fell. "Sadly, trying to rebuild our funds quickly cost me and my partners our ship and livelihood."

Grauffis had heard enough. He stood up to leave and extended his hand, which Harkaman took and shook. "I'll have to give this careful consideration. I'll contact you in a day or two when I've made up my mind."

IV

Harkaman spent an anxious two days waiting in the cheap spaceport hotel he was sharing with his comrades. He made certain that at least one person was always in the room to answer the viewphone if anyone called. Everyone but Vann Larch was currently out looking for work. Vann Larch was painting on a canvas, while he was doing a poor job of concentrating on the journal he was reading. Selling Vann Larch's paintings was bringing in more stellars than all of the temporary work everyone else had found.

He almost catapulted out of his chair when he heard the viewphone chime. "Hello, Harkaman here."

"It's me, Rovard Grauffis," a voice replied, gruffly. "I believe you may be the right man to captain the Duke's ship, but I can't hire you on my own. You'll have to come back to Gram with me on the Duke's hyperyacht and talk with Himself and the other investors. Is that doable?"

"Yes. When do you want to leave, Sir Rovard?"

"Is two hours too soon?"

"No sir. I'll be at the spaceport in an hour and a half. What about my officers?"

"You can find new ones on Gram," Grauffis said.

"Not experienced ones," he rebutted. "These men are hand-picked and have proven their mettle. Besides, they're my partners: it's a package deal."

Grauffis paused, looking thoughtful. "What the Gehenna, it won't cost us anything to bring them along. Can they make it on time?"

Harkaman laughed. "Count on it."

He quickly screened Alvyn Karffard and told him to gather what was left of the crew and meet him at the spaceport.

"So the Gram party came through?" Karffard asked.

"Sort of. We're headed for Gram for an audition."

"It beats sticking around here. Do you think you'll to get to captain their new ship?"

"Yes, if I jump through the right hoops."

"Well, then, start jumping!" Alvyn said with a laugh.

Now, all he Harkaman to do was convince the investors on Gram that he still had what it took to raid the Old Federation and bring home the bacon. During the ninety-five hour journey to Gram, he spent most of his time going over his journals to pick the ideal spot to launch a series of raids that would not only cement his authority as a top captain, but be profitable enough that he could use his shares to eventually purchase another ship. He had a good list drawn up by the time they arrived at Wardshavenport. On top of that, he'd even come up with what he thought might be the ideal base world—Tanith.

Gram

I

1716 A.E.

After disembarking, they were taken to the Excelsior, obviously one of the finest hotels in Wardshaven, where they were given the keys to a penthouse suite. In the contragravity lift, Baron Grauffis informed Harkaman that Duke Angus owned the hotel and reserved this suite for visiting dignitaries and good friends. It was a far cry from the dingy quarters they'd shared on Quernbiter; he had a good feeling about the way things were going for the first time since the loss of the *Corisande*.

It was early evening and the two of them had just finished a fine dinner at the hotel restaurant. Before saying goodnight, Grauffis said he'd see him in the morning. "First, we'll tour the Gorram shipyard, then I'll show you the *Enterprise*—Angus's pride and joy! I think you'll like her, Harkaman. Hell, you're gonna love her! Then I'll take you to the Duke's mansion for lunch, and you can meet Duke Angus and the rest of the investors."

For the first time in months, Harkaman went to sleep with a light heart and no worries pressing down upon him.

The next morning, Sir Alex Gorram himself gave Harkaman, Duke Angus and Rovard Grauffis a personal tour of the two-thousand foot hypership named the *Enterprise*. The most prominent of the Xipototec Investors accompanied them: Sesar Karvall, an industrial baron; Burt Sandrasan, Karvall's brother-in-law; Lothar Ffayle, a rotund banker; Nikkolay Trask, a lawyer; and Count Hilgrim Viallo, a prominent businessman and Baron Rathmore, a gentleman adventurer. They all oohed and aahed at the craftsmanship and the commanding presence of the huge ship. The inside, especially the bridge, was a bit too luxurious for his taste. But it was a solid ship with a first class weapons inventory.

"Nice work," he said to Gorram. "I haven't seen any better work, even on Excalibur. I see it's already spaced out at least once."

Gorram's face split into a smile. "Yes, I took the helm for a quick shakedown cruise around the system. I can say in all honesty, she's the finest ship to come out of our yards."

Harkaman gave a nod of approval; he, too, believed a man should take pride in his work.

Back in Gorram's private office, he asked pointedly if any of the investors had any questions.

Lothar Ffayle, the rotund banker, spoke first: "Captain Harkaman, I'd like to know just how long you believe it will take for us to recoup our investment?"

Several of the men laughed nervously. He noticed that Nikkolay Trask appeared to be the most interested in his reply. *Probably mortgaged down to his socks*, he thought. "Good question. Do you want the comforting answer or the honest one?"

Eyes widened all around.

"The honest one," Duke Angus growled.

"First off, there are no guarantees on a Space Viking multiple-planet blitz. On a quick hit-and-grab raid, looting a handful of worlds, a good ship can pull in thirty to fifty million stellars, sometimes more. That is, if you can find the right worlds to hit."

There were smiles at that announcement.

"Hit the wrong ones and you can lose your shirt, or maybe even your ship. I plan to avoid those."

There was an uncomfortable titter of laughter.

"The more profitable target worlds," he continued, "are also the best defended. So a ship usually has to hit the repair docks after a good run, and that can cost a few million stellars depending on the damage. Even with no ship damage, just restocking supplies, replacing weapons stores and missiles and updating engines and other ship's systems can run from four hundred thousand to a million stellars. The crux of the matter is: It doesn't matter how good or powerful your ship is, if you don't know which planets to raid and which ones to stay away from, you're not going to make any money. And that's where my expertise is second to none."

"How is that?" Angus asked, everyone else deferring to the Duke.

He went on to give them a brief summary of his years of raiding Neobarbarian worlds, then expounded on his diligent search through various sources for the best and most up-to-date information on the many planets of the Old Federation.

"Well, you talk a good job, Captain," Duke Angus said. "And you've certainly given us better answers than the other captains we've interviewed."

All the investors nodded their heads in agreement.

"And Rovard seems to believe that you can shoot stellars out your arse."

That led to some uncomfortable laughter.

"Does anyone else have anything to say?" the Duke asked.

No one was foolish enough to reply.

"Then, we are agreed. Captain Harkaman, you will be the first captain of the *Enterprise*."

"Thank you, Your Grace," he said with smile, taking the proffered hand to seal the deal.

A bottle of Colada champagne was uncorked and everyone had a drink, most of them congratulating him on his new job. He thought the champagne was the correct choice of beverage, since Colada was his birth world and good omen of things to come. He knew one thing for sure; his raids had better prove successful or he might lose both his command and his head, if Duke Angus had anything to do with it.

II

The next morning Harkaman awoke with a slight hangover and a feeling that finally things were beginning to go his way. There was an incoming call on the viewscreen and he suddenly felt a lump deep down in his stomach.

He wondered what was up when he saw Rovard Grauffis' face fill the screen. "Good morning."

Grauffis grunted; he looked as bedraggled as Harkaman felt. "Otto, the Duke wants to talk with you in private."

"Okay, Rovard. I'll need a few minutes to get cleaned up and dressed."

"Fine. I'll meet you in the restaurant for breakfast."

Grauffis, though a little worse for wear, seemed to be his usual gruff self. Maybe it was just an informal meeting without the interference of the other investors. He hoped so; he'd had enough bad news to last a lifetime.

They had a quick breakfast, then Rovard took him in his aircar to the Ward Tower, the highest building in Wardshaven. They flew onto the landing deck on the fiftieth level and the Duke's henchman escorted him to Angus' private office. It was surprisingly austere; he'd imagined it would appear more like a Neobarb king's royal presence chamber. *Maybe it's just for business?*

Angus, looking a bit like a gnome perching on a stool, sat on a chair half-again higher than the one Rovard had directed him to sit on. Like many small men, Angus appeared to have a bit of an inferiority complex.

"I invited you here for a private audience, Captain, because I didn't want any interference from the other Xipototec Adventure investors. Some of them are timid, like the Trask boy, while others are too aggressive—they even talk of raiding one of the civilized worlds!"

The Duke leaned back and lit a cigarette.

He decided that meant it would be all right for him to smoke and took out his pipe. The Duke didn't object and he packed and tamped it while thinking over what he was about to say. He didn't want to insult anyone, but it didn't appear to be Angus's idea so he decided it was best to be direct.

"Attacking a civilized world is not only a bad move, but suicidal, Your Grace. What your investors don't realize is that worlds like Isis and Odin all have their own navies. It would take a large fleet indeed to tackle any one of them, and might very well bring retribution from the others. The last thing any of the civilized worlds want is to be vulnerable to a Space Viking raid. Any such attack could very well result in a combined Aton, Odin, Baldur, Vishnu and Isis armada against the Sword-Worlds."

The Duke looked positively worried. "You mean if they were attacked, they might come here? Is that really a possibility? I always heard that Aton and Odin were deadly enemies."

"If sufficiently provoked, that could change in an eye blink—and, believe me, an attack on a civilized world by a Space Viking fleet would be a provocation of such magnitude it might very well force the civilized worlds to combine their might against their common foe. The result would be disastrous for the entire Helm!"

Duke Angus shuddered. "That's the last thing I want. I need money and lots of it; not more trouble. I've got enough troubles here on Gram with all its fractious lords and long-held grudges over territorial boundaries."

Harkaman had heard stories about the curse of the Blackcliffe's, the Duke's family. While placid on the surface, underneath Gram was seething with political discontent and madness. No wonder people were so anxious to get off-world. Sadly, too many of the Sword-Worlds were ruled by unstable leaders or incompetent ones. He wondered if that, in and of itself, was an indictment of Sword-World industrial feudalism.

The Duke threw his hand to one side, as though to dismiss the issue. "What I wanted to discuss with you in private is the site we've picked for our base world in the Old Federation. Upon the advice of several advisors, I have selected Xipototec as the site. What are your thoughts, Captain?"

Harkaman had given this a lot of thought ever since he'd learned the expedition into the Old Federation was called the Xipototec Adventure. From Angus' manner, he knew he had to be very careful on just how he presented his ideas. The Duke was the kind of hot-head, know-it-all who, when he lost his temper became completely irrational. "It's an obvious choice for someone who's never been to Xipototec. Have you, Your Grace?"

"No, I was basing my selection on what Baron Rathmore told me. He's been on two or three raiding parties and made enough money on those raids to become an investor."

"If the Baron has only been on a few trips into the Old Federation, I doubt he has the knowledge to make an informed decision about something as important as your base world." The implication being that he did. It was also obvious that while the expedition was called the Xipototec Adventure, it was Angus, not the investors who called the shots.

Duke Angus nodded. "What do you know of Xipototec?"

"First, the planet is very distant from its star, which is an A-type—very hot. The saving grace is the world has a lot of water. Grimm's Star is also very young and life only appeared on Xipototec within the last hundred million or so years, which is very recent. The local life forms are primitive and mostly sea based."

He lit his pipe and drew down on it. "It was originally colonized by a religious group calling themselves the Jan Dharma—a strongly pacifist religion, originating on Terra. They believe in spiritual salvation through enlightenment. The religion emphasizes non-violence against all life. The Janis left Osiris because there were growing rumors of war and they wanted to get as far away from any future conflict as possible. They selected Xipototec because it was farthest world, at that time, from the heart of the Federation. Plus, it has no natural fauna. Although it is a big world, 1.4 Galactic Standard in size; it has a gravity of .9 Galactic Standard, meaning it has very few metals and no valuable deposits of radioactive ores and rare earth elements. This was important to the original settlers, since Xipototec would offer little incentive for outsiders to visit."

Angus looked concerned, as if he could see where this was going.

"Xipototec took very well to transplanted Terran flora and fauna, especially since there were no competing plants or animal life. The colonists were careful to only import those insects and birds absolutely necessary for the plant life to flourish. Under their stewardship the land became very lush and grows a *lot* of foodstuffs, especially grains and cereals. Over the millennia this has led to an enormous population growth, making this world an ideal place for slavers but not much else.

He noticed Angus, while looking more concerned, did not seem to be getting angry. He continued:

"The last I heard the population was over twelve billion. The world has nothing else to offer but passive workers who make malleable slaves. Technologically, it's been stuck at a pre-industrial level ever since the Federation collapsed. The few weapons they have, mostly for protecting themselves from wild boars, are spears and long knives. Not that the Xipototectites would ever use a weapon in anger, not even to protect themselves and their families."

Angus' face turned beet red. "Rathmore said it was a peaceful place where we'd find lots of cheap labor. He said their silks and embroidered clothes are prized throughout the Old Federation."

"Maybe, but how much are textiles and silks worth? Not the kind of stellars you need to pay off the investors. Plus, the locals are worthless as workers because they're only useful for hewing and carrying—we've got robots and contragravity sleds to that. You can't use them as fighters; they won't even lift a hand to protect themselves! Taking slaves is for ships that have fallen on hard times; there's no profit to it, since none of the civilized, or even half-civilized, worlds allow slavery. Only backwater planets buy them. And they don't pay much. On top of that, the spaceport there is a complete wreck. I don't know of any base world without a working spaceport for landing and repairs. To rebuild the spaceport would cost north of fifty million stellars."

"Fifty million! Rathmore sure sold me a bum ticket," Angus said, visibly restraining his temper. "I'm glad you set me straight before we traveled there and learned the truth. Do you have an alternate selection for a base?"

"Tanith. It's what is known as a fringe world, that is, another one of the last planets colonized by the Federation before the Big Break-up. I raided there right after I took command of the *Corisande*; it wasn't a profitable stop. Tanith is uncivilized; technologically, it's still in the waterwheel/gunpowder stage. In the Space Viking vernacular, it's known as a chicken-stealing world, with little loot to be obtained, which means it won't be visited very often by other Space Vikings. But the locals are fighters and many of them, if needed, can be recruited and trained as ground fighters.

"And it has a spaceport with minimal damage, which only needs to be cleaned up to be put back in use. Tanith's located some three thousand hours from Gram; it's in an area where there aren't any nearby base worlds. However, there are a lot of nearby worlds that could be raided profitably. Overall, it's an excellent place for your Old Federation base world."

Angus gave a sigh of relief. "It sounds like a much better choice than Xipototec. How long will it take you to get a crew together, Captain?"

"I've got my men working on it right now. I'll need a deposit of a hundred thousand stellars to set up operations. I brought along my bridge crew but I'll need to recruit around three hundred crewmen to handle the ship along with five hundred ground fighters."

"Good." Angus paused to open a desk and take out some bills. He handed ten of them to Harkaman, saying, "These are ten-thousand stellar notes. I suggest you use these to set up an account at the Planetary Bank of Gram. I'll screen Lothar Ffayle and let him know you're coming."

As the Duke left, Harkaman hard him muttering, "If that bastard Rathmore wasn't an investor, I'd put him in jail and throw away the key…."

III

Using the Duke's advance, it took Otto Harkaman and Alvyn Karffard only a few weeks to put together an experienced crew for the *Enterprise*, including hiring some five hundred ground fighters. It appeared that everyone on Gram was excited about the Tanith Adventure, as it was now called, and he'd had to turn qualified people away. The only dark cloud on the horizon was that the Duke wanted his henchman, Rovard Grauffis, to act as commander of the ground forces. On the other hand, it could have been a lot worse; Duke Angus might have wanted to take over and lead the expedition himself!

He reminded himself to be thankful for what he could control and not worry about people and things out of his authority. Once they were space-bound, then he would be firmly in charge.

Now, he had to dress and get ready for a pre-wedding party at the Karvall mansion. Attendance was mandatory since it was the union of the farming and ranching barony of Traskon and the Karvall steel mills. Since both houses were now allied with Duke Angus, it was practically a public holiday. Almost all of the city's businesses and industries had closed down to celebrate the event. There would be celebrations throughout Wardshaven for the next two days. It was another symbol, like the *Enterprise* herself, of Angus' growing power and ambition.

Fortunately, the bridegroom was Baron Lucas Trask of Traskon, not the weak-chinned Nikkolay who was an investor in the Tanith Adventure.

Harkaman had just finished pinning his cravat, which was the local style of formal dress, when Baron Grauffis knocked at his door. He wore his gold braided Space Viking captain's jacket. *Have to look the part*, he thought. As they left the hotel, he noticed that the place was empty other than the desk clerk. *They do take their holidays seriously here*, he noted.

The reception was held at Sesar Karvall's mansion at the outskirts of Wardshaven. Grauffis had the airtaxi drop them off at the gate. Two guardsmen, wearing the black and yellow of the House of Karvall, bowed and then quickly opened the door. It was obvious that Grauffis was well-known and respected by the Karvall retainers.

They stopped to shake hands and talk to Sesar Karvall, their host. He had some questions about the Tanith Adventure.

"Captain, isn't it getting to be a little late in the game to wrest fortunes out of the Old Federation? I hear more Space Vikings are returning home without a lot to show for their efforts."

"My answer would have to be: yes and no."

That got a chuckle out of the older man.

"The short answer is: there's still a lot of loot left in the Old Federation. However, many worlds have been plucked down to their bare bones."

Sesar paused as a gorgeous young woman approached him and whispered into his ear. He turned, saying, "Captain, this is my daughter Elaine—the bride-to-be."

He bowed. "Glad you meet you, Lady Elaine. I'm Otto Harkaman, soon to be captain of the *Enterprise*."

She smiled, lighting up the garden. "Yes, it's the talk of the town. I hear about nothing else but the Tanith Adventure these days, even at the beauty shops!"

They all got a good laugh out of that.

"Gentlemen continue," she said. "I've got to find Lucas."

"Nice meeting you, Lady Elaine," he said as she passed by and went up the escalator.

Sesar turned back to him. "So what's the answer, Captain, if so many worlds have been plucked clean, as you put forward?"

"Better research, sir. I've spent the last several decades traveling around and through the Old Federation, visiting different worlds, talking with other captains, studying old logs, going through libraries and reading memoirs. There are still valuable target worlds out there; they're just not low-hanging fruit anymore. One has to dig them up, or combine with other like-minded captains and raid the more advanced worlds in squadrons."

"Sounds expensive, Captain. And, I suspect, few captains are willing to spend the time and money on research as you have done."

He nodded. "I agree. And more and more expeditions into the Old Federation will end in failure or poor results."

"After hearing you talk, young man, I'm glad you're the captain the Duke chose to helm his ship. You should have seen some of the other choices, like his crazy nephew."

Out of the corner of his eye, Harkaman saw Rovard Grauffis with a young man he hadn't met before. From the comments of passersby, he took him to be the bridegroom. He was a tall man, although not as tall as himself. He had blond hair, a neatly trimmed beard and strong features, unlike his cousin. He also had a commanding presence that Nikkolay lacked. It appeared Grauffis was bringing him along for a meet.

"Lucas, this is Captain Harkaman," Rovard Grauffis said.

"Pleased to meet you, Captain."

"A pleasure, Lord Trask," he opined. "I've met your lovely bride-to-be, and now that I've met you, let me congratulate both."

They shook hands then Trask had a word with the bartending robot, who gave him a glass of wine.

"You're not an investor in the Tanith Adventure, are you?" he asked.

"No, I'm not. I've left that pleasure to my cousin, Nikkolay."

He had to stifle a laugh. Obviously, Lucas was the brains of the clan.

"Lord Trask does not approve of the Tanith Adventure," young Basil Gorram, son of Alex, said scornfully. "He thinks we should stay home and produce wealth, instead of exporting robbery and murder to the Old Federation for it."

He held his emotions in check. It wouldn't do to insult the man of the hour and one of the Duke's most important liegeman. He unobtrusively shifted his drink to his left hand, just in case things got out of hand.

"Well, our operations are definable as robbery and murder," he agreed. "Space Vikings are professional robbers and murderers. And you object? Perhaps you find me personally objectionable?"

"I wouldn't have shaken your hand nor had a drink with you if I did. I don't care how many planets you raid or cities you sack, or how many innocents, if that's what they are, you massacre in the Old Federation. You couldn't possibly do anything worse than those people have been doing to one another for the past ten centuries. What I object to is the way you're raiding the Sword-Worlds."

"You're crazy!" Basil Gorram exploded.

There were few things that annoyed him more than being told he was crazy just because he suggested something that wasn't current wisdom. He found himself annoyed now even though it was another man who was being accused.

"Young man," he reproved, "the conversation was between Lord Trask and me. And when somebody makes a statement you don't understand, don't tell him he's crazy. Ask him what he means. What *do* you mean, Lord Trask?"

"You should know; you've just raided Gram for eight hundred of our best men. You've raided me for close to forty vaqueros, farm-workers, lumbermen, machine-operators, and I doubt I'll be able to replace them with as good." He turned to the elder Gorram. "Alex, how many have you lost to Captain Harkaman?"

Lord Trask then spoke to all of the employers in the room, having them detail all the personnel they had lost. It was an impressive list. Harkaman had raided this planet for a lot of good men. He could have mentioned that most of them undoubtedly left because he was offering an opportunity for better pay and faster advancement in life by being a Space Viking, rather than staying on Gram. But, he decided to keep his mouth shut. He was quite impressed with Lord Trask. Clearly, he was a very bright man and there was a lot of truth in what he was saying.

He turned to Basil Gorram. "You see, the gentleman isn't crazy, at all. That's what happened to the Terran Federation, by the way. The good men all left to colonize, and the stuffed shirts and yes-men and herd-followers and safety-firsters stayed on Terra and tried to govern the galaxy."

"Well, maybe this is all new to you, Captain," Rovard Grauffis said, his mouth twisted, "but Lucas Trask's dirge for the Decline and Fall of the Sword-Worlds is an old song to the rest of us. I have too much to do to stay here and argue with him."

Lothar Ffayle threw his two cents in: "All you're saying, Lucas, is that we're expanding. You want us to sit here and build up population pressure like Terra in the First Century?"

"With three and a half billion people spread out on twelve planets? They had that many on Terra alone. And it took us eight centuries to reach that."

Harkaman nodded. Trask was right, just like Spain during the Age of Discovery, the Sword-Worlds were decivilizing. It was easier to steal goods than to make them. They continued their argument, or discussion, depending on one perspective, when he got an uneasy feeling at the back of his shoulders. Unthinkingly, he reached for the pistol he usually wore on his belt.

People were quickly advancing to the escalators. Voices were rising. News cars were circling above, like vultures—a Terran imported bird that seemed to flourish on every habitable world. *Maybe a fight?* Otto asked himself.

"Some drunk being bounced," Nikkolay, Lucas' cousin, commented. "Sesar's let all Wardshaven in here, today. But, Lucas, this Tanith Adventure; we're not making any hit-and-run raid. We're taking over a whole planet; it'll be another Sword-World in forty or fifty years."

They continued their discussion, but Harkaman was too distracted by the possibility of a fight to pay much attention. *Am I bored and looking for a diversion*, he wondered. Then he became aware that they were talking about other parts of Gram that apparently not as civilized as Wardshaven.

"Why, there's a miserable little war down in Southmain Continent that's been going on for over two centuries."

"That's probably where Dunnan's going to take that army of his," the robot-manufacturing baron said. "I hope it gets wiped out, and Dunnan with it."

Dunnan, where had he heard that name before? Oh yes, Grauffis had mentioned him. The Duke's nephew, apparently not a favorite either. He'd told the Duke that he'd gather his ground fighters and put paid to Dunnan's account, but he'd turned him down—something about a blood relationship.

"You don't have to go to Southmain; just go to Glaspyth," somebody else said.

"Well, if we don't get a planetary monarchy to keep order, this planet will decivilize like anything in the Old Federation."

"Oh, *come*, Lucas!" Alex Gorram protested. "That's pulling it out too far."

"Yes, for one thing, we don't have the Neobarbarians," somebody said. "And if they ever came out here, we'd blow them to Em-See-Square in nothing flat. Might be a good thing if they did, too; it would stop us squabbling among ourselves."

Harkaman looked at him in surprise. "Just who do you think the Neobarbarians are, anyhow?" he asked. "Some race of invading nomads, Attila's Huns in spaceships?"

"Well, isn't that who the Neobarbs are?" Gorram asked.

"Nifflheim, no! There aren't a dozen and a half planets in the Old Federation that still have hyperdrive, and they're all civilized. That's if 'civilized' is what Gilgamesh is," he added. "These are homemade barbarians. Workers and peasants who revolted to seize and divide the wealth and then found they'd smashed the means of production and killed off all the technical brains. Survivors on planets hit during the Interstellar Wars, from the Eleventh to the Thirteenth Centuries, who lost the machinery of civilization. Followers of political leaders on local-dictatorship planets. Companies of mercenaries thrown out of employment and living by pillage. Religious fanatics following self-anointed prophets."

"You think we don't have plenty of Neobarbarian material here on Gram?" Trask demanded. "If you do, take a look around."

"Glaspyth," somebody said.

"That collection of over-ripe gallows-fruit Andray Dunnan's recruited," Rathmore mentioned.

Alex Gorram was grumbling that his shipyard was full of them; agitators stirring up trouble, trying to organize a strike to get rid of the robots.

"Yes," Harkaman pounced on that last. "I know of at least forty instances, on a dozen and a half planets, in the last eight centuries, of anti-technological movements. They had them on Terra, back as far as the Second Century Pre-Atomic Era. And after Venus seceded from the First Federation, before the Second Federation was organized."

"You're interested in history?" Rathmore asked.

"A hobby. All spacemen have hobbies. There's very little work aboard ship in hyperspace; boredom is the worst enemy. My guns-and-missiles officer, Vann Larch, is a painter. Most of his work was lost with the *Corisande* on Durendal, but he kept us from starving a few times on Quernbiter by painting pictures and selling them. My hyperspatial astrogator, Guatt Kirbey, composes music; he tries to express the mathematics of hyperspatial theory in musical terms. I don't care much for it, myself," he admitted. "I study history. You know, it's odd; practically everything that's happened on any of the inhabited planets happened on Terra before the first spaceship."

Suddenly a hush fell over the garden. All he could hear was the clank of the robo bartender. People were huddled over by the landing-stage escalators.

He was about to comment, but then he saw five or six of Sesar Karvall's uniformed guardsmen run past. They were helmeted and in bulletproof armor; one was carrying an auto-rifle, while the rest carried knobbed truncheons. He finished his drink and set it down.

"Let's go," Harkaman said. "Our host is calling up his troops; I think the guests ought to find battle-stations, too."

IV

A crowd of well-dressed rubberneckers were flooding the landing-stage, blocking the Karvall guardsmen who were trying to board the escalators. Four Interplanetary news-service cars hovered above, searchlights stabbing down to illuminate circles of thronging party goers.

The guards sergeant pleaded: "Please, ladies and gentlemen; your pardon, noble sir," but was unable to break through the milling crowd.

Otto Harkaman cried, "By Satan's Black Mass, make way here! Let these guards pass." He shoved his way past two gentlemen, who turned to protest—one with his fists raised—until they saw his size. He pushed his way to the front of the landing stage, where Rovard Grauffis, Sesar Karvall, Alex Gorram and Burt Sandrasan stood frozen.

Facing them were four men in black cloaks who stood with their backs to the escalators. From their demeanor, Harkaman could tell that two of them were retainers, hired gunsels. He wondered what they were doing at a wedding.

At the forefront, was a thin man with a pointed face and a pencil moustache. His eyes were wide open—all but popping out of his head. His mouth was twitching and grimacing. At his side was a taller man with black beard and a frozen look on his face—like a bisonoid caught in a ground car's headlights.

"You lie!" the man was shouting. "You lie damnably, in your stinking teeth, all of you! You've intercepted every message she's tried to send me."

The man turned out to be Andray Dunnan, Duke Angus' nephew. He spewed forth a series of statements about how Lady Elaine really loved him and that she was being forced into marriage with Lord Trask. Sesar Karvall and Rovard Grauffis tried without success to convince him otherwise and, failing that, to convince his friend—who was referred to as Sir Nevil—to get him out of the room before Duke Angus arrived. It was clear to Otto that Dunnan was stark raving mad and living in a complete dream world.

Finally, Lady Elaine arrived, attended by a variety of matrons, all with shawls draped over their heads, which seemed to signify rejection. She demolished Dunnan's claims, telling him she'd sent no messages, didn't love him and that she was marrying Lucas Trask of her own free will.

This caused an immediate change in Dunnan's demeanor; he called her a harlot, his uncle a usurper and accused everyone present of scheming against him and denying him his rights. Finally, his friend Sir Nevil succeeded in convincing two nearby retainers to help him drag Dunnan away, with the man cursing and screaming all the while.

Trask's face was a mask of restrained anger.

"Lucas, he's crazy," Sesar Karvall was insisting. "Elaine hasn't spoken fifty words to him since he came back from his last voyage—"

Trask visibly restrained himself, then laughed and put a hand on Karvall's shoulder. "I know that, Sesar. You don't think, do you, that I need assurance of it?"

"Crazy, I'll say he's crazy," Rovard Grauffis offered. "Did you hear what he said about his rights? Wait till his Grace hears about that."

"Does he lay claim to the ducal throne, Sir Rovard?" Harkaman asked, sharply and seriously.

"Oh, he claims that his mother was born a year and a half before Duke Angus and the true date of her birth falsified to give Angus the succession. Why, his present Grace was three years old when she was born. I was old Duke Fergus' esquire; I carried Angus on my shoulders when Andray Dunnan's mother was presented to the lords and barons the day after she was born."

"Of course he's crazy," Alex Gorram agreed. "I don't know why the Duke doesn't have him put under psychiatric treatment."

"I'd put him under treatment," Harkaman said, drawing a finger across under his beard. "Crazy men who pretend to thrones are bombs that ought to be deactivated, before they blow things up."

"We couldn't do that," Grauffis said. "After all, he's Duke Angus' nephew—"

"I could do it," Harkaman said. "He only has three hundred men in this company of his. Why you people ever let him recruit them Satan only knows," he parenthesized. "I have eight hundred; five hundred groundfighters. I'd like to see how they shape up in combat before we space out. I can have them ready for action in two hours, and it'd be all over before midnight."

"No, Captain Harkaman; his Grace would never permit it," Grauffis vetoed. "You have no idea of the political harm that would do among the independent lords on whom we're counting for support. You weren't here on Gram when Duke Ridgerd of Didreksburg had his sister Sancia's second husband poisoned—"

Harkaman was beginning to get the idea that the Duke was wrong about a lot of things. He was beginning to wonder what constraints he was going to find himself under as captain of the *Enterprise.*

I'll be damned if I'm going to bow and scrape before the wisdom of Angus, he decided. *Even if it costs me my new ship!*

V

When Otto Harkaman had first arrived, Grauffis had told him: "You're to be part of the ducal party."

As he'd suspected, this affair was much more than just a wedding celebration, but a celebration of the Duke's growing authority. And, he, as captain of the *Enterprise*, was another symbol of that power.

They went up the escalator and joined up with the duke's followers, behind a squad of guards dressed in red and yellow, with gilded helmets and ceremonial halberds. An esquire held aloft the Sword of State, preceding Duke Angus and his council, Harkaman tucked safely at the rear.

The recorded music was suddenly cut off and a fanfare came out of speakers. A hush fell over the crowd. The ducal party, with Lucas Trask, began to move down the escalator. The crowd erupted in cheers as they descended. News-service aircars hovered above. They reached the end of the central walkway, halted and deployed.

Karvall's minions in black and flame-yellow appeared across the terrace. The music started up again, playing the courtly "Nobles' Wedding March."

Sesar Karvall, with Elaine on his arm, wearing a shawl of black and yellow was followed by the bridesmaids, led by Lady Lavina Karvall. Finally they halted, ten yards apart, in front of the Duke.

Harkaman found the wedding ceremony interesting, not the least because it was short. He hadn't attended any other wedding, even while growing up on Colada. His sister had not married until after he left home. Space Vikings, while they were active, rarely married. They spent too little time at home and while away there were lots of temptations. Plus, there was always a good chance they might not return; many Space Vikings' bones were interred on distant worlds.

He had never found a woman he'd wanted to spend the rest of his life with. Looking at the lovely Elaine in her wedding dress, he determined that Lucas Trask was a lucky man. The love of such a woman might even change the course of his life....

At last, the ceremony was coming to an end: "And do you, and your houses, avow us, Angus, Duke of Wardshaven, to be your sovereign prince, and pledge fealty to us and to our legitimate and lawful successors?"

"We do." Not only Lucas and Elaine answered, but all the throng in the gardens, answered, the spectators in shouts. Someone, with a very loud voice, cried out: "*Long live Angus the First of Gram!*"

The Duke acted as if he hadn't heard the proclamation and continued with the ceremony: "And we, Angus, do confer upon you two, and your houses, the right to wear our badge as you see fit, and pledge ourself to maintain your rights against any and all who may presume to invade them. And we declare that this marriage between you two, and this agreement between your respective houses, does please us, and we avow you two, Lucas and Elaine, to be lawfully wed, and who so questions this marriage challenges us, in our teeth and to our despite."

That wasn't the wording Harkaman expected from a ducal lord. It was the formula employed by a planetary king. Well, there was no doubt about it now; Angus was making his bid for the crown of Gram. He suspected this whole event had been orchestrated by Angus, right down to the interloper who cried: "Long live Angus the first of Gram."

Honestly, Harkaman didn't like the Duke, who he'd found to be arrogant and pompous. Once he was enthroned, he suspected his followers, the poor bastards, were going to get much more than they bargained for. It was fortunate he'd be light-years away before the happy event occurred.

Once the Tanith base world was set up and working, he figured there would be very little reason for him ever to return to Gram. Yes, he would fulfill his sworn obligations, and conduct all the raids the ships' owners wanted, but he would make a point of staying as far away from Angus as he could arrange. He knew he wouldn't be able to put up with Angus' hectoring and bad temper; it would be best for everyone that they stayed far apart. At least, until he could afford to buy another ship. He decided right then, he'd name her "Corisande II."

He watched as Lord Lucas stepped forward and draped the shawl in Trask colors over Lady Elaine's—now Baroness Trask's—shoulders, then took her in his arms. The cheering roared forth once more, then the firing of the pom-pom in celebration.

After the ceremony, Harkaman had a glass of Baldur honey-rum—a tipple imported by some Space Viking—while he watched the new couple finish their toasts and shake hands with everyone circling them.

One of the news cars, painted orange and blue, dropped down upon the landing stage. *Now, that's odd*, he thought.

At the foot of the escalator, Elaine kicked off her gilded slippers and the bride and groom stepped onto the escalator and turned about. The bridesmaids rushed forward grabbing for the slippers, turning it into a meleé. After tossing the bridal bouquet, Elaine blew kisses to the crowd while Lucas shook his clasped hands over his head as they went up the escalator.

As the newlywed couple turned and stepped off, the orange and blue aircar dropped down directly in front of them. Harkaman rose to his feet and started running toward the escalator. He pushed two rubberneckers aside and vaulted up the moving stairway. When he reached the top of the ramp, he couldn't see who was inside the car, but someone had opened the window and was tilting the barrel of a submachine gun out of it.

There was the harsh burp of repeated gunfire. He watched as Lucas tripped his bride and brought her down. A man stepped out of the car and began firing downward. He could see bright blossoms of blood on both bride and groom. Then chaos erupted. The man slipped back inside and the aircar sped off. Several of the guards were firing at the retreating car. Somebody wearing the Duke's livery, from the distance it appeared to be Rovard Grauffis, was trying to organize the guards and form a posse. He pushed his way over to the Baron's side, bumping people to the right and left.

VI

Things quickly went from bad to worse. Lady Elaine was dead while Lord Trask was badly injured and in the hospital recovering from several serious gunshot wounds. Sesar Karvall had been badly wounded trying to reach his daughter; his prognosis was grim. Then Harkaman learned the shooter, the madman Andray Dunnan, had returned to the Gorram shipyards and stolen the *Enterprise*. The ship had hyperspaced out of the system off to who knew where. So much for his dreams, and possibly Duke Angus's as well.

He met with his officers in one of the hotel conference rooms. Everyone looked depressed.

"What are we going to do now?" Alvyn Karffard asked.

"I don't know," Harkaman said, shaking his head wearily. "Heads are going to roll at Gorram Spaceyards; apparently some of the people working there were in on the grab. Bribes were offered and taken; I wouldn't want to be in the head of security's shoes!"

"That doesn't do us much good," Vann Larch noted. "Besides, that crazy fool had several hundred armed mercenaries with him. Not much the spaceyard people could have done to stop him. There are all kinds of rumors running through the city, some of them blaming this Omfray character. Next, they'll be blaming the Gilgameshers; after all, there was a Gilgamesh ship in port."

Harkaman nodded. It was unusual to see a Gilgamesher trader on one of the Sword-Worlds, but when there was a coronation or big celebration going on, one or two of them usually showed up. They had noses like bloodhounds for a quick buck, or they had the best intelligence network in Terro-human space.

"How long before they blame us?" Sharll Renner exclaimed.

"We don't have to worry about that," Harkaman replied. "I had a talk with Baron Grauffis, the Duke's agent, and we're in the clear—at least as far as the Duke's concerned. In fact, he was as apologetic as all get-out. Our hotel bill and all our expenses will remain on his tab."

"Well, that's a relief," Larch said. He could take it easy for a while and paint for fun, not profit.

"What about our case against the Trans-World Bank on Dagon?" Guatt Kirbey asked.

"I still haven't heard a word," he said. Knowing how slow the wheels of justice turn, it could be years before a settlement was reached. "Besides, at best we'll only get thirty to forty million stellars, which is nowhere near what we need to buy another ship."

"So where do we go from here?" Paul Koreff asked.

"I'm supposed to meet with Duke Angus tomorrow. I should have a better idea by then."

Sir Rovard Grauffis himself came to the hotel to chauffer him to the meet with Duke Angus. They met in the same conference room as before. Only this time, the Duke looked apologetic, handing Harkaman a tumbler of Baldur honey-rum before directing him to a chair.

His thin face was gaunt; it looked like Angus hadn't slept for a week. "This was a complete and utter disaster! I'm embarrassed, Captain. I let my familial feelings overshadow my instincts. I should have had that boy confined and put in a safe place years ago. He not only hurt me, but, after murdering Sesar's daughter, he almost killed one of my most valuable liegemen. And, poor Lucas! By the gods, that young man has lost everything."

"Don't take all the blame, Your Grace," Harkaman said. "Dunnan owes us all a great debt. If I had another ship, I'd be after him myself."

"Do you think he can be found?"

He shrugged his shoulders. "Good question, Your Grace. The Old Federation's a big place to hide in. He could be anywhere. Even on one of the Sword-Worlds. I think one could spend a lifetime searching for him and still come up empty-handed. On the other hand, he could be at the next planet stop."

"That's what I was afraid of," Angus replied with a frown. "I'm sure you're wondering what is to happen to yourself and your crew."

"Yes, Your Grace. Things haven't worked out too well here on Gram."

"Don't despair, Captain. I haven't changed my mind about raiding the Old Federation. It's just going to take longer, that's all."

"What do you have in mind?" he asked, feeling somewhat revived; at least, until he found out what Angus' plans were.

"I've already talked with Raff Anhowler, Alex Gorram's Chief Operating Officer, and he's going to start working on the second ship, as soon as I can raise the funds. I want you boys to stick around until she's finished, all on my tab."

"That could be a long time. I heard it took a year to build the *Enterprise*."

"True," the Duke said. "But the shipyard is all tooled up now; Alex has already laid the keel for a second ship. It could be done in less than six Galactic Standard months."

Harkaman wondered if this was another pie-in-the-sky scheme.

With taxes as high as the populace would put up with in Wardshaven, where was Angus going to get the stellars he needed? However, he was still here on Angus' sufferance, so he sucked it up and said, "That's good news, Your Grace. I'm sure my partners will be relieved. Let me know if there is anything I can do to help speed matters up."

VII

A week later Rovard Grauffis screened him, asking if he wanted to visit Lucas Trask.

"Of course," Harkaman replied. "How is he doing?"

"Much better. Awake almost half the day. The head medico says he'll be out and about in another week"

Considering Trask's injuries, he doubted that.

He followed Grauffis into the white room. Lucas was lying in a hospital bed, looking pale and disheveled. He was attempting to light a cigarette, showing difficulty aligning cigarette and lighter.

Harkaman leaned over and lit it for him. "How are you feeling?"

"I've felt better," Lucas said, wryly. "I can't wait to get out of here."

He nodded. "I've done my share of hospital-time. One of the downsides of being a professional Space Viking."

Lucas made a hacking sort of laugh. "Ouch, that hurt! I'd ask you about the rest of the downsides, but I don't think I could survive the laughs."

Trask turned to Grauffis and asked, "What happened? And where's Dunnan?"

"He pirated the *Enterprise*," Grauffis told him. "He had that company of mercenaries of his, and he'd bribed some of the people at the Gorram shipyards. I thought Alex would kill his chief of security when he found out what had happened. We can't prove anything—we're trying hard enough to—but we're sure Omfray of Glaspyth furnished the money. He's been denying it just a shade too emphatically."

"Then the whole thing was planned in advance?"

"Taking the ship was; he must have been planning that for months before he started recruiting that company. I think he meant to do it the night before the wedding. Then he tried to persuade the Lady-Demoiselle Elaine to elope with him—he seems to have actually thought that was possible—and when she humiliated him, he decided to kill both of you first."

Grauffis turned to Harkaman, "As long as I live, I'll regret not taking you at your word and accepting your offer, then."

He wished he had. His men would have disposed of Dunnan and his band permanently, and he'd now be off in hyperspace and on his way to the Old Federation aboard the *Enterprise*. Despite his own distress, he couldn't help but notice the look of despair that had come over Lucas' face when Rovard had mentioned Lady Elaine's name. The poor bastard had it a lot worse than he did.

"How did he get hold of that Westlands Telecast and Teleprint car?" Lucas asked.

"Oh," Grauffis replied. "The morning of the wedding, he screened Westlands' editorial office and told them he had the inside story on the marriage and why the Duke was sponsoring it. Made it sound as though there was some scandal; insisted that a reporter come to Dunnan House for a face-to-face interview. They sent a man, and that was the last they saw him alive; our people found his body at Dunnan House when we were searching the place afterward. We found the car at the shipyard; it had taken a couple of hits from the guns at Karvall House, but you know what these press-cars are built to stand. He went directly to the shipyard, where his men already held the *Enterprise*; as soon as he arrived, she lifted out."

Lucas stared at the cigarette between his fingers. With an obvious and painful movement, he leaned forward to crush it out.

"Rovard, how soon will that second ship be finished?"

Grauffis laughed bitterly. "Building the *Enterprise* took everything we had. The duchy's on the edge of bankruptcy now. We stopped work on the second ship six months ago because we didn't have enough money to keep on with her and still get the *Enterprise* finished. We were expecting the *Enterprise* to make enough in the Old Federation to finish the second one. Then, with two ships and a base on Tanith, the money would begin coming in instead of going out. But now—"

Harkaman had to hold back a string of curses. Angus hadn't given him the full story, just left him hanging. "It leaves me where I was on Quernbiter. Worse. King Valgard was going to help the Elmersans, and I'd have gotten a command in that. It's too late for that now."

Trask picked up his cane and used it to push himself to his feet. The broken leg had mended, but he was still weak.

He moved into a position where he could prop Trask up if he started to fall.

Trask took a few tottering steps, paused to lean on the cane, and then forced himself on to the open window and stood for a moment staring out. Then he turned.

"Captain Harkaman, it might be that you could still get a command, here on Gram. That's if you don't mind commanding under me as owner-aboard. I am going hunting for Andray Dunnan."

He only had to think about that for a moment. "I'd count it an honor, Lord Trask. But where will you get a ship?"

"She's half-finished now. You already have a crew for her. Duke Angus can finish her for me, and pay for it by pledging his new barony of Traskon."

Rovard Grauffis jaw dropped. "You mean, you'll trade Traskon for that ship?" he demanded.

"Finished, equipped and ready for space, yes."

"The Duke will agree to that," Grauffis said promptly. "But, Lucas; Traskon is all you own—your title, your land, your revenues…."

"If I have a ship, I won't need them. I am turning Space Viking."

Harkaman stood up and roared his approval.

Grauffis looked at him, his mouth still slightly open.

"Lucas Trask—Space Viking," he said. "Now I've heard everything."

"That was another Lucas Trask, Rovard. He's dead, now."

VIII

After he left Trask's hospital room, first on Harkaman's list of things to do was to inform his partners of their new posting. He suspected they'd be grateful; Gram's hospitality and entertainments were growing threadbare. Once he learned of Trask's deal with him and his crew, he suspected Duke Angus would cut off their line of credit and their welcome. He screened his exec and set up a meet at his hotel suite.

Alvyn Karffard and Guatt Kirbey were the first to arrive. He waited patiently until the rest arrived. Most had glum faces as if they expected the worst.

"I take it you have news?" Karffard asked.

Harkaman nodded. "Lord Trask is going to buy the hypership currently under construction at Gorram Spaceyards."

They all perked up.

"He wants me to be the captain and—of course—you all will be offered positions at your current rank and at established shipboard pay rates for said rank."

Karffard, Paul Koreff and Sharll Renner looked pleased, while Vann Larch and Guatt Kirbey looked disappointed.

He looked at Larch and asked, "What's the matter?"

Larch sighed. "After owning our own ship, this is a step backwards."

Karffard interjected, "But, at least, it's a job on a ship where we're all together."

They all nodded in agreement to that point.

Karffard added, "And it's a first-rate ship. We were all but salivating to get a position aboard the *Enterprise*. The only thing different is the man in charge. With Angus running things, we'd of had to put up with

Rovard Grauffis, the kind of leader who doesn't know much about what he's doing, resents advice and thinks he knows it all. I could see rough sailing ahead. Although, I don't know if being under Trask is any better.... Now we're set to ship out with an owner who also knows nothing about warships or planetary raids, and on top of that recently lost his new wife. What's the story there, Captain?"

"Since Trask has been in the hospital I've gotten a chance to get to know him," he said. "He's an honorable man who's been dishonorably used. He wants to get revenge on the madman who murdered his wife and attacked his friends. He's also got the wherewithal to pay for his own ship, which we certainly do not." Harkaman paused to look around at his seated crewmen.

Not one of them made a peep.

He continued, "Lucas Trask wants revenge. We want—no, need—a hypership with the capability to conduct raids. He has one, no one else here on Gram does; so, we need him more than he needs us."

They all nodded.

"I'm not sure where this journey will take us, or how much fighting there'll be. But it's not going to be dull. And we'll get the usual officer shares if there's any plunder."

"That's good to know," Karffard said. "The way you said Trask was talking at the pre-wedding party, I wasn't sure if there'd be any loot at all...."

"The Lucas Trask leaving the hospital is not the same man who entered it on his back. He's bitter, he's angry and he's determined to get revenge. And I plan to help him get it. If anyone objects, let him speak now!"

"But how certain are you that he'll permit raids?" Koreff asked.

Harkaman set down his drink. "First, Trask knows we've hired a lot of ground fighters, some of them inexperienced. He's going to want to cure that problem right away, and as we all know: the best way to gain experience is to raid a few Old Federation worlds"

"Right."

"Plus, he needs to test his new ship and its weapon systems before we go up against the *Enterprise*. So, Trask is going to need a space battle or two. And, if we can't make those raids and battles turn a good profit; well, then this isn't the bunch I've spent the last ten years fighting across the Old Federation with!"

End